D0481269

Treasured Vows

Also by Cathy Maxwell
in Large Print:

The Seduction of an English Lady
The Lady Is Tempted
The Wedding Wager
Flanna and the Lawman

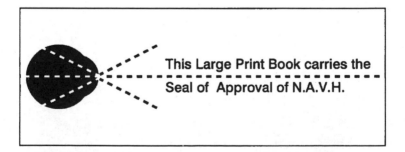

Treasured Vows

CATHY MAXWELL

WHEELER
PUBLISHING

Published in 2005 by arrangement with Avon Books, an imprint of HarperCollins Publishers Inc.

Wheeler Large Print Hardcover.

The text of this Large Print edition is unabridged. Other aspects of the book may vary from the original edition.

Set in 16 pt. Plantin by Al Chase.

Printed in the United States on permanent paper.

Library of Congress Cataloging-in-Publication Data

Maxwell, Cathy.
    Treasured vows / Cathy Maxwell.
        p. cm.
    ISBN 1-58724-885-9 (lg. print : hc : alk. paper)
    1. Inheritance and succession — Fiction.   2. Fathers and daughters — Fiction.   3. Guardian and ward — Fiction.
    4. Explorers — Fiction.   5. Large type books.   I. Title.
    PS3563.A8996T74 2005
        813'.6—dc22   2004061165

For Marvin and Sally Wollen,
with love

As the Founder/CEO of NAVH, the only national health agency solely devoted to those who, although not totally blind, have an eye disease which could lead to serious visual impairment, I am pleased to recognize Thorndike Press★ as one of the leading publishers in the large print field.

Founded in 1954 in San Francisco to prepare large print textbooks for partially seeing children, NAVH became the pioneer and standard setting agency in the preparation of large type.

Today, those publishers who meet our standards carry the prestigious "Seal of Approval" indicating high quality large print. We are delighted that Thorndike Press is one of the publishers whose titles meet these standards. We are also pleased to recognize the significant contribution Thorndike Press is making in this important and growing field.

Lorraine H. Marchi, L.H.D.
Founder/CEO
NAVH

★ Thorndike Press encompasses the following imprints: Thorndike, Wheeler, Walker and Large Print Press.

Dear Reader

Treasured Vows is still my favorite of the books I've written. I love Phadra Abbott. I admire her audacity, her resiliency, and her vulnerability.

Is she out of step with Regency heroines? I don't think so. The Regency was a time of vivid characters and boundless opportunity. Like many of us, Phadra comes to an awakening — if she intends to live life to its fullest, it's going to have to be up to her. What she knows of the world has been from books. Now, she's ready to see for herself.

Many people ask about Phadra's name. It is pronounced "fay-dra," like the Phaedra of myth, but that isn't where I took the name (which has been spelled many different ways over the centuries). My Phadra is named after a young girl who died of child abuse around the time I wrote the book. Her death haunted me. That Phadra never had a chance. My Phadra would.

I took a risk in writing the character of

Grant Morgan. He's a banker. Yes, that's right, a banker. Grant is amazingly steady. In fact, he's so steady, he does need a shake-up, and Phadra, with her scarves and toe bells, is exactly the right person to challenge him at every turn.

She dances on dreams; he is rooted in reality. Someplace in between love happens. I hope you adore them as much as I do.

All my best,

Cathy Maxwell

Rousseau declares that a woman should never, for a moment, feel herself independent, that she should be governed by fear to exercise her natural cunning, and made a coquettish slave in order to render her a more alluring object of desire, a *sweeter* companion of man, whenever he chooses to relax himself. . . . What nonsense!

A Vindication of the Rights of Woman
Mary Wollstonecraft (1759–1797)

Chapter 1

May 1810

Bankers and body snatchers, Phadra Abbott decided grimly, they were one and the same.

Standing in the office's window alcove, she turned her head and looked at Sir Cecil Evans, a member of the Bank of England's Court of Directors, letting all of her anger flow from her eyes.

Sir Cecil reacted as if her glance scalded him. His fingers fumbled and dropped the letter opener he'd been playing with onto his desk. He'd been nervously toying with the dratted thing for the past ten minutes while they waited. His bushy brows came together in a frown, and he huddled down deeper over his desk as if he could shut out her presence. "It wasn't *all* my fault," he muttered. "Your father had a hand in the matter."

Phadra snorted but said nothing, not trusting herself to speak. Ignoring her companion Henny's look of concern, she gave them all her back and stared with unseeing eyes out the window.

Two hours. That was all the time that had elapsed since Sir Cecil had delivered the news of her financial ruin and her carefully constructed world had come crashing down around her. She took a deep breath, steadying herself. She wouldn't give up. Not yet.

When the banker had finished his confession, he'd added that he held hopes that there was a way out of "this tangled web your father and I wove for you" — as if he wouldn't also go to debtor's prison with her.

He probably wouldn't. He had money, whereas she was bankrupt and would be held responsible for her father's debts as well as her own.

Dear God, she had no desire to see the inside of a prison.

A sharp knock broke the silence of the room. "Come in," Sir Cecil said, his voice squeaking on the first word. He cleared his throat and repeated his command in a firmer tone.

He's more nervous than I am, Phadra thought, and realized that she'd been holding out some hope, some prayer, that this was all an elaborate hoax and she'd return home to find her life intact. *I must be strong. I must be brave.* She repeated the litany to herself and then turned to face the one man Sir Cecil felt could contrive a way out of these dire circumstances. He'd even gone so far as to describe Grant Morgan as the sharpest mind in England.

She wondered what Morgan was doing involved with Sir Cecil if he was so intelligent, but wisely held her tongue.

The door opened and a respectful young secretary announced, "Mr. Morgan, sir."

"Good!" The word exploded out of Sir Cecil as he rose and walked around the desk to greet his visitor, who was without question one of the most handsome men Phadra had ever laid eyes on. "Morgan, thank you for coming."

Grant Morgan had a profile — and a body — like those Michelangelo had loved to sculpt. He met Sir Cecil halfway into the room and took his hand. "I'm sorry I couldn't answer your summons sooner, sir. I had to finish some accounts on the Scottish question for Deveril."

His low, deep voice was pleasing to Phadra's ear. A good voice for an actor.

But it wasn't just the looks or the voice that captured her attention so completely. The man had presence. Why would anyone so young — he must have been in his early thirties — and so devilishly good-looking lock himself up in a stuffy bank?

Ignoring Henny's whispered "Oh, my" of admiration, Phadra closed her own gaping mouth and let her artist's eye for detail take over. Physically attractive he might be, but he had banker's eyes, steel-gray and direct, as if they could see right through a person. Nor did she admire the short, conservative style of his thick, dark hair or the fact that his well-tailored dark blue coat and buff trousers allowed no personal flair. He wore his clothes almost as if they were a uniform.

Sir Cecil turned to her. "Let me introduce you to Miss Phadra Abbott. She is the daughter of Sir Julius Abbott."

"The explorer?" Mr. Morgan asked.

Phadra was impressed. "You've heard of my father?"

"I read his book. Of course, that was several years ago."

"At least twelve. It was published the last time he was in England . . . that I know of." She struggled to keep the bitterness out of her voice.

"Sir Julius has an account with the bank," Sir Cecil said.

"He does?" The news apparently surprised the younger man.

Sir Cecil looked away, as if embarrassed. "It is one I handle personally."

Mr. Morgan's silvery eyes narrowed as if he sensed the unspoken in Sir Cecil's statement. He looked at Phadra and then back to his colleague. "I see."

He did see, Phadra realized, and that only made her angrier. If he knew Sir Cecil for the bumbling, incompetent fool she now knew him to be, why hadn't he done something sooner? Before she'd been ruined?

As if wanting to cover the moment of realization, Sir Cecil hurried to introduce Henny, who sat in a chair to his right. "And this is Mrs. Henrietta Shaunessy, Miss Abbott's companion."

The banker dutifully took her offered hand and bowed over it while Henny cooed in her throaty voice, "Please call me Henny."

Phadra shot her a cross look. There were times when Henny's heyday as an opera dancer was a little too apparent, but this was the first time it had embarrassed Phadra. Henny smiled back, unrepentant, and tucked a dyed red curl back under her bonnet.

Her flirtation seemed to have no impact on Mr. Morgan. He released her hand with a tight, pleasant smile and turned his attention to his colleague. "You need my help," he stated, confirming Phadra's suspicion that this wasn't the first time Sir Cecil had turned to Mr. Morgan for help. She looked out the window, biting back a harsh accusation.

"Yes, yes," Sir Cecil said. "Please, Miss Abbott, Morgan, be seated. This will take some explaining."

"I'm fine where I am," Phadra said. "Be seated, Mr. Morgan. Sir Cecil takes his time in telling a story," she added dryly.

Her touch of sarcasm caught Grant off guard, and he gave her a closer look. She'd returned to the window alcove, her arms tightly crossed against her chest and her chin lifted in defiant pride.

When he'd first entered the room, he thought her a child because of the way her hair curled freely down to her waist. Now the sunlight of the May afternoon captured and highlighted those unruly flaxen curls. This was no child but a young woman in her twenties, he'd hazard to guess, whose dark blue eyes flashed with the promise of a spirited intelligence and challenged him directly, without the restraints of false modesty so common among debutantes these days.

In fact, dressed as she was in a vivid

purple high-waisted tunic that flowed gracefully to her feet and emphasized the round firmness of her breasts, she looked more like a bold Saxon princess than the well-bred daughter of a knight. The wide bronze bracelets on her wrists and the gold circlet around her head enhanced that impression. A very unconventional style.

Perhaps a very unconventional woman.

"What service can I perform for you, Sir Cecil?" he asked, dragging his gaze away from Miss Abbott. He didn't sit, as she'd ordered.

Sir Cecil cleared his throat, took a deep breath, worked his eyebrows up and down as if considering the best way to approach the subject, opened his mouth to speak, and then closed it again with a frown.

Grant prodded, "Whatever it is, sir, I am sure I can help you."

Instead of offering encouragement, his words seemed to deepen Sir Cecil's anxiety. Grant thought he detected tears, which the man blinked back. "Sir Cecil, whatever is wrong?"

The cool, husky voice from the window gave him his answer. "He's embezzled from the bank and is afraid to tell you."

The words shocked Grant. He looked from the proud woman in the window back to the older man. "Sir Cecil?" he started, almost afraid to ask if it was true.

"It wasn't exactly like that," Sir Cecil said.

Grant wanted to sigh with relief. "You didn't embezzle."

"Well, that isn't exactly right, either."

Grant felt uneasy. "You'd better explain, sir."

"I just managed to work the books a bit to my advantage in order to finance Sir Julius's last expedition." His words came out in a rush of breath.

Grant sat down. He'd embezzled.

Sir Cecil finally raised his ruddy face to Grant. "I shouldn't have done it."

You're right, Grant wanted to shout. During the eight years he'd been with the bank, he'd almost made a career of extricating Sir Cecil from his bad business dealings. But he'd never thought the man would stoop to stealing. "What exactly have you done?"

Sir Cecil studied his thumbnail as if it were a work of art.

Finally Miss Abbott said, "My father, the famous explorer" — again he detected the touch of sarcasm in her tone — "and Sir Cecil, the trusted banker, defrauded the Bank of England to raise money for a *treasure hunt*."

Sir Cecil jumped to his feet and faced his accuser. "It exists, I tell you. Hikuptah's treasure is real."

"Who is Hikuptah?" Grant asked.

"A very wealthy and powerful Egyptian priest who lived around the time of Alexander the Great," Sir Cecil answered. "Julius stumbled on the story in some papers written by a Greek merchant. He'd purchased the papers from an antiquities dealer years ago, before Miss Abbott was born."

Grant stole a look at the young woman, who now stared out the window, her arms wrapped around her waist.

"Morgan, you must understand, Hikuptah was rich! Wealthy beyond imagination," Sir Cecil practically crowed. "The Greek had been a friend of Hikuptah and, in true shopkeeper fashion, had documented everything he saw delivered into the man's tomb for the afterlife. You can't imagine what was in there!" He waved his hands in the air as if conjuring the treasures of the tomb before them. "Solid gold plates for eating in the spirit world, baskets woven out of silver and gold, sapphires as big as goose eggs, crowns encrusted with every stone known to man. All of it sitting there waiting for someone with daring to come and take it." He gave a happy laugh. "And Julius had discovered directions to the tomb. Everything was in the Greek's letter."

Grant leaned forward in his chair. "Let me see if I understand this correctly, sir. Are you saying that Sir Julius wasn't an explorer at all but a *grave robber?*"

Miss Abbott gave a sharp bark of laughter. Sir Cecil's smile abruptly turned to a frown. His eyebrows came together. "No, no! We would have shared what knowledge we'd gained."

"And how does the bank fit into this —" Grant searched his mind for a seemly word. "— endeavor?"

"The bank *financed* their grave robbery," Miss Abbott responded audaciously.

Grant returned her brazenness with a measuring gaze of his own. He didn't admire bold women and wondered if Miss Abbott was one of those females who didn't understand her place in society. She had the look. "Perhaps we should continue this conversation in private, sir."

At that she marched toward him, her chin tilted up in defiance. "In private? About *my* father and *my* future? I don't think so, Mr. Morgan."

But Grant didn't hear her clearly. His attention was distracted by the tinkling of bells, apparently coming from the floor. He'd heard it earlier, when he'd entered the room. Curious, he bent over in his chair and searched around the room until his gaze fell on the petite toes that peeked out at him from beneath Miss Abbott's gauzy purple skirts.

"Do you like Phadra's sandals?" Mrs. Shaunessy asked. She'd bent over as well, and now Grant discovered her practically nose to nose with him. He sat up abruptly.

Mrs. Shaunessy followed him up. She smiled and proudly announced, "She designed them herself. She designs all of her own clothing. Very original, I think. Phadra darling, lift your skirts a bit and show Mr. Morgan your pretty sandals with your little toe rings and their bells."

"Toe bells?" Grant repeated, surprised by a slow heat stealing up his neck. Normally nothing ruffled his composure, and yet there he was, blushing like a callow youth at the sight of Miss Abbott's toes.

"Henny, I am not going to lift my skirts for this man," she protested, and then her own cheeks turned pink at the double entendre of her words.

Grant forced the discussion back to business. "Explain to me, Sir Cecil, exactly what happened."

Sir Cecil, who had also been contemplating Miss Abbott's toes, looked up and cleared his throat. "We had to finance the expedition. It was all very innocent at first. We were determined to keep this all private, so I gave Julius everything I could spare for a stake in the treasure, and he raised a good share of the funds by marrying Mary Milford."

He slid an uncomfortable look in Miss Abbott's direction. "Mary was an heiress. Her fortune was not a prodigious one, but she had enough to spare and no kin to lay claims. Julius married her and, when we had the money together, left on the first ship for Cairo."

"Leaving his pregnant wife behind in England," Miss Abbott added softly. "Please understand, Mr. Morgan, that at this time, everything they did was all very legal —"

"Yes," Sir Cecil readily agreed. "We didn't do anything wrong."

"— although a person could question the morality of marrying a young woman for her money and then abandoning her," she finished.

"She wasn't abandoned," Sir Cecil snapped, as if they'd had this argument before. "She had the benefit of his ring and his name." Turning his back to her, he continued, "Julius spent years looking in Egypt for that tomb. Time had erased most landmarks, and the sands were constantly shifting. He had to bribe everyone, from the workers, who were impossibly lazy beasts, to every government official, including the French." He lifted his hands in the air. "A lesser man would have given up years earlier, but not Julius. He didn't stop until he *found* it, the tomb of Hikuptah."

Sir Cecil sank down into his chair behind his desk. "But grave robbers — real robbers, not men like us — had beaten him to the treasure. Can you imagine what Julius felt, Morgan? To have made so many sacrifices, only to discover the treasure gone, stolen?"

"So he returned to England?" Grant asked.

"He was preparing to return," Sir Cecil said. "Our money was used up, finished. Then one of the agents he had worked with over the years came to him in the middle of the night. He'd discovered a French deserter dying of fever with a story Julius should hear. Julius hurried to the man's deathbed."

Sir Cecil stared off into space as if he could see the scene between Sir Julius and the deserter. "The Frenchman was one of

23

the men who had broken into the tomb. He and three other soldiers had come across the tomb by accident. They stole the treasure, deserted the army, and headed up the Nile, hoping to escape Napoleon's long arm. The trip was a disaster. All of the men contracted fever, and three died of it. The last man, alone and frightened, hid the treasure and headed back to civilization. But he died in Julius's arms." He smiled disarmingly. "Of course, that was after he'd given Julius a rudimentary description of where the treasure was hidden."

"But Sir Julius had no more money for a search," Grant said.

"We were so close," Sir Cecil answered, pinching his thumb and index finger together. "We couldn't give up. Not at that point. It's true, though, that we needed more money. The bank already had the Abbott emeralds and would sell them to pay his debt once it became known that he was penniless. I wasn't much further away from dun territory myself."

"The Abbott emeralds were also the collateral my father used to secure a living for my mother and myself through the bank," Miss Abbott explained to Grant. "They were our only means of support."

"Yes," Sir Cecil agreed. The word hung

in the air for a few seconds, and then he continued in a rush, as if he suddenly felt a need to make a clean breast of everything, "One night over a brandy bottle, we hatched the idea of replacing the real emeralds with paste copies. After all, no one really knew about them, since I had managed to keep this account relatively to myself."

Grant's sense of foreboding grew stronger.

"So," Sir Cecil said, "I borrowed the real emeralds from the vault and sold them."

"Borrowed?" Grant choked on the word.

"He does have a funny way of looking at thievery, doesn't he?" Miss Abbott asked.

Slamming his palm down on his desk, Sir Cecil rose and turned toward her. "I didn't steal anything. We are going to pay it all back as soon as Julius returns. He wasn't supposed to be gone this long. He was supposed to find that damned treasure and come home."

"How long has he been gone?" Grant asked.

"Nine years," Sir Cecil said.

"Nine years!" The words shot out of Grant. "Have you lost all sense of reason? Do you realize what you've lost for some wild tale of a tomb full of treasure?"

"I wouldn't have lost a thing if *she'd* stayed where she was supposed to and not upset the scheme of things," Sir Cecil returned heatedly, pointing his finger at Miss Abbott.

"Stayed where I was?" She placed her hands on her hips. "I'd been in that boarding school for the last sixteen years, since the day after my mother died. And I'd still be rotting there if I hadn't taken matters into my own hands."

"Who has been responsible for you since your mother's death?" Grant asked.

"The Bank of England is my official guardian," she replied, seemingly angry that he didn't know the answer.

"We are?" Grant turned to Sir Cecil. "Isn't that unusual?"

Sir Cecil shrugged. "Julius and I didn't know what else to do with her."

"Heaven forbid that my father should take responsibility for his only child," Miss Abbott said.

Sir Cecil defended his friend. "Well, you were fine."

"Fine?" she exclaimed. Sir Cecil backed up as she stalked him in her anger, her toe bells accentuating each step. "Do you know what it was like to be cloistered in that boarding school without benefit of friends or family? With nowhere to go on holidays? No one to turn to when I'd finished my studies and watched all of the other girls leave to go out in the world? I had to stay behind. To *wait* for my father and the Bank of England. Thankfully, someone introduced me to Mary Wollstonecraft and her ideas on women's independence, or I'd still be back at Miss Agatha's in my serge uniform — waiting."

"And we wouldn't be in this bloody mess, either!" Sir Cecil shot back, finally standing his ground. His hands shook with anger as he reached down to scoop up a handful of papers from his desk. "Do you know what these are, Morgan? Bills. Bills she's run up since she checked herself out of that boarding school six months ago and set up her own establishment without so much as a by-your-leave. Even hired her own companion —"

"I had to have a proper chaperone — something you never spent a moment worrying about," Miss Abbott said.

Sir Cecil ignored her, caught up in his tirade. "She's been holding 'salons' for starving pamphleteers and poets. Paying a hundred and fifty pounds a night to feed them strawberries and champagne."

"It's important for the reputation of my salons that I serve the very best —"

"And do you know what they discuss, Grant? Atheism!"

"I've explained to you before, Sir Cecil," she said, "that it is not *atheism* to discuss modern theology."

Sir Cecil looked down his nose at her and frowned. "Are you a vicar?"

"Of course not."

"Then you have no business discussing such matters out of church!" he declared. He turned to Grant. "And they go on and on about the Enlightenment and silly nonsense such as letting women own property and having a voice in government!"

Miss Abbott bit each word off as she said, "Those ideas aren't silly —"

"In short, this woman runs through money she doesn't have the way a thirsty man gulps water, and she spends it on radicals and insurrectionists!" Sir Cecil let the bills fall through his fingers and onto the desk for emphasis.

"Money I don't have?" Miss Abbott clenched her fists as if she'd have liked to box his ears. Her body practically quivered with anger. "Oh, that is a rich one, Sir Cecil. I had money secured with the Abbott emeralds until you decided to steal my inheritance."

"I didn't steal anything. Your father made that decision."

"Or so you say!"

Sir Cecil's eyes opened so wide they looked as though they would pop out of his head. "No one has ever questioned my integrity —"

"Ha!"

Grant stepped between them. "This isn't getting us anywhere. You're both on your way to debtor's prison once the auditors discover the jewels are paste."

"And they will," Sir Cecil said to Miss Abbott, leaning around Grant to throw one last accusation at her head, "since you have alerted them by overspending your accounts."

Miss Abbott faced Grant, her expression bleak but her voice reasoned and sober. "It's not my fault. I thought I had money. I didn't expect my father to leave me penniless."

Grant admired her ability to face reality without hysterics, unlike others of her sex. She repudiated his assumption with her next words. "And when I see him, I shall ask him why."

"When you see him?" Grant repeated.

"Yes. You see, while Sir Cecil has been hashing history, I think I have the solution to our problems." She raised her head proudly. "I shall lead an expedition to search for my father."

Sir Cecil burst into laughter, practically doubling over and slapping his knees. "Don't you think that if Julius was alive, he would have returned by now?"

Her eyes narrowed. "If my father were dead, I would know it. Here." She touched her heart. "We are of the same flesh, the same blood. I know he's alive — and he may need our help." She turned to Grant. "One of my reasons for coming to London was to mount an expedition to search for him. I used my salons as a way to meet people who could help me." She ignored Sir Cecil's snort of disbelief. "It is more important now than it was before for us to find him."

"How do you propose to pay for this?" Sir Cecil asked. "I haven't got the blunt to pay for hack fare home, let alone such an expedition, and you don't have enough to cover your rent."

"Surely the bank —," she started.

"Will have us both clapped in irons if they know about this," Sir Cecil finished.

Miss Abbott slowly closed her mouth, her brow furrowed in concern.

Sir Cecil came around the desk to face him. "Morgan, you have to help me. I know I shouldn't have done it, but a man can make a mistake, can't he?"

Only if it's not discovered, Grant thought,

shaking his head. He knew better than anyone the number of times Sir Cecil's greed had exceeded his responsibleness. Except that maybe this time Sir Cecil might have taken that one step too far. For years he'd covered for Sir Cecil with his own funds and would do so again, because in spite of his bumbling, the man had the power to recommend Grant for a seat on the Bank's Court of Directors and the one thing he worked for with every breath he took: a knighthood.

Almost as if reading Grant's thoughts, Sir Cecil said, "I understand that I have often asked a great deal of you, Grant. Some might even think that I was implicating you in this affair by confessing all to you."

Grant acknowledged that fact with his silence.

Sir Cecil appeared to choose his next words carefully. "Perhaps it would help you to know that I have considered you almost as a son. In fact, I would favorably consider your suit if you were interested in my Miranda's hand in marriage."

His words shocked Grant. He marry Lady Miranda, Sir Cecil's only daughter? The seat on the Court of Directors would be his. This was his moment — his opportunity, his Rubicon.

"Would you be interested in my daughter's hand?"

Sir Grant. He struggled to keep the excitement from his voice. "I'd be honored to marry your daughter."

Miss Abbott's mocking voice destroyed the import of the moment. "And what will your daughter have to say about the matter? Perhaps she won't appreciate being sacrificed to Mr. Morgan in exchange for your sins, sir."

"My Miranda knows her place in the world, Miss Abbott." Sir Cecil practically growled the words out.

"What place? The role of chattel? I don't envy your daughter *her* place."

Sir Cecil looked as if he would have an apoplectic fit until Mrs. Shaunessy interrupted, "Phadra dear, not all women are as independent as you care to be. Mr. Morgan is an unusually fine-looking man. Lady Miranda could do worse."

In response Miss Abbott cocked her head and gave him a slow perusal, as if questioning Mrs. Shaunessy's judgment. For the second time in their interview, he felt his face grow warm. Nor did he appreciate the laughter dancing in Miss Abbott's eyes.

The woman was bold. Damned bold.

"Are you finished?" he asked. "Or shall I turn around?"

She laughed, completely unaffected by his rudeness. "Perhaps I should ask Sir Cecil to check your teeth."

Her words robbed him of speech, and that apparently pleased her. "I think I would value interesting conversation over looks," she said lightly. "Not that it is my concern. I know nothing of your conversational abilities, Mr. Morgan, but I admit you are pleasing to look at. Quite extraordinary, actually." She grinned up at him.

That rebellious tilt of her chin irritated him. He forced a smile. "Do you think I lack wits, Miss Abbott?"

Her eyes grew wide in feigned innocence. "Why, I'm waiting for a demonstration, Mr. Morgan. After all, Sir Cecil has hailed you as our savior — and his heir apparent. Save us. Please."

She was ridiculing him! Grant felt his temper stretch almost to the breaking point. Then, in the span of a moment, the solution to their problems — and a fitting turn of the tables on Miss Abbott — became blindingly clear. She was a challenging opponent, but he held the winning card.

"Sir Cecil, is the bank still Miss Abbott's guardian?" he asked.

Sir Cecil took a moment to ponder the question. "I'm not certain. Julius had the papers drawn up to state that we are her legal guardians until she turns five and twenty."

"And have you reached your majority yet, Miss Abbott?" Grant asked.

Uncertainty replaced the laughter in her eyes. "I don't reach my majority for another seven months," she answered stiffly.

Grant smiled, enjoying himself now. "Then I have the perfect solution. One that should see both you and Sir Cecil free and clear."

"And that is?" she asked, arching an eyebrow.

"Marriage," he answered succinctly.

She clearly didn't understand. Her expression turned slightly bored. "Yours, Mr. Morgan?"

He smiled, savoring the moment. "No, Miss Abbott, yours."

Chapter 2

"Have you lost your senses?" Lady Evans asked her husband, her strident voice carrying through the heavy paneled door at Evans House. Furious at being forced to accept the Evanses' charity while they sponsored her on the marriage mart, Phadra shifted uncomfortably in her straight-backed chair. A portmanteau with a few necessities sat at her feet.

After the discussion at the bank, Sir Cecil had taken her and Henny back to her beloved townhouse, where they'd gathered a few articles of clothing. Sir Cecil hadn't given them time to linger but had hurried them to Evans House.

Now she and Henny sat in the hallway as if they were shopkeepers and not guests in this home. They'd been relegated there by the imperious Lady Evans after Sir Cecil had introduced her and Henny. Lady Evans had taken one look down her nose at her houseguests and announced, "I must talk to Sir Cecil. Alone."

Henny had sat down with uncharacteristic docility, but Phadra had stood, angry and humiliated by the woman's rudeness. Her proud show of defiance didn't stop Lady Evans from shutting the door in her face.

Eventually she had no choice but to sit — and listen to Sir Cecil plead his case.

What a pathetic man.

Lady Evans heaved a loud sigh. Phadra could imagine her massive bosom heaving with long-suffering righteousness while the salt-and-pepper hair piled regally on top of her head shook to mirror her disappointment. "Once again you've let your overgenerous heart get in the way of good common sense. Look at the woman! She's well past a marriageable age. We'd practically have to buy her a husband."

Phadra's cheeks burned with embarrassment, and she slid a glance at the footman awaiting his master's summons at his post by the paneled door to see if he'd heard his mistress. He maintained his stoic countenance while Henny snored lightly next to her. Dear Henny. She could fall asleep anywhere, anytime. Phadra reached over and tucked the folds of her Indian silk shawl around the kind woman, who served as her only confidante and companion.

Inside the room, Lady Evans was asking, as if struck by a new and important thought, "She's not an heiress, is she?"

"Well, no —"

"I thought not! And I assume that she has no family, or else they'd see to her come out?"

"Yes, yes. As a matter of fact, she does have family. She has a father. You do remember my good friend Julius?"

"Sir Julius! That rapscallion? This is his daughter? Now I understand why she's so odd. Were my eyes deceiving me, or is she wearing sandals in the middle of the afternoon? And Miss Abbott's companion. Can you believe the *red* of that woman's hair?"

Phadra glared at the paneled door and laid the blame for Lady Evans's rudeness squarely on the head of Grant Morgan. If it hadn't been for him and his highhanded ways, she would not be sitting here right at this moment. She squeezed her hands tightly in her lap . . . wishing she held his neck between them.

Lady Evans continued, caught up in her tirade, "Furthermore, what of your own daughter?"

"Actually, Beatrice, that is the beauty —"

"Are you so lost to sensibility that you

would have me sponsor another chit on the marriage mart when your own daughter hasn't taken? Although I would never say such a thing to our precious Miranda."

"I've found a match for Miranda. One I'm sure will please you."

"You have?" she asked, her voice alive with surprise. "Whom?"

"Grant Morgan."

"Grant Morgan? Grant Morgan." Lady Evans tested the name as if it was unfamiliar to her. "Do we know a Grant Morgan?"

Phadra smiled. She'd love for the haughty Mr. Morgan to hear Lady Evans's total lack of recognition at the sound of his name.

"From the bank," Sir Cecil said. "He's been to our home several times. Good-looking lad. Smart one."

Lady Evans must have finally recognized the name, for she said in a horrified tone, "Not Jason Morgan's son!"

"Beatrice —"

"You've gone mad!" Her voice went up an octave. "How can you expect me to turn my precious Miranda over to Jason Morgan, the Lord of Love?"

"Jason Morgan is dead, Beatrice."

"The sins of the father rest upon the head of the child," she declared. "The man wasn't good *ton*. Oh, he was a handsome one, I'll grant you that. He was killed in a duel, wasn't he?"

"Yes, I believe —"

"And left *no* fortune. He'd gambled it all away. *Everyone* knows that."

"Grant has restored —"

"And this is the family you want our one and only daughter to marry into?"

"Grant is nothing like his father," Sir Cecil protested. "I mean, he looks very much like Jason, but that is where all similarity ends."

"He has bad blood in him," his wife hissed.

"Drat it all, Beatrice. Listen to me! In the eight years I've known him, I've never seen the lad let spirits cross his lips — not even ale. Furthermore, he's seen to the marriages of his three sisters to good, honorable men and managed to put together a modest fortune. When I think about it, we need his investment acumen in the family."

"He has no title."

"He'll earn one. I'll see to it. Furthermore, his family background is suitable. He's related to the Archbishop of Canterbury, and his mother was Marlborough's second cousin," he responded dutifully, as if he'd anticipated this topic.

Lady Evans was unimpressed. "But the

man has no prospects beyond being a banker."

"Beatrice, *I'm* a banker."

"You are a member of the Court of Directors."

"Grant Morgan has one of the sharpest minds in England today," Sir Cecil said. "If it weren't for his father's almost legendary reputation as a blackguard, Grant wouldn't be at the bank but would be building a powerful political career. The man's got the brains to be prime minister, if he had a care to, but instead he works for the Bank of England and does a jolly good job of it, too! Even the Court's governor acknowledges that he is one of the best."

His impassioned defense apparently didn't sway Lady Evans. "Miranda can do better. Lord Phipps has been paying particular attention to her. He is eminently eligible, is connected to the War Office, and has an income of five thousand a year."

"Grant will marry Miranda, Beatrice —"

"No! Absolutely not. She can bring in Lord Phipps. I know it."

There was a long silence. Phadra could imagine Lady Evans defiantly staring down her husband. She had no doubt that Lady Evans won every argument between the two — and that meant her problems were solved. She felt a surge of elation. Lady Evans would succeed where she had not.

Perhaps she should see if she could enlist Lady Evans's help in mounting a search for her father.

She smiled in happy anticipation. Any second now, Sir Cecil would open the door and announce that Phadra would not be welcome in his home. She started to nudge Henny to wake her — and then Sir Cecil's next words stopped her with her elbow in midair.

"Beatrice," he said in a voice that vibrated with great import, "I believe there are a few home truths you must understand."

Those were the last words Phadra heard. No matter how hard she strained, she couldn't hear another word that passed between the two without actually getting up from her chair and putting her ear to the keyhole — and she wasn't about to do that. Not with the footman standing present.

Sir Cecil was doing most of the talking. She could hear his low, serious mumbling. Obviously he'd decided to make a clean breast of the matter and confess the story of the Abbott emeralds to his wife.

All she heard of Lady Evans's resonant voice were loud gasps and stifled cries. At one point Sir Cecil rang for a maid, who went in and out of the room and returned again holding her lady's hartshorn. Phadra couldn't picture Lady Evans swooning, but the maid acted very concerned.

At long last the door slowly opened. This time Phadra did elbow Henny, who came awake with a snort. Lady Evans stood in the doorway, looking down on them, her lips pursed as if she'd just taken a bad-tasting physic.

Refusing to be intimidated, Phadra rose to her feet.

The two women faced each other, while Sir Cecil hovered anxiously behind his wife and Henny rubbed her eyes. Lady Evans spoke first, her eyes cold and uninviting. "Welcome to Evans House, my dear. I'll show you to your room."

Phadra's heart sank to her feet.

She was trapped.

Lady Evans sent for the housekeeper, Mrs. Mullins, and ordered her to see to a room for Henny. Mrs. Mullins bobbed a curtsey and led Henny down the hall. Lady Evans then turned to Phadra. "Follow me."

The footman picked up Phadra's bag and waited respectfully for her to follow his mistress. Phadra discovered she had no choice but to trail after Lady Evans feeling like a condemned man on his way to the gallows.

The bells on her toes didn't sound so merry now, especially when Lady Evans paused on the first step of the staircase and looked over her shoulder at Phadra. "Bells will never do." Her words had the ring of an official edict.

Lady Evans turned and started climbing the steps. "Tomorrow, first thing, we will go to the dressmaker for decent clothing and to the cobbler for decent shoes. I do not expect to see you attired in such outlandish costumes ever again. Marrying you off is going to be hard enough as it is. Do I make myself plain?"

Phadra refused to answer. She might have to suffer Lady Evans's tyranny, but she'd be a mutinous pupil — at least until she thought of a way out of these impossible circumstances. Instead she asked, "Where is Henny's room?"

Lady Evans paused before one of the doorways in the wide, elegant hallway. "In the servants' quarters."

"But she isn't a servant."

"She is in this house," Lady Evans countered, and, turning the door handle, opened the door and stepped into the room.

Fighting the urge to turn on her heel and run, Phadra followed her hostess into the bedroom. The room was appointed in bland

43

shades of blue. Phadra was conscious of how vivid her purple tunic dress must look against such a background.

"Put her valise on the table," Lady Evans instructed the footman, who dutifully did as he was told and then bowed out of the room, shutting the door behind him.

Phadra turned her attention from the large canopied bed and outdated heavy furniture to find Lady Evans studying her with an unpleasant smile frozen on her lips. Phadra matched the woman's haughty look.

"I don't approve of you," Lady Evans said at last.

"I don't care if you do or not," Phadra answered, and had the satisfaction of seeing the woman blink in surprise.

But it didn't make her feel good. She would much rather get along with Lady Evans than battle with her. However, her years at Miss Agatha's had taught her the only way to battle a she-cat was to show a few claws of her own.

To Phadra's relief, Lady Evans's tone of voice turned more civil. "This room shares a connecting door with Miranda's room. Who knows? Perhaps the two of you will become friends."

Not a chance, Phadra thought, and saw her sentiments echoed on Lady Evans's face.

Lady Evans walked over and rapped on the connecting door before calling out in a silly falsetto, "Miranda darling, may I come in? I have good news for you."

The door was opened by a maid in a mobcap who bobbed a curtsey as Lady Evans stepped through the door. "Mama?" came a young woman's voice from inside the room.

Lady Evans beckoned Phadra forward. Entering the room, Phadra found it decorated in a flamboyant style of rose and gold. Rose bed curtains hung from a massive canopy in the center of the room, and three huge armoires stood like silent sentinels around the room's perimeter. An open one was stuffed with dresses made of gorgeous silks and velvets. Dainty porcelains, perfume flasks, and silver bottles sat on the vanity at which Miranda, a very pretty golden blonde, had been sitting and letting her maid attend to her hair before her mother had interrupted her toilette.

Having seen Sir Cecil's wealth, and knowing what little she did about fashionable marriages, Phadra found it hard to believe that Miranda had not yet had an offer. The young woman, who must have been just a year or two younger than herself, was all that could be considered perfect in a young society miss.

"Mama," Miranda said again as she gracefully rose and welcomed her mother with a small hug. "What good news do you have for me?"

"My pet, this is our new houseguest, Miss Phadra Abbott. Your father and I will be introducing her into society."

Miranda looked from her mother to Phadra. Her wide blue, limpid eyes didn't miss a thing, Phadra thought, and for the third time that day she was conscious of someone staring at her toes.

Miranda smiled. "Oh, welcome," she said pleasantly. She turned to her mother. "Was this your news?"

"Did you have a good day?" Lady Evans asked, the smile on her face looking somewhat forced.

"I spent it with Cousin Sophie. She is becoming quite a bore, really." She rolled her eyes. "She goes on and on about how any day, any moment, she is expecting an offer. She's certain that Dangerfield is going to ask for her hand. I've warned her that she has been out for only a year and shouldn't have such high hopes, but" — she shrugged her elegant shoulders — "I only say it to be kind. Let's be honest: Sophie doesn't have a prayer at all of contracting any alliance, es-

46

pecially one as good as Dangerfield. She's got those buck teeth, and Dangerfield knows he can do better. You must see her, Phadra. Her two front teeth are very pronounced. Very unattractive," she finished, giving her own appearance a sweeping glance of approval in the glass over the vanity.

Lady Evans took a very deep breath before surprising Phadra by announcing to everyone in the room, "Well, my good news is that your father has accepted a contract for your hand in marriage."

Miranda seemed both surprised and delighted. "Lord Phipps has called on Father." She clapped her hands together. "I'm so happy."

"Well . . . no, not exactly," Lady Evans answered, the lines of her face crinkling with worry. "Oh, dear, Miranda. Perhaps you'd better sit while I tell you this."

"Tell me what?" The joyful certainty in her daughter's eyes turned to confusion. "Mama, what's wrong? Father hasn't bungled this, has he?"

Lady Evans blanched. "My dear, you are contracted to wed a Mr. Grant Morgan." Her words came out in a rush. "He's a gentleman your father knows at the bank."

Phadra watched the sweet, pleasant expression on Miranda's face change with the swiftness of rolling storm clouds. "Mr. Grant Morgan? A *Mister?*" she asked, her voice deceptively calm.

Lady Evans nodded, the salt-and-pepper curls bobbing, her expression tight. "He will present himself shortly to ask formally for your hand."

Miranda stared as if she hadn't heard her mother. "My father wants to marry me off to a *Mister?*" Her voice began increasing in volume. "Didn't you tell him about Lord Phipps? Didn't you tell him I had more *suitable* prospects?"

The maid and Lady Evans stepped back, leaving Phadra standing in the forefront. Phadra wondered briefly why they had done so — until the young woman, in a sudden, rash action, swept all of the glass bottles and pretty things from her vanity with such force that some hit the wall and broke.

"I won't do it!" she shrieked as the scent of lily of the valley filled the air. "I won't marry a plain Mister. I want to marry Lord Phipps. Father can't make me marry a stupid banker. Do you hear?" For emphasis, she crossed over to her bed and with one firm yank of her hand pulled down the bed curtains and flung them with surprising strength at her mother — but it was Phadra who caught them, taking a step back under their weight. Meanwhile Miranda beat her feet in an angry staccato on the India carpet. "I won't have it! I won't!" Her pretty face began turning beet red with anger.

A knock at the door interrupted her tirade.

"Who is it?" Miranda shouted, and stood there breathing in great gulps of air.

The footman's voice trembled slightly as he answered. "I have a message from Lady St. George and Lady Sophie."

Before anyone in the room could react, a woman's voice spoke up from the other side of the door, "Beatrice, open up. I have the most incredible news! I can't wait to tell you."

Lady Evans's eyes opened wide with alarm. "It's Louise and Sophie."

Miranda immediately snapped out of her tantrum. "What do they want?" she whispered.

"I don't know," Lady Evans answered. "Quick, let's get this room cleaned up." With surprising strength, she swept the bed curtains out of Phadra's arms and stashed them under the bed. The maid and Miranda picked up the bottles. Miranda pushed her bottles in the maid's arms and then shoved the woman off into a small room that,

Phadra surmised, had to be the water closet.

"Come in," Lady Evans managed to call out even as the door flew open. In rushed an almost exact copy of Lady Evans, with the same massive bosom. She was followed by a pretty brunette with a pronounced, but not unattractive, overbite.

"I have the most incredible news!" the woman Phadra assumed to be Lady St. George announced.

"Something that couldn't wait until dinner this evening, Louise?" Lady Evans asked.

"My dear sister. My dear niece," Lady St. George intoned in a dramatic voice, moving around the room to embrace Lady Evans and Miranda. "This news is so important that it must be shared right away. Isn't that right, Sophie?"

Sophie smiled shyly and didn't answer. Her mother obviously didn't expect her to.

Lady St. George started to hug Phadra but stopped herself, startled by her presence. "Do I know you?"

Before Phadra could answer, Lady Evans announced, "She's our guest. Miss Abbott, this is my sister, Lady St. George, and her daughter Lady Sophie. This is Miss Phadra Abbott, the daughter of Sir Julius Abbott."

"Oh," Lady St. George responded

without interest. Her gaze traveled from the top of Phadra's head and her circlet of gold to the tips of her toes. "What an unusual costume, dear. Is it foreign?" Before Phadra could answer, she turned to her sister and declared, "I have news of great import! But first, tell me, who is that *incredibly* handsome man sitting in your yellow parlor, Beatrice?"

"Handsome man?" Lady Evans was obviously puzzled.

"Yes," Sophie chimed in, her face flushing with shy excitement. "He's gorgeous. I've never seen the like. We met him when we first arrived, and he's so tall he practically fills up the doorway."

There was only one man who matched that description whom Phadra knew and who might also be cooling his heels in Lady Evans's parlor. "Mr. Morgan," she whispered to her hostess.

"Morgan?" Lady Evans repeated blankly, and then caught herself. "Ah, yes, Mr. Morgan." She shot a glance at her daughter, who glared back, her lower lip protruding in a mutinous pout.

Lady Evans evidently thought the time had come to get off the subject of Morgan. "What brings you to visit, Louise?"

Lady St. George smiled, her attention

brought back to the purpose of her journey. Clapping her gloved hands together, she announced, "It's the most marvelous news! Sophie has contracted an alliance."

"What?" Lady Evans and Miranda asked at the same time.

The fingers of Lady St. George's hands fluttered to punctuate her words. "An alliance. Lord Dangerfield has come up to scratch and asked for our little Sophie. Isn't it wonderful?"

"We're talking about a September wedding," Lady Sophie added, blushing with happiness.

"I wanted you and Miranda to be the first to hear our happy news," Lady St. George went on. "Can you imagine, an offer this soon? After all, Sophie has been out only a year, and Miranda has been out — how long has it been? Three years? Well, we never expected Sophie to land such a glorious catch. Imagine, Lord Dangerfield."

She put a hand to her breast as if so much happiness was overwhelming. "I feel as though there is so much to do, and I don't even know where to begin. Wait until you go through it, Beatrice. Oh, I know that you've gone through a wedding when your son was married, but it is a completely different matter to be the mother of the bride.

So much planning. But you'll find your opportunity soon. After all, Miranda has had three seasons. I'm sure she'll find a husband soon." She stopped and sniffed the air. "By the way, this room smells heavenly."

Lady Evans and Miranda stood frozen, their smiles plastered on their faces.

Lady Evans found her voice first. "Well, what . . . wonderful . . . news," she managed to choke out.

Sophie blushed deeper. "I knew you would be happy for me, Aunt Beatrice."

"Oh, I am," Lady Evans said, though she looked as if she was about to cry.

"And you, Miranda?" Sophie turned toward her cousin. "Aren't you happy for me, too?"

Miranda looked like she'd rather plunge a knife in her own heart than wish her cousin happiness. For a moment expectancy hung in the air. Phadra feared they were about to have a repeat of Miranda's tantrum and realized that her mother feared the same thing.

Miranda looked at her mother and then at Phadra. Her frown, so much like her father's, grew deeper.

Phadra held her breath.

The frown flattened — and then slowly turned into a dazzling smile. "Of course I am happy for you, cousin," Miranda said, her smile now as lovely and pleasant as a summer day. Lady Evans gave an audible sigh of relief that turned to a gasp of surprise as Miranda went on, "And you can be happy for me, too."

"We can?" Lady St. George asked, caught off guard.

"Why, yes," Miranda responded. "Mother, haven't you told Aunt Louise?"

"Told her what?" Lady Evans asked blankly.

"About *my* offer," Miranda said in a low, slightly angry tone.

It took Lady Evans a second to understand. When she did, her puzzled expression curled up into a smile. "Yes. Oh, yes, you need to wish Miranda happiness, Louise!"

"I do? Whatever for?"

Lady Evans smiled. She crossed to stand next to her daughter. Their arms linked in an unspoken bond. "Remember that glorious man in my yellow parlor?"

"He'd be hard to forget," Lady St. George said with a sly smile.

"He is Miranda's fiancé."

Lady Miranda and Mr. Morgan spent fifteen minutes together in the yellow parlor.

Everyone in the household, including Phadra and Henny, lined up in the hallway outside.

At last the door opened and Mr. Morgan walked out with a blushing Miranda on his arm. They looked the perfect couple with his dark masculine looks and her cool golden blondness. He announced ceremoniously that Lady Miranda had made him "the happiest man in London" by accepting his proposal of marriage.

Miranda lowered her eyes demurely. "You are very kind to say so, Grant."

Grant. Phadra thought his Christian name sounded strange on Miranda's lips.

The servants clapped while Lady Evans and Lady St. George embraced each other and wept. However, a few minutes later, Lady St. George pointed out to her daughter in a carrying voice, "He doesn't have a title."

Immediately Miranda's back stiffened. A jovial Sir Cecil, as if sensing danger, hastened the family members, of which Phadra was included, into the dining room for a toast to the couple's happiness.

But Phadra felt like an outsider. Listening to the relatives laughing and toasting the future of their daughters, she suddenly felt very alone.

"I trust that your moving in with the Evanses has gone smoothly," Mr. Morgan's deep voice said from beside her.

Phadra looked up at him, feeling unaccountably angry with him. "Would it matter?"

His eyebrows came together in concern. "Miss Abbott, I sensed earlier today that you believe I'm your enemy. I'm not. I truly want to do what is best for you."

"Then why don't you listen to what I have to say?"

"About what? Leading a search for your father?"

"I think it's possible."

He studied her for a moment, as if debating an answer, and then looked away. "Perhaps, but it isn't feasible at this time." She sensed that he didn't believe his own words. He looked back down at her. "Of course, if you marry a man with the right resources, anything is possible."

"We obviously hold a difference of opinion, Mr. Morgan. I think marriage should be something more than a sham."

His eyes hardened, and she noticed that they darkened with emotion. "Marriage is a perfectly respectable way for a person to advance in this world."

Phadra held up her hand. "You may call a

cold, impartial alliance a marriage. I cut to the heart of the matter and call it a farce."

His eyes flashed. "You are naive, Miss Abbott. I like to think that Lady Miranda and I will make a good marriage, one based upon mutual respect and not upon strong, often errant, emotions."

"Now that sounds boring," Phadra retorted before thinking of the wisdom of her words.

He looked as if she'd slapped him, and he took a step back, as if needing to remove himself from her presence. "You don't believe I'm good enough for Lady Miranda?"

The gravity in his tone startled Phadra. An angry muscle worked in the side of his jaw. But then some little mischievous imp inside her, recalling Miranda's house-shaking tantrum, caused her to say, "Oh, no, Mr. Morgan. If anything, I think the two of you are very well suited for each other."

"You do?" he asked, and then his eyes narrowed, as if he suspected a hidden meaning.

"You do what?" Miranda asked, coming up behind them.

"Miss Abbott thinks you will make a beautiful bride," Mr. Morgan said smoothly, surprising Phadra by the honeyed warmth in his voice. Miranda preened under the compliment, and Phadra found herself more than irritated with him.

"What are you going to do with my possessions, Mr. Morgan?" she asked, her words now clipped and businesslike.

Her sudden change of topic appeared to surprise him. He glanced at Miranda, as if to see whether she needed to be included in the conversation. She was no longer listening. Sophie had started talking about her engagement ball, and Miranda had stepped away from them and joined the little group around Sophie.

"Most of them will be auctioned," he answered.

Suddenly she felt a painful sense of loss. "All of them?"

He paused, seeming to want to soften the blow. "Most of them. I'm sorry."

"Why should you be sorry? I'm the one who ran up the debts — or at least part of them." She couldn't keep the bitterness from her voice and had to look away, her eyes blinking back the sting of tears. "May I at least have my books?"

"I will see what I can do."

"Thank you," Phadra said, the sound coming out in a whisper as she realized how difficult things were going to be. Her reversal of fortune had happened so fast that

58

when she and Henny had returned to her townhouse with Sir Cecil to pack a bag, she hadn't been able to think of what she was losing. Fortunately she'd had the presence of mind to pack her small silver box, with the few mementos it held of her mother like the emerald earrings and pin that matched the set in the bank's vault, but she hadn't thought to bring anything else.

Such as her books. Or the wooden horse that her father had sent to her mother years ago on the occasion of Phadra's birth. That, along with her debts, was her only link to her father. Could she ask for the wooden horse also? She had no idea how matters worked with creditors and bankers.

Unfortunately Sir Cecil interrupted any further discussion by announcing that an engagement ball would be held the next month in Grant and Miranda's honor. Miranda squealed her delight.

"Phadra . . . Phadra, wake up."

Phadra came awake slowly. Morning couldn't have arrived this quickly. Again she felt someone shake her shoulder.

There was light in the room. In the dim recesses of her sleep-fogged brain, Phadra knew that it was still night. The light shone from the connecting door between her

59

room and Miranda's.

"Miranda?"

"Yes, it's me." The mattress shifted slightly under Miranda's weight as she sat down. "Phadra, you have to make me a promise."

"Promise?"

"Yes. I need your help."

Phadra rubbed her face, trying to wake up. "For what?"

"I need you to go with me to the exhibit at the Royal Academy tomorrow."

"Of course. Fine," Phadra agreed, already laying her head back down on the pillow.

"Good," came Miranda's voice. Her silhouette was defined sharply against the light coming from her room. "Then you can keep Grant Morgan occupied at the exhibit while I keep my assignation with Lord Phipps."

Chapter 3

The next afternoon Grant, anxious to get to know his fiancée better, was impatient to be on his way to Evans House to escort Lady Miranda through the exhibit at the Royal Academy. However, he felt the delicate matter of preparing Miss Abbott's furniture and belongings for auction should be handled by him personally.

He rapped with the head of his walking stick on the black lacquered door of Miss Abbott's smart London townhouse. The sound echoed inside the building. Behind him, waiting patiently, stood two gentlemen from a respectable auction house.

He smiled at them.

They smiled back.

He rapped again . . . and smiled at the gentlemen.

He was just getting ready to rap on the door a third time when the door opened slowly — but Grant wasn't prepared for the apparition that met his eyes.

A Turkish pasha, dressed in yellow-and-blue harem pants, a brocade jacket, and a turban decorated with turquoise ostrich plumes, stood in the doorway. In the sonorous tones of an English butler, he asked, "May I help you?"

Grant looked from the tip of the man's nodding plumes down to his good, sturdy English shoes and their shiny buckles before he found his voice. "I'm with the Bank of England. I'm here on behalf of Miss Phadra Abbott." He held out his card.

Taking Grant's card, the Turk asked eagerly, "How is Miss Abbott? Jem and I have been worried."

Grant didn't know what to make of the man's familiarity. He looked over his shoulder at the two auction-house men. They waited patiently, acting as though it were not unusual for him to be having a conversation with a butler dressed for a masquerade. "May I come in?" Grant asked.

"Oh! Yes, sir, please enter." The butler held the door open wider.

Grant stepped into the cramped space that passed for a hallway in most London homes. Besides the butler, there was a footman in the same outlandish garb, who moved up onto the first step of the staircase as the auction-house men crowded in behind Grant. "These gentlemen are from the auction firm of Booth and Peabody. They are here to appraise the contents of this establishment."

The eagerness left the butler's face. "Miss Abbott isn't returning?"

"No," Grant replied soberly.

"She's fine, isn't she?" the footman, whom Grant surmised was named Jem, asked.

Surprised that both servants were more concerned for their mistress's welfare than for their own, Grant answered, "Yes, she's fine, although she has suffered a temporary financial setback." He didn't quite understand why he felt it necessary to honey-coat the exact truth. That thought brought to his mind another unpleasant task he had to perform. He turned to the butler. "I need a word in private with all the servants."

"There's just myself and Jem, sir. Miss Abbott would bring in a cook and a maid if she was holding a salon, but other than that, Henny, Jem, and I managed most matters for Miss Abbott."

"And your name is?" Grant asked.

"Wallace, sir."

"Wallace, which room shall we use to talk in private?"

The butler pulled his turban off his head to reveal a shock of snow-white hair. He nodded at a door. "There's the receiving room."

"Please give us a moment," Grant said to the other men, who nodded gravely. Without waiting for the servants, Grant opened the door and stepped into the room — and then stopped.

The initial impact of the room's outrageous decor stunned him. The sky-blue walls met a ceiling painted pale yellow and crisscrossed with an azure and sea-green Moorish lattice design. Crimson sofas and Egyptian-style cross-framed chairs, embellished with gold leaf, provided the seating. Carved wooden sphinxes served as table and sofa legs, while brass lanterns, much like those that could be seen in pictures of Turkish palaces, hung from the ceiling. The light scent of incense perfumed the air.

He instantly recognized the furniture from the descriptions he'd read on several of Miss Abbott's bills. On the mantel sat a clock that he knew she had paid £325 for. He moved closer to study it. The clock's face was set into the carved figure of a half-naked Isis. Her full breasts cuddled the numeral 12.

"Unusual, isn't it, sir?" Wallace said.

"Henny always called it rubbish, but Miss Abbott claimed it was a work of art. She said it was classical."

"Like your livery?" Grant asked dryly.

Wallace's face broke into a big grin. "Oh, no, sir. She termed our livery 'original.' "

Grant smiled and looked around the room again. Now he saw that it held a certain grace, a certain flair. Like Phadra Abbott herself.

"Miss Abbott is one of the best patrons I've ever worked for," the butler was saying.

His words brought Grant back to his unpleasant task. He'd discovered that the best way to deliver bad news was to be direct. He stated baldly, "Unfortunately, as her guardian, I must regretfully inform you that your services will no longer be needed."

"You're her guardian, sir?" Wallace asked. His eyebrows came together in a fierce frown.

"Yes, I am," Grant answered. "As a representative of the Bank of England, I bear responsibility for her."

"Well, then, sir, it is high time you saw to your responsibilities!" the butler practically roared, and shoved Grant in the shoulder.

"I beg your pardon," Grant began, confused by the man's anger.

"You certainly should beg it," Wallace

snapped. "That young woman has been given far too much freedom. She believed every shark's story in London and would have found herself up to her pretty neck in ugly tricks if we hadn't kept her out of trouble." He leaned forward, both fists clenched, and for a moment Grant thought he was going to have a fistfight on his hands. "It's about time, I say, that you owned up to your responsibility and took a hand in her affairs — although I won't hesitate to tell you that I think less of you as a man for waiting until the wolf is at the door."

As a banker who'd worked his way up through the ranks, and as the head of a household, Grant had sacked many individuals, both at work and at home. He'd seen his share of angry reactions, but he'd never had an employee defend the employer before. He raised a conciliatory hand, but Jem jumped in before he could speak. "Wallace is right! Miss Phadra is one of the kindest, good people I know. Men like you should be hung at Tyburn for leaving defenseless women to their own devices —"

"I'm just her banker," Grant finally managed to get in.

Wallace shoved Grant again, his lip curling with disgust. "Yes, and just like Henny says, you all are a lot of bloody grave robbers."

66

That insult was going a step too far. "Is that what Mrs. Shaunessy says?" Grant said. "Or yourself?"

"Meself," the butler announced with a trace of the street in his voice. "*I* say you are a bloody grave robber for leaving a poor, defenseless woman to her own devices, and I've a good mind to give you a taste of me fist." He raised a beefy fist that made Grant realize that this man was no ordinary butler.

"And after he gives you a popper, I plan on landing one on you, too!" Jem chimed in.

"Don't wait your turn," Grant snapped. "Come on, both of you! I'll not stand here and be called names by two ostlers dressed up like Turks and passing themselves off as decent British servants."

Wallace's face turned livid. He put up his fives in a traditional boxing stance. There was no doubt in Grant's mind that the man had seen the ring. Well, he could throw a good punch or two himself.

"Get 'im, Wallace," Jem yelled. "You show 'im wot's wot!"

The two men circled each other. Wallace's right came out in a sharp jab. Grant ducked and felt the wind from the swing over his head. What he didn't plan on was Wallace's left catching him in the stomach. Fortunately he was stepping back

67

when the man's punch caught him.

But Wallace's uppercut caught him square in the jaw.

The bone-rattling pain made Grant see red. His first punch hit the butler square on the nose; his second snapped the man's head back. Wallace staggered backward. Grant followed him, grabbed a handful of his pasha costume at the neck, and dragged the man up forward, his right arm pulled back, ready to land another bruising punch.

The sight of blood coming from the man's nose brought Grant to his senses. What had come over him? Wallace wobbled slightly but steadied himself by holding on to Grant's arm. Both Grant and Wallace were breathing heavily.

He looked past Jem, who stared in surprise at the now-open door to the receiving room. The gentlemen from the auction house leaned through the doorway, openly gawking at the scene in front of them. They couldn't have raised their eyebrows any higher.

Slowly Grant lowered his right arm. He untangled his fingers from the brocade of the butler's pasha jacket and stepped back before glancing over at the auction-house men, who nodded and mumbled some apologies about entering without being invited and then bowed out of the room, shutting the door behind them.

Grant cleared his throat, feeling very awkward. "I owe you an apology, Wallace. I normally don't lose my temper like that."

Wallace had pulled out a handkerchief and was dabbing at his nose. "There's no apology necessary, guv'nor. We both lost our heads. Miss Abbott can do that to a man."

"Miss Abbott had nothing to do with it," Grant replied. "She wasn't even in the room."

"She don't have to be," came the answer. Wallace held out his bloodied handkerchief. "Here, sir, you have blood on your neck-cloth."

"And the back of your sleeve is torn," Jem added, his eyes holding new respect for Grant. "If I may say, sir, you swing a good punch."

"Aye, sir," Wallace said. "It's not often a man staggers me with a facer, and you can take a punch, too. Do you follow the sport?"

Refusing with a shake of his head Wallace's offer to share his handkerchief, Grant reached under his arm and felt the tear along the seam of his sleeve. He'd have to return home and change before meeting Lady Miranda. Wallace's question distracted him. "No, no, I don't. I boxed some when I was up at Oxford, but that's the last of it. I'm a banker." He looked at the two servants. "I'm really a very rational man. I don't brawl with servants."

Both men nodded, although their expressions let Grant know they saw nothing wrong with a brawl or two. Wallace said, "We know you are a gentleman, sir, even if you can throw a punch. You might need to a time or two if you are going to look after Miss Abbott," he finished stoutly.

"How many times do I have to tell you that she has nothing to do with this?" Grant asked, completely exasperated with the two men.

"Till you convince yourself," Wallace answered. "Besides, sir, we mean no disrespect. We just want to make sure that you do your duty to Miss Abbott."

The two men looked so sober and honest in their concern for their mistress that Grant had the urge to explain to them that he had just taken over her account, that he wouldn't let anything happen to her. Instead he found himself asking, "Are you two men interested in working for me?"

Their jaws dropped open.

Grant had surprised himself too . . . but then when he thought about it, it made sense. "I'll be getting married soon and will need more household help, especially since four months ago my sister Jane married a clergyman from Essex and took our butler, Hankins, with her. Now I need a butler and could use a footman, too."

"And how much are the wages?" Wallace asked, suddenly a man of business himself.

"Twenty pounds for each of you," Grant said. "I'll pay Jem the same, since he will have to find his own lodgings."

Wallace looked at Jem, who shrugged. Then he turned to Grant and said, "Thirty pounds."

Grant frowned. The rascal was lucky he was offering him a job at all. "Twenty-five, and I never want to see you in that costume again."

"Done, sir. We will accept your employment."

A few minutes later Grant sent Jem and Wallace to his house, asking Jem to return with a clean shirt and fresh jacket for him. He then opened up the receiving room to the auction-house men, who went about their grim business efficiently.

Grant roamed through the empty house. No other room was decorated with the reckless abandon of the receiving room — until he came to what he knew must be Miss

71

Abbott's bedroom. He hesitated in the doorway, and then pushed the door open with his fingertips.

The walls and the ceiling were all painted a lovely sky blue. White bed curtains and bedclothes gave him the impression that he was stepping into the heavens. Even the bedposts and wardrobe were painted white. The only color in the room was provided by a stack of books on her night table.

He remembered her request to let her keep her books. Curious, he walked toward the night table and ran his finger down the spines. Philosophy. History. His sisters' tastes ran more toward melodrama and romantic novels, whereas Miss Abbott's apparently coincided with his own.

The book on the top was lying open, face down. Grant read the title: *A Vindication of the Rights of Woman.* Unfamiliar with the author, Mary Wollstonecraft, he picked the book up and turned it over.

It was obvious that this was a much-read and valued book. The pages were no longer clean and fresh, and their corners were turned down to mark particular passages. Without thinking, Grant flipped through several pages, reading various paragraphs.

He didn't argue with the author's opinions. After all, his sisters had railed about the inequalities of men and women under English law for years — and he agreed with much they said. But a treatise urging women to search for true freedom and demand educational equality with men would not help Miss Abbott. She was to be sold to the highest bidder.

For the second time that day he felt a stab of guilt. The men in her life had not taken care of her the way he believed they should have — and now she would be the one to pay.

Next to the stack of books sat a wooden carving of a proud, defiant stallion with its front hooves pawing the air. The carver had been skilled. He'd captured the spirit and beauty of the beast in a piece of golden wood.

Grant picked up the carving and, in his mind, weighed it against the books.

At last he set the book back down on the table, placed the horse in his pocket, and left the room. Outside the door, he ran into one of the estimators. "There are some books on the table," Grant said. "Sell them."

Phadra rocketed out of her room at Evans House like Chinese fireworks. After having spent hours being pinned, pulled, and pushed by Lady Evans and her dressmakers, she was sure she had no sanity left.

She was beginning to believe that debtor's prison would be preferable to enduring another round of fittings.

"You're late," she snapped at Mr. Morgan when he finally made his appearance to take them to the Royal Academy.

He stared at her, his eyes wide in disbelief. "Miss Abbott?"

She gave him a small mocking curtsey. "I'm not surprised you don't recognize me. I barely recognize myself. But then, you are one of the henchmen."

"Henchmen?"

"Yes," she replied, her voice sharp with anger. "You are part of the plot to turn me into a pattern copy of every other lady walking through society today, no matter what I think, what I feel, or how I look."

"You're upset."

"Whyever not? Look at me!" Phadra turned in a circle so he would receive the full impact of her outfit. "I look ridiculous in this. It's all the dressmaker had ready to wear, but Lady Evans ordered three more cut just like it."

He stepped back and surveyed her critically. "Actually, you look quite . . . fetching."

"In a pig's eye," Phadra said. She waved her arms wildly. "I look like a dwarf in these fussy ruffles. Plus the cream color makes me look washed out and sickly, but Lady Evans insisted all my clothing be debutante whites and pastels because that is what an unmarried woman wears." She held out a slippered foot. "I *caan't* wear *saandaals*," she said, imitating Lady Evans's tones. "I must wear shoes. Why? Well, not because I find these little leather things comfortable, but because that is what is expected by *society*. Who is Society, anyway, and why does it care what I have on my feet when there are so many other more important matters to think upon?"

It felt good to vent her frustration, and she sensed her anger ebbing. In fact, it soothed her wounded pride that Mr. Morgan appeared to enjoy her recitation of the trials she had suffered that morning. She raised her hands to either side of the brim of her hat. "This hat's outrageous. I'm like a horse with blinders and have to turn my head in order to see anything fully. I've had this hat on for only five minutes and already I have a crick in my neck. And you should see my hair underneath it."

"They didn't cut it?" he asked, sounding genuinely alarmed.

"They tried. But I wouldn't let them. Every time Lady Evans's maid came toward me with scissors, I held her off with the fireplace poker."

"The devil you did," he said, starting to laugh at her story.

"I most certainly did!" she declared, striking a noble pose. "But still they rolled and pinned it up until I feel almost bald. I tell you, sir, that we should forget sending the army after Napoleon and send society matrons and dressmakers. We'd have him licked in a trice."

Mr. Morgan burst out in laughter, glorious and rich. The transformation of his features stunned Phadra. If anything, he became more handsome, and she hadn't thought that possible. She found herself laughing, too, pleased that he enjoyed her humor.

He studied her for a moment with his sparkling gray eyes. "I'm glad they didn't cut your hair."

Dear heavens, had he paid her a compliment? The warm regard in his statement brought a sudden rush of heat to her cheeks. Thankful now that the bonnet hid her face, she made a pretense of smoothing the fit of her gloves, feeling light-headed, giddy.

Phadra didn't know what to do. She said

the first coherent thought to cross her mind. "Miranda should be down in a moment. I don't know what could be keeping her." She glanced up and away from him, suddenly shy of his silvery gaze.

"Women do take their time preparing to go out, Miss Abbott. It seems to be a cardinal sin of your sex."

"I beg your pardon?" Her gaze shot up to meet his squarely.

"Please, I mean it not as an insult but rather as a statement of fact."

"Of fact? Based upon what? Your study of the nature of women? Let me point out that I was here on time. You were not." She discovered that it felt good to argue with him and push away those disturbing feelings his presence could arouse.

"I have three sisters, Miss Abbott," he announced with a certain amount of smug satisfaction. "I found it prudent — no, *necessary* to tell them we were leaving a half hour earlier than the actual time in order to arrive anywhere *on* time. Experience, not fancy, has taught me the truth of that statement."

"Perhaps you would have found them ready on time if you'd let them know what you expected rather than play silly games with them."

He hated the way she talked down to him, as if he were a schoolboy, but held his tongue. His goal that day wasn't to match wits with Miss Abbott but to spend time with his future wife. His voice sounded a little too stiff, even to his own ears, when he said, "I wasn't aware that you were accompanying us."

"Miranda invited me. Is that *agreeable* to you?" Miss Abbott didn't look at him, but made a great pretense of pulling at her gloves, as if she found them uncomfortable.

"Yes, of course." What else could he say?

Grant had to admit that her dress looked to be more to Lady Evans's tastes than to Miss Abbott's. For a moment his mind conjured up the proud young woman she had been the day before in that flowing deep purple tunic.

He erased the image from his mind.

Then he remembered the wooden horse in his pocket and pulled it out. "I almost forgot. I picked this up at your home."

Her eyes lit up at the sight of the horse. She took it from him with both hands and pressed it close to her chest. "Thank you so much." Her words were filled with genuine emotion. "I can't tell you how important this small piece is to me. I've had it since childhood."

She held the carving in her hands and studied it for a moment before looking back up at him. Her deep, magnetic blue eyes were luminous with unshed tears as she asked, "Were you able to save any of my books? There was one in particular I would so like to have."

Grant's sense of pleasure died. "No. I couldn't bring the books." He looked away, unable to face his lie with that startling gaze on him.

The door to the room flew open, and Miranda burst in, radiant in a peach silk dress with a matching leghorn bonnet that suited her features perfectly. "Grant," she said lazily, pulling on her gloves, "I hope I haven't kept you waiting overlong." She stopped in the center of the room and made a silly moue at him as if to beg his forgiveness. He had the feeling she'd practiced that particular expression in the mirror.

Gallantly he replied, "Waiting for you, my lady, is an honor." He bent over the hand she held out to him.

That was prettily done, Phadra wanted to snap at him, but she held her tongue. She knew she appeared a drab goose next to Miranda, but she didn't understand why Mr. Morgan's marked attentions to Miranda irritated her. Not wanting to examine those feelings too closely, she said, "Excuse me for a moment; I need to run this up to my room."

"What is that?" Miranda asked, noticing the object in her hand.

"It is a wooden horse my father gave me. Mr. Morgan was kind enough to bring it to me from my old home."

"Grant," Miranda purred his name in a slightly petulant voice, "did you bring me anything?"

Phadra left the room on that question, half hoping Miranda would give him a dose of her temper — something she'd witnessed again that morning when Miranda demanded that her mother have dresses made for her, too. Let Mr. Morgan talk his way around that!

He must have succeeded in sweetening Miranda's mood, since the ride to the Royal Academy in the elegant coach he had hired for the occasion was uneventful. Because of the decided chill in the spring air and the threat of rain, the exhibit rooms were more crowded than usual. The Royal Academy was one of Phadra's favorite places to visit, and she came often. This day, though, she noticed something peculiar. Walking alongside the maid in the couple's wake, she noticed that heads turned and people stopped to watch the banker and Miranda as they passed.

At first she assumed people stared at them because of Miranda. Miranda must have thought so, too. She started to preen with all of the silent attention.

However, a few minutes later, Phadra changed her opinion. The heads turning as the couple walked by were women's heads — and they weren't admiring Miranda but savoring the chiseled good looks of Grant Morgan.

Phadra covered her lips with her fingertips to keep from bursting out into laughter. The banker acted as if he didn't notice the admiring glances and sly smiles. In fact, he was so extremely solicitous of his fiancée and her silly prattle that Phadra doubted Miranda would be able to free herself from him to keep her meeting with Lord Phipps.

She was wrong.

In a few minutes Miranda announced with the right touch of delicacy that she would have to excuse herself from their party for a few minutes to attend to necessities.

"Do you need me to go with you, Miranda?" Phadra asked, unable to stop herself from toying with her hostess.

"No," Miranda answered with false

sweetness and angry eyes. "My maid will accompany me."

In a second Phadra and Mr. Morgan stood alone, but Phadra wasn't laughing anymore. It was unsettling to be standing in public next to a man she, and everyone else in the room, thought more attractive than herself.

He spoke first. "I've never been to the Royal Academy or any of its exhibits before. Have you?"

That question brought Phadra out of her shyness immediately. "It was the first place I visited when I reached London. You don't admire art, Mr. Morgan?"

"It's not a question of admiration, Miss Abbott. I've had little time in my life to walk around looking at pictures."

At that moment a striking young matron in a very stylish gown accidentally bumped into Mr. Morgan's arm. She murmured an excuse and moved on, but Phadra caught her coy sidelong glance toward Mr. Morgan. A beat later, he bent and picked up a glove from the floor. He looked directly at the woman. "Excuse me, madam, but I believe you dropped this."

"Did I?" the woman said in a slow, inviting voice. "Then I thank you for returning it." Her fingers stroked the banker's hands as she took the glove from him.

Mr. Morgan gave her a short, cool bow, slipped his hand under Phadra's elbow, and — was it her imagination? — pulled her closer to his body. He directed the two of them out of the room and into another.

Phadra sensed movement behind them as women started to follow them into the next room. The whole situation was astounding. Every ounce of her experience had taught her that men did the pursuing, not vice versa. She looked over her shoulder and noticed that the forward young woman hadn't yet given up the pursuit. If Miranda was smart, she would hurry back and protect her territory, Phadra decided irritably. She whispered to him, "Is it always like this for you?"

He looked down at her, his expression tense. "Like what?"

She was caught off guard at how close his face was to hers. Heavens, she could see his whisker line and smell the clean, slightly spicy scent of shaving soap. She heard herself repeat dumbly, "Like what?" Then she blinked as if to break the spell. Perhaps this was the closest she'd ever been to a man — except for Alexei Popov, the poet, who attended her salons, drank all of her champagne, and one time had chased her around the table, managing to kiss her once before Wallace threw him out into the street — but she certainly didn't have to act as smitten as the other women at the exhibit. "Like these women practically offering themselves to you," she replied curtly.

Again the set of his jaw tightened. "If I ignore them, they will eventually go away. Besides, I am already escorting a young lady."

Struck by the absurdity of the situation, Phadra found her sense of humor. "Obviously I don't intimidate them."

Mr. Morgan saw no humor in the matter. "Miss Abbott, can we concentrate on the art?"

Phadra looked up in surprise. "You're embarrassed by all this."

He frowned, his eyes practically boring holes in the picture before them, which was of a naked shepherdess and two randy satyrs, but Phadra doubted if he saw a thing. "I don't know what you are talking about."

"I'm talking about the fact that there are women staring at you as though you were marzipan and they'd love to gobble you up."

To her delight, a slow blush stained his cheeks, and she realized that in spite of his extraordinary good looks, the man was actually modest. He tightened his hold on her elbow and pulled her even closer. "Will you stop it? They will go away if we ignore them."

Phadra almost choked on a bubble of laughter. "You understand that most men would kill to have so much attention paid to them? I tell you, if we could bottle what you have, my money problems would be solved."

He pulled away as if her words stung him, but she grabbed hold of his arm. "Please, Mr. Morgan, don't be cross with me. I'm only teasing. However, if you share your father's looks, I now understand his reputation as the Lord of Love," she said, inadvertently referring to the information she had learned eavesdropping on Lady Evans the previous day.

His eyes narrowed at her use of the title. "I am not a rake," he said angrily, his voice so low only she could hear him. "Nor am I unprincipled or unbridled in my passions. I don't trade on my looks." He bent down over her until they practically breathed the same air. "I work hard for my living and my rewards, Miss Abbott. I take my position with the bank, my family, and my engagement to Miranda very seriously. Yes, I want a title, but I also want to have a successful *marriage*. And my purpose in being here today is not to be ogled by a gaggle of females but to have the opportunity to acquaint myself better with my fiancée."

His vehemence startled Phadra. But she heard something else in his voice, too — the mention of his father caused him pain, made him angry.

She could have cut out her tongue for being so flippant. She would have told him so, too, except that when she looked up at him, he was no longer paying attention to her.

Instead he was staring over her head into the next room. Phadra turned to look in the same direction and saw that he was looking at a mirror that reflected the corners of that room. It also captured Miranda leaning against a door frame in easy nonchalance, basking in the admiration of a short, slightly rotund man who could only be Lord Phipps.

Chapter 4

Phadra's gaze went from Lord Phipps's reflection to Mr. Morgan. She didn't know what to say.

Mr. Morgan straightened his broad shoulders, looking more like a lord than did the man Miranda was flirting with. He forced his attention to the painting on the wall in front of them, his eyes icy, an angry muscle twitching in his jaw.

Phadra felt betrayed for him. "I'm sorry," she whispered.

"For what?" he asked, his tone offhand, almost bored.

She didn't answer.

After several long moments of silence, he asked, "You think I should be upset that I saw Miranda talking to Lord Phipps?"

"You know him?" she asked, surprised.

"I know him."

But do you know Miranda would jilt you if Lord Phipps crooked his finger? she wanted to ask, but held her tongue. He studied the painting in silence.

Phadra sensed that seeing Miranda with Lord Phipps was more upsetting to him than he wanted to admit.

She understood the pride that made him pretend all was well. She just hadn't expected to find that Grant Morgan, the banker, had an Achilles heel.

At last he spoke. "You are unfamiliar with the ways of the aristocracy, Miss Abbott. Fidelity in marriage is not a necessity. Miranda is free to go her own way as long as she is discreet."

"You're lying," she said softly.

He turned his head to look down at her then, his eyes the deep gray of hard steel. "What I do, what I think, is no business of yours."

"It's not," she conceded. "Except that I understand what it means to lie to yourself. To pretend things are right when they are actually terribly wrong."

"Miss Abbott, I am not here to argue with you but to enjoy the art." He spoke the words through clenched teeth.

"And to acquaint yourself better with your fiancée. Aren't those the words you used with me not more than several minutes ago?"

For a second she realized that she was behaving recklessly, but it had become important to her that he see the folly of marrying Miranda. The words, filled with passion, poured out of her.

"My mother had one of those marriages. You heard Sir Cecil yesterday. My father married her only for her money, and that is the way he treated her, as a piece of property that a landlord stops by and checks on from time to time. I can count on one hand the number of times I saw my father. Mother lived a lonely life, pretending her husband cared when he didn't. Looking back, I honestly believe that she didn't die of any disease other than a feeling of uselessness and neglect."

"And yet you want to lead a search to find this prodigal father?" His lips curled in mocking humor.

"Yes. Because I want to see him. I *have* to see him, to see the look on his face, to see if he recognizes me. If I don't, a part of me is always going to be trapped the way my mother was." She'd stepped close to him as she spoke, the vehemence and truth of her words surprising even her. Suddenly remembering that they were in public, she moved back.

She hadn't meant to reveal so much of herself to him. Or to anyone.

Feeling self-conscious, she shot a sidelong glance around the room to see if anyone was staring. The other occupants of the room seemed interested only in their own conversations or the paintings displayed on the walls. She relaxed slightly but could not bring herself to look up at Mr. Morgan.

He took her arm and led her away from where Miranda was enjoying her tryst. When he spoke, his voice was low and thoughtful. "I've learned, Miss Abbott, through hard and bitter experience, that the child can never escape the sins of the father. He can try . . . but he will not succeed."

He led them through a small hallway and into another room. Phadra no longer noticed if women were watching him. Her whole being was centered around listening to his deep, melodic voice.

Mr. Morgan stopped in a secluded corner. "I don't want my children to live with the sins of my father. I will marry Miranda and I will earn my title. My son will not be ashamed of me."

His words hung in the air between them.

"Then marry Miranda, if that is what you want," she answered, choosing her words carefully. "But I *want* to see my father. I must."

Phadra looked away for a moment, drawing on every last measure of her composure. Then she turned back to him. "You see, I've thought about this long and hard. I think love is important. I think that having someone who loves and cares for you makes a difference. After spending years without love since my mother's death, I want to find it again." Her gaze met his squarely. "You may marry to secure your position in the world, but I've already witnessed that sort of bartered life, and I don't want it. I don't want to be like you."

"Like me?" He laughed softly, without humor. "You're naive, Miss Abbott, to think that love between a man and a woman is that important or that it can sustain itself through the eternity promised in a marriage vow."

His verdict stung. "Perhaps we should change the vow to state 'until death do us part or three years, whichever comes first,' " she replied tartly.

He laughed, the sound carrying no mirth. "You learn quickly, Miss Abbott."

"You're a cold man, Mr. Morgan."

"Yes, but I will get my title," he drawled cynically.

"And at what cost, Mr. Morgan?"

"I'll sleep with a clear conscience."

"Yes, and whom will your wife be sleeping with?" she snapped without thinking. Immediately she regretted her words.

His mouth flattened grimly. He leaned closer to her. "You are too bold, Miss Abbott. Trust me, when Miranda comes to my bed, she'll never *want* to leave it."

No.

Phadra couldn't imagine any woman wanting to leave his bed. Her mind was filled with the image of this man and what he was boasting of.

Her mouth went dry.

Phadra could see her reflection in his hard, angry eyes. Every fiber of her being suddenly sensed how close he was to her — the long, lean line of his jaw, the outline of his whiskers, the curve of his lower lip. The other exhibit-goers, the room, and the day all seemed to fade away.

Tension hung in the air between them.

But it wasn't animosity.

His voice sounded as though it came to her from a distance when he said, "I believe we should consider returning to Evans House." He stepped away from her.

Phadra felt the wild, inexplicable emotion that had coursed through her drain away suddenly.

He hadn't felt it. He couldn't have felt what she'd just experienced because he was still in control of his senses. Still reasonable. Still the banker.

And she was the silly goose who, for one forbidden moment, had felt the closest thing to desire that she'd ever felt for a man — a man whom every woman lusted after! Maybe this whole situation of her father's leaving her penniless and on the marriage block was affecting her mind.

"Yes," she agreed stiffly. "It is time to return."

He looked as if he was about to move toward her, but then he held his position. "I realize it may be hard for you to fathom, but I do have your best interests at heart. I would like to think —"

He never got a chance to say what he thought because Miranda's shrill voice interrupted him. "I found you." Her face was flushed, and she smiled as if she carried a wonderful secret.

Phadra didn't dare judge her, because at Miranda's appearance she felt her own cheeks overheat, as if she'd been standing too close to a fire . . . or had a guilty secret of her own. She discovered herself staring at the wood flooring and her new kid slippers, which peeked out from under the satin skirt.

Miranda prattled on, describing the people she'd encountered while looking for him and Phadra. She didn't mention Lord Phipps.

Phadra mustered the courage to slide a glance up at Mr. Morgan. Gone was the raw, open emotion of only moments before, and in its place he wore his banker's face, a look of tolerant accommodation, as he dutifully listened to Miranda.

That was the expression he would wear the rest of his life, Phadra thought.

The thought depressed her, and as she and the maid followed the couple out of the Royal Academy, she vowed that the same fate would not befall her.

"There you are," Sir Cecil's voice boomed at them as they walked through the front door of Evans House. He stepped out of the yellow parlor, a glass of port in one hand, and waved them inside. "Come in, Phadra. Come in. I have someone for you to meet. Morgan, you too. Come in and meet these gentlemen."

Gentlemen? Phadra slowly untied the ribbons of her bonnet and let the ends hang down. She turned to dart a look of uncertainty at Mr. Morgan. He shrugged slightly and signaled her forward with his eyes.

Sir Cecil had already gone into the yellow parlor. Phadra followed him in cautiously. Her feeling of trepidation grew with each step.

The yellow parlor was so called because of Lady Evans's choice of colors for the room and for its sunny location on the eastern side of Evans House. Phadra imagined that it could be a lovely golden room. However, that day, with the overcast sky and the threat of rain, the room's colors appeared muddy and dismal.

Sir Cecil stood in the middle of the room, his face beaming with pride. He was flanked by two men, each looking as different from the other as day is to night. Lady Evans hovered nearby, her expression anxious.

"Miss Abbott, I would like you to meet Squire Blaney of Fowlmere, Cambridgeshire," Sir Cecil announced, introducing her to the small, wizened man on his right. Squire Blaney's face, except for a hooked nose, was lost under the moth-eaten bagwig covering his head. He looked as though he'd gotten dressed in the same clothes he'd worn to go to London twenty years before. His velvet knee breeches hung loosely around knobby knees, and his silk stockings were no longer white but a yellowish gray. He smelled of camphor and dogs.

The squire grinned a toothless grin and inclined his head, his eyes devouring her as if she were a sweetmeat. Phadra took a small step backward.

"Blaney runs a string of racing dogs, the best in England," Sir Cecil said.

The squire looked up at Sir Cecil. "What did you say?" he asked in a loud voice.

Sir Cecil leaned over to place his mouth closer to Squire Blaney's ear. "I said, you run a string of racing dogs," he shouted.

"I don't raise hogs," the squire practically shouted back, and Phadra realized that this was the man's normal tone of voice. "I raise *dogs*."

"This is Miss Abbott," Sir Cecil shouted again.

The squire made a courtly bow, almost losing his balance. "It's a pleasure to meet you, Miss Babbitt." He turned to lean close to Sir Cecil and said in a voice that was only slightly softer than his shout, "Actually, I like my women with a little more meat on them. Women are like bitches. With a little fat on them and a good stud, you can breed litter after litter." He pointed a callused finger past Phadra and at Miranda. "I'd prefer to marry that one."

Miranda choked with indignation. Sir Cecil hastily interjected that Lady Miranda was already spoken for by Mr. Morgan and physically turned the man so that he could see the size and breadth of the tall banker who stood to the side, a silent witness.

"Oh, well," Squire Blaney said, and then turned his rheumy eyes to study Phadra a moment. He frowned, as if struggling with disappointment. "I guess I could fatten her up," he conceded.

Miranda tried to stifle her laughter by covering her mouth with her hand. Unsuccessful, she mumbled an excuse to the guests and practically ran from the room, the sounds of her footsteps and laughter carrying in her wake.

As if to cover for her daughter's rudeness, Lady Evans came up from behind Sir Cecil and pulled the other man forward. "This is Mr. Jules Woodlac," she gushed. "And this is his mother, Mrs. Lawrence Woodlac." She stepped aside so that Phadra could see the huge woman whose presence had been hidden by the three men standing in front of her.

Her bulk took up most of the settee. She didn't acknowledge Phadra but reached for a small cake on a tray in front of her.

Phadra's gaze shifted back to the young man. He was passably good-looking, with sweeping dark curls, soulful brown eyes, and an upturned nose, though his dark features and all-black clothing emphasized his pasty complexion.

"It is a pleasure to meet you, Mr. Woodlac," Phadra forced herself to say. She held out her hand.

"And you," he replied as if those two words required a great deal of effort. He took her hand in his long, slender, almost white one and gave hers a limp squeeze.

His hand felt cold and clammy. She pulled hers back.

With a bright smile on her face, Lady Evans said, "Jules's father owns several mills in Ireland. Someday Jules will inherit all of them."

The young man's expression didn't change, even as he said, "Actually, I prefer to think of myself as a poet."

"What did he say?" Squire Blaney shouted. "What are you talking about?"

Sir Cecil clapped his hands together and, ignoring the squire, said, "Isn't that interesting? A poet! Miss Abbott is interested in poetry, aren't you, my dear?"

"Yes, I'm very fond of *good* poetry," Phadra demurred.

"Oh, see, you have something in common!" Lady Evans said. She looked over her shoulder as if searching for Mrs.

Woodlac's approval. The woman didn't look up but stuffed the last bit of cake into her mouth.

"Tell me, Miss Abbott, do you think about death?" Mr. Woodlac asked in an expressionless tone.

"Breath?" Squire Blaney asked in his carrying voice. "Does Miss Babbitt need a breath? What's the matter with her?" He turned and looked up expectantly at Sir Cecil as though he'd been about to purchase a prize hunting dog and found that it might have a defect.

Phadra felt ready to explode. Who did Sir Cecil think he was, foisting her off on these two dregs? And Mr. Morgan! What role did he play in this folly? Her temper barely under control, she said to the two would-be suitors, "Would you excuse me? I need a moment to remove my bonnet." *And put distance between myself and Mr. Morgan before I throttle him and the Evanses,* she added to herself.

She didn't wait for an answer but turned on her heel, left the room, and marched up the stairs, giving her anger free rein. Oh, yes, she had a word or two for Sir Cecil — and Mr. Morgan. Mr. Morgan in particular! To think she had started to believe that he held some regard, some respect, for her.

Did he think she would let either of those two potential husbands touch her? Phadra gave a shiver of disgust. She knew she wasn't a beauty, but she wasn't a toad, either!

She had just reached the first landing, out of sight to anyone in the hall, when she heard Mr. Morgan's voice. "What is the meaning of this nonsense, Sir Cecil?"

Phadra froze, straining to hear the answer.

"What nonsense?" Sir Cecil's voice asked.

"Of trying to palm off those two idiots on Miss Abbott!"

"Beatrice and I are merely trying to find her a husband. Wasn't that the plan?"

"The plan was," Mr. Morgan's voice said heatedly, "to find her a *suitable* husband. Blaney has to be all of seventy, and I don't think Woodlac is old enough to have seen his majority."

"He's young, I'll admit that fact. But he's over sixteen."

"What? He's seventeen?" Morgan snorted his disbelief.

"Those men are both suitable," Sir Cecil objected. "True, Blaney's a miser through and through, but he has more gold in his mattress than most people have in the bank, and that would suit our purpose —"

"*Our* purpose?" Morgan asked archly, as if to distance himself from the crime.

"— and Lawrence Woodlac, Jules's father, is rich beyond belief, plus he'd pay anything for an heir." His tone turned confidential. "Actually, Lawrence is a bit worried about his son. I mean, you may have noticed the boy is a bit queer in the head and maybe not all a man should be. However, if Phadra manages to breed a brat by him, Lawrence would make her rich beyond her dreams. He wants an heir."

"You sound as coarse as that old goat of a squire," Mr. Morgan answered.

The sound of a closing door warned Phadra that someone might be coming. Silently she hurried up the last few steps as Miranda appeared at the top of the staircase. Miranda smiled like a cat lapping cream as the two of them passed. "Tearing yourself away from two such earnest suitors so quickly?"

"One of them seems to prefer you," Phadra said evenly.

"I already have a suitor," came the smug reply. With a bounce of her curls, Miranda disappeared around the turn in the staircase.

And you'll make life hell for him, Phadra

thought as she turned the handle of her door and entered her room.

Practically ripping the hat off her head, Phadra threw the thing at the door.

A knock sounded. "Come in," Phadra called.

In came Annie, the maid Lady Evans had assigned to her. "Miss, is everything all right?"

It was on the tip of Phadra's tongue to shout, "No, everything is all wrong!" but then she realized that taking out her frustration on Annie wasn't a solution.

There had to be an answer to her problems. She had to think, to use her wits.

"Here, miss, let me brush out your hair. You've lost a few pins. You have to be careful when you remove your bonnet."

Phadra sat down at the chair in front of her mirror and for five wonderful minutes Annie brushed her hair out. Then she started to pin it back up again.

Phadra raised her hands to stop her. "Do we have to?"

The maid's gaze met hers in the mirror. "It's Lady Evans's orders, miss."

Lowering her arms, Phadra frowned in the mirror. She hated wearing her hair pinned up. However, the hairstyle was so ugly that maybe it would scare Jules

Woodlac and Squire Blaney away. All she had to do was thwart Lord and Lady Evans until she'd thought of a plan to either extricate herself from debt or find her father.

Her gaze moved from her own image to her bedside table, searching for the wooden horse, which she had left there.

The horse wasn't there.

Phadra rose to her feet, heedless of Annie, who was just about to stick another pin in her hair, and walked over to the bedside table.

She found the horse, but its front legs no longer pawed the air. They'd been snapped off. The head had been hit against the night table until it had splintered into pieces.

There was only one person Phadra could think of who could have done something this petty, this spiteful, this vicious. She picked up the pieces in her hand and stormed out of her room.

A footman opened the doors to the yellow parlor, so Phadra didn't have to stop until she stood in front of Miranda, who made a charming picture in blue silk, sitting in a chair opposite Mrs. Woodlac. Phadra dumped the pieces of the horse in her lap.

"What is this?" Miranda asked, her eyes wide, as if seeing the horse for the first time.

For a second Phadra's conviction wavered, but then she saw the laughter lurking deep in Miranda's eyes. "You tell me," Phadra said, her voice low and taut with the force of her anger.

"Was this your little horse?" Miranda tilted her head and slid a sly gaze up at Phadra before asking innocently, "However did it end up in so many pieces? Or was it that cheaply made?"

Phadra wanted to punch her. She forced herself to keep her arms at her side, her fists clenching handfuls of her skirt in an effort to exert control over her emotions. She'd never hated anyone the way she hated Miranda Evans at that moment.

But she also knew there wasn't anything she could do to Miranda.

What was worse, Miranda knew it, too. Her eyes glowed with challenge. With slow, deliberate movements, she brushed her hand against her skirt, sweeping the pieces of wood onto the floor. "I don't like things that are broken," she said. "Do you?"

Phadra stared at the pieces lying on the India carpet. "It was my only link with my father," she said, as if she could make Miranda understand the magnitude of her hateful act.

Miranda shrugged and looked away. Phadra fought the urge to shake her, to make her understand. She knew it would be no use. People like Miranda, who had everything they wanted, didn't understand what it meant to have little.

Slowly, almost as if in a dream, Phadra looked around the room at the people who had witnessed this scene. She saw Lord and Lady Evans, the footman and butler, Jules and his gluttonous mother, and Squire Blaney, who'd cupped a hand to his ear as if to pick up every sound he could. Finally she forced herself to look up at Mr. Morgan. He had come over to pick up the pieces of the horse, and now held them out in his hand. She hated the expression on his face — one of pity for her.

Phadra drew in a deep breath and held her head as high as any duchess. "Throw it away. I don't want it." She walked out of the room, refusing to look back.

But her composure didn't last past the door of her bedroom. Once inside, she collapsed like a wet sugar cake and stayed there until all of her tears were spent. She cried for her mother, for the changes in her life, and for all the opportunities she had to give up. She cried for a father who didn't care. And for a life that stretched long and bleak ahead of her.

When Annie tapped at the door, wanting

to know if she needed help preparing for bed or would like a bowl of soup, Phadra sent her away. She didn't want anyone to see her that way — not even Henny, whom she also turned away shortly after Annie's visit.

That night, drained of all emotion, she lay in the middle of her bed listening to the steady sound of rain falling outside her window. Never in her life had she felt so completely lost and alone. She fell asleep to the sound of rain.

Phadra woke the next morning feeling as though she'd been squeezed through a cider press. Henny appeared in her room shortly after Annie had brought a cup of coffee and spent part of the morning trying to cheer her. Phadra didn't say much. Her will, her energy to tackle life no matter what odds, had disappeared as if it had never existed.

Then the package arrived.

Annie didn't know who had delivered it. "A boy brought it. Mayhap there's a card inside that will tell who sent it."

Phadra turned the package in her hands. She didn't recognize the bold, slashing handwriting on the outside, nor was there any message on it other than her name.

"Aren't you going to open it?" Henny asked.

"I don't know. I haven't received many gifts in my life," Phadra confessed.

"Me neither." Annie's eyes were bright with excitement, as if she were the one receiving the present. "That's what makes them so special. Go on, miss. Open it up."

Carefully Phadra untied the string and then slowly unfolded the brown paper wrapping. For a moment, when she saw the contents, she forgot to breathe . . . and then slowly, almost reverently, she ran her fingers over the buttery soft leather of a much-read, much-cherished copy of Mary Wollstonecraft's *A Vindication of the Rights of Woman.*

Chapter 5

Phadra knew that Mr. Morgan had sent the book. She'd eliminated all other possibilities. Henny was with her, Wallace and Jem didn't read and wouldn't have been aware of what the book meant to her, and her other acquaintances didn't know about her abrupt reversal of fortune.

Remembering Miranda's jealousy, Phadra let four days pass before she attempted to thank him.

He was coming down the hallway from Sir Cecil's study, looking more handsome than she had remembered when she'd mentally rehearsed this meeting. He'd already finished with his fifteen-minute formal call on Miranda and was heading for the front door.

Feeling a little foolish for setting up a clandestine meeting, and aware that her heart was beating a rather strange tattoo, Phadra called his name softly. She had to repeat it before he checked his long, athletic stride. He stopped and listened.

Placing a hand to her stomach to steady her nerves, Phadra pulled the dining room door open a little wider so that he could see her. He turned at the sound of creaking hinges.

"Miss Abbott?"

"Mr. Morgan, may I have a moment of your time?" Phadra was relieved her voice didn't shake. "In private."

He looked at her uncertainly and then shot a cautious glance up the hall. Phadra could hear the noises of visitors in the yellow parlor — the clink of china and the low hum of gossip. It hadn't escaped her attention that recently Lady St. George, Sophie, and several of Miranda's friends had made it a point to present themselves at Evans House at approximately the same hour as Mr. Morgan's punctual visits.

He appeared to weigh the consequences. His hesitation made her feel brazen, but her pride urged her to continue. "For a moment," she added, and lifted her chin to let him know that it was of no importance to her if he came or not.

When he reluctantly murmured, "For a moment," Phadra felt a stab of panic. She held the door open while he slipped through. He shut the door quietly.

Afraid that he could hear the hammering of her heart in the quiet of the dining room, Phadra turned and walked toward the door that led into the smaller dining room the family used regularly. At the doorway she stopped to see if he followed.

The tense expression on his face told her he didn't think this was a good idea.

What did he think she was going to do, anyway? Irritated, she turned and went into the other room, her kid slippers gliding quietly across the hardwood floor.

A moment later she heard his heavier footsteps follow.

Along the wall overlooking the garden was a long bank of tall French windows, one of them open and leading into the garden. Phadra went through the French window and down the steps into a small, private herb garden.

Grant wondered where she was leading him as she disappeared through the door. He followed her and then stopped, poised on the window steps.

Miss Abbott stood on the gravel path cutting through the garden, waiting for him. Her dress was much the same as the one she had worn to the Royal Academy, except it was a light rose color. With her pale hair, it would have made her appear almost fragile were it not for the vibrant enamel blue of her eyes and the determined set of her chin.

Her lively corkscrew curls had escaped the maid's attempt at a fashionable coiffure. The spring sun kissed those curling tendrils, creating a gentle halo. She stood waiting for him like a proud young goddess.

He suddenly realized that following her to this private haven was not a wise idea.

"I wanted to thank you." Phadra had to force herself to speak the words. Seeing him standing on the steps, as imperious and reserved as a lord, intimidated her. She wondered if she had made a mistake by seeking him out to thank him in private.

"For what?" he asked in his cool banker's voice.

"For the book." She clasped her hands in front of her, sure that he would notice how nervous she was if she didn't hold them tightly. "It meant a great deal to me . . . and came at the time I needed it most."

"It wasn't a gift," Grant said abruptly, intensely aware that somewhere deep inside him his body responded to her low, musical voice — that he'd been listening for it these last four days on his visits to Miranda. "It belongs to you."

"But you had the power to return it, and you did so. For that I thank you."

For a moment Grant forgot to breathe. He no longer heard the hum of bees encouraging the lavender to grow or felt the sun on his head and shoulders.

Everything about him was concentrated on the petite, regal figure of Phadra Abbott standing before him — but then she'd rarely been far from his thoughts since she'd defied him at the Royal Academy.

He didn't want to feel this way. He didn't want to stand there in the herb-scented spring air and remember the day when she'd broken through his wall of caution and restraint.

He didn't want to remember that for one mad moment she'd tempted him, as no woman had tempted him before, to lean over and taste her lips. Or that he was alone in the garden with her right at that moment and could easily cross over to her, slip his hand around her trim waist, and draw her to him.

She wouldn't resist. Whether she knew it or not, every part of her, from her newly shod toes to her full, firm lower lip and shining blue eyes, begged him to do just that.

For a long, painful span of time, the hot, sporting blood of his father warred with the man he wanted to become.

"Think nothing of it," he said, his voice curt and businesslike, and then he ducked back through the French window and left the garden, running from her as if the hounds of hell snapped at his heels.

Phadra stood motionless a long time after he'd left. Deep inside her, a sad, wise voice said that it was all for the best.

"Damn it all, Grant. How much longer is it going to take to find a husband for this filly?" Sir Cecil grumbled as he walked into Grant's private office unannounced. "She's been under my roof for two weeks."

"Do you refer to Miss Abbott?" Grant asked without looking up from the reports and advertisements of properties being offered for sale that he had been studying. He planned on purchasing a country estate just as soon as he married and received his knighthood.

However, if the truth were known, he wasn't enamored of his future wife. There were sheep brighter than Miranda Evans, and, now that he knew her better, her clandestine attempts to throw herself at Lord Phipps inspired apathy in him rather than jealousy.

Sir Cecil brought his hands down on the papers, forcing Grant to look up at him.

"Don't think I don't know why Blaney cried off. He was interested in the chit until he had a visit from you."

"Squire Blaney treats his dogs better than he would a wife."

"He is rich."

"I'm not going to marry her off to someone I wouldn't let call on one of my own sisters."

"The problem with you, Morgan, is that you've too much of a conscience." Sir Cecil emphasized his words by pounding his palm against Grant's desk. "If you expect to succeed in the bank or in this world, then you are going to have to think with your head and not rely on emotion."

"How interesting," Grant drawled, "I'll have to inform Gladbury at the Royal Exchange. He told me this morning that I had no heart whatsoever."

But Sir Cecil wasn't listening. He pushed away from the desk and started pacing. "I ran into Harry Jenkins on my way in today. He asked how an auction we'd held in the name of a Sir Julius Abbott went. Said he hadn't heard of the account — well, you know how the man is," Sir Cecil said with a wave of his hand. "Damn nosy."

Now he had Grant's complete attention. "What did you tell him?"

"Fine, I said, fine. What else could I say?" He stopped and looked at Grant. "Did it go off well?"

"Well enough. We managed to take care of her most pressing debts. However, there is still the matter of replacing the ten thousand pounds for the emeralds," he reminded Sir Cecil.

"We've got to marry Phadra Abbott off. I can't cover it. I've been in dun territory for years," Sir Cecil said in a small, desperate voice.

Yes, Grant thought, *we have to marry Phadra Abbott off* — or his hell-born agreement to marry Lady Miranda would be for naught.

Phadra sat curled up in a chair in her bedroom. She and Henny had managed a visit to the lending library, and she wanted to do nothing more that afternoon than forget her problems in a good book on Roman history.

Unfortunately Miranda was having another fit in her room. Phadra tried to shut out the whining and concentrate on the book — then she heard her name mentioned.

Nothing could have stopped her from putting the book aside and rising from the chair. She didn't have to lean too close to the door to hear Miranda's plaintive voice. "I have to have more time. I know William will come up to scratch."

"There is no more time," Lady Evans said. "Your engagement ball is this Wednesday."

"One more chance. I demand it."

"Miranda, child, I don't see how we can stall Mr. Morgan any longer. He expects the announcement to be in the papers the following morning."

"I just don't think I can stand having Sophie outrank me! I can't stand it!" Suddenly there came a loud crash. Phadra jumped.

But this time Lady Evans didn't seem to have patience with Miranda. "Stop it. Stop destroying the furniture now and face reality."

Miranda broke down into big, gulping sobs that made Phadra wonder if the girl wasn't a touch mad.

"Miranda, you have to control yourself," her mother urged. "You can't go on this way."

Eventually her heartrending sobs subsided a little. Lady Evans went on in a voice of patient authority, "You will marry Grant Morgan. He's a good man, certainly an uncommonly handsome one, and your father promises to see him knighted soon after your wedding."

"A knighthood." Miranda made a spitting sound. "Dangerfield has a better title than that."

"Then maybe you should set your cap for Sophie's lad."

"You know I don't stand a chance with him. I lost my temper at Aunt Elizabeth's soiree and hit that maid over the head with her tray. Dangerfield is the one who helped the maid up from the floor." She heaved a sigh and said, "He acted as if I'd whacked some duchess over the head."

"Oh, I remember," Lady Evans said, sounding as if she was reliving the horror of that incident.

"Mother, please, I know I can bring in Lord Phipps."

There was a long silence. Finally Lady Evans said, "Mr. Morgan has two gentlemen he wants to introduce to Phadra and has suggested we host a small dinner party. We could invite Lord Phipps."

Miranda clapped her hands together. "Yes!"

"Mind you, it will be upright and respectable. I'll have no more of your flitting around meeting Phipps behind your father's back. If you can't bring him up to scratch during the dinner party, then prepare to be a knight's lady."

Phadra returned to her chair. She pulled her book onto her lap but didn't read. Instead she stared off into space, thinking.

So. Mr. Morgan had been searching on her behalf.

She wondered what kind of man he thought suitable for her.

The evening of the dinner party, Grant had to admit that Miranda looked stunning. She wore a dress made of expensive Valenciennes lace and silk, the white elegance making her appear almost regal.

In contrast, Miss Abbott wore one of the ruffly dresses Lady Evans had chosen. It seemed to hide her figure better than sackcloth. Her unruly hair had been pulled back tightly.

He'd rarely had the opportunity to see her these past weeks, but he'd heard her. Almost every day she played the pianoforte in the Evanses' music room.

Once he'd cracked open the music room door and silently watched her as she bent over the instrument, her concentration so intense that she didn't appear to notice he was there. Phadra Abbott lacked Miranda's superior musicianship. Her mistakes had

118

been loud and obvious, but she'd worked at the music with the dedication of a person who enjoyed the endeavor. Every note, even the wrong ones, had conveyed her understanding of the beauty and feeling of the piece.

That day she'd worn her hair down and loosely tied with a ribbon at the nape of her neck. The late-afternoon light streaming through the window next to the piano had touched her hair gently, causing it to gleam. Her long fingers had moved across the keys, stopping after each bad chord while she chastised herself for not playing better.

She wasn't a classic beauty, not with her upturned nose and that almost unmanageable hair, but there was something special about her. She was like a vibrant star that had its own sense of life. The problem was, women like Phadra Abbott found it difficult to conform; without the benefit of wealth, they would be hard to marry off.

Grant frowned, his mind now in the present. Not only did he not like Miss Abbott's tightly pinned hairstyle, but also he was not pleased to see Lord Phipps seated right next to her.

Phadra was aware of Grant Morgan the moment he stepped into the room. Even before the other guests moved and shifted in response to his incredible good looks and air of authority, she'd sensed his presence — just as she had that afternoon in the music room when he'd watched her play.

She looked up slowly and discovered that her senses had not lied. Mr. Morgan's tall frame filled the door. For the briefest of moments their gazes met. The butler announced him — and the two men accompanying him. It was only then that Phadra noticed his companions.

Thomas Jamison was an attractive man about twenty years older than herself. Captain William Duroy was perhaps the same age as Mr. Morgan and quite dashing in his white and gold uniform.

Her suitors. A soft, nervous fluttering in her stomach warned her that she wasn't ready for this. These men were nothing like the fops Sir Cecil had attempted to foist off on her. It took all her willpower to stand rooted to her place on the carpet and not make a mad dash for her room.

Lady Evans charged forward. "Mr. Morgan," she said, drawing out the words. "You've arrived at last. Pray introduce me to your guests."

She then took them around and introduced them to the other guests: Lord Phipps, Lord Dangerfield, Sophie and Lord and Lady St. George, Miranda's friends Lady Roberta Carr and Lady Margaret Nicely, and Sir Cecil's son and heir, Mr. Reginald Evans, and his wife, Deborah. Deborah was a sweet-looking young lady with cherry cheeks, whereas Mr. Evans — or Reggie, as he insisted everyone call him — was a miniature of his father, only with a head of dark curly hair.

"Morgan!" Lord Phipps said in his booming voice. "Good to see you." He stood and looked up at the banker in clear and complete awe.

Mr. Morgan bowed slightly in Lord Phipps's direction. "Good evening, Phipps. It is good to see you again."

Phadra didn't know who was more surprised by his familiarity with his lordship, herself or the Evanses — who all stared in open-mouthed surprise.

"You *know* each other?" Lady Evans asked.

"Of course I know Morgan!" Lord Phipps said. "Best swordsman in London. We patronize the same school." He nodded at the banker. "I heartily enjoyed that match you had with Woolford. I never liked the man; too high in the instep even for an earl." He looked at the rest of the company. "His forcing a challenge on Morgan was the best thing that could have happened. Morgan hit him on the fourth disengage. The man didn't even see Morgan's sword move. Like lightning." The affable Lord Phipps turned his attention to the two men with Mr. Morgan. "Have you seen Morgan fence? Marvelous swordsman. I'd wager he's the best in England."

"Many times," Captain Duroy answered. "We've long claimed Morgan is more of a Corinthian than a banker."

"I like that!" Lord Phipps declared before breaking into loud laughter. He reached up and, with an air of bonhomie, clapped Mr. Morgan on the back. "But then, swordplay runs in the family, doesn't it? They say no one could match your father."

Mr. Morgan smiled, a tight expression devoid of emotion, and answered lightly, "Someone did."

Lord Phipps's ruddy cheeks turned even redder. The conversation in the room had ceased, and Phadra realized that she wasn't the only one listening intently to every word the men were saying.

Lady Roberta leaned close to Lady St. George and asked in a low voice, "Who was his father?" Lady St. George obligingly whispered a hurried reply, and Lady Roberta's eyes grew wide with recognition.

Phadra dearly wished she could have heard what Lady St. George had said.

As if to cover the breach, Mr. Jamison asked politely, "Do you fence, Lord Phipps?"

"A little," he answered, "although I'm not in Morgan's class. Unfortunately, my time is not my own these days."

Mr. Morgan explained, "Lord Phipps is at Whitehall."

"I'm practically chained to my desk waiting for Napoleon's next move," the portly lord confessed.

"Phipps is a genius at moving supplies and troops to where they are needed," Mr. Morgan said.

"With your help," Lord Phipps added, his face flushing with pleasure at Mr. Morgan's compliment. "We couldn't have managed to sail the first ship across the channel without your understanding of how to work the financial markets to our advantage."

Captain Duroy nodded. "There isn't free time for any of us as long as Boney rules the Continent." The three other men agreed soberly with his pronouncement.

Mr. Morgan cleared his throat and changed the subject. "William, Thomas, I'd like to introduce you to Miss Phadra Abbott. Miss Abbott, this is Captain Wil-

liam Duroy, with the 7th Hussars, and
Thomas Jamison, a university officer at
Cambridge."

Phadra felt herself blush like a lower-
school girl. She held out her hand, and the
gentlemen made their bows graciously.

Before conversation could resume
beyond the pleasantries, the butler entered
and in a stately voice announced dinner.

Lord Phipps turned to Phadra. "May I
escort you into the dining room?"

His request startled her. Her gaze flew to
Lady Evans. Miranda stood behind her
mother, frowning.

Phadra realized she had no other course
of action than to place her hand on his arm.
Walking into the dining room, she could
feel Miranda's angry eyes boring two holes
in her back.

Fortunately, once inside the dining room,
Lady Evans separated them and seated
Phadra between Mr. Jamison and Captain
Duroy. Miranda took a seat next to Lord
Phipps.

Mr. Morgan was seated between Lady
Margaret and Lady Roberta, who batted
their eyelashes at him as if he were Apollo
come to earth. His lack of title didn't seem
to dampen their spirits, Phadra noticed.

One servant had been assigned to every

three guests, so the serving of the soup went quickly enough. Lady Evans attempted small talk. "So, Mr. Jamison. You teach?"

"Yes, history."

"Oh. How pleasant for you," Lady Evans said, and then beamed at Phadra as if to say, *Don't you like him?*

Phadra knew she should pick up the thread of conversation, but she suddenly felt awkward playing this debutante role. She was relieved when Lord Phipps interrupted. He leaned over Miranda, breaking all the rules of etiquette Lady Evans had drummed into Phadra over the last several days, and asked, "Tell me, Miss Abbott, is it true you are new to London?"

Phadra met the young lord's eager gaze and then glanced at Miranda. Forced by Lord Phipps to lean back in her chair, Miranda held her soup spoon over her bowl, her fingers curling like talons around the handle.

Something about the almost malevolent promise in Miranda's eyes angered Phadra. She graced Lord Phipps with what she hoped was a dazzling smile and answered, "My family is originally from London, and I have only just returned six months ago."

Captain Duroy started to make a comment, but before he could get a word out,

Lord Phipps blurted out, "Do you believe in fate, Miss Abbott?" He stared at her as if her every move fascinated him.

Everyone at the table looked from him to Phadra, waiting for her answer to his rather unorthodox question. Phadra didn't mind tweaking Miranda's nose once, but Lord Phipps was taking it too far. Miranda's smile looked frozen on her face — a dangerous sign.

Sensing the danger, Lady Evans quickly chimed in, "So, did you enjoy the war on the Peninsula, Captain?"

The inane diversion didn't work. Miranda's voice, silky and low, commanded attention, "You surprise me, Lord Phipps. I didn't imagine you had a taste toward the bluestocking."

Lord Phipps sat back in his chair. "Miss Abbott likes books?" He frowned and looked down the table at Phadra as if reconsidering his opinion of her.

"Yes, she owns several," Miranda purred. "Let's see, Miss Abbott, how many years have you attended school? Almost fifteen?"

Phadra smiled at Miranda to let her know that she knew what Miranda was doing — and it didn't matter. Her superior education didn't embarrass her. Furthermore, she had no interest in Lord Phipps. "Yes, fifteen, including the four years that I taught at Miss Agatha's Scientific Academy."

Mr. Jamison leaned forward. "That's very interesting. I have six children, and I think education is almost as important for my daughters as it is for my sons. Miss Agatha's has a very good reputation."

"Yes, but not as good a reputation as Cambridge holds. Tell me, sir, don't you think it is time Cambridge opened its doors to women?" Phadra asked.

"Whatever for?" Mr. Jamison asked, appearing to be surprised by the idea. "My personal observation is that schools such as Miss Agatha's prepare a young woman for her role as wife and mother better than the academic rigors of Cambridge."

Warming up to a debate on one of her favorite topics, Phadra couldn't possibly hold her tongue. "If that's our only goal in educating women, then you all would be better off marrying butlers!" She set her spoon down. "I believe there is more to being a wife and a mother than knowing how to ply a needle or dance a tarantella."

"But it is not necessary for Cambridge to open its doors to us," interjected Lady Margaret. "I know I wouldn't want to go there." She smiled sweetly at Mr. Jamison.

"But another woman might," Phadra

said. "Why should she be denied the opportunity because *you* don't wish to go?"

"Because that is not our place," Lady Roberta answered. "Our place is in being mothers and helpmeets." She looked to Mr. Morgan as if to seek his approval, but he ignored her. He appeared to be studiously examining the ceiling medallions on the far side of the room.

"Exactly," Phadra agreed. "And wouldn't we be better suited for our roles if we were educated? Wouldn't we be better able to raise our children to be strong citizens of this great nation of ours, and be more entertaining companions to our husbands, if we understood the world, its history, and the forces that govern it?"

"How would that make us more entertaining?" Lady Roberta asked, her expression blank. "I find this conversation boring."

"Yes —" Mr. Morgan started to interject, but Phadra wasn't ready to let it go.

"Lady Roberta, someday your youth will be gone." When the young woman seemed shocked at the thought, Phadra quickly added, "But if you have developed your mind, then the world will always hold a wealth of opportunities."

"If I lose my looks, Miss Abbott, I'd

rather be dead," Lady Roberta replied.

"And that is a silly sentiment, my lady," Phadra shot back. "There's more to you and to me than our looks. We have minds."

"Ah, now we come to the crux of the problem," Mr. Jamison said. "The truth is, women are not known for wisdom."

"Women are wise," Phadra said quietly, struggling to keep her temper. "We make wise decisions for the good of our families all the time, and what is good for our families is good for this country. In fact, two women have served as reigning monarchs and helped to make England great."

"They were aberrations, not the rule," declared Captain Duroy. "I for one don't want my women to be like Boadicea or Elizabeth. Of course, history tells us that Elizabeth was more like a man than a woman."

"History tells us no such thing," Phadra fired back, his ignorance helping to make her point, "because I have read history and I know that the men of her time respected her. And matters such as the misinterpretation of history are part of the reason a woman should be educated — so that she can determine what is *truth* and what is *fiction*."

Mr. Jamison's expression turned cold. "I for one have always considered women a

129

special breed apart from men. I admire them for their beauty and, in some measure, their intellect."

"That's right!" Reggie declared. "We love them for what they look like outside their heads, not what's going on inside their heads." He gave his wife an aren't-I-clever smile, and Phadra noticed that she, poor creature, actually nodded her approval to him!

Mrs. Evans's willing acceptance of her husband's dominance made Phadra throw caution aside. She leaned toward the lady. "Why can't a woman be lovely on the outside *and* educated and intelligent on the inside? Why is it always an either-or situation?"

Mrs. Evans's eyes opened wide. She turned to her mother-in-law. "I don't have an answer," she whispered with a touch of panic.

Phadra smiled at the innocent woman. "I don't expect you to answer, Mrs. Evans. There is no reasonable answer. But the truth is, God gave men and women equal minds —"

"Now, I don't know if I agree with that," Reggie, the humorist, chimed in.

"— but men have made laws and rules to keep women from using them." She looked around the table, noticing that Mr. Morgan had again returned to examining the ceiling medallions. Well, let him! She didn't need him to defend her position!

She addressed the younger women at the table with all the passion in her being. "Captain Duroy doesn't berate Mr. Morgan for choosing a career as a banker over the military. Nor does either of those two men chastise Mr. Jamison for choosing the academic life or suggest his time would be better spent at home with his children."

"Of course not," Lady Miranda said. "He is a man. It's a woman's place to stay in the home."

"Think about it!" Phadra snapped back. "A man has the freedom to take care of his children *and* have a career. Any career of his choosing! Whereas women have only two choices: to marry or not to marry. And there are those who would speculate that we have no worth at all if we can't manage to capture a husband. Our lives could be so much richer and rewarding *if we were educated.*" She turned to Mr. Jamison. "The idea that women are not bright enough for higher education is nonsense, and any rules that keep them from attending England's best schools ought to be declared invalid."

"Invalid?" Mrs. Evans said. She looked at

her husband. "What does that mean?"

Phadra wasn't about to let Reggie steer his wife wrong. She quickly interjected, "It means that some rules *should* be broken."

Mrs. Evans stared at her with a blank expression. Phadra desperately wanted her to understand. She searched her mind for an illustration. "Some rules we should follow. We shouldn't murder people or steal things. If we do murder and steal, people would be hurt. This is a rule, or law, we should follow." Mrs. Evans bobbed her head in agreement.

Phadra smiled, hoping she could phrase this so that Mrs. Evans, and all sitting at the table, understood. "There are other rules that really have no basis other than someone's decision that things should be done a certain way." She lifted her soup spoon. "For example, it is a rule of etiquette that we eat soup with a spoon." Mrs. Evans nodded again.

"But what if we didn't?" Phadra asked. "Is anyone harmed by our action if we don't? Does it make a difference if I pick up my soup bowl like this" — she lifted her bowl up, cradling it in both her hands — "and drink from it like so?" Without hesitation, she placed her lips to the edge of the bowl and swallowed some lukewarm soup.

She set the bowl down with a flourish. "See. I broke a rule, but no one was hurt. The rule has no merit because it wasn't that important."

But something had happened. Dead silence met her pronouncement. Mrs. Evans, Lady Evans, and all the other ladies around the table stared at Phadra as if she'd committed a mortal sin.

And the uncomfortable thought struck Phadra that maybe she'd gone *too* far in her effort to prove her point.

Chapter 6

Phadra placed her spoon next to her bowl and forced herself to complete the point of her demonstration in a much softer tone. "If Cambridge allowed women to attend, I think the country might actually be the better for it."

No response.

She looked from stunned face to stunned face and realized that she had crossed an imaginary line and had no idea how to return to the other side. Worse, Miranda was positively gloating.

"Perhaps Miss Abbott is correct," came Mr. Morgan's deep voice. "Perhaps we could do with fewer rules."

Lord Phipps turned to him, a look of interest in his eyes. "What do you mean, Morgan?"

Mr. Morgan shrugged. "There are times I find myself bored with the expected. Who needs a soup spoon?" To the shock of everyone — including Phadra — he threw the spoon over his shoulder. It hit the wall and clattered to the floor. He then picked up his soup bowl and, after lifting it in her direction as if in a toast, drank from the rim.

Phadra's mouth dropped open in shock. Mr. Morgan, elegant and handsome in his black evening clothes, was the last person she'd expected to do something so outrageous — or to support her outspoken behavior. Evidently everyone else at the table agreed with her. Except for Lord Phipps.

His lordship raised his eyebrows and broke into a big grin. "I tire of rules, too! Down with the tyranny of etiquette and the stuffiness of dining rooms. I've had enough!" He tossed his spoon over his shoulder where it was caught in midair by an alert footman and lifted his soup bowl. "To you, Miss Abbott, for setting us free." Putting his lips to the edge of his bowl, he slurped noisily. Reggie Evans laughingly seconded the toast, threw his spoon *at* a footman, who dodged in time, and drank from his own bowl.

It was on the tip of Phadra's tongue to explain that to use a soup spoon or not to use a soup spoon was not the point of her demonstration. However, one look at the horror-stricken expression on Lady Evans's face as she watched her carefully planned dinner party turn into chaos convinced Phadra that this was not the time to call attention to the fact that it was she, Phadra, who had started this nonsense.

Mr. Morgan turned to his friends. "Duroy, Jamison, won't you join us?" he asked.

Mr. Jamison frowned, and Phadra sensed that he'd rather plunge his butter knife into his breast than take part in this inanity. However, Captain Duroy met the challenge. He rose to his feet and raised his bowl. "To Grant Morgan and his fiancée, the lovely Lady Miranda. May they share a long and happy life together."

"What?" Lord Phipps said, looking up from his soup bowl. He turned to Miranda, a dribble of soup on his chin. "You and Morgan are going to tie the parson's knot?"

Lady Evans uttered a soft, frantic gasp.

"Oh, I thought everyone knew," Lady St. George said with mild surprise.

Lady Miranda sat still, as if she'd been hit by lightning and couldn't move, let alone comprehend Lord Phipps's question . . . and then, ever so slowly, she turned her head to stare in shock at Phadra. Phadra leaned back in her chair, preparing herself for the worst.

"Oh, Miranda, that is wonderful news!"

said her sister-in-law, Mrs. Evans, her voice breaking the silence. Lady Margaret and Lady Roberta added their congratulations. It couldn't have been lost on Miranda, Phadra hoped, that there was more than a touch of envy in their voices.

"To Morgan and Lady Miranda!" Lord Phipps cried, his exuberant voice bouncing off the dining room ceiling, and raised his bowl once more.

With such a toast, there was nothing to do but for everyone to lift their soup bowls and drink.

Reggie discovered he could blow bubbles in his soup, and his wife giggled at his antics. Lord Phipps was so charmed that he too tried his luck at blowing bubbles in the oxtail soup, and blew some soup up his nose. Lord Dangerfield sat back, apparently amazed by all of this. Finally he raised his bowl and silently toasted Lady Sophie, who blushed and raised her own bowl to shyly salute him.

The older couples looked as though they would rather have their hands cut off than touch their soup bowls.

Miranda appeared to bask in the attention, her lips curved into a charming smile that never touched her eyes. Phadra noticed that her hand was clenching her soup so tightly her knuckles turned white.

At last everyone appeared to tire of the soup, and the footmen stepped forward to remove the bowls and prepare for the next course. Lady Evans leaned forward, the ostrich plumes of her headdress bobbing, and said, "Well, that was entertaining." She looked directly at Phadra. "I wonder what we'll do for the next course."

After dinner, the women left the men to their port and adjourned to the yellow parlor. Grant waited until Sir Cecil had nodded to the butler to serve before excusing himself from the company. No one would miss him. He'd discovered that his nondrinking presence was not always appreciated by men interested in emptying a bottle.

He didn't even bother to check the drawing room, to which the women had retired. Phadra Abbott wouldn't be there. When the women had left the dining room, it was obvious they considered Miss Abbott a leper in their midst. Nor did he think she would escape to her bedroom.

He walked down the hallway to the back of the house, where a set of doors led to the walled garden. He took the garden's gravel path and found Miss Abbott where he thought she'd be, sitting on one of a trio of benches in the heart of the garden. She was so deep in thought that she didn't appear to hear his approach. She sat as poised and graceful as a classic Greek sculpture, the moonlight turning her hair to silken silver and her skin to alabaster.

Grant stepped out of the shadows. "When I didn't see you with the others, I assumed you would be out here."

She appeared startled at the sound of his voice. Her gaze met his, and then she looked away. "I thought you would be with the men, enjoying your port." There was no mistaking the bitterness in her voice. She resented his intrusion of her privacy.

He sat on the bench across from her and said lightly, "I tired of Reggie's jokes about men who don't drink."

The expression in her large eyes turned sad. "I suppose we're both outsiders, aren't we?" He didn't get a chance to answer because she went on, her voice very serious, "This isn't going to work, you know."

"What isn't going to work?"

"Marrying me off. Tonight was my first introduction to society, and you saw what I did. I always get carried away. I always do the wrong thing."

"Miss Abbott —"

"I made a fool of myself."

"You weren't a complete failure."

"I wasn't a total success."

"Did you want to be?"

Her eyes widened at his question. Then she blinked and looked off into the garden as if considering this issue for the first time. "Yes," she said slowly. "Yes, I did. I was nervous before the party, and Henny told me everything would go well. Of course, she also warned me to keep my opinions to myself." She smiled ruefully. "I didn't follow her advice."

"The courses after the soup went well," he pointed out in a mild attempt at humor.

"Do you think Lady Evans will remember that?" She took a long, deep breath before asking him, "Why did you come to my rescue? Why didn't you just let me die a peaceful social death and be done with it? I'll warn you now, I can't change. No matter what the situation, I always end up speaking my mind. Even in school, my tongue made me an outcast. My imagination runs away from me, and then . . ." She gave a small laugh. "I can't believe *you* drank straight from your bowl."

"You make it sound as though I was playing St. George."

"Trust me," she said, giving a nod toward

the house, "the dragons have their heads together in the drawing room. You are probably being painted just as black as I am right now."

"Miss Abbott, I know how you feel —"

"You couldn't possibly," she interjected. "You can't know how it feels." Her eyes gleamed with tears in the moonlight, and she averted her face. "I don't feel particularly well, Mr. Morgan." She rose. "Perhaps the night air isn't the best thing for me. I hope you'll excuse me if I retire to my room," she said, already starting to walk away from him.

He pursued her. "Is that it, then?" he asked. "You're going to accept defeat and run to the safety of your room? I thought Phadra Abbott had more spirit than that."

She stopped, the gravel crunching underneath her kid slippers as she turned to face him. "You don't understand."

"Oh, yes, I do. You're talking about your father again." He snorted. "Miss Abbott, having a father doesn't guarantee that everything in your world will go fine or stop you from making a fool of yourself."

She lifted her chin proudly. Her refusal to see her father as a selfish scoundrel angered Grant.

"You want to know about fathers, Miss

Abbott? Let me tell you about mine. Noble blood flowed through his veins, but he carried no title. Of course, that didn't stop him from acting like a lord. He was a great swordsman and an outstanding horseman. He was educated at Eton, and his friends represented all of the noble houses of Europe. He gambled, ran up huge debts, drank too much —" Grant paused for a moment, "And made love to other men's wives. That was his career, drinking and making love to women."

She gasped lightly at his admission, as he knew she would. "Did I shock you, Miss Abbott?" He "tsked" softly. "You are provincial. It is the duty of great would-be lords such as my father to spread himself out among women. It demonstrated that he was a man, and, to be honest, women melted in his presence. It's funny, but I don't remember him as handsome. Perhaps that is because I didn't like him."

"You didn't like your father?" she asked. She spoke as if the idea was completely foreign to her.

"It's an unnatural thing when the child doesn't love the parent, isn't it? Everything I've been taught from my prayer book to my primer says that I must love him and give him filial devotion . . . and for years I tried to. Not that my father demanded my love or even loyalty — he was far too self-absorbed to need anyone else's approval other than his own."

"You sound so bitter."

He looked up at her. "Do I?" For a second he looked into the dark shadows of the tree, looking straight into the past, seeing the memories, the demons that sometimes haunted him, even there in the fragrant peace of the garden. "Yes, I am," he said quietly.

"Why?"

"You always have a question, don't you, Miss Abbott?"

"How else will I understand, Mr. Morgan?"

Grant sat down on one of the garden seats. He shouldn't answer her. He never talked about it, but . . . He started speaking, needing to tell her, needing to let someone understand. "It started at Eton. The first day I was there." He could recall it all perfectly, the smell of books, slate and chalk, the shuffling of the older students as one by one they noticed. "I looked across the schoolroom, and there sat a boy who looked almost exactly like me."

She didn't understand, so he explained, "This was no cursory likeness. The boy and

I were close enough in looks to have come from the same womb. He was a marquess's son, heir to a grand estate, and held a title of his own. I was the son of a titleless gentleman whose very name made the other boys' mothers whisper behind their hands and their fathers threaten to withdraw their sons from the school if I remained. In fact, there had been some question about my even being accepted at Eton because of my father's reputation. Fortunately, my mother was related to Marlborough, and he spoke on my behalf."

"Are you going to tell me that boys can be as cruel as girls?"

He laughed. She evidently understood. "They can be worse. One day the boy's mother visited the school but didn't ask to see her son. Instead she asked to see me. When I went into the headmaster's office to meet her, she burst into laughter and told me I was better-looking than my father. That night, my half-brother and his mates gave me the worst beating of my life."

She sat down on the bench beside him. "No! What did you do?"

"Learned to fight back."

"Did you say anything to your father about your resemblance to this boy?"

"Of course. There was a part of me that

wanted him to deny the truth. I loved my mother and still had a child's deeply held opinion that my father must love her, too." He looked at her. "Life is very simple when we are children."

If she understood his point, she gave no sign but asked instead, "What did your father say?"

Grant shrugged. "He laughed."

"He laughed?"

"He informed me that he didn't understand what I was upset about."

"I think he was the one who didn't understand!" she said, her spirited indignation returning. Grant smiled. Phadra Abbott loved to champion causes.

He almost hated to destroy her illusions. "No, he made me understand. That night he took me to his favorite brothel and purchased a girl for me."

Her eyes widened in shock. "What did he want you to understand?"

"How to be a man, Miss Abbott. The type of man he thought I should be."

"And did you become a man?"

He wondered if this young woman, cloistered for so long in a girls' school, really had any idea of what they were discussing. In his mind's eye he could recall the features of the prostitute, who had been little older than himself, and his blundering attempts to make his father proud of him . . . his own confusion. He erased the night from his mind and responded coldly, "I wanted to please my father."

She frowned, as if she wasn't certain that she had heard him correctly. "But you were so young."

He laughed, the sound without mirth. "Trust me, Miss Abbott, I learned it all at my father's knee — gambling, drinking, whoring."

She sat back, sliding him a shrewd glance. "But you are not like him today."

"No," he agreed softly. "When I turned seventeen, I came home on holiday and found my mother dying. She had a brain sickness and had been ill for months."

"And no one told you?"

Grant leaned forward, resting his elbows on his thighs, finding the memories almost too painful to recall. "My uncle, who was looking after my mother and sisters, didn't see fit to tell me because he considered me too much of the 'devil's own image.' He never got along with my father." His uncle's words still had the power to hurt. "Father knew Mother was ill, but he hadn't gotten around to paying her a visit. I remember that she lay in the middle of her big bed, calling his name over and over. She didn't even recognize me."

Miss Abbott surprised him by laying a hand on his shoulder. The gesture was strangely comforting. "What did you do?"

"I went looking for him — and I found him. He and a crony had picked up a young girl on the street. They had raped her. A young girl." He stood abruptly, feeling a need to put distance between himself and Miss Abbott's compassion. "You can't imagine the things they did."

The memory was too real, too vivid. He ran a hand through his hair and took a deep, steadying breath. "That's when I knew I didn't want to be like my father." He turned to her and added quietly, "And I'm not."

"What happened to the girl?" Miss Abbott asked softly.

"I took her home. Her family had to call the physician . . . but I don't know what happened to her. She had a brother who was a lieutenant in the Horse Guards, though. He called Father out and ran him through. The rumor is that Father showed up for the duel drunk. I don't doubt it."

"Did he ever see your mother before —"

"No. She died two weeks later. It was just as well. The man was a bastard."

She studied him quietly with that direct,

clear gaze of hers. Finally he broke the silence. "Trying to picture me as a rake?" he asked, hearing more bitterness in his voice than he'd intended.

"No," she responded softly. "I'm seeing you as a man desperately trying to be the opposite of his father and yet headed in the same direction."

The verdict shocked him. "What do you mean?" he demanded.

She rose to her feet. "I mean that you want so desperately to prove yourself different from your father that you'd even marry a woman for whom you have no affection whatsoever."

Her audacity stunned him. No one had ever delivered a crueler insult. "You don't know what you are saying," he said when he found control of his voice. "I am not offering Miranda *carte blanche*, Miss Abbott. I am offering her my *name*."

"Mr. Morgan, perhaps I am overstepping myself in saying this, but Miranda has a *problem*." She tapped her temple with two fingers. "And I can't believe you don't see it as clearly as I do. You're a fool to marry her — especially for no other reason than to buy a title to prove yourself different from your father."

Grant stared at her hard for a long minute

before responding, "You're right, Miss Abbott."

She blinked in surprise. "I am?"

"Yes, you *are* overstepping yourself. Furthermore, *I'm* the fool for unburdening myself to you." He practically ground the words out.

She sat down on the bench, carefully erect. A cloud covered the moon, and he couldn't read her expression.

He looked away. Damn her! She'd insulted him — so why did he feel guilty? Finally he said, "I didn't come out here to argue." He sat on the bench opposite her. "I wanted you to know that I understand how it feels not to fit in." He paused a moment and added, "I also know how important it is to you to believe that your father must feel something for you."

When she spoke, her voice came out hoarse with pent-up emotion. "Then let me go."

"What?"

"I said, let me go."

"The bank has a responsibility to you. I can't."

"Yes, you can." Her eyes sparkled in the moonlight as she challenged him, "If you understand even a little of what I feel, then you should know how I long to free myself from this." She gestured to the house and surrounding garden.

"So you can do what? Run up bills you can't pay? Or find your father? Haven't you understood anything of what I just told you? *The man's not worth it.*"

"Why? Because you say so? I don't know that! And I have to find out for myself." She dropped to her knees in front of him. "Don't you understand? You know who your father is. You rejected him. But I don't know. My common sense tells me that he can't have my best interests at heart, but I'll never know until I meet him." She touched her hand to her breast. "It's something in here, deep inside me, that needs to meet him. To look into his eyes. To hear his voice."

"Even if he's a bloody scoundrel?"

"Yes," she said softly. "Perhaps after I meet him, I won't want him in my life . . . but I have to know."

A part of him wanted to grant her deepest wish. She had that effect on him. He rose and walked a few steps away, again feeling the need to put distance between them.

"It's virtually impossible to reunite you with him," he said curtly.

"Only because you keep saying it is," she said, rising to her feet.

"You must understand, I'm acting in your best interests —"

"A pox on my best interests!" she shouted, her voice carrying in the night. He looked toward the house. She did, too, and then lowered her voice to say with equal heat, "It certainly can't be in my best interests to be forced into a marriage I don't want. And if you tell me one more time that it is an acceptable solution, I shall scream and pull my hair out. You may marry for money, sir, but I want nothing to do with it."

The woman never gave up! "You know, Miss Abbott, you can be quite infuriating."

She arched an eyebrow. "So can you, Mr. Morgan. So can you."

Grant caught himself smiling. She was more stubborn than a barrister and twice as intelligent. A man would never be bored with Phadra Abbott in his life. Finally he confessed, "I have tried to think of another way."

She looked at him with surprise. "You have?"

"But I haven't been successful. The problem is time. The activity in your accounts has drawn attention. We need to replace the funds for the emeralds before the end of the year."

"I could take a position as a governess. I could work off the debt."

"I don't think —"

"Yes, I can."

"Miss Abbott, it would take years for you to earn enough to pay back the amount the emeralds were sold for. Don't look for help from Sir Cecil. The man's made several unwise business decisions and is barely making ends meet, in spite of all this." He nodded his head toward the house.

"Then I'll pay back *all* of it."

"Ten thousand pounds?"

She sank down onto a bench. "I had no idea they cost that much," she said in a small voice.

"It was an incredible set of stones."

Miss Abbott looked off into the distance as if evaluating her future. Grant didn't like the determined set of her chin and wasn't surprised when she looked at him intently and announced, "I'll do it. I will find a way to pay back the debt. I can write. I can teach. I may even try my luck on the stage, as Henny did."

"No," he said emphatically.

"Why not?" she asked with some exasperation. "It's a solution. There has to be another way besides marriage. Trust me, I'm not marriageable material."

"That's not true," he answered, surprised she would even say such a thing. "Right now, standing in the garden with the moonlight all around you, you look very marriageable."

Miss Abbott's mouth dropped open, as if she couldn't believe he'd said those words.

He couldn't believe he'd said them, either. Grant shifted, suddenly uneasy.

A voice calling his name interrupted his thoughts. Lady Roberta had come out into the garden from the back doorway of the house. She hurried toward him, throwing a shawl around her shoulders.

Thankful for the interruption, Grant walked up the path to meet her. "Is something wrong?"

"Nothing's wrong . . . other than that we missed you. I noticed that you didn't come out from the dining room with the other men." Her lips formed a lovely little moue before she asked, "What have you been doing out here by yourself?"

"By myself?" Grant turned toward the shrubs that encircled the benches. Miss Abbott was not in sight. Had she slipped away or was she hiding? He realized that it didn't matter — in fact, it would be better if no one knew they'd been out there together. When he turned back around, he almost bumped into Lady Roberta, who had moved quite close to him. He took a step backward. "Did you come to take me inside?"

She smiled, her invitation clear. "I was hoping I could convince you to give me a tour of the garden."

Grant placed a hand on each of her shoulders and turned her in the direction of the house. "I'm sure Miranda is waiting for us."

Lady Roberta dug in her heels and pulled him back with surprising strength. "She's not. When I left the parlor, she and Lord Phipps were very cozy."

The idea that Miranda was once again throwing herself at Phipps irritated Grant. He also thought of what Miss Abbott would say if she'd overheard this conversation or if she'd been serious when she said that she didn't think Miranda was quite right in the head.

He dismissed the idea even as he almost forcibly dragged the pouting Lady Roberta to the house. Furthermore, he had to put Phadra Abbott out of his mind.

But that was easier said than done. Especially since he found her in the drawing room when he and Lady Roberta rejoined the rest of the company. There must be a side door he didn't know about.

He frowned. Lord Phipps no longer attended Miranda but sat next to Miss Abbott. The two appeared deeply involved in conversation until she looked up, her gaze meeting his. He could tell that she still considered herself mistress of her fate.

Grant felt his jaw tighten at her stubborn refusal to listen to reason. At that moment a smiling Sir Cecil, benevolent from food and drink, walked up and nudged him in the ribs before whispering, "Might be a match. Phipps has got the blunt to pay off the emeralds and then some, hasn't he? And he loved all that soup-drinking nonsense!"

Chapter 7

Monday afternoon Grant was so immersed in his work that he didn't hear the door to his private office swing open until a voice said, "You work too hard."

Startled, Grant looked up and saw William Duroy in his smart-looking uniform standing in the doorway. "William," he said, pleased to see him. "What brings you here?" he asked, pulling out his watch from his waistcoat. It was 1:39. Replacing his watch, Grant sat back in his chair and stretched, feeling his muscles unkink themselves up and down his back. "I didn't think you rose before two when you were on leave, and your uniform puts me to shame as I sit here working. Is it a holiday? Has the king demanded your presence?" He grinned. "Or has Napoleon landed and you've come to warn me?"

"I paid a morning call on Miss Abbott."

The grin froze on Grant's face. "Miss Abbott? You called on her . . . this morning?"

William laughed happily. "Now I've shocked you. Not only am I at your office before two, but I've been courting."

"Courting . . . ?" Grant groped for words. "I'm — surprised."

"Oh, I am, too. I didn't know what to think the other night. I mean, with all that nonsense about women going on to university."

"She meant what she said," Grant interjected, feeling a sudden need to make sure William understood.

"I'm sure she does," he agreed. "And I admit that at first I was put off by it. Thomas too. He was still grumbling when we parted company. He went on and on about how the first thing women will want is entry to university and then next they'll expect seats in Parliament. Can you imagine a female prime minister? It might be just what the government needs to act against Napoleon!" He laughed again, the sound light-hearted. He stepped to Grant's desk and placed a hand on its polished surface. "However, after the party I couldn't get her off my mind."

Grant shifted uncomfortably.

"I find the fact that she has strong ideals refreshing," William said.

"You do?"

"I do," William reaffirmed before moving with restless energy around the room. "Too many women do nothing more than parrot one's words. But Phadra Abbott is original, her ideas thoughtful, her manner direct. In short, she is like no other woman I've met — except for my mother. Did I ever tell you that my mother always wanted to teach? Just like Miss Abbott."

"No, you've never said a word to me about your mother," Grant answered, feeling irrationally cross.

"Well, my mother is a headstrong woman, and I adore her that way. My father always told us boys that when the time came to choose a wife, we should do what he did and find someone with some spirit, some intelligence."

"He said that, did he?"

"Yes. He said a woman like that could keep a man interested not only in the bedroom but out of the bedroom as well."

"William —," Grant started, not certain he wanted to hear his friend talk about Miss Abbott and bedrooms.

"Oh, I never thought there was another woman with Mother's verve and energy."

"Verve?"

"Yes! That special something that is so hard to define. I've looked, but I'd never

met anyone just like her . . . until last night."
William's eyes took on a dreamy look, something that Grant had never thought possible for the pragmatic military man. He sat down on the arm of the chair in front of Grant's desk. "My call on Miss Abbott this morning only confirmed what I'd suspected. She's intelligent. Spirited. Noble. Beautiful."

"Beautiful?" Grant admitted she was uncommonly attractive, but beautiful?

"Those eyes," William went on as if he hadn't heard him. "They are like windows to her soul. You can read everything going on in her lively mind through those eyes. And her figure . . . so enticing . . ." He lifted a hand to draw a curved shape in the air and smiled.

Grant didn't like the smile any more than he liked the fact that William had seen what he himself had noticed. "I don't know what you're talking about," he said stiffly.

William sighed before focusing again on his friend. "Grant, you can't have turned into that much of a monk! Oh, I admit, I didn't see it all at first. That outfit she was wearing hid a great deal. It was grossly unattractive, and I have no idea why she doesn't choose a more becoming style. But I'm not blind. Phadra Abbott has a figure any man

159

would like to explore."

Grant felt hot, indignant color steal up his neck.

"And that hair," William continued, staring into space as if transfixed. "I don't like the style of it. I found myself sitting across from her in the parlor today and wondering what it would be like if she took the pins out of it and set it free. I bet it hangs down to her waist. All wild and curly."

Grant's fingers tingled as if they could feel those lively, silky curls. He rose suddenly and walked over to the window. It took him a second to find his voice. "She's deeply in debt."

"What?" William asked. Grant's voice seemed to have brought him out of a trance.

Grant turned, his hands clasped behind his back, his face set in his sternest banker expression. "She's deeply in debt," he repeated.

"I know that. You told Thomas and me before you introduced her to us. Ten thousand pounds, isn't it?"

"Fifteen," Grant lied, fueled by an irrational urge to dampen William's enthusiasm.

His friend was silent a moment, as if mulling this information over in his mind. "I believe she's worth it," he finally said.

That wasn't the answer Grant had expected. "William, think sensibly. You don't know her at all."

The young officer winked slyly. "But what I know, I like excessively."

Before Grant could think of a comment — something other than crossing over to his friend and shaking him senseless — William asked, "What's the matter with you? I thought you wanted to find a suitor for Miss Abbott. I gained the impression that you were even desperate to find a husband for her." He stood and spread his hands. "Well, here I am. And if she accepts my suit, we'll name the first baby after you."

The first baby? Grant frowned.

"Is something the matter?" William asked, his expression puzzled.

Grant shook his head. What the devil *was* the matter with him? "No. Nothing." He forced a smile. "Name the first baby after me? What if it's a girl?"

William laughed, his good humor restored, "Grantwina?"

Grant found himself smiling at that bit of foolishness and dismissed the idea with a wave of his hand.

William looked down at his hands, which held his cockaded hat with its jaunty red and yellow plumes. His eyes turned pensive.

"Your friendship has meant a great deal to me over the years."

"As I value yours," Grant answered sincerely. He walked back to his desk and sat down, steepling his fingers in front of him.

William's expression turned serious. "We've known each since our first day at Eton together. I know better than most how hard you've worked and how much you want a title. Grant, I firmly believe you'll get it someday. So I hope you'll not believe that I'm crossing the line of friendship when I tell you that I think you should reconsider your engagement to Lady Miranda."

"What do you mean?" Grant asked, caution edging his tone.

William's eyes didn't meet Grant's gaze as he said, "I've heard things."

The words hung in the air between them. Grant didn't have to ask him what he meant. William was not the first friend to take him aside, and then there had been Miss Abbott's suggestion that perhaps Miranda wasn't well . . .

Grant pushed his own reservations aside. Enough people knew of his intentions toward Miranda that there was no honorable way to withdraw his suit without creating a scandal — something Grant could not afford if he wanted his knighthood. He shook his head. "I'm committed."

William looked as though he was about to say something, but then apparently thought better of it. When he spoke, his voice was again carefree. "Come with me to my club."

Where they would run into more friends who would take him aside and act as if he were marrying one of *Macbeth*'s witches and not the very lovely and aristocratic Miranda Evans. Grant waved toward the papers on his desk. "I can't."

"Not even for an afternoon? This may be our last chance to enjoy ourselves as bachelors."

Grant shook his head. It wasn't only the work. He needed some time alone. Why was the idea of William and Miss Abbott together so unsettling?

William studied him for a moment before saying, "Suit yourself."

Grant felt guilty. "Will I see you at the ball?"

William smiled. "When your engagement is announced? Absolutely. Who knows? We cavalry officers are a dashing lot. Perhaps I'll have swept Miss Abbott off her feet by then, and we can make a double engagement announcement."

"That would be good," Grant managed to croak out.

If William noticed his lack of enthusiasm, he gave no indication. He placed his hat underneath his arm and with a salute left Grant's office.

Grant sat still for several long moments analyzing the feelings churning within him. He should be pleased William planned to make an offer for Phadra Abbott. After all, he thought of William almost as a brother. Miss Abbott would be marrying a good man.

Sir Cecil burst into Grant's office without announcing himself. "Oh, good, you're here. Just ran into that Captain Duroy again. Met him this morning when he paid a call to our precious Phadra. Did he have anything particular he wanted to say to you?"

"He wanted me to go to his club with him this afternoon," Grant answered, not certain why he didn't want to tell Sir Cecil of William's intentions toward Miss Abbott.

That wasn't the answer Sir Cecil wanted. The corners of his mouth turned down as he leaned against the door frame. "Well, he probably couldn't afford her debts."

"His father is Malcolm Duroy of Yorkshire."

"The nabob?"

"Exactly. His father made the family's

fortune, but they all work. William chose the military. His brothers run the family concerns."

Sir Cecil stood up straight, his eyes dancing with excitement. "Well, now, this is interesting. Duroy and Phipps. Our little Phadra is making a good showing for herself."

"Phipps?"

"Phadra received a huge bouquet of posies from him this morning." Sir Cecil clapped his hands together. "When do you think you can hook one and reel him in? Phipps would be nice. He has excellent connections, but I don't know how Miranda will handle it." Then he flushed, realizing what bit of information he had inadvertently let slip.

Grant felt the muscles in his jaw tense. Did the man think he was a fool and completely blind to Miranda's machinations over the past few weeks? It was on the tip of his tongue to tell Evans he didn't give a bloody damn about Miranda's feelings over Phipps, but he reined in his pride and swallowed the angry retort. When he had his title and seat on the Court of Directors, then he would be his own man and could speak his mind to Sir Cecil. Until then he would play the game. He made himself answer calmly, "I'll talk to William. Perhaps we can announce both engagements Wednesday night."

"Excellent!" Sir Cecil started to leave but then stopped and turned back to Grant. "I can't tell you how much I appreciate your handling this little matter of the emeralds and all for me, Grant. I know you're coming into the family through the back door, but I want you to know that I consider you an asset to the Evans name."

Realizing Sir Cecil was waiting for a response, Grant managed a dutiful "Thank you, my lord."

The words tasted sour in his mouth.

It didn't help matters when, an hour later, Sir Cecil left for the day. His secretary appeared in Grant's office with a stack of papers and instructions from Sir Cecil to review them for him.

Several times during the afternoon Grant told himself that it didn't matter. After all he had no plans for the evening. Miranda planned to attend Almack's, the very exclusive supper club that would never let the son of Jason Morgan walk through its portal — and he sensed she knew it.

Well let her have her last fling, he thought grimly, signing Sir Cecil's name to another report and throwing it on top of the high stack of finished work. After their engagement was announced, she'd discover herself just as unwelcome at Almack's.

He sat back in his chair and rubbed his temples, dismissing the thought as uncharitable — and not the best way to start a marriage. He rarely got headaches, but all day, for some reason, something had not seemed right to him.

The oil on his desk lamp burned low when the note from Elrad the goldsmith came. The man wanted to see Grant immediately, that evening.

Grant pulled out his watch. 8:13. He was ready for his supper and his bed, but he'd done bank business, and personal business, with Elrad for years and respected him. Pulling on his double-breasted dress coat, he left for the goldsmith's shop on Cranbourne Street.

Elrad answered Grant's knock on the establishment's door himself. "Thank you for coming so quickly," he said, the long chestnut curls on either side of his head bobbing with his bow.

"You said it was urgent."

"It is. My father is furious, but I told him I would take it up with you and you would make everything right."

"Make what right?" Grant asked. The tension in his body increased.

"Come. I'll show you." Elrad led Grant through the shop to the back room. Three lamps burned brightly from a table. Their combined light lit a goldsmith's velvet cloth and several pieces of jewelry.

Some inner sense warned Grant he wasn't going to like what Elrad was about to show him. He slowly took the steps to the table. On the cloth lay a set of emerald earrings and a large emerald ring. Grant picked up the ring and held it to the light. The deep-colored gems sparkled and winked at him.

Emeralds.

The settings of the earrings and ring matched the Abbott emeralds that sat in a vault in the Bank of England. "They're beautiful," he murmured.

"They're fake," came the harsh voice of Mordecai. The older man stepped into the light. Bright anger shone in his eyes.

"How can you be so certain?" Grant asked cautiously, placing the ring back on the cloth. He turned to face Elrad's father.

Mordecai gave him a slow smile, his eyes glittering with knowledge. "Because I made the paste copies."

Grant's heart went still. Seeing no sense in pretense if Mordecai already knew the

168

truth of the Abbott emeralds, he asked, "How did you get these?"

Mordecai adjusted his robe and sat down on the high stool in front of the table. His fingers lightly touched the jewelry pieces as he talked. "My son purchased them. He didn't realize they were clever forgeries until he showed them to me this evening." He gave a slight smile. "I do good work."

"Did Sir Cecil bring them in?" Grant asked.

Elrad answered, "No, a young woman brought them in."

"A woman!" Grant exclaimed.

"Yes, Miss Phadra Abbott. She said the pieces had been in her family for generations and she wanted to sell them," Elrad said.

Grant felt his face flush with anger. So the minx had been holding a thing or two back from him. "When did she do this?"

"It was early in the afternoon. About one-thirty," Elrad said.

"Was anyone with her?" Grant asked.

"No, she came in alone." He shrugged. "I've already confessed to my father, and I might as well tell you the same. All I saw was the sapphire blue of her eyes. I wasn't thinking straight."

Mordecai gave a world-weary sigh and

shook his head. "He's young; she was blond," he explained to Grant, as if Grant himself was immune to that same set of large blue eyes. "He even paid her too much."

"I thought they were a flawless set, and she was dressed like a gentlewoman of quality," Elrad said, bright spots of color burning on his cheeks.

Mordecai waved a dismissive hand toward his son. "My question is, what is Mr. Morgan going to do?"

"Why me?" Grant asked, his voice tight. "Why not Sir Cecil?"

"He's a fool," Mordecai answered. "And I don't think he has the money to repay me."

"Whereas you think I do," Grant said.

Mordecai bowed his head, acknowledging the truth of Grant's statement. "You are an honorable man and a man who handles important, delicate matters for your bank. I am correct in assuming that this is delicate business, no?" His shrewd eyes studied Grant's face as if gauging his reaction.

Grant smiled coolly. "I appreciate your discretion, Mordecai. How much do I write the draft on my account for?"

"Five hundred pounds," Mordecai answered.

"Five hundred pounds!" The words burst out of Grant before he could think. "What is she going to do with five hundred pounds?"

Mordecai smiled benignly. "For that, my friend, you will have to ask Miss Abbott."

Grant had every intention of doing exactly that. Immediately.

The lamps of Evans House glowed brightly through the foggy evening. Grant took the front steps two at a time and pounded the door knocker against the heavy door.

A second later a footman opened the door, saw who stood on the step, and blanched before slamming the door shut in Grant's face.

What the devil was going on? Grant knocked again with such force he could have splintered the wood.

The door swung open again, and Mrs. Shaunessy flew out and threw her arms around his neck. "Mr. Morgan, praise heaven you've come."

"What's going on here?" Grant demanded as he pried the woman off him and walked into the house.

Mrs. Shaunessy shut the door behind him, and Grant found himself surrounded by servants, including the stone-faced butler. "It's Phadra," Mrs. Shaunessy cried out, and leaned against the door as if she was ready to faint.

"Stop acting as though this is a theater production," Grant ordered, catching the redhead by an elbow and making her keep her balance. "What about Miss Abbott?"

"She ran away!" Mrs. Shaunessy said.

"Ran away?" Grant repeated blankly. He looked from her to the butler, who silently nodded. "Where are the Evanses?"

"Out!" Mrs. Shaunessy exclaimed. "Sir Cecil is off to his club, and Lady Evans went with Lady Miranda out to dinner with friends and then to Almack's."

"Maybe we should talk about this in private," Grant muttered, suddenly realizing that almost all of the Evanses' servants had crowded into the hallway and were watching Mrs. Shaunessy's theatrics with intense interest.

Mrs. Shaunessy waved her hand. "They all know that Phadra's run off. There are no secrets here, Mr. Morgan," she said in a ringing voice. "And I'll also tell you that every one of them is loyal to Phadra."

"That's right, Mr. Morgan," said the housekeeper, stepping forward. "We all respect and admire Miss Abbott. She's a saint, and there isn't a one of us who would do a thing to hurt her."

Not for the first time did it strike Grant that Phadra Abbott had a way with servants. He ran his hand through his hair in exasperation and took a deep breath. "All right. What makes you think Miss Abbott has run away and isn't with Lady Evans and Miranda?"

"Because they can't stand her!" Mrs. Shaunessy declared as if Grant were simpleminded.

"Mrs. Shaunessy —" Grant started.

"It's true!" Mrs. Shaunessy gave a shiver of indignation. "You should have heard Lady Miranda carrying on today when the flowers arrived for my dear Phadra. I think she would have murdered my poor girl if it hadn't been for the footmen."

Grant frowned at such nonsense until he noticed that the footmen and the butler were nodding in agreement with Mrs. Shaunessy. "All right. So she is not with them. Where else could she be? There has to be a reasonable explanation."

Mrs. Shaunessy grabbed the lapels of his jacket. "I tell you, she has run away!"

He pushed her arms away. "Mrs. Shaunessy, please come to your senses and think rationally. Where would she go?" *With five hundred pounds,* he added silently.

Mrs. Shaunessy opened her mouth to speak and then just as quickly shut it. She shook her head. From the mutterings of the other servants, no one else had any idea, either.

Then a clear young voice rang out from the back of the crowd. "I think I know where she went."

"Who said that?" Grant asked, and the servants pushed forward a young woman in a claret-colored uniform, white apron, and mobcap until she stood in front of him. "What is your name?"

The maid made an awkward curtsey. "Annie, sir. I'm Miss Abbott's abigail." She twisted her apron nervously with her hands.

"Where do you think Miss Abbott has gone?" he asked.

"I think she has gone to find her father," she announced.

If Grant had been whacked in the head with a hammer, he couldn't have been more surprised.

The problem was, the maid's comment made sense . . . if one knew Phadra Abbott.

"Why do you think this, Annie?" he asked softly.

Annie swallowed. "She wants to see her father. It's a need inside of her. I understand it. My father died when I was a babe. That need to know is very powerful."

Powerful enough to make her do something this foolhardy? Grant turned to Mrs. Shaunessy. "When was the last time you saw Miss Abbott?"

"This morning, after she received the flowers. And after that nice young captain paid his call."

Grant looked at Annie. "When was the last time you saw her?"

"This morning, when I helped her dress. When I knocked on her door later, after Captain Duroy's visit, she said she was ill and didn't want to be disturbed."

"She told me the same thing," Mrs. Shaunessy said. "Turns out she'd bundled up some clothes and put them under the bedclothes to make it look as though she was sleeping. I just discovered her absence an hour ago when I went to her room to insist that she eat something."

So Elrad had been the last one to see her, and that was earlier in the afternoon. Grant wondered if she was really foolish enough to think she could make it to Egypt on five hundred pounds.

Yes, she was. She'd left Miss Agatha's Scientific Academy with less. He knew because he'd checked the records.

"What are you going to do?" Mrs.

Shaunessy asked, her voice rising hysterically. "She'll be ruined once Lord and Lady Evans discover she's gone. No decent man will marry her. And you *know* what that means," she finished in a dramatic whispered aside to Grant.

He certainly did know what that meant. His marriage to Miranda would be for naught, since Sir Cecil could end up sitting in prison with Miss Abbott beside him — and Grant too, if he wasn't careful.

"Do, Mrs. Shaunessy? Why, I'm going to go find her," Grant promised, his voice steely with determination. "Tonight." He looked around the hallway at the servants. Their expressions were full of sober concern. "If she is not returned to Evans House before her absence is discovered, her reputation will be ruined and all doors will be closed to her. Do you understand? For her own good, we must all keep her absence a secret until I can return with her."

To a man, all the servants nodded. The housekeeper said, "Mr. Morgan, I speak for all of us. You bring that young woman back safe from harm and you can count on us. We won't breathe a word of this to another living soul."

"Thank you," Grant acknowledged curtly, thinking at the same time that it was futile. Servants never kept secrets, and yet he had no choice. Everything, including Miss Abbott's safety and his title, hung in the balance. He had to find her before it was too late.

Mrs. Shaunessy threw her arms around him in a surprisingly strong hug. "You are a good man, Mr. Morgan, no matter what Phadra says. I know you will bring her home safe and sound."

Grant removed her arms from around his neck and promised to endeavor to do so.

Later, after he'd traveled from post house to post house in the foggy night asking if anyone had seen a young woman matching Miss Abbott's description, he found his fears for her safety dwindling. As his anger neared the boiling point, he wondered instead who was going to protect Miss Abbott from him once he found her!

Chapter 8

By the time the private mail coach pulled into the torch-lit inn yard, Phadra felt jostled black and blue. Crammed into the cheap seats on top of the coach between an onion-eating preacher and a heavyset tinker, she didn't know which was rattled more — her brain or her person.

The foggy weather threatened a storm, which she hoped would hold off until she arrived in Portsmouth the next afternoon. She didn't relish riding the coach in the rain. Already her head ached from the number of times the guard had blown his horn — to show off his musical ability, no doubt! — and a few times the coachman's whip had nicked off some of the feathers on her bonnet. One passenger sitting knee to knee across from her lost his entire hat to the coachman's whip when it was flicked off his head and disappeared into the wake of dust behind the coach.

Still, the stop irritated her. After almost

four hours of travel, the coach moved too slowly for her. Her mind reviewed the precautions she'd taken earlier in the day to delay her absence from being discovered. It had to be nigh onto midnight now. At this point, only Henny might have discovered her absence, and she could trust Henny.

The one person she couldn't trust was Grant Morgan. When he found out she'd run away, he'd be furious. Especially since the Evanses might then refuse his suit for her daughter. She felt a small measure of satisfaction at the thought that she was saving him from a marriage to Miranda. "One day he'll thank me. Heavens, he should thank me now," she said. When the preacher looked up, she was surprised to find she'd spoken out loud.

"Excuse me, miss," he said, the onion on his breath almost overpowering.

Phadra raised her hand palm up and shook her head. "I was indulging in woolgathering."

"No, I mean excuse me," the preacher corrected. "I have to step around you. We only have the time they take to change the horses to grab a bite to eat, and everyone else has left us."

"Oh. Well, here, step around me," Phadra offered, and pulled her skirts back.

The preacher didn't stand on ceremony but stepped over her legs and climbed down the side of the coach.

At the thought of food Phadra's stomach growled noisily, and she realized it would feel good to have her feet on solid ground. Carefully she moved to the side and climbed down the ladder, searching with her foot for each rung.

This trip was a far cry from the one she'd made to London several months earlier. Then she'd thought herself a young woman of means and had hired a private coach with outriders. Mr. Morgan would probably have winced at the expense.

Her feet had just touched the ground when a pair of large hands clasped her waist.

"Here. Let me help you watch your step, darlin'," a husky man's voice said in her ear.

Phadra immediately recognized him as the musical guard. "I'm fine, thank you," she said coldly, and gripped the ladder rail tightly.

"Oh, I'm sure you are," he cooed in her ear. She could feel, even through her heavy wool cloak, his fingers moving up to stroke the undersides of her breasts.

Her heart stopped. Fear that he'd feel the layer of pound notes she'd hidden in the secret pocket of her cloak warred with anger at the liberty he was taking with her person. She'd stayed up until the wee hours the night before, fashioning that pocket and plotting her escape from Evans House. She knew that as a woman traveling alone she was in a vulnerable position, but she had decided that the risks must be taken.

Now she questioned that decision.

A whip cracked. "Watty, there's no time for that," the coachman shouted. "Leave the passengers alone and help me see to these horses."

The guard growled something under his breath and gave one of her breasts a light squeeze before turning away from her. Phadra almost collapsed with relief. She set her feet on the ground and hurried toward the inn.

The five hundred pounds made her feel rich, but she knew she had to take every economy she could in order to finance her search for her father.

Phadra rubbed the back of her neck, trying to ease the tension. If she understood the information she'd gotten in London, the *Queen's Bounty* was scheduled to sail for the Mediterranean Friday morning with the tide. She planned to be on that ship.

She was almost to the inn's front door when she heard the pounding of a horse and rider entering the inn yard. Sparing only a momentary backward glance for the new arrival, Phadra noted the horse's lathered flank. The animal had been ridden hard. She felt sorry for the horse and wondered vaguely where the rider was going in such a hurry.

A blink of an eye later, her full attention was captured by a man's voice saying, "Seven shillings for the table. Seven shillings." The gray-haired innkeeper guarded the door, his hand held out expectantly.

Inside the common room, the other passengers were already greedily helping themselves to a round of cheese and loaves of bread at a table set in one corner of the room.

Again her stomach rumbled, but Phadra reminded herself that she must follow the strictest economies. She lifted her chin. "Seven shillings for a piece of cheese and bread?"

"Aye, seven shillings and no less. I don't haggle," the innkeeper said.

Phadra wondered if she could manage to go without until Portsmouth.

Seeing her indecision, the innkeeper turned his attention to the other passengers. Two men were trying to put cheese in their pockets. "No food out the door, mind you," he called, and walked over to confront them.

Phadra frowned. A piece of ripe, sharp cheese would taste good, and Portsmouth was hours away. The scent of freshly baked bread nearly made her dizzy. She was about to reach into the hidden pocket of her cloak to remove some money when she heard heavy, purposeful footsteps coming up behind her. A large hand came down on her shoulder.

This time the guard's advances didn't frighten her. "Didn't the coachman tell you to leave me alone?" she snapped in her haughtiest voice before turning. All other words died in her throat . . . for she stared into the hard silver eyes of Grant Morgan.

"Surprised to see me?" he drawled.

Surprised was a mild word for what Phadra felt. *Shocked* came to mind. *Horrified* might be a better description. "What are you doing here?" she asked, her words coming out as little more than a hoarse whisper.

Reflections of the flames from the lamps flanking the doorway danced in his eyes like twin devils. The dark shadow of his whiskers, his wind-tossed hair, and the fog around him added to his sinister appearance. He had been the rider on the horse she'd noticed, and he seemed to be a far cry from the man who had graced the Evanses' drawing room over the last several weeks.

"Come," he ordered, taking her arm in a steel grip. "I'm taking you back before your absence is discovered." Without another word he picked her up and threw her over his shoulder like a sack of grain.

Phadra lost her breath as the world reeled beneath her. By the time she'd gathered her senses, she was being carried unceremoniously out into the inn yard.

"Who do you think you — What are you — Let me down this second, you brigand!" She began kicking her heels and beating his back with her fists.

"What goes on here?" demanded the innkeeper's gruff voice.

Phadra raised her head to look back toward the inn door. "Please, you must help me!" she shouted. "He's taking me against my will!"

At that moment the coachman cried, "All ready!" — the signal for the passengers to return to the coach or be left behind. The other passengers gathered behind the innkeeper, pushing him out the door in their hurry to board the waiting coach. Several servants led by a matronly woman in a mobcap followed them, attracted by

Phadra's shouting. That was all the encouragement she needed to keep hollering.

As if her ranting and kicking had no impact on him at all, Mr. Morgan turned to face the innkeeper. "I need to hire a coach and team."

The innkeeper's attention, momentarily distracted by his desire to make sure the passengers didn't leave with food, turned to the couple making the racket in front of his establishment. "A team, you say?"

"No!" Phadra shouted. "He's kidnapping me. He's taking me to London against my will. I've paid my passage to Portsmouth. I don't want to go back to London." She kicked her feet harder, wishing she could manage to do some damage to Mr. Morgan, who acted as if her struggles were merely a minor irritation.

"Kidnapping?" the mobcapped woman said, her eyes growing wide with alarm. "Oh, Edwin, I don't think that's right. Not if she's paid her fare." Several passengers stopped to watch a moment, although the majority made their way to the coach.

The innkeeper looked from Phadra's face to Mr. Morgan's. "See here, sir. My wife's right. You can't just remove any passenger off any coach that you want, not if she's paid her passage. Isn't that right, Hobbs?"

"Isn't what right?" Hobbs, the coachman, asked, looking up from the harness he'd been checking.

The innkeeper gestured toward Mr. Morgan. "A man can't just ride in here and make off with one of the passengers, can he?" The passengers watched silently from their seats, but the servants and stable hands murmured softly amongst themselves.

His words appeared to penetrate Hobbs's mind. He stepped closer to Mr. Morgan and bent to peer up at Phadra's face under her bonnet. "You're the girl with Watty," he said with a hint of disgust in his voice, making the connection to his earlier rescue of her.

Phadra glared at him. "That wasn't my fault! The man accosted me."

Hobbs turned to the innkeeper. "I don't know. I have mail to get through, and I'm running late." He cracked his whip to stress his importance.

The innkeeper's wife charged forward. "You stay right there, Hobbs," she commanded. "I think there's a law against it! I don't think a man can walk up and throw any woman he wants over his shoulder and walk off. Not if she's paid her fare. That's not right."

"Unless he has a good reason to throw the woman over his shoulder," the innkeeper mused, as if this were a salient point. He addressed Grant. "Do you have a good reason, sir?"

Grant didn't give a damn about reasons. He was bloody tired, and every muscle in his body ached from the bruising chase Miss Abbott had forced him to undertake.

Now that he'd found her, he was feeling a bit short of tact . . . and yet he could see from the faces in the crowd that these people weren't the type to listen to an explanation about banks and guardianships. If he wasn't careful, they would put Miss Abbott back on the coach and he'd have to chase her to Portsmouth. He'd fight every man jack of them with his bare fists before he'd let that happen.

The woman's words made Miss Abbott twist and wriggle all the more. Grant decided to take command of the situation.

Flipping her off his shoulder so that her feet hit the ground hard — a movement that caught her by surprise and, thankfully, temporarily deprived her of speech — he clapped his hands down on her shoulders to hold her in place and announced, "She's my wife."

Grant didn't know whose shocked gasp

was the loudest: the innkeeper's wife's, the passengers', or Miss Abbott's. He'd chosen the right words. Immediately the crowd's favor swung from the runaway to him.

He played the jilted husband to the hilt. "She's running away to join her lover —"

"My lover?" Miss Abbott spit out, obviously finding her voice.

"— a *sailor*," Grant continued, as if she hadn't even spoken.

The crowd gave a murmur of disapproval. Several voices whispered in knowing tones.

Grant nodded his head. "He's so completely turned her head with his foreign talk and pretty baubles that she's running away to meet him in Portsmouth, leaving me behind with the children."

"Children?" the innkeeper's wife said, her voice soft with dismay.

"Children?" Miss Abbott shouted. She jerked away and turned to confront him, her hands on her hips.

"Aye, Phadra *darling*," Grant said, laying his act of lovesick husband on thick. "You must come back before they wake up wondering where their mother ran off to. Tonight little Miranda called and called to you before she finally cried herself to sleep."

"Oh, I bet *little* Miranda cried out my name," Miss Abbott shot back. She straightened the bonnet that tilted over her eyes, the ribbons hanging completely undone — and then almost immediately realized that it had been the wrong thing to say.

The innkeeper's wife asked in a horrified voice, "Are you unnatural? Are you unmoved by the cries of your child?"

Phadra turned to the woman. "Trust me, Miranda doesn't worry about me at all."

"But she's your *child*," the innkeeper's wife said, bristling with righteous indignation. "A child needs its mother."

"It's not like that —," she started to explain, but a snap of the whip cut her off.

"I've had enough of this!" the coachman announced. "I've got the mail to get through." He turned on his heel and marched toward the waiting coach.

"Wait!" Phadra cried, starting to move after him. "I'm going with you."

Mr. Morgan stepped in front of her, his hands reaching down to grab her wrists. "No, darling, don't leave me," he cried dramatically. "The children and I need you."

Phadra thought she could murder him. She doubled her fists and would have punched him in the nose if his superior strength hadn't been able to hold her flailing arms at bay. "Let go of me, you —

you —" She searched for a name bad enough to call him. "You rat! You scum! You *banker!*"

"Phadra, does this mean you don't love me anymore?" he asked in his subservient-husband voice. She could see the laughter in his quicksilver eyes.

"I hate you," she muttered, and moved in closer to him to give him a kick in the shins.

"It's all for the best, dear," he answered, his words coming out in puffs as he dodged her kicking feet. He turned her in his arms and held her firmly in place, then looked at the innkeeper. "Now, about that rig I need to hire . . ."

"Jim, hitch up a team," the innkeeper commanded. "This man has to get to London before dawn." He turned toward Mr. Morgan, his manner solicitous. "Are you sure you can manage her, sir?"

"Aye," Mr. Morgan assured him grandly even as Phadra managed to connect her booted foot with his shin. He grunted, his hold breaking, and she pushed away to run after the mail coach, her bonnet tumbling off her head in her haste.

"Wait!" she cried, dismayed to see the coachman swing up into his place. She had to get on that coach. She had to! Suddenly she felt strong arms around her waist, pulling her back to him.

She prepared to fight, balling her hands into fists. But then Mr. Morgan did something she never would have anticipated in a million years.

Instead of grabbing her arms again, instead of holding her prisoner, instead of any of the dozens of things he could have done that she was prepared to guard herself against, he did the unexpected.

He kissed her.

Phadra didn't even realize it until his lips came down on hers, and when she started to gasp in surprise, she found her mouth locked with his. His action startled her. She started to struggle until a part of her realized this was actually very pleasant, a far cry from Popov the poet's wet, sloppy kisses.

Grant Morgan tasted of the night fog, of hidden secrets, and of something so incredible that Phadra found him impossible to resist. She leaned into him, her mouth now exploring his, timidly at first but then more boldly. His hold on her relaxed. No longer did he grip her arms; rather, he caressed her back, bringing her closer into the strength and protection of his arms — and the kiss deepened in magic ways that Phadra had never imagined possible. She wrapped her arms around his neck and held on for everything she was worth.

From the dim recesses of what was left of her mind, she heard the blast of the guard's horn and a crack of the whip as the mail coach took off into the night without her.

Phadra was only vaguely aware that he had pulled his lips away from hers. She leaned forward, anxious to return to his melting kisses, when she heard him say clearly and succinctly to the innkeeper, "Is the team ready?"

"That it is, sir," the innkeeper confirmed as a small two-passenger post chaise and a team of horses rolled forward into the torch-light.

Phadra shoved against his body with all her might. He freed her this time. *And why not?* she thought furiously. The coach to Portsmouth was gone and with it her hopes.

She turned to the innkeeper angrily. "How dare you believe him over me! How dare you let him lie to you? There is no sailor! This man has no rights over me at all."

"It appeared to me that you gave him a good number of rights a moment ago," the man replied sagely. "And you should count your blessings. If you were my wife, I would have beaten you."

Phadra had a few choice words to say

about *that* — until a round of guffaws and giggles from the maids and stable hands made her realize that her complete and absolute humiliation had had a rather large audience. Her cheeks flamed. How could she have responded so wantonly to Grant Morgan?

The force of his kiss had shaken her to the very root of her being, but he stood there calm and unruffled. Sweet Mary, she was no more levelheaded than any of the silly women who dropped their gloves for him or flirted openly.

Phadra picked up her bonnet from the dust at her feet. Her head held high, she said, "This isn't over yet."

"No," he agreed soberly, his eyes hard and determined. "We're not back in London. Back to *little* Miranda."

Phadra's palm itched to slap him — but she wouldn't give him the satisfaction. "You had better watch what you wish for, Mr. Morgan. You may get your wish."

With that grim announcement, she squared her shoulders and marched proudly to the waiting post chaise, its coach lamps lit for the dangerous night journey.

Phadra sat as close to the coach door as she could, her bonnet in her lap. That still didn't mean that her body didn't touch Mr. Morgan's after he'd settled with the innkeeper and climbed into the coach. For once she wished that he weren't such a large man.

She also wished he weren't such a *masculine* man. The taste of his kiss still haunted her.

After a half hour of traveling he broke the icy silence. "Is something wrong?" She could feel him turn toward her in the darkness.

"Wrong?" Phadra put anger into the word. "Why should anything be wrong? I mean, just because you made a fool of me in public with your lies and your *deceit* —"

"I was acting for your own good."

"Oh! That's a rich one. *Whose* good? Be honest, Mr. Morgan. You came after me to save your arranged marriage to a spoiled, petted woman, who has no idea of decency or good manners, so that you can earn a title. Well, you have earned a title in my esteem. Lord of Lies! How do you like that one?"

He snorted. Obviously he didn't like that one at all, and Phadra felt a small measure of satisfaction.

When he spoke again, the tone of his voice was conciliatory, as if he was negotiating a difficult business transaction. "Miss Abbott, I'm aware of how much you wish to make contact with your father. However, the trip you were planning is dangerous, especially for a young woman alone —"

"It's my life. My choice."

"I can appreciate that sentiment. However —"

"Save me from your 'howevers.' I'm sick of 'howevers.' All my life I've had people pretend to agree with me and then tack on 'however.' " Her tone changed to mimic Miss Agatha's squeaky high voice. " 'Yes, Miss Abbott, you are very bright and could study Greek; *however,* it is not an acceptable language for a young woman's studies.' " She dropped her voice in an imitation of Lady Evans's round tones. " 'Hooow becoming that dress is on you, Phadra. *However,* it is not the mooode. We don't *want* to be *different,* do we?' "

She turned to where he sat in the rolling coach. "But you're the worst," she said. "I think you genuinely do see and hear me, but still you give me a 'however' because you want everything nice and neat. You *know* what Lord Evans is guilty of, and yet you play his game and cater to his daughter because of what *you* want. But the devil take me about what I want! I want to see my father —"

"And you will, when he returns."

"Don't pretend with me, Mr. Morgan. You don't even believe he is alive. *But I do.*" She leaned closer to him in the dark, the better to make her point, conscious of the firm, muscular tightness of his thigh beneath her palm — before she quickly moved it. "I have a *dream*, Mr. Morgan, that is just as important to me as the dreams you hold are to you. I want to find my father. I need to find him. There is no compromise to that dream, no 'however.' " She threw herself back in the seat as far away from him as she could manage. The energy and spirit so necessary to her hopes and dreams drained from her body, to be replaced by an almost overwhelming sadness. She wrapped the bonnet's ribbons around her hands before she added quietly, "It's something I have to do . . . or I'll never feel complete."

He didn't answer. She wished she could see his face, read his expression. Her open show of emotion embarrassed her. When, she wondered, had been the last time that she had revealed herself so completely to another human being?

She couldn't remember.

They rode in silence for a while. Then his deep voice came to her through the night: "I'm sorry."

Well, what did I expect? Phadra thought ruefully.

He continued, "But I can't let you go off alone. It's too dangerous. However —" He paused briefly after the word before he continued. "There are other resources to explore that may help you find your father. Letters, reports from men who have been in that part of the world."

"I've talked to some men with the Royal Geographic Society since I've come to London. No one has heard of or from him."

He said in a measured, thoughtful voice, "Most of the members of the Royal Geographic Society are chair-bound explorers. I have contacts through the bank — merchants, military men and others — who may have had word of Sir Julius during their travels. We could contact them."

Phadra turned to him. "You would do that? You would help me?"

He made an impatient sound. "Of course. I bear no animosity toward you. I covered the payment for the fake emeralds and chased after you tonight not to teach you a lesson but because I care what happens to you."

When he said, "I care what happens to you," Phadra noticed he used the tone of voice one would use to express affection for a sister or other female relative. The sting of hurt surprised her.

"Let's see if we understand each other," he said slowly. "I'm here because I don't want you ruined. Whether you believe it or not, a young woman's reputation is of value to her. If Mrs. Shaunessy hadn't told me —"

"Henny! She alerted you to my absence?" Phadra felt betrayed.

"Yes, but don't hold it against her. She knows what a dangerous world it is out there and was only concerned for your safety." When she made no comment, he continued, "She'll be waiting for us at the servants' entrance of Evans House. If all goes well, we should arrive in London before dawn and be able to sneak you in without the Evanses' being the wiser. You are going to have to marry, Miss Abbott. I know you are not ready, but you must understand that someday you will want to, just as my sisters eventually wanted to. Unfortunately you must do this sooner than you wish, thanks to Lord Evans and your father's exploits, but believe me when I say I'm committed to finding a companion who is acceptable to you."

Phadra leaned her elbow against the door and rested her head on her forearm. He didn't understand. He didn't *want* to understand. She felt tired, defeated.

"Captain Duroy is planning to make an offer for you," he added.

Phadra didn't answer. What could she say? She demanded her freedom; he attempted to placate her by telling her she had a serious suitor for her hand. Was he deliberately being obtuse, or was it a trait of his gender in general?

"Miss Abbott?"

"Mr. Morgan?" she answered sarcastically, and then heaved a heavy sigh. "So the emeralds were fake," she said as if stating a fact.

"Yes."

"I wondered."

A long pause drifted between them before he asked, "Aren't you going to thank me for covering your debt? The goldsmith could have contacted the magistrate instead."

"Yes," she agreed, but added, "However, I would have been long gone by then."

It wasn't the answer he'd wanted. She could almost feel him staring at her through the dark.

She closed her eyes, wishing she could completely shut out the disturbing nearness of his presence. She forced herself to think instead of the goldsmith. He'd been a kind young man, and she had felt the worst sort of criminal in deceiving him. It had crossed her mind that the emerald pieces she'd received from her mother might also be fake. But she didn't want to believe that her father could so thoroughly cheat both her and her mother.

The pressure of tears pushed against her closed eyelids. *Not now. Not in front of him.*

Why couldn't she put this behind her? In a sense she knew Mr. Morgan was right. No good would come out of a direct confrontation with her father.

He gave an exasperated sigh, as if annoyed by her silence. "What do you want? I'm doing my best —"

The sound of a pistol shot interrupted him. A cry of alarm came from outside the post chaise. It sounded as if it came from the postboy, Jim. The loud, gruff voice of a highwayman answered her unspoken question by declaring, "Stand and deliver!"

Chapter 9

In the dark, Grant Morgan's hand came down on her arm, and he squeezed as if commanding her to be silent. The human contact quelled the panic she felt rising inside of her. Dear Lord, what had the brigands done to the poor postboy?

"Come out, guv'nor, and bring your lady with that wad of pound notes she has in her pocket, and we'll let you go with your lives," the gruff voice commanded.

Mr. Morgan was silent for a moment, as if weighing the consequences. He wasn't a man who liked to be forced to do another's bidding. She knew how he felt. She wasn't about to climb out of the coach and calmly turn over the balance of her five hundred pounds!

"I'm not getting out," she whispered.

"Do you plan on fighting them off by yourself?"

"I have no intention of just handing my money over to them without a fight!"

"Whose money?" he asked dryly.

"Mine," she snapped. "Your money purchased fake emeralds from the goldsmith."

"I wondered how you'd justify that to yourself," he muttered before reaching across her and placing his hand on the door handle.

Phadra boldly covered his hand with hers. "This is everything I have in the world. I'm *not* giving up without a fight!" She wished she could see his face.

"Then you are free to stay in this coach and let them blow holes in your hide, but I for one value my life over pound notes." He turned the handle and pushed open the door.

In the dark, foggy night, the coach lamps cast an eerie light over the figures of three masked and hooded highwaymen. One stood holding a brace of pistols aimed at the door. Two others sat on horseback like silent specters. The horses impatiently stamped their hooves, their legs disappearing into the drifting fog along the ground. Phadra raised her hand to her throat, wishing that he'd never opened the coach door.

Mr. Morgan climbed out of the coach first, holding his hands in the air. He then turned and offered her his hand. Suddenly

Phadra realized she didn't want a pistol hole in her "hide," as he'd succinctly put it. She placed her trembling hand in his. His touch was reassuring and warm. It gave her the courage to climb down the step and onto the hard, fog-shrouded ground.

"I'm pleased that you listen to reason, guv'nor," said one of the highwaymen, who appeared to be the leader.

At that moment another masked man, breathing heavily, came crashing into the circle of light. "I couldn't catch the boy," he reported between panting breaths.

The leader cut him off with a movement of his hand. "It won't matter. There isn't anyplace he can go to around here for help." He looked at Phadra and the banker. "Give us your purse, man, and remember to move your hands slowly. The light is dim, and I wouldn't want my friend's pistol to go off."

Mr. Morgan reached into the inside pocket of his coat and pulled out a flat purse. He tossed it to the leader, who caught it easily.

"And now you, miss. We'll be taking that roll of notes."

Something snapped inside Phadra. How dare these men come and think they could dance off with every shilling she had in the world? She lifted her chin defiantly. "No."

Mr. Morgan muttered under his breath, "I should have known better than to think this would be easy."

But Phadra's attention was focused on the leader. His eyes glittered like hard diamonds at her open show of defiance. "I didn't ask, woman. I ordered. Give me your money." For emphasis, the man holding the pistols raised them menacingly.

Phadra gazed at him shrewdly, her mind working quickly. "You know I have money, don't you?" She didn't give the leader time to answer but charged on. "The guard on that other coach is working with you. That's why he ran his hands all over me. He tipped you off to my money. Why, you men were probably in the inn yard."

She took a step forward and, in a voice filled with righteousness, demanded, "How many other poor passengers have you robbed? How many unsuspecting women has that poor excuse for a man accosted?"

The leader answered her questions by pulling out a pistol of his own. "You know, guv'nor, you should teach your woman to keep her mouth shut." He lifted the gun so that its barrel was aimed directly at her and said, "We can't have her going around telling tales on our friend Watty, can we?"

At that moment Mr. Morgan jumped between her and the leader, exclaiming in a high, shrill voice that didn't sound like him at all, "Miss Abbott, *how* many times do I have to tell you to keep your mouth shut?" He stepped forward, his manner foppish as he waved his hands in the air. "I have to talk to her and talk to her," he complained in that amazing falsetto voice. "She never listens to reason. Doesn't listen at all!"

A handkerchief appeared in his hand, and he fluttered it nervously before using it to dab his forehead. "I think there really is only one thing we can do with her," he announced in a worrisome voice before breaking into the silliest giggles Phadra had ever heard. She couldn't fathom what was the matter with him. He acted as if he'd gone mad.

The highwaymen looked at each other and then started laughing, as if enjoying a show. Their leader shifted in his saddle and waved his pistol at Mr. Morgan before asking good-naturedly, "And what is it we can do with her, lad? Or should I say *laddie?*" He guffawed at his pun, and the others joined him.

The man holding the pistols looked up at his comrades. "Watty didn't tell us about this!"

Mr. Morgan laughed loudest of all. His

high-pitched "tee-hee" annoyed Phadra. He even bent over and slapped his knees with mirth. "That's very clever!" he said. "Very clever," he repeated, only this time his handkerchief-wielding hand had turned into a large fist, and it connected with the jaw of the man holding the pistols. With a lightning-fast movement, Mr. Morgan grabbed one of the arms of the staggering man and pointed one of the pistols at the leader just as the man pulled the trigger of his gun.

The barrel spit fire, the acrid scent of gunpowder filled the air, and the ball found its mark, striking the leader with enough force to topple him from his horse. His own weapon discharged harmlessly into the air. The animals reared in alarm.

"Miss Abbott, get down!" ordered the very masculine voice of Grant Morgan.

"It was a trick!" she exclaimed with pleasure, ignoring his command.

Mr. Morgan didn't answer but quickly turned with the second pistol that the highwayman had been holding and fired it in the direction of the other man on foot, who ran into the darkness. "Miss Abbott, can't you do anything I tell you to do?" Mr. Morgan roared before his concentration was completely claimed by the man in his arms and a bout of fisticuffs.

Phadra doubled her own fists, wishing to jump into the fray. When the other mounted highwayman moved to help his friend, she stooped down and picked up rocks, throwing them at him. Her pebble missiles weren't dangerous, but they caused the man's horse to rear and prance, threatening to unseat the rider.

Suddenly, through the dust and fog, Phadra saw the man fighting with Mr. Morgan break free and run into the woods. Mr. Morgan didn't chase him but turned his attention to the mounted man.

Phadra watched open-mouthed as Mr. Morgan reached up toward this new attacker, using brute strength to make the nervous horse back away. The highwayman shouted and reached into his coat.

"Grant, he's armed," Phadra shouted, and boldly reached up herself to pull on the man's coat. Her action startled both the man and the horse, which backed up and reared slightly at this new aggression. The man had to use both his hands to keep his seat on the horse. With a shove of his elbow, he hit Phadra in the chin and pushed her away.

Grant Morgan's face went livid with fury when he saw her fall back. With murder in his eyes, he reached to grapple the man from his horse.

The explosion of a pistol broke through the chaos. The horse screamed and jumped forward, taking his rider with him. Still lying on the ground where she'd fallen, Phadra watched in shocked horror as Grant Morgan jerked in response to the shot and then fell to the ground.

The leader of the highwaymen sat up slowly, as if crippled by pain, the pistol in his hand still smoking. The rider didn't waste time but circled back to reach the leader and heaved him onto the back of the horse. Together the two men charged away into the night.

Phadra didn't care where they went or whether they would come back. She crawled on hands and knees to Mr. Morgan. "Grant? Grant, speak to me."

He didn't move. She reached to touch him and then drew her hand back. Blood stained the back of his coat. The shot had gone in his upper back. "No, Grant, no!" she cried, moving to rip a strip of her petticoat to staunch the flow of blood. "I'm so sorry. This is all my fault. I should have given them the money. I should have listened to you."

Tears poured down her cheeks as her

208

hand came back with the cloth covered with dark, fresh blood. The stain on the cloth spread — and that was when she realized that it wasn't only her tears she felt dripping onto her arms but also the start of the steady rain that had threatened all evening and now had begun to fall.

Quickly she pressed the cloth back against the wound and then struggled out of her wool cloak, wrapping it around him to protect him from the rain. Her fingers pressed against the roll of banknotes, and she felt a stab of guilt. She forced herself to keep working, whispering, "I mustn't panic. I must be brave. I must have courage."

"Miss Abbott, are you quoting Mary Wollstonecraft again?"

Phadra's eyes opened wide at the sound of his voice. "You're alive!" she cried, reaching down for him as he started to turn over and sit up.

He sat for a moment, the rain plastering his hair to his head, before he grumbled, "The next time a man holding a gun asks for your money, *give it to him!*"

Phadra didn't know whether to laugh or cry — so she did a combination of both. "I will. I solemnly promise."

"I'll hold you to that promise," he said, and got to his feet with her help. Alarmed,

Phadra realized that he must be losing a good measure of blood.

"Help me up into the coach, will you?" he grunted.

"You must be in terrible pain," she said, placing his arm around her shoulder.

His lips twisted into a grimace. "I've been better."

They'd just reached the shelter of the coach when a timid voice called out, "Hello? Is everyone all right?"

Phadra leaned over Mr. Morgan's body protectively. Her voice a whisper, she asked, "Who is that?"

"The postboy, I imagine," he said, and then raised his voice to call, "Jim?"

"Aye, sir," came the answer. A moment later the postboy stepped into the flickering light cast by the coach lamps. He stopped dead in his tracks at the sight of his two passengers. "I'm sorry I ran."

"No, you were a smart lad and saved your life. Here, come help me," Mr. Morgan commanded. "I need help getting my jacket off."

Phadra climbed into the coach and had Mr. Morgan sit on the step, his booted legs hanging out of the door. Working together, she and Jim removed his jacket and his lawn shirt. Mr. Morgan reached around to feel the hole.

"It's in the fleshy part right under the arm. Damn, it didn't go through."

"What didn't go through?" Phadra asked, busily tearing her petticoats into strips to make a bandage.

"The ball. The shot is still in there. He got me in the back."

"At least he didn't hit anything vital," Jim said. "I can see the hole from back here. You need to have the ball removed, sir."

"Bind the wound. It'll stop the bleeding," Mr. Morgan ordered.

Phadra had removed her cloak so that she could move freely. Now she reached around his chest and started binding the wound tightly. His blood stained the bodice of her dress. She spoke to the postboy as she worked. "Jim, we must go for a doctor immediately."

Grant countermanded her order. "We're not stopping for any doctor. I'll be all right until we get to London. We must be there before dawn."

"But your wound!" Phadra protested.

"Get us to London before first light and I'll throw in five guineas for you," Mr. Morgan said to Jim.

"Take us to a doctor and I'll give you five hundred pounds," Phadra shot back.

"You wouldn't dare!" Mr. Morgan roared.

"Yes, I would. And you should save your energy. You're going to need it until we can get you to a doctor and have him look at this wound."

"It'll wait until morning after I return you to Evans House," Mr. Morgan said.

"It will not!" she snapped. "I know little about wounds, but I do know that riding around the countryside in the rain is not a remedy. And you have to get that ball out."

"She's right, sir. That ball can only be causing you pain, and may even poison you."

Mr. Morgan frowned so fiercely, the postboy backed away until he stood out in the rain. Suddenly Mr. Morgan's shoulders sagged and he leaned back into the coach against the seat. His face looked pale in the darkness of the coach.

"Jim," Phadra said, "where is the nearest doctor?" She rose up on her knees and with Jim's help pulled Mr. Morgan into the coach, crushing her bonnet in the process.

"There's Dr. Blounder, but it would be closer to take him back to the inn. Mr. Allen, the innkeeper, has a good steady hand."

"Then get us back to the inn," Phadra ordered. She took another look at Mr. Morgan's face. He'd closed his eyes. She turned

212

to Jim, angry that he hadn't started moving yet. "Did you hear me?" The shrillness of her voice spurred the young man to move. She slammed the door shut, protecting them from the rain, and struggled to maintain her composure.

Mr. Morgan's voice came to her in the dark. "You shouldn't have yelled at the lad."

The two of them sat in the cramped space on the floor. Phadra busied herself by wrapping her wool cloak around his shoulders. She kept her voice light. "Why is it that no matter what I do, you always find fault?"

"It's my role, Miss Abbott. I'm your banker." She could hear the dry humor in his tired voice.

"Have you ever considered that perhaps you take your responsibilities too seriously?" she teased back, but her voice shook on the last words, and one of the tears she'd been struggling to control escaped and ran down her cheek.

Jim was turning the team and coach on the road, a maneuver that caused the post chaise to sway and jerk. Mr. Morgan hissed slightly in pain, a response to the jarring his body received.

She reached up and placed her arms around him. "Lie back against me, Mr.

Morgan." He didn't fight her but slowly slumped against her, his body rolling with the movement of the coach. Phadra closed her eyes for a second, sending a silent blessing to Jim for moving them toward their destination with all possible haste.

At first she held her hands in the air as if afraid to touch him, but then she gingerly lowered her arms, feeling his body beneath her hands. She readjusted her cloak, tucking it closer around him. He didn't move, even when she let her fingers touch his wet curls and push them back from his brow. She knew he needed to rest. The less he moved, the better.

His slow, drowsy voice startled her. "Did you realize that you used my Christian name, Miss Abbott?"

"I beg you pardon?"

"My name," he said in a voice so low, she had to bend to catch the words. "You called me Grant."

The news surprised Phadra until she realized she had shouted his name once when the fighting had been its heaviest and again later when he'd been wounded. At the time, it had seemed perfectly right and natural.

She sat back, one hand resting against his brow, another wrapped protectively around his shoulders. "So I did, Mr. Morgan," she replied quietly, certain that he had lapsed into unconsciousness and could no longer hear her. "So I did."

The barking of dogs signaled to her that they were at the inn. Jim yelled for help and then set the brake and ran up to the inn door, pounding on it madly. Soon Phadra heard the voice of the innkeeper. He threw open the coach door and took Mr. Morgan from her arms with the help of another servant.

Phadra followed behind them anxiously.

Inside the inn, the innkeeper had Mr. Morgan laid out on the same trestle table he'd used to serve the coach passengers cheese and bread. Ordering Jim to hold the lamp high so he'd have enough light to see, he cut off the bandages with a good-sized knife. While his master probed the wound, Jim told the story of the mail coach guard's duplicity and how Mr. Morgan had fought off four highwaymen.

Mr. Morgan came to his senses with a hiss when the innkeeper poked the wound. He insisted on sitting up. For a brief moment his silver-gray eyes, dazed with pain, met Phadra's gaze.

The innkeeper looked over his shoulder and didn't hide his look of disgust at seeing the "errant wife." Phadra felt her cheeks flame.

"What is going on here, Mr. Allen?" the innkeeper's wife called out. She came down the stairs in her mob-cap, dressing gown, and shawl.

"The lad, the one from earlier, has a pistol shot in him from a run-in with highwaymen."

She gasped. "Never, you say!" She quickly came down the stair and crossed over to Mr. Morgan, pausing for a moment to give Phadra a disapproving stare.

"You can feel the ball?" Mr. Allen asked his patient.

Mr. Morgan nodded, sweat beading his forehead. "It must be near the bone. Otherwise it would have gone through."

"Well, you're lucky the blighter wasn't a better shot," Mr. Allen said.

"I would have been luckier if he hadn't shot at all," Mr. Morgan said dryly.

The innkeeper gave him a grave smile. "You still have your sense of humor. Keep it. We'll have to cauterize the wound after we get the ball out. It's never good to take chances. Jim, go get my whisky. Mind you, not the good bottle but the rotgut. It cleans better and works faster," he explained to Mr. Morgan. "When we get done, I'll let

216

you have a swig from the good bottle — not that you'll be able to taste the difference at that point."

Phadra didn't understand what he meant, but Mr. Morgan nodded. Mrs. Allen brought a bowl over as well as a wicked-looking set of sharp tongs. Taking the bottle from Jim, her husband poured a good portion of the whiskey over the tongs and ordered Jim to build the fire a bit higher and place an iron rod in it. Mrs. Allen swirled a clean cloth through the whiskey in the bowl and made a pad of the cloth.

The innkeeper looked over his shoulder at Phadra. "Get over here, lass, and do your share. It will take every one of us to hold him down."

"It's not necessary to include her in this," Mr. Morgan protested.

"I want to help," Phadra said, coming to his side. Mrs. Allen looked down her nose at Phadra, obviously unwelcoming.

Mr. Allen held the bottle out to Mr. Morgan. "Better take a swig, lad. If the ball is lost in the flesh or touching the bone, you'll go wild with pain. I'll not be fighting you to get it out."

"He doesn't drink," Phadra said, feeling a need to explain.

"He will now," Mr. Allen answered.

"We've nothing else for the pain."

Mr. Morgan took a healthy drink. He rocked back, wheezing and sputtering.

"Aye, it's raw stuff," the innkeeper commiserated, "but like I said, it works fast." He began probing the wound with his fingers, and Mr. Morgan needed no further encouragement to drink the liquor.

"The ball ripped into you," Mr. Allen said. "But once we fix you up, a big man like you will be up and about in no time."

Mr. Morgan took another draw on the bottle. His gaze started to lose its keen edge, although the lines of pain were still etched plainly around the corners of his mouth. Phadra reached for his hand and gave it a reassuring squeeze. He clasped hers in response and tilted the bottle up once more.

Phadra tried to smile, but it was difficult. The sight of him acting with anything less than his usual steely control frightened her. He closed his eyes and leaned his head against her shoulder.

"You're about ready, aren't you, lad?" Mr. Allen asked. He didn't wait for an answer but nodded to Jim and the other servant. They quietly moved him around on the table and stretched him out flat.

"The table's cold," Mr. Morgan complained before laying his cheek against it.

He still held her hand.

Phadra looked up at Mr. Allen, who was in the act of removing the whiskey-cleaned tongs. "Is there something you want me to do?" she asked.

"No, lass. You're doing the best thing you can for him by holding his hand. But mind you, in a second it will seem like the hardest job of all." With those words, he didn't waste another motion but plunged the pressed-together tongs into the wound and started searching for the ball.

Phadra knew at what moment Mr. Morgan felt the tongs, because his strong, long fingers almost crushed hers. The fingers of his other hand bent around the edge of the table until the knuckles turned white. Mrs. Allen stood over him, using the whiskey-soaked cloth in her hand to wipe away the blood and keep the wound clean. At the first douse of whiskey into the wound, Mr. Morgan reached out with his free hand and wrapped it around the hand Phadra already held. Phadra squeezed back, offering him what little comfort she could.

They worked over him for several minutes more in the yellow lamplight. The servants held down his arms and legs. The pain was more than Grant had anticipated, even with the edge of it dulled by the whiskey coursing through his system. He could feel the ball hit bone when the tongs found it but missed grabbing it. The innkeeper swore and then pressed in again, determined to remove the lead.

Grant tasted his own blood as he bit down on his bottom lip, and the taste mingled with the smell of his fear and blood. Why hadn't they given him a piece of leather or something for him to bite down on so that he didn't unman himself and scream from the pain of it?

The only thing that saved him from losing control was Miss Abbott's hands wrapped around his and the fear in her large blue eyes. They looked large and frightened, and her hair curled everywhere without a care for pins or convention.

He wanted to tell her that it would be all right, that he would recover. But as he opened his mouth to speak, pain shot through him as the red-hot poker gouged into the deepest part of the wound. His breath came out in a hiss, and his vision clouded.

She gripped his hands harder and laid her cool, smooth cheek against his forehead. Before his world turned to black, he felt a wetness that could only be her tears, and he heard her soft, husky voice whispering over and over, "I'm sorry. I am so, so sorry."

"Has he passed out?" Mr. Allen asked.

Phadra nodded mutely.

"They always do when they feel the rod." He set the heated rod he'd used to cleanse and cauterize the wound back on the brick before the hearth, lifted the whiskey bottle, and took a drink himself. "It's never easy."

Mrs. Allen set the bowl aside, poured some more whiskey on a clean pad of cloth, and placed it on the wound. She then started to wrap a bandage around his chest and back, with Jim and the other servant lifting Mr. Morgan to help her get the bandage around him.

"We'll take him upstairs to one of the empty rooms and get him out of the rest of these wet clothes," Mrs. Allen said while she worked. "He's going to have fever shortly. He's lost a good measure of blood. But he needs fever before he can get better. I've found that always to be the case, haven't you, Mr. Allen?"

Her husband grunted his agreement and took another long pull on the whiskey bottle. The nails of his hands were stained with Mr. Morgan's blood.

Mrs. Allen continued, her hands busy tying the bandage off into a tight knot, "Someone will have to keep bathing him so we can keep the fever under control."

"I'll do it," Phadra answered. Mr. Morgan's hands no longer clenched hers tightly but lay relaxed in her palms, his fingers slack.

Mrs. Allen let her eyes drift from Phadra's face down to where her hands held his. Her gaze met Phadra's. "So," she said softly, "have you decided to be a wife to him after all?"

Phadra rose slowly, her conviction firm. "Yes."

Chapter 10

Mrs. Allen gave a nod of approval. Phadra sighed inwardly with relief.

"Take the other candle and follow us," the older woman ordered, lifting up the lantern from the table.

Mr. Allen and the servants hoisted Mr. Morgan up, none too gently, and followed her through the common room and down a back hallway. Phadra picked up the candle and hurried to follow. Almost out the door, she remembered her cloak — with the five hundred pounds. She retrieved it and practically had to run to catch up with them.

They'd already started up the narrow back staircase when Jim held them up for a moment so that he could shift his hold on Mr. Morgan's thigh and stomach. Mr. Morgan moaned.

"You don't think we're hurting him?" Phadra asked anxiously.

"Poo!" Mrs. Allen said, opening the door to a room located near the top of the stairs.

"A strong, healthy man like him should recover with only a scar to remind him of this night. Though it's too bad that we don't have a bit of laudanum. He'll have a restless night." She held the door open for the men carrying him.

The room was small, with only enough space for the bed, a small chair, and a chest with a washbasin sitting on top. Mrs. Allen pulled down the covers, and the men dumped Mr. Morgan onto the mattress as if glad to be relieved of their load. Phadra waited for Jim and Mr. Allen, who muttered something in passing about needing his sleep, to leave the room before she entered.

"Toby," Mrs. Allen said to the other young servant, "go fetch us a bucket of fresh water." Before the lad ran to do her bidding, she added, "From the rain barrel, mind you." She turned to Phadra. "It'll be fresher that way, and cooler."

Phadra's attention was completely focused on the half-naked man who seemed to fill the bed. He lay face down on the pillow. The golden wash of lamplight highlighted the planes of his back and shoulders and the curve of his buttocks in his fashionably snug doeskin trousers. The bandage cut like a sash across his back and shoulder. His outstretched arms and large hands with long, tapered fingers — swordsman's hands — hung over the sides.

"Are you all right?" Mrs. Allen asked, cocking her head and giving Phadra a hard stare.

"What?" Phadra came to her senses. "Yes, yes. Oh, yes," she repeated, feeling foolish. She'd been ogling. The man lay half-dead on the bed because of her and, with God as her witness, she'd been staring at him like a Haymarket Theatre doxy! Her face flamed with color.

Mrs. Allen stepped forward and put the back of her palm against Phadra's cheek. "You may be a little warm yourself." She tilted Phadra's chin up toward the lamp hanging on a peg on the wall. "We need to get you out of your wet clothes."

"I'm fine," Phadra protested.

Mrs. Allen didn't look convinced but changed the subject. "With all the commotion and nonsense, I didn't catch your name, lass."

"Phadra Abbott."

She'd responded without thinking and realized her error when Mrs. Allen said, "So, you and Mr. Abbott have had quite a change in plans. I hope someone is there for the children."

Mr. Abbott! Phadra prayed she didn't

make another blunder. "Uh . . . we have a companion who watches them."

"Oh?" Mrs. Allen said. The knowledge that they had a companion for their child seemed to raise their standing in her eyes. "Well, that's good." She seemed about to ask more questions, but the servant claimed her attention when he returned with the bucket of water. "Toby, put the bucket next to the chest and then off to bed with you. Dawn will come early."

The lad did as he was told, pulling his forelock as he backed out the door. It was only then, when they were alone, that Phadra confessed, "I have no clothes."

"No clothes?" Mrs. Allen frowned.

"My portmanteau went off with the mail coach. I just remembered I lost it."

Mrs. Allen waved a dismissive hand. "I probably have something you can use for tonight. And I'll get some cloths for you to bathe him with." She nodded toward Mr. Morgan.

"Bathe him?" Phadra choked over the words.

"In case the fever comes, you'll need some way to bring it down. Trust me, more men have died from the fever than the wound," Mrs. Allen responded matter-of-factly. "I'll go get the cloths now while you get him out of those wet clothes." With that, she turned on her heel and bustled out of the room, pulling the door shut firmly behind her.

Phadra stared open-mouthed at the closed door. Slowly she turned to look at Mr. Morgan, still unconscious on the bed. She shut her mouth and drew a deep breath, letting it out slowly.

This wasn't actually what she'd bargained for, but she was certain Mrs. Allen was right. The night air and their wet clothes were not a healthy combination. "Approach this scientifically," she muttered under her breath. "Like a study of a plant or animal."

The first *scientific* step she took was to pull off his boots. She thought it would be a safe move, except they didn't come off easily and required her to straddle each of his legs and use her whole body as leverage to remove them.

Removing boots was child's play compared to taking off his stockings. Phadra had never thought of feet as being particularly intimate . . . until her fingers brushed against the bottom of his bare foot and he reacted, his toes curling ticklishly. When she rolled the other stocking down his ankle and over his heel, he pushed her off the bed with his other foot.

Suspicious that he had done it on purpose, Phadra popped her head up over the edge of the bed and glared at him, expecting to find him grinning at her. Instead he slept on. The white pillow emphasized the dark shadow of his beard line and his strong, masculine features.

He truly was a beautiful man, she thought as she pushed herself up from the floor and rose to her feet. Beautiful from his dark curly hair to his well-formed legs . . . and then she realized that it was her job now to take the trousers off those legs. The room suddenly seemed unbearably hot.

"You're allowing your sensibilities to run wild," she reasoned out loud. "The man has passed out." She ran her fingers through her unruly curls and pulled them back from her face. The pins had long since disappeared. "Keep this scientific," she muttered.

So. The scientific question: How did men remove their pants?

Nothing in her experience had taught her about the intricacies of male clothing. Phadra closed her eyes for modesty's sake and slipped a hand around each side of his waist, feeling the waistband. Buttons!

She started unbuttoning the buttons that formed a row on either side of his hip, unconsciously holding her breath all the while.

That task done, she started to pull down the wet trousers at the waist but discovered that she had to open her eyes. The sight of a new expanse of bare skin stopped her actions.

He didn't wear undergarments. The discovery was a revelation. She'd never imagined a banker without undergarments.

Phadra stood up. She didn't know if she could go through with it . . . and then Mrs. Allen would come back and see Mr. Morgan still dressed and Phadra close to tears . . .

An idea came to her.

Quickly Phadra pulled and tugged the quilt from beneath his body. With a flick of her wrists, she threw the quilt over him and then, her hands under the quilt, pulled down his trousers. The tricky part was maneuvering them down his legs. She found she needed to use both her hands to move the soft, wet leather over his knees and down his calves. Even keeping her movements as economical and practical as possible, she couldn't escape the feel of his warm skin under her hand. Heavens, the man had more curve to his calves than she had to hers! Frustrated, she finally lifted the quilt up and over her head to see into the murky darkness and get the job done.

"Mrs. Abbott! What are you doing?"

Phadra pulled her head out from under the quilt sharply. Mrs. Allen stood in the doorway, holding cloths, a nightgown, a cup, and a brandy bottle in her arms. She seemed taken aback by the sight of Phadra climbing around on top of Mr. Morgan under the covers. Phadra could feel her face flood with hot color.

"I had to — uh, get these off." She'd worked the trousers down and over his feet, and now she pulled them out from under the quilt.

Mrs. Allen raised her eyebrows in patent disbelief.

Phadra made a great show of shaking the trousers out. "They are more wet than I thought. I, uh, hope they don't shrink." She forced herself to look at Mrs. Allen.

The innkeeper's lady didn't answer immediately but crossed over to the bed. She eyed the wet leather. "You never can tell."

"That's what I thought," Phadra answered, desperate to make conversation and cover the terrible awkwardness she felt. "You never can tell," she echoed, and attempted a smile that felt more like a grimace.

Then, to her horror, Mrs. Allen placed the cloths on the chair at his bedside and, lifting an edge of the quilt, threw it off Mr.

Morgan, who stirred as the air hit him.

Phadra raised her eyes to the corner of the ceiling.

"Why, Mrs. Abbott, your face is as red as a beet. Are you sure you are feeling well?"

"I'm just very modest," Phadra managed to answer, her fingers still tingling from where they'd brushed down the line of his body.

Mrs. Allen opened her eyes wide with surprise. "Modest?" she said. She looked at Phadra and then at the nude Mr. Morgan. The surprise turned to revelation. "Oh!" She reached over to give Phadra's arm a reassuring squeeze. "There's no reason to be embarrassed on my account, lass. I've seen what he has many a time before. It's an innkeeper's life and part of providing people with lodging." Suddenly her eyes took on a twinkle. " 'Course, I admit that what he has is better than most. He's a fine-looking man. Your sailor *must* really be something if you would run away from what's stretched out on the bed there."

Phadra didn't know how to react and felt herself blushing even more furiously.

"Oh now, see, I've made matters worse," Mrs. Allen said. "It's my country ways." She heaved a sigh. "Here, let me help you out of those wet clothes." She practically turned Phadra around and began unbuttoning her dress. "Maybe what you two need is another baby."

"Why would we need that?" Phadra started to turn, but Mrs. Allen was already helping her pull her dress down off her shoulders.

"Children help a marriage, make it grow a bit."

Phadra thought of her mother and father and rejected the woman's theory. "I wouldn't consider it a solution." Her dress fell to her feet. She stepped out of it and reached down to pick it up. A moment later she was out of what was left of her damp undergarments and in a voluminous cotton nightgown.

"This is one of my old ones. It's seen better days, but it will get you through the night," Mrs. Allen said. She pushed back Phadra's curls, a motherly gesture. "I know it's none of my affair, but sometimes after a couple has been married awhile, things don't look as good as they did before they posted the banns. It's not my place to speak, and Mr. Allen would be the first to tell me so. He always says that an innkeeper should keep his nose out of the guests' way. But I watched your face as we pulled the piece of lead out of him. You care for this man."

Her last simple sentence went straight to Phadra's heart. Did she care for Grant Morgan? "Mrs. Allen, you don't understand —"

"Oh, I understand more than a little. Sometimes things are hard between a man and a woman. We don't see things as clearly as we should, and it takes another person, on the outside, to help us see."

Phadra had an insane urge to laugh and cry at the same time. She covered her lips with her fingers and with her other hand gave the innkeeper's wife a half hug.

"And I'll tell you something else," Mrs. Allen whispered in her ear. "That man cares for you, too. Oh, I can tell he's a bit gruff and high-handed, but he cares."

Phadra didn't know what to say. In the morning she'd probably tell Mr. Morgan what Mrs. Allen had said and they would laugh. But tonight . . . tonight, the woman's conclusions were very comforting.

They parted company on the best of terms. Before she left with the wet clothes to be dried for the morrow, Mrs. Allen told Phadra to pour a little of the brandy in a cup and mix it with some water. "Give this to him every once in a while to help him sleep. I don't know if it does much good, but then, it's never harmed anyone."

Phadra smiled at her country wisdom and wished her a good night. At last she and Mr. Morgan were alone. Outside the room's shuttered window, the soft rain hit the tile roof and ran down the eaves.

Phadra stifled a yawn and reached to feel his brow. Warm, but not hot.

She pulled the chair over beside the bed, poured water from the bucket into the basin, and dipped a cloth into it. The cool water felt good against her hand. She pressed it against the back of his neck and the side of his face, as Mrs. Allen had demonstrated.

He didn't react but instead slept peacefully, his body rising and falling with his breathing. Again Phadra soaked the cloth and stroked it across his brow.

She did it not so much for him but for herself: a penance of sorts and a balm for her guilt-laden mind.

Grant shifted, searching for a better position on the bed. He never slept on his stomach, but when he turned on one side, the pain in his shoulder roused him.

He frowned, but it took him a minute or two to remember what was wrong with his arm. The room was dark except for the light from a candle in a lamp hanging from a peg on the wall.

His mouth tasted of whiskey and something else . . . brandy. He'd never had a head for liquor. When he raised his head, the world spun slightly.

He dropped his head back to the pillow, too tired to fight the dizziness. He was about to drift off to sleep when his senses told him something was not completely correct about the room. He looked around. The glow of the single candle shone on a mass of flaxen curls lying on the mattress not more than a hand's width from his face.

Miss Abbott.

In spite of the pain in his shoulder, Grant rolled to his right side and slowly, almost reverently, lifted his left hand to bury his fingers in the wild mass of curls.

Dear Lord, they felt every bit as silky as he had imagined. He detected the scent of wildflowers and sunshine that always seemed to be a part of her, a scent that even in his liquor-soaked state he identified with Phadra Abbott.

The head beneath his hand lifted, and he found himself staring into her eyes. She blinked and wet her lips with the tip of her tongue. The gesture was so sweet and sensual that he was sure he had to be dreaming.

Grant reached out, his movements limited and slow, and traced with the tip of his finger the path her tongue had just taken.

Her lips parted in surprise . . . and she swallowed, a movement he followed with the back of his hand down the smooth column of her neck.

It didn't hurt his arm to be stretched out this way, and he let it rest heavily on her shoulder, his fingers touching the back of her neck beneath that shimmering cascade of hair.

Her eyes opened wider at his boldness, and she made as if to pull back. That was when he noticed that she was sitting in a chair by the side of the bed. With his hand cupping the back of her neck, he held her in place. "I fell asleep," she said in a husky whisper, as if admitting a sin.

He smiled lazily. The sound of her low, musical voice pleased him.

She started to pull away again, but still he held her, so she reached up and put a cool hand against his head. "You're running a slight fever."

"Yes," he agreed, although the fever he was talking about wasn't coming from his forehead.

His answer appeared to alarm her. Again she started to pull away. "Let me put some cool compresses against your head. That will make you feel better."

"No, it won't," he told her softly.

"It won't?" she asked, worry edging her voice. "Then what can I do?"

"This," he answered, and pulled her head closer to his while he pushed up with his good arm and brought his lips to hers. She tasted every bit as good as she had earlier that evening when he'd kissed her in the inn yard, and, after a moment's startled hesitation, she relaxed and kissed him back.

Phadra's mind was reeling from the intimacy of the kiss. From the moment he'd touched her hair and traced the line of her jaw, she'd wanted him to kiss her. He tasted of smoky whiskey and sensual promises. She relaxed, enjoying the textures of his body.

His whiskered jaw brushed against the side of her cheek as he pulled her off the chair and onto the bed beside him. His lips brushed her hair and then her ear, a sensation that shot straight through her.

Dear Lord, she was the one who needed a cool compress! No one had the right to feel this way. But when she shifted to move, he kissed her neck and lower jaw, blazing a path back to her lips, and she was caught once again in his spell.

He'd pulled her body against his, and now Phadra felt the rough hairs of his legs and his strong muscles as he pressed against her. Dimly she was aware that her nightgown was up around her thighs . . . but she didn't care.

Phadra snuggled against him, wanting to be as close to him as possible, especially when he whispered in her ear, "What you do to me, love . . ."

And then, with a sigh of deep satisfaction, he fell asleep holding her in his arms, his hand cupping her breast.

A moment later Phadra too closed her eyes.

The pounding on the door echoed the pounding in his head. Grant stirred restlessly.

He moved his hand and winced at the sharp, stiff pain in his arm. Memories flooded his mind. Memories of fake emeralds, highwaymen, and caressing the breasts of Phadra Abbott.

Grant opened his eyes, wide awake now. Rays of bright sunlight filtered in through the slats of the shuttered window. He didn't know what time it was, but the day must be well advanced. Curled up next to him, Miss Abbott stretched and then resettled herself closer to him with a contented sigh, oblivious to the knocking.

She shifted again, and he felt her bare legs brush against his. The soft, feminine curve of her naked hip pressed up against him, and his body responded with a will of its own.

"Grant Morgan, you bloody fool, what have you done?" he swore softly. His head felt like a thundercloud, his mouth tasted of dry cotton and stale liquor — and yet, after the fight with the highwaymen, he remembered little except the pain.

At that moment the knocking stopped. He lifted his head off the pillow and stared at the door, holding his breath as the handle turned.

The door opened . . . and, as if his worst possible nightmare had come true, in marched Sir Cecil and Lady Evans.

Chapter 11

"I believe, Sir Cecil, that we have a matter to discuss."

Phadra heard Grant Morgan's words and the serious manner in which he said them. She didn't open her eyes. She didn't want to. She'd already heard Lady Evans's loud denunciations and Mrs. Allen's claims that she hadn't known Mr. and Mrs. *Abbott* were not married.

No, she had no desire to open her eyes and see how Mr. Morgan accepted *that* one. So she feigned sleep, listening to Sir Cecil's courteous "I await your pleasure." There was an edge to the way he said those words, though, as if the most important ones were left unsaid.

Until the door shut and his hand came down upon her shoulder, she'd thought that Mr. Morgan wasn't aware that she was awake. "You can open your eyes now, Miss Abbott. The wolves are at bay. For now," he added under his breath.

Phadra complied and discovered herself staring directly into his hard silver eyes. He was angry.

Aware that she lay half-naked and tangled in the sheets, she managed to sit up and pull the voluminous gown down over her legs with as much dignity as she could muster. He warily watched her movements.

"How is your shoulder?" she asked primly.

He grunted a response.

"Oh," Phadra answered, as if he'd said something intelligible.

A knock sounded at the door.

Mr. Morgan shocked Phadra by leaping out of the bed, heedless of his nakedness, and crossing to the door. He kneaded his wounded shoulder as he called out, "Who's there?"

A man's voice answered, "It's the innkeeper. I have your clothes."

Mr. Morgan opened the door only wide enough for the clothes to be handed to him. Phadra realized that she was staring at his bare buttocks and looked away.

"They're still damp," Mr. Morgan commented.

"I'm not surprised," Phadra replied tightly, concentrating on the bedpost knob.

"Why, Miss Abbott, you're blushing — or

should I say *Mrs. Abbott?*"

"I knew you'd be upset about the Mr. Abbott! I knew it." She turned to him without thinking and then almost gave a sigh of relief when she discovered that the pile of clothing he held with his one good arm covered a good portion — or at least the most important part — of his anatomy. She focused her attention on his face. "And yes, sir, I find this situation somewhat embarrassing."

"Somewhat?" he mocked.

"We've done nothing wrong. There is no reason for you to be angry with me."

In answer, he threw the clothes in a heap on the chair before pulling out his doeskin breeches with a disregard of her presence that shocked her. Then he sat on the bed and started dressing.

A student of Miss Agatha's, if she was a proper young woman, would have looked away. And Phadra did look away — but not until she'd secretly satisfied her curiosity. He was beautiful. She followed the line of his body with his eyes . . . until her eyes met his.

"Are you enjoying yourself?" he asked rudely, standing and pulling his breeches up around his waist. He buttoned the buttons before turning and facing her, a hand on his hip. Self-consciously Phadra raised a hand to her hair, which was wild and tangled.

He drew in a deep breath and ran a hand through his hair. "I'm not angry with you. It's myself I blame." Spying his boots, he pulled his stockings out of the clothing pile and then sat down on the edge of the same chair to put on first them and then the boots. "Damned boots are probably ruined."

Phadra swung her legs around so that she could sit on the edge of the bed. "Blame yourself for what?" she pressed, afraid of the answer.

Grant made a great pretense of stamping his feet into his boots before turning to her, his expression bitter. "For this." The wave of his hand encompassed the room and the bed with its rumpled sheets. Suddenly his brows came together. He crossed to the window and threw open the shutters. The late-afternoon light of an overcast day filled the room.

He turned to her, his eyes burning like two live coals. "I didn't hurt you, did I?" The words sounded unnaturally forced.

"Hurt me?" she repeated blankly. He watched her closely. "No, you didn't *hurt* me," she said. She took a step toward him. "Mr. Morgan, I don't know what you're thinking, but I assure you that I was as much a party to what happened between us as —" She paused for a second, as if debating her next words, before finishing quietly, "As you were."

His lips curled in derision. "Oh, I have no doubt I was involved. It's in my blood, you know." He crossed in front of her to pick up his shirt from the chair.

"What exactly does that mean?"

He shoved his head through the neck of the shirt and carefully pulled his wounded arm through the sleeve, refusing her silent offer of help before answering. "I took advantage of you. You're an innocent, or you were," he amended, tucking the shirttail into his breeches.

An innocent? She burst into laughter. "I hate to disillusion you, Mr. Morgan, but you did not seduce me."

"Oh, you just hopped into my bed on your own?"

Phadra felt her cheeks burn with color. "No, it wasn't quite like that."

"So who made the first move, you or myself?"

She hated the question. "You did." Then she added, "But I was the one who removed your clothing."

He flashed her a look from under his dark

lashes. "How daring of you," he mocked. "Can I expect a *carte blanche?*"

"It wasn't like that," she said, stung by his sarcasm. "Nothing happened between us."

"Nothing?" he demanded.

"Except that you kissed me," she confessed tightly. *But oh, what a kiss,* she wanted to add.

Silence.

"You don't remember the kiss?" She sat down on the bed, stunned by the revelation.

"Miss Abbott." He knelt down on the floor in front of her. "I don't want to hurt you . . . but a man doesn't have to have his brain engaged for what happened between us. Especially a Morgan," he added in a quiet voice.

"What does that mean?" Her chest felt as heavy as stone.

His handsome face with its dark shadow of whiskers was so close, almost as close as it had been when he'd stroked her hair during the night. "It means I don't remember what happened between us," he said.

Phadra pulled away from him.

He reached out and picked up the brandy bottle sitting on the floor, looking to see how much remained in it. With a guilty start, Phadra realized that she had dosed him rather liberally the night before in her concern that he not suffer much pain. He set the bottle down.

Grant closed his eyes, drew in a deep breath, and leaned his arm on the mattress. He was handling this badly. An image played in his mind of her body next to his, her scent filling his senses.

He stood abruptly, shocked by the vividness of the image. But he knew what he had to do. He looked at her standing in the window, the sun highlighting her glorious curls.

He forced himself to say the words. "Miss Abbott, would you do me the honor of becoming my wife?"

Her head snapped round to him. "What?" Her question came out as little more than a whisper.

Grant straightened his shoulders. "I'm asking you to marry me."

She stared at him, her eyes turning hard and bright. "Why are you doing this?"

That wasn't the answer he expected. "The reason should be as obvious as those rumpled sheets and your state of undress."

"All we did was kiss."

"And I woke up with you half-naked and in my arms. That should be reason enough."

"Not to me. You're betrothed to another woman."

"I assure you, Sir Cecil no longer thinks of me as a suitable candidate for his daughter's hand. In fact, I am confident that at this very moment Sir Cecil is waiting for me to make the arrangements for our marriage."

Phadra studied him for a moment. When she'd first heard him ask her to marry him, her heart had stopped beating — until she'd turned to face him. The stern expression on his face and the almost military stiffness of his body would have been more suited to a man facing a firing squad than to a doting suitor.

Could it be that he loved Miranda? Phadra dismissed that idea immediately. She asked, "What about your title? What about your future?"

"It's of no consequence."

Phadra's lips parted in surprise at his answer. "No consequence? How can something that you've dreamed about and worked for — even going so far as to barter your soul in a marriage to Miranda Evans — be suddenly of *no consequence?*"

His eyes snapped with anger. "That, Miss Abbott, is my affair."

"Your affair?" Her anger swept aside any hurt she might have felt. "You ask me to marry you and then chastise me for questioning your motives?"

"My motives?" he repeated blankly, as if she were speaking gibberish.

"Well, I won't have it," she announced briskly. "Your suit is rejected, Mr. Morgan. I will not marry you. Good day."

He stared at her open-mouthed, as if she'd just struck him.

Phadra looked at him haughtily. "You may leave the room. Our interview is over. I acquit you from any further obligation to me."

"You *acquit* me?"

"I pray never to see you again," she said plainly.

The expression on his face changed from *noblesse oblige* to dumbfounded anger. "Madam, you mistake the matter. You have no choice."

"Yes, I do, and I've *made* it."

His temper exploded like lightning cracking open the heavens. "In God's name, woman, you could drive a man to madness." He started toward her but then appeared to change his mind. He crossed the room to stand far away from her. His next words were clear and succinct. "You do not have a choice."

"Yes, I do."

"No! You do not." He pointed an angry

finger at the bed. "If a man did to one of my sisters what I did to you last night, I would kill him. *After* I'd seen them married!"

"Then I should thank the heavens that I have no overbearing male relative to avenge my honor, because I have no desire to enter into a marriage of convenience." *Especially with you,* she wanted to add. A man who couldn't even remember kissing her the night before!

"What? You wish to live a scandal? To be ostracized from polite society?"

Phadra tilted her chin proudly. "Nothing happened last night for which either of us should apologize. Furthermore, a woman today can take a lover and still find doors open to her —"

"Only the doors of a bawdy house!"

"That's not true!" she shot back. "Mary Wollstonecraft had a lover. She even had a child by him —"

With a roar, Grant crossed the room in three steps to stand in front of her. "Don't quote that heretical woman to me right now! I wish with all my being that you'd never heard her name or that of her abominable book."

"There! That's the reason we can't be married. I could *never* marry a man who thought he could exercise such control over

249

me. I will read what I wish, think what I wish, and —"

"Be married before this day is out," he growled.

"You can't make me," she spat back, her body almost shaking with the force of her anger.

His eyes blazed with angry intensity, but when he spoke, his voice was controlled and tight. "I can and I will. The Bank of England is your guardian, and with or without your permission they will countenance our marriage."

They stood toe to toe, his large frame looming over her, but Phadra refused to be cowed. "It won't be legal. I'll never sign the license!"

"You won't need to. Sir Cecil can sign for you as your guardian. The marriage will be legal."

"That's not true!"

"Who would challenge it? No judge would set the marriage aside in light of the compromising position the Evanses found you in this afternoon — with witnesses, no less!"

The truth of his words shocked her. Now she understood the nuances in his brief conversation with Sir Cecil earlier. She stepped away from him, suddenly struck by something else. For all her brave words, Phadra didn't really want to play the fallen woman. She'd met courtesans among her artist friends, but everything in her upbringing, from what she'd learned at her mother's knee to the dictums heard at Miss Agatha's, had preached the ruin of a woman choosing such a road.

She went back to the window and stared out at the gray clouds. "What about the emeralds? Don't we still have a problem there?"

He took so long to answer that she feared he hadn't heard the question. Finally he said, "I'll pay the debt."

"Can you?" She turned to him in surprise.

"I can." With those words, Grant realized completely all that he'd lost. The money he'd planned to spend for an estate in the country would go to pay for an ill-fated treasure hunt and fake emeralds. The dream of a title appeared an impossibility now. Furthermore, enough people knew of his plans to marry Miranda that there would be talk, especially when he suddenly turned up in London married to Phadra, and the gossips would whisper that the apple never falls far from the tree. The set of his jaw hardened at the thought. He had to keep his temper. Too much scandal, and even his present position at the bank could be in jeopardy.

He looked at the petite woman swimming in the oversized nightgown. The light from the window framed her silhouette. She was a far cry from the aristocratic wife he'd planned to marry one day.

And yet even now his traitorous body responded to her. He damned his bad blood.

Bluntly he said, "I need to see Sir Cecil."

She didn't acknowledge him, but continued staring as if dazed by the turn of events. For the first time he wondered if she too had regrets. Had she long held dreams about the man she would choose to marry, dreams that must now be let go?

Hardening his resolve, he crossed to the door and turned the handle, not surprised to catch the innkeepers and Lady Evans scrambling away from the door. With one last look over his shoulder at the silent woman inside the room, he left, closing the door behind him.

Lady Evans gave Phadra only a half hour to brood before she burst into the room, trying to act like a ray of sunshine. "Well," she announced, rolling the *l*'s, as was her habit, "you can't continue to be a slugabed. We need to get you dressed. Did you hear that rider take off from the inn yard? He's on his way to London to procure a special license."

Phadra turned slowly from the window. "A special license?"

Lady Evans smiled without mirth. "You can be married this very evening, here at this inn, as soon as the messenger returns. Mr. Morgan has made all the arrangements."

"What if the messenger is unable to purchase the license?" Phadra asked.

"Oh, but he will," Lady Evans assured her. "Mr. Morgan is related to the Archbishop of Canterbury, who, I'm sure, given the family history, will be only too glad to see his nephew do the honorable thing."

"Aren't you the least bit concerned about what Miranda will have to say?"

Lady Evans looked at Phadra as if amazed she would even suggest such a concern. "My dear, Miranda will count herself lucky to be rid of such an undesirable match. Furthermore, the engagement was never formally announced. There were no commitments. Of course, the engagement ball is scheduled for tomorrow evening, but I'll think of a way out of that." She smiled then, a smile that didn't reach the avarice in her eyes, before adding, "Sir Cecil feels this is the best thing that could happen to us.

After all, Grant Morgan is a very clever young man. With his help, no one will discover my husband's small indiscretion. He may even be of future help to us, if he wants to ensure our silence in this affair."

Phadra slid Lady Evans a suspicious look. "What do you mean by that?"

All the pretense in Lady Evans's manner disappeared. "Grant values his position with the bank. He'll be only too happy to see the debts paid in full and keep his own neck out of debtor's prison."

"But that's not right. Sir Cecil helped plan the emeralds' theft. He should pay his share!"

With malicious satisfaction Lady Evans responded, "My dear, life is rarely fair." The pile of clothing on the chair then caught her attention. "Oh, gracious, these things will be hopelessly wrinkled, and I do so love this ruffled muslin dress on you. We'll have to see that it is aired and pressed. We can't have you looking anything less than your best for your bridegroom, can we?" She gave Phadra her sweetest smile.

The messenger sent to London didn't return until well past midnight. Phadra sat still and tense on a hard high-backed chair, her hands tightly clasped in front of her. She prayed that something had happened to prevent the man from purchasing the license.

A knock sounded at the door a brief second before Lady Evans and Mrs. Allen entered the room. "Arise, Phadra. Your moment has come," Lady Evans announced.

"I love weddings," Mrs. Allen confided, her mobcap bobbing in excitement.

Phadra was tempted to offer Mrs. Allen her place in the event but decided that it was not the time for sarcasm.

She'd thought long and hard over the past hours. Her childhood dreams had been spent fantasizing about her reunion with her father. Marriage had always been something distant and not quite attainable. Even over the past weeks, when she'd been presented with suitors, it had never seemed a reality.

Now she was marrying a man she barely knew. A man who was marrying her out of honor only, with none of the other, finer emotions. A man who could now be blackmailed because of her.

Phadra fought an almost overwhelming sense of panic. Her knees buckled, and she sat back down in the chair.

"Miss Abbott, are you all right?" Mrs. Allen asked.

"Of course she's all right," Lady Evans snapped.

"Yes, I'm fine, aren't I?" Phadra said, directing her statement to Lady Evans and letting the force of her anger at being bullied into this marriage show in her eyes.

Her irritation had no impact on Lady Evans, who smiled benignly. "Phadra, dear, I thought you were going to pin up your hair. It is more proper to do so."

"I like it down."

"Your husband will expect you to do what is proper and fitting in a wife," Lady Evans lectured. "He will want you to wear it up so you do not attract attention to yourself by being different."

"It would look more formal, dear," Mrs. Allen said. "I'll have Toby run out and cut some flowers in my garden. We can put a few in your hair, and it will make everything all the more special."

She was so earnest, so anxious for all to go off well, that Phadra couldn't turn her down. Fifteen minutes later, with Mrs. Allen's help, Phadra had her hair pinned on top of her head in a fashionable style that looked better on her with the cornflowers tucked between her curls. They even brightened the fussy muslin walking dress.

Mrs. Allen also fashioned a small nosegay

of cornflowers and roses for Phadra to carry. Opening the door for Phadra, she whispered, "You look beautiful."

Phadra doubted that. She'd seen her reflection in the mirror, and her features appeared strained and pale. Still, she appreciated the kindness the woman showed her by saying so.

Lady Evans was already downstairs in the inn's private room, standing next to her husband and a man wearing the somber garb of a vicar. Off to one side, his head almost touching the low ceiling, the candlelight casting his long shadow against the walls, stood Grant Morgan, looking more handsome than she could have possibly imagined.

He wore the same clothes, but his appearance didn't seem wrinkled or soiled, as she felt hers did. The doeskin breeches hugged the long, lean lines of his thighs, and his boots were freshly polished. His coat appeared to be molded to his broad shoulders yet still managed to hide the bulk of his bandage.

Mrs. Allen nudged Phadra to take her place next to him. Phadra was conscious of the clean scent of his shaving soap and the snowy white of his neckcloth, which emphasized the squareness of his jaw.

She felt perfectly dowdy standing next to him.

"Phadra," he said, her name sounding perfectly right and natural on his lips, "this is the Reverend Rawls-Hicks."

She nodded, not able to trust her voice.

Mr. Rawls-Hicks smiled and readjusted the gold-framed reading lenses that perched on the bridge of his nose. "Please don't be anxious, Miss Abbott. These circumstances are unusual, but I've seen many a fine marriage evolve out of less-than-auspicious beginnings."

He didn't wait for a response but opened his prayer book and in the voice of command asked Grant to take her hand in his. "It's a nice touch," he explained.

Grant did as he asked, conscious that her hand was cold, her motions stiff and formal. She looked like a child bride, with her unruly curls in that tight hairstyle and the dress's oversized ruffles concealing her figure. He wished she'd worn her hair down.

For a brief moment he remembered exactly the feel of his fingers in her hair, the touch of his lips possessing hers, and he gave her hand a gentle squeeze.

The warm reassurance of his hand around hers steadied her resolve. As the vicar said

the opening words of the marriage ceremony, Phadra raised her gaze to him. He
looked so handsome, so strong and invin-
cible, standing beside her.

For a second she forgot the angry words
between them. She wanted to let herself believe, even for just a moment, that a man
like this could love her.

The vicar said, "Grant Morgan, wilt thou
have this woman to be thy wedded wife, to
live together after God's ordinance in the
holy estate of matrimony? Wilt thou love
her, comfort her, honor and keep her in
sickness and in health; and, forsaking all
others, keep thee only unto her, so long as
ye both shall live?"

Phadra watched, almost as if witnessing a
miracle, as Grant replied in a steady voice,
"I will."

"Phadra Abbott, wilt thou have this man
to be thy wedded husband, to live together
after God's ordinance in the holy estate of
matrimony? Wilt thou love him, comfort
him, obey him, honor and keep him in sickness and in health; and, forsaking all others,
keep thee only unto him, so long as ye both
shall live?"

Her first impulse was to throw the
nosegay in the air and run from the room, to
run so hard and so fast that no one would

ever catch her or find her.

But she couldn't. Not with Grant Morgan holding her hand so tightly that she could swear he'd read her mind. Her mouth went dry. He squeezed her hand, a silent command to answer. She forced herself to swallow and whispered, "I will."

She sensed a collective sigh in the room. Her gaze darted up to Grant. His expression remained formally impassive — until the time came for him to pledge his troth.

Then he looked at her, the expression in his gray eyes somber and enigmatic. His deep masculine voice was firm and resolute as he promised to cherish her "until death us do part."

Phadra repeated her part, but she didn't look at him as she said it. Even as she whispered the words "to love and to cherish," she couldn't believe this was happening. Any second now she expected him to change his mind, to deny that they had shared more than a kiss — and yet she finished her piece without interruption.

The wonder of it shocked her.

The Reverend Rawls-Hicks said, "And now it's time for the ring." He looked over his spectacles at them. "Do you have a ring, or should I pass over that part?"

Grant surprised Phadra by announcing,

"I have a ring." Releasing her hand, he reached inside his pocket, pulled out a cloth, and offered it to the vicar. Inside the folds of the cloth were the emerald earrings and ring she'd sold to the goldsmith. Mr. Rawls-Hicks took the ring, and Grant refolded the earrings in their cloth and put them back in his pocket.

"Lovely," the vicar murmured, holding the emerald up to the candlelight. Phadra watched, still in shock at the turn of events, as the clergyman blessed the ring and then passed it to Grant, who held it out for her left hand. She knew it would fit. It had been her mother's wedding ring.

That had been the last of her father's betrayals — he'd even sold the emeralds from his wife's wedding ring.

Slowly, respectfully, Grant slipped the ring down over the third finger of her left hand. Silent tears escaped Phadra's defenses and rolled down her cheeks, tears for herself, tears for her mother. She didn't realize they were there until Grant lifted his hand and with the back of his fingers brushed them away.

The vicar still spoke the words of the ceremony, but Phadra no longer listened. Instead she focused on the planes and hollows of her husband's face in the dancing candlelight and the grim set of his mouth.

She felt ashamed. True, she had no desire to live a mockery of a marriage like her mother's, and yet this man had shown her more openness and honesty in the short time she'd known him than her father had over a lifetime.

She had to explain, to make him understand the tears. "The emerald's fake," she whispered. The words came out even deeper and hoarser than her natural huskiness.

"I know," he replied. "But the gold is good —"

At that moment the Reverend Rawls-Hicks announced, "Those whom God hath joined together, let no man put asunder."

"— and solid."

Chapter 12

The Reverend Rawls-Hicks pronounced them man and wife.

With the words still hanging in the air, Lady Evans chimed in briskly, "Well, I'm glad that's over. Now we can all head back to London." She pulled on her gloves as she turned to Phadra. "Sir Cecil and I have discussed the matter with Grant, Phadra, and we think it best that we go ahead and hold the ball tomorrow evening — no, wait. It'll be held *this* evening." She placed a hand to her head as if overwhelmed by the thought. Finally, with a dramatic sigh, she finished, "Well, we must simply do what we must do. Grant agrees with us that we should use this occasion to announce your marriage."

"Announce my marriage at Miranda's ball?" Phadra asked blankly. Certainly she would discover all of this was an elaborate hoax.

Lady Evans dismissed the concern with a wave of her gloved hand. "Miranda won't give it a second thought." For a moment her attention was diverted by the bellowing of her husband, who had turned on his heel and headed for his carriage the minute the ceremony was finished. The wide-eyed innkeeper and his wife scurried to obey the summons. When Sir Cecil called for his wife the second time, she winced at the sound of his voice but did not hurry to comply with his command. Instead she turned to Phadra and picked up the threads of the conversation. "We'll have it put out that Sir Cecil and I discovered that we just couldn't give our approval to such a poor match. Everyone will understand." She frowned in mock concern before leaning closer to Phadra and confiding, "After all, *no one* wants their bloodlines tainted by the Morgans."

Phadra glanced at Grant to see if he'd heard Lady Evans. He was handing several pound notes to the vicar, who slipped them discreetly into his pocket. As if feeling her eyes upon him, Grant looked up. The expression on his face betrayed no emotion, but she sensed he'd heard.

A sudden, fierce loyalty welled up inside her. She had just been united with Grant Morgan before God. She vowed he'd never be sorry for this forced union.

Tilting her chin with pride, Phadra answered in a perfect imitation of the frostiest of society matrons, "Lady Evans, I'd advise you to say no such thing."

Her ladyship turned to her with a look of surprise, then, her eyes narrowed with interest and her voice silky with challenge, she asked, "Or you will do what?"

"Nothing," came Grant's firm reply.

Lady Evans looked from Grant to Phadra, who was standing in stunned silence, and gloated. Placing her hat upon her head and tying the ribbons, she said, "Then I suppose I will see you this evening, Phadra. Around seven." With a swish of her skirts she left the room.

Slowly Phadra turned to Grant. He met her gaze squarely, his expression stern.

"I give you my best wishes," Mr. Rawls-Hicks said awkwardly, as if wanting to fill the silence. He reached out and gave Phadra's hand, tightly clenched around the bridal nosegay, a shake. Then he wasted no more time removing himself from the room.

They were alone.

Grant knew he'd blundered. He shouldn't have corrected her in front of that vicious harpy Lady Evans, but he said, "I will not have you say anything to discredit her."

The flash of challenge in his wife's blue eyes warned him that he'd gone at it the wrong way. "Even if she runs around town discrediting you?"

"Yes."

Phadra pulled back from him, her expressive eyes rebellious. He sighed exasperatedly and ran a hand through his hair. He should have known better. His sisters would never have accepted his orders blindly, either. Why had he assumed a wife would be different?

"You can't let her say whatever she wishes and not counter with the truth," she said.

Grant hated having to explain himself — especially when he sensed that the truth would diminish his stature in her eyes. *Well, she might as well learn now*, he thought. "I can and I will," he said curtly. "Furthermore, I expect you to do the same."

"Why?" she demanded.

"Because she's the wife of one of my employers." He took a step away from her, irritated that she'd made him voice those words, before turning and asking, "What is the matter with you? Why do you always demand explanations? Isn't it enough that I tell you not to do something?"

Phadra didn't bat an eye. "No."

He stared at her as if not sure he'd heard

her correctly. Phadra shifted nervously, conscious that she wasn't getting their marriage off to the best possible start, but believing passionately in her right to express her opinion.

She attempted to diffuse the situation. "I don't believe that just because you and Sir Cecil work at the same bank, it gives Lady Evans license to trample over the truth, let alone other people's feelings."

"And what truth is she trampling?"

"That they rejected your suit for Miranda. Trust me, Sir Cecil was overjoyed that you or anyone would take Miranda off his hands. And our marriage had nothing to do with your family!"

His brows came together. "Oh, that's right," he said sarcastically. "Let's have the *truth* bandied about — that you ran away from your guardians and that I, in my attempt to return you to them, seduced you, thereby jilting my fiancée. Yes, that sounds much better!"

"That's not the truth and you know it!" Phadra said, coming toward him.

"Oh? Don't tell me that you seduced me!"

Phadra narrowed her eyes at him. "I think we've had this argument already."

"The point is, the truth is just as unsavory as whatever story Lady Evans puts out. Be-

267

lieve me, Phadra, you didn't get a bargain out of this marriage. There will be gossip. My goal is to keep it from becoming a scandal, and in order to do that I need Sir Cecil's goodwill. Furthermore, I see no need to drag Miranda's name down with us. Do you understand?"

"I understand that you will be at the Evanses' mercy. That they can say or do anything they please," she answered tartly, angry at having to swallow this injustice.

"That's your pride talking. After you've been a Morgan for a while, you'll learn to ignore the barbs from the society matrons," he answered stiffly. As if the matter between them was resolved, he picked up her cloak and, taking her arm, led her out of the room.

Phadra allowed herself to be led. Something about his solemn reserve disturbed her. "Does your shoulder hurt?"

"Like the very devil," he answered without looking at her. He guided them through the inn's hall toward the front door. "I'm anxious to get into our coach and catch a few hours of sleep before we reach London."

She pulled up short. Through the inn's open front door, torchlight revealed a post chaise and team waiting for them. "We're going back tonight? Do you think it wise?

268

You tell me your shoulder bothers you." And she wanted nothing more right then than to return to their little room, shut the door on the world . . . and have him hold her, kiss her, hug her as he'd done the previous night.

The need for his touch shocked her. She took a step back.

Grant spoke with the patience a parent would reserve for a child. "Phadra, I have to be at the bank on the morrow. I need to announce our marriage to the directors before the ball. . . ." He allowed his voice to trail off, but Phadra caught the unspoken meaning.

"Before the gossip reaches them first, you mean," she finished. The realization of how deeply he must regret their marriage sobered her. She had to force herself to take each step toward the waiting coach . . . and her destiny.

Grant heard the disappointment in her voice. He opened the door to the chaise and helped her in. Phadra slid across the seat, away from him. He could feel her pulling away. He climbed into the chaise and sat beside her, the confines too close for them to sit very far apart. After rapping on the roof to signal the postboy to start the journey, he attempted to explain. "Phadra, this will be a difficult time." The post chaise took off with a jerk that threw her against him. He clenched his teeth against the pain as she jostled his wounded shoulder.

She quickly pushed herself away and asked coldly, "And if they do hear the gossip before you can talk to them?"

Grant didn't answer immediately. He felt the shift of the coach as it rolled out of the inn yard and onto the road to London. Finally he said, "I could lose my position with the bank —"

"I see."

"Do you?" he asked, irritated by her interruption. "There will be people who will put the worst possible cast on the matter. Junior men who covet my position —"

She interrupted him again. "What are you warning me about?" He could feel her staring at him in the dark.

Grant ran a hand through his hair. "I'm not warning you —," he began, then stopped himself. "Yes, I am warning you. People can be cruel, but I think we can weather the storm if we present a respectable picture, if we stand together. The gossip will die down."

The gossip. He knew how hard it was to live down gossip. He knew the shame of having everyone know your secrets. Instead he said, "After all, this isn't the worst scandal London has witnessed. It'll be a momentary diversion."

Phadra was thankful that he couldn't see her face in the dark, for her cheeks burned with embarrassment. He hadn't wanted this marriage . . . any more than her father had wanted a child. Only Grant wouldn't desert her as her father had — even if the marriage ruined him.

She didn't know if she would be able to speak, but she forced herself. "I shouldn't have run away." Her voice came out as little more than a whisper. "Here. Take what is left of the five hundred pounds."

Grant heard in her voice what she didn't want him to know — how much saying those words aloud cost her pride. "Keep it." He almost reached over to her in the dark, but something held him back. It wouldn't do any good. He'd already made a muddle of everything. Why couldn't he have left her alone the night before? Even now, hearing her voice in the dark, his body responded. The image of taking her right there in the close confines of the rolling post chaise almost robbed him of breath.

His father would have done so, had he been in the same position.

Instead Grant moved closer to the door

and concentrated on the dull, throbbing pain in his shoulder. She wouldn't be sorry she married him, he vowed. And he would protect her. He knew what to avoid. He'd steer them through this scandal.

All he had to do was stay in control.

Phadra woke in stages. She no longer felt the roll and sway of the carriage; slowly, as she became aware of her surroundings, she realized that she was in a bedroom.

She sat up on the large, comfortable mattress of a four-poster bed. She was still dressed in the clothes she'd worn in the post chaise, except that her shoes had been removed. Peering over the edge of the mattress, she saw them sitting in perfect alignment by the side of the bed.

Phadra slid off the high four-poster, using the steps set at the side of the bed to climb down. Something about the room seemed vaguely familiar. Almost as if in a dream, she crossed to the window, her feet soundless on the thick carpet, and pulled open the drapes. Daylight flooded the room. Phadra blinked and looked out onto the street.

She didn't recognize the neighborhood, with its neat brick row houses lining the streets. There was much of London she hadn't explored yet, but she knew by the genteel appointments and wrought-iron fences that she was in one of the better neighborhoods.

She turned and looked around the room. It was not overlarge. The bed dominated it. The colors were deep, evergreen with hints of brown. A masculine room. The lines of the bed, the washstand, and the dresser were plainly styled, but Phadra found them exceptionally tasteful. In fact, the whole room was pleasing to her in spite of its outward masculinity.

Suddenly she realized what seemed so familiar to her. The air smelled of the shaving soap used by Grant Morgan.

Phadra looked down at her left hand. The fake emerald on her wedding ring winked back at her in the summer morning sun.

She walked over to the dresser. On top sat three miniatures of women who she assumed must be his sisters since they bore a striking resemblance to her husband.

Her husband . . .

She looked around the room, seeing it with new eyes now that she realized that it was the intimate domain of her husband. It fit Grant's personality. Tasteful, understated, not an item in the room that didn't serve a useful purpose.

She didn't feel uncomfortable in it.

She turned her gaze to the bed. The feather pillow on the other side of the bed was indented as if someone had rested there. Hot color flooded her cheeks as she realized that she hadn't been the only one in the bed that night. Could he have —

A discreet knock at the door interrupted her thoughts. For a moment Phadra panicked. Catching sight of herself in the mirror over the washstand, she decided she didn't want anyone to see her. The dress was wrinkled almost beyond repair; her hair hung in a mass of tangles and curls. The knock sounded again, this time more insistent. "Who's there?" Phadra called.

"Wallace, madam," came the crisp answer.

"Wallace?" she repeated in disbelief.

The door opened.

"Wallace!" Phadra cried in glad recognition. She stopped herself just short of throwing a big hug around his neck. "What are you doing here?"

The burly butler, now dressed in somber black and white livery instead of the more flamboyant style she had chosen and carrying a small silver tray, smiled. "I'm in Mr. Morgan's service. Jem and I both have been since Mr. Morgan closed up your house in Soho Square."

"He never said a word to me."

A knowing smile stretched across Wallace's face. "Mayhap he'd planned on bringing home a different bride."

Hot color flooded her cheeks.

"Here now, Miss Abbott — I mean, Mrs. Morgan, don't be that way about it. Jem and I are proud as punch to be back in your employ." He lowered his voice to a confidential level. "Better than that *other* one, I can tell you."

"Who, Miranda? What do you know of her?"

Wallace stood to his full height. "When your employer is about to marry a new mistress, a smart servant finds out everything he can about her." He didn't have to say anything further. What he'd discovered was etched in the frown lines of his face. He indicated the small silver tray he held and the single card on it bearing Miranda's name. "She's waiting in the parlor and demands a word with you. And the master left this message for you." With his other hand he offered a heavy bond envelope.

Phadra stared at Miranda's calling card on the silver salver as if it were a live thing. She shook the fanciful idea from her head, but reached instead for the envelope. The letter was addressed to her in Grant's bold handwriting. She broke the seal.

Phadra,
Wanted to let you sleep. Will return
this evening and escort you to the ball.
Lady Evans expects us at seven. Have
sent for your clothing from Evans
House. Will expect you to be ready and
appropriately attired at half past six.
                              G. Morgan

Phadra reread the note and blinked. At
first she'd been pleasantly surprised by the
sight of her name written in his strong
script, but the curtness of the note took her
aback . . . and what did he mean by "appropriately attired"? She frowned.

"Is everything all right, madam?"

Phadra looked up at Wallace's concerned
face and answered in a distracted manner,
"Yes, everything's fine. I'm just overtired,"
and then realized it was true.

"You did come in late last night. Mr.
Morgan carried you in from the coach and
said you didn't stir."

She gave him a sharp glance, "He carried
me in? With his shoulder wound?"

Wallace shrugged. "That's what he told
me this morning when he informed me of
your marriage. He should have woken me. I

would have helped, but he said he hadn't had a problem. He's a strong man. He should have been in the military instead of wasting away in a bank." He gave a meaningful look at the card on the silver dish. "She insists that she is going to wait for you."

Phadra pushed aside the distracting idea of Grant's carrying her to his bed and turned her thoughts to Miranda. What in the world could she want? "What time is it?"

"A quarter past ten."

"I didn't think she rose before noon," Phadra muttered, and then made a decision. "Wallace," she said grandly, "please convey to her my sincere apologies, but I am not ready to receive guests. I don't have anything to wear other than this, and it is hopelessly wrinkled."

"Lady Miranda ordered me to convey her express apologies for the early hour, but she feels she must see you this morning. She has also delivered trunks with your clothing from Evans House. Jem is out in the hall with her footman, waiting for your permission to bring the trunks in."

Phadra looked around Grant's orderly but relatively small room. As if reading her mind, Wallace answered, "Mr. Morgan did say for you to be in this room. There's three other bedrooms, but they lack furnishings, since he gave each of his sisters the furniture upon their marriages. He hasn't replaced it because he was planning to move to the country after the wedding and thought she'd like to choose the furniture." Immediately he realized his possible blunder. He added almost apologetically, "He's a frugal one. Keeps a tight rein on the expenses. Doesn't spend unless he has to."

Remembering that Grant was now responsible for her debts, Phadra couldn't stop herself from murmuring under her breath, "And he is about to become more frugal."

"I beg your pardon, madam?"

"It's nothing, Wallace," she demurred with a wave of her hand.

Wallace looked over his shoulder, as if expecting someone to be eavesdropping on their conversation, and then whispered, "You've done right by this marriage, Miss Abbott — I mean, Mrs. Morgan. He's a man with big plans."

"Really?" Phadra was intensely curious about anything that had to do with Grant Morgan.

The butler needed no more encouragement to continue. "He doesn't spend money unless he has to. Puts it to better use.

In the funds." Wallace winked. "He's a smart one. He's given me a tip or two, and already it has borne fruit. I've made more than a couple of quid listening to him."

Phadra blinked. She wasn't so much surprised that Grant knew how to invest money as she was that he and the earthy Wallace seemed to be on such close terms.

His manner changed abruptly as he turned into the butler again. "Shall I tell Lady Miranda you will be down presently?"

Phadra grimaced. She didn't look forward to the interview. "Yes." She raised a hand to her hair. "Once I straighten this out. If I'm lucky, it may take an hour or two."

Wallace gave her a big smile. "It's good to be working for you again, Miss Abbott. Mr. Morgan keeps his brush in his top drawer." He nodded toward the dresser.

She was to use Grant's brush? She shot a guilty glance at the dresser drawer. Nothing made her feel more like a wife than the manservant's easy acceptance that she and her husband should share toiletries.

Wallace opened the bedroom door and ordered the men with her trunks to enter. Jem, hale and hearty, brought in a trunk packed with her clothes from the days before her move to Evans House; Lady

Evans had insisted that it be banished to the attic. The Evanses' footman brought in another trunk, which she assumed must contain the ruffled cottons and satins Lady Evans had chosen for her. She knew the servant, but when she nodded a greeting, he looked away, his ruddy complexion turning a shade redder.

Jem was busy talking to her about the milliner's assistant he wanted to marry, who he thought would make an excellent lady's maid for Phadra. Phadra's attention, however, was on the Evanses' footman and the almost sheepish way he handed over the key to the newest trunk to her. It was then that she remembered that the key to her old trunk, the one full of the clothing she'd designed herself, was in the portmanteau that had gone off to Portsmouth with the mail coach. It didn't matter. Grant wouldn't consider any of the clothes in that trunk "appropriate."

She interrupted Jem's prattle. "Wallace, tell Lady Miranda that I will present myself as soon as I have had a chance to dress."

With a snap of his fingers, Wallace motioned Jem and the footman out of the room before he bowed and followed.

Phadra crossed to the trunk with her clothes from Evans House — her "appropriate" attire — and unlocked it. On top of the neatly folded clothing, like an old reliable friend, lay her copy of Mary Wollstonecraft's book. Phadra picked it up, letting her fingers run across the leather binding lovingly. She put it on top of the dresser next to the pictures of Grant's sisters. It looked right there, and suddenly Phadra felt a sense of security that she'd never known before.

She wanted to stay here, to belong here and have her portrait sitting on the dresser beside those of his sisters — and, perhaps, to build a marriage based upon mutual respect.

But first she had to suffer through the interview with Miranda. She turned her attention back to the trunk and pulled out the first dress her fingers touched, a white muslin day dress that completely washed out her features. Lady Evans had insisted she have it in her wardrobe. Phadra hated the dress but decided to wear it so that Miranda would not be left waiting any longer than necessary.

She shook the dress out and then realized something was wrong. The skirt separated in long shreds. She looked at the bodice. It too had long gashes, making it completely unwearable.

Quickly Phadra drew out the other

clothing in the trunk. Dress after dress had been treated in this manner. Even her undergarments had been sliced and shredded, making them virtually unwearable. The outrage of it filled her with fury.

She had nothing to wear — and at that very moment Miranda Evans was probably standing in the parlor smiling at this one last dirty trick.

Without a care for her hair or wrinkled dress, Phadra marched out of the bedroom in a blind rage and stomped down the stairs to the lower floor. The Evanses' footman and Miranda's maid saw her first and huddled against the wall closest to the front door. Wallace took one look at the expression on her face and her tightly clenched fists and indicated with a nod which closed door led to the parlor. Then he motioned for Jem to open the door for her — but Phadra reached it first.

She turned the door handle and shoved the door open, pleased that it hit the wall with a resounding bang. Miranda stood in the middle of the room. Phadra slammed the door shut and then slowly approached the woman.

Miranda smiled pleasantly. "Phadra, you look absolutely horrible. Couldn't you have taken a moment to change? You look as though you slept in those clothes."

"You piece of baggage," Phadra said, her voice vibrating with anger. "What possessed you to pull this trick?"

Miranda's eyes glinted with malice. "You took him from me."

"Took him from you?" Phadra asked, dumbfounded. "You didn't even want him. If Lord Phipps had made an offer, you would have jilted Grant Morgan without a second's hesitation. You let one and all know you thought he was beneath you."

Miranda stepped toward her, the anger of her mania burning bright in her eyes. "He was mine! He was promised to me, and he was mine to do with as I wished."

Phadra stood her ground. "Yours? You make him sound like a pet. Well, he's not. The circumstances of our marriage might have been unusual — which I'm *sure* your mother has explained to you — but they were unavoidable, and right now I'm glad! Marriage to you would have been a living hell, and no man, certainly not Grant Morgan, deserves that!"

Miranda's face turned an unnatural shade of red, and her body began to shake. For a brief moment Phadra wondered if she had gone too far.

"I hate you." Miranda's voice seemed to

come from deep inside her. It rolled out with hideous resonance. "Ever since you came into my life, everything has gone wrong. But it is going to end here!" Her lovely face contorted with rage, Miranda shouldered Phadra aside and crossed to the door. "I'll destroy both of you. I can do it *and I will.* Tonight all the *ton* will know Grant Morgan for the pretender he is. By the time I am through with him, no one will receive him!"

Phadra moved toward her. "Miranda, if you want to blame someone, blame me! It was my foolishness that led us to this pass. It's all my fault. Not Grant's. He's only tried to do what is right and honorable in this mess."

"He shouldn't have married you!"

The words hurt — especially because Phadra feared Grant agreed with her. "What would you have had him do? He had to marry me." The words tasted bitter when said out loud. "He had no choice."

"It's your fault." Miranda's lip protruded peevishly, but the anger in her features softened slightly.

Phadra agreed readily, "That's right. It's my fault. Not Grant's."

"But it doesn't matter," Miranda snapped. "I'll see you both turned out —"

Dear God, Phadra thought as the other young woman spoke, could Miranda not know about the emerald fiasco? Was she mad enough to destroy her own father in order to wreak revenge on Grant? But Miranda's next words commanded Phadra's complete attention.

"— just like Mama turned out that vulgar woman who pretended to be your chaperone."

"Henny?" Phadra's alarm turned to quiet, deadly anger. "What have you done to Henny?"

Miranda's lip curled into a sneer. "She's out on the streets. I hope the dogs get her." She turned the handle on the door and opened it. "Good day to you, *Mrs.* Morgan. I pray you find something *suitable* to wear this evening." She turned to make her exit.

"Stop right there," Phadra ordered in a cold, hard voice.

Miranda looked back over her shoulder. Raising a scornful eyebrow as if to ask who dared to speak to her in such a manner, she turned to face Phadra.

Phadra lifted her chin. "Normally, Miranda, you have the good sense to save your tantrums for servants and people you think you can bully. Well, you've missed your mark this time. I'm not afraid of you.

Do your worst, Miranda Evans."

Miranda's lips parted in surprise. Then her mouth tightened into a thin, hard smile. "So be it. I look forward to seeing you at the ball." With a swish of her skirts she turned on her heel and left the house.

Phadra waited until she heard the door slam behind the she-devil before stepping out in the hallway, where her servants stared with wide eyes at the door. "Wallace, Henny has been turned out by the Evanses. I know you two are close. Do you think you could find her?"

"Aye," Wallace conceded. "I know a place or two she'd turn to if she was in trouble."

"Then find her. Immediately," Phadra ordered calmly, "and bring her here. As for you, Jem —"

The footman stepped forward, pulling his forelock. "Yes, madam?"

"Follow me upstairs. I need you to break into my old trunk."

"Yes, madam." He pulled his forelock again.

She continued issuing orders as she started up the stairs. "And contact your milliner's assistant. Tell her I do find myself in need of a lady's maid. I want her now, today, as soon as possible. Her wages are not an issue."

Jem shot a look back over his shoulder at Wallace, who shrugged a silent answer.

"Is something wrong, Jem?" She stopped, surprised that he wasn't behind her.

The servant shot a guilty look at Wallace before saying, "No, madam. It's just . . ."

"It's just what?" she prodded.

Jem gave another glance back at Wallace before saying boldly, "I just wanted to know if everything is all right."

Phadra gifted them with a radiant smile. She leaned over the banister. "Everything is wonderful. In fact, for the first time since I entered Sir Cecil's office and discovered my financial affairs completely in shambles, I feel like myself again. I feel strong. I feel powerful." She finished triumphantly, "I feel like going to a ball!"

Chapter 13

Grant walked out of the bank and stood for a moment on the steps, finally able to give rein to the anger that had been building slowly and steadily all day. The scowl he allowed himself was so fierce, two gentlemen walking down Threadneedle Street took one look at his face and crossed the road as if anxious to avoid his path.

He had just had the most frustrating day of his career at the bank. It was almost as if the moment he'd become a married man, his carefully constructed world had immediately started to collapse. No, he amended, that had happened the first moment he'd laid eyes on Phadra Abbott in Sir Cecil's office.

Tongues all over town were already wagging about his mysterious absence and sudden marriage. Before he'd been able to contact all the bank's directors discreetly, most had heard the news while visiting their various clubs and had already passed judgment. His supporters admitted openly that it would have been a better move for his career for him to have married Miranda Evans. His enemies, with their own protégés to promote, congratulated him with such cheerful goodwill that Grant knew his marriage to Phadra had already been declared by consensus a disaster.

His fist tightened around his walking stick. Unwilling to wait for a hack, he started walking home. He needed to stretch his legs and work off his anger. It felt good to be moving even in the close heat of the summer evening.

But it wasn't the lukewarm reception of his marriage that made him so angry. That very afternoon Lord Phipps had come to him seeking help from the bank. The government needed more money to fight Napoleon. Once, in the past, Grant had suggested to Phipps that the government should obtain its funds through the Bank of England. Now Whitehall was interested — and Grant couldn't get anyone at the bank to think about anything except his ill-conceived marriage.

A crier announced the hour. Half past six. He was going to be late. He hated to be late. He walked faster, his mind working furiously while his legs ate up stretches of the pavement.

Not for the first time did he feel frustrated by his position with the bank. World events placed the bank on the threshold of a new age, a new economy, but the Court of Directors didn't seem to understand how rapidly changes were taking place in the world. They clung to tenets that were dead and best buried, dismissing most of his ideas as too radical.

Coming to an abrupt halt, he discovered his mental tirade had carried him to the steps of his home. For a moment he closed his eyes. What else could go wrong?

And then he thought of Phadra.

No matter what he'd done that day, she was never far from his thoughts — especially when he'd quietly transferred the necessary funds from his accounts to the Abbott account and then closed it. With a few simple pen strokes, the debt was paid. In full. And his modest fortune had suffered a severe setback.

He bounded up the steps. Wallace opened the door.

"I'm late, Wallace," Grant growled.

"I'm aware of that, sir."

He handed the butler his curly-brim beaver. "Better have Jem run over to Evans House with a message that we are running behind. Also, I hired a rig from Tilbury. It

290

should be right on my heels, since I ordered it for half past the hour. If I'd been thinking, I would have had them pick me up at the bank, but hindsight is always clearer, isn't it?"

"That's often the case, sir." Wallace passed the hat to Jem, the action making Grant realize that he didn't need two servants, and now he couldn't afford them. Still, he'd grown very fond of this pair of characters.

He pushed his financial worries aside and started toward the stairs to change into evening dress when a movement inside the parlor caught his attention. He moved toward the door.

Waiting in the parlor, her hands clasped in front of her, her head bowed in the picture of wifely submission, stood Phadra. Yards and yards of sapphire silk shot through with threads of gold and wrapped in the Eastern style of a sari covered her hair, shoulders, and arms. Layers of the same silk flowed down to her feet and swept the ground.

When she raised her magnificent eyes — which were the clear blue of stained glass — his breath caught in his throat. "You're beautiful." His words came out in a whisper.

The compliment brought a soft rose tinge to her cheeks, which made her seem even more like a beautiful, devoted houri. She answered him with a shy smile, as though uncertain whether or not she'd heard him correctly, and his mouth went dry. For the first time in his life Grant understood why a man would want to keep a harem, a way to keep a woman all to himself and not share her with another.

Someone pounded the knocker on the front door, startling him out of his reverie. Surprised to discover that he was leaning against the door frame, he straightened.

"It's the coachman from Tilbury," Wallace said a second later. "Your rig is outside, sir."

"My rig?" Grant repeated blankly, and then came to his senses. He turned to Phadra. "I ordered a coach to take us to Evans House."

"That's good," she said. For a second, hearing her low, husky voice, his mind conjured an image of her lying beside him, answering his kisses with a passion that rivaled his own . . .

He shook his head. Now was not the time. But later? He was suddenly anxious to rush over to Evans House, dance twice around the room, and return with his wife to his hearth — and his bed.

"I need to change." His voice came out a bit higher than he'd intended. He cleared his throat and added, "I'll be down in a minute."

He started up the stairs, but she stopped him. "Grant, there's something I should tell you."

He turned around. "Phadra, is something wrong?"

She took a deep breath and said in a rush of words, "The Evanses threw Henny out into the street and I sent Wallace to rescue her and I've told her that she may make her home with us for however long she wants to and I hope you agree."

Her torrent of words both surprised and delighted him. Little did she know that the sight of her standing there looking so lovely in the soft candlelight made it difficult for him to refuse her anything. "Of course, Phadra. We'll make room for her. We may not be able to pay her a wage —"

"You've paid off the emeralds." Her words came out in a whisper, her eyes growing wider as the magnitude of what he'd done hit her.

When she looked at him that way, he felt absurdly gallant, as if he'd slain the dragon and rescued the damsel. He forced himself to return to reality once again. "I'd better change. It's almost seven and we're late enough as it is." He turned and climbed the stairs.

The second he left, Phadra wanted to collapse in relief. That had been almost too easy — and she was immediately struck by guilt. The amount he'd had to pay to meet her debts had to have been staggering. She should have told him about the lady's maid.

She should have told him about the fight with Miranda.

She wrapped the sari closer around her, feeling a chill in spite of the evening's warmth. She *should* let him see her dress before they left the house. But he'd make her change, and she wasn't going to give in to Miranda. Not now. Not ever. But . . . he might be very upset.

Fifteen minutes later Grant came down the stairs, and the sight of him in his elegant evening wear of black coat and tails struck any idea of confession from her mind. So well did the tailored black coat emphasize his broad shoulders and masculine good looks that Phadra was certain no one would even notice if she was in the room, let alone what she was wearing. For one wild, almost painful moment, the memory of her body nestled next to his assaulted her senses.

Grant placed her hand on his arm. "We'll be home early, Wallace," he said, leading her out the door.

On the top step Phadra stopped and drew in a gasp. "Where did that come from?" Before her in the evening twilight sat an elegant black and gold coach drawn by a perfectly matched team of grays.

Grant laughed as if happy that he'd surprised her. She stared at him, smitten by the sound of his laughter, until he pulled on her hand eagerly, urging her to hurry down the steps. "I felt that as long as we were going to be the talk of the evening, we might as well make a good show of it. It's a beauty, isn't it? I've always dreamed of owning one like this."

He helped her into the coach, and she sat back in the cushioned seat, reveling in the soft butternut-colored leather upholstery. "I feel like a queen."

He climbed in beside her, his thigh brushing against her leg. "Only a queen could afford to own one of these."

"Can we afford it?" The words popped out of her mouth without thinking.

"Yes. Tonight." He rapped on the roof, signaling for the coachman to start, before turning to her. "Phadra, don't worry. I'm not a pauper yet."

"I feel guilty. You had plans, other things that you wanted to do with that money." She looked out the coach window and made a pretense of studying the passing street scene before adding quietly, "Such as buying a coach like this."

He reached over and took her hand in his, and Phadra discovered she had to struggle to regulate her breathing. The confines of the coach suddenly seemed impossibly close. She turned toward him and discovered that his face was close to hers, closer than she had thought. She had never realized how deep and inviting his silver-gray eyes could be.

"Don't worry," he murmured. His thumb stroked her palm, and Phadra wondered how she could even think, let alone worry. "I think if we practice economies, we'll be fine."

"Fine," she repeated blankly. He smelled of spicy shaving soap, a scent Phadra had enjoyed all afternoon while she'd prepared for him in . . . their . . . bedroom. She couldn't have moved away even if she'd wanted to — which she didn't.

His lips moved. "When I first saw you this evening, I recalled the first time we'd met. You were wearing purple, the deep, rich color of royalty, and your hair curled down around your shoulders." He raised her hand to his lips and lightly kissed the tips of her fingers. "In fact, so vividly could I recall our first meeting, I almost thought that when we walked out to the coach I could hear the sound of those silly little toe bells you wore."

Phadra opened her eyes wide and pulled back slightly. "Silly?"

Grant frowned. "Well, unconventional." He leaned toward her.

Phadra scooted a little away from him and self-consciously tucked her sandaled feet beneath her skirts. The movement sent the damning soft tinkling of tiny bells into the air.

Grant stopped moving. It was as though he'd been turned to stone.

At that moment the coach pulled up in front of Evans House. A footman stationed at the end of the walkway to the house opened the door for Phadra, and she quickly climbed out. Without waiting for Grant, she walked toward the door, her toe bells jingling with every step.

She didn't get very far before Grant's hand caught her elbow and turned her around to face him. "You're wearing them!"

She lifted her chin. "What if I am?"

"I specifically ordered you to don *appropriate* attire."

"And what exactly does that mean?"

"It means that a *lady* doesn't wear toe bells."

Phadra straightened her shoulders, announcing, "A lady wears anything she wishes."

"Not if her husband commands her not to!"

"Did you say *husband,* sir, or *jailer?*"

"Phadra," he warned, and took a step away in complete exasperation before exploding, "I wish I had a dungeon to throw you in. A deep, dark place where I could keep you until you started to develop some common sense!"

Phadra felt her temper bubble to the surface. "How archaic! How ridiculous!" She stomped up the steps, glad that the bells rang with every step. "If that is your attitude, we should never have married!"

"Now there you may have a point," he answered, his long legs enabling him to pass her on the steps. "I thought that I was marrying a woman of class and distinction, not some termagant who wouldn't have enough sense to follow her husband's orders!"

Phadra wasn't about to let him reach the

front door before her. She did not trail behind a man like chattel! The sari slid off her head and down past one bare shoulder, but she made it to the top step at the same second he reached it. She stared up at him with defiance.

Grant looked over, his eyes hard and angry — and then his mouth dropped open. "Your shoulder is bare!"

Phadra had the satisfaction of looking at him as if he'd turned into the village idiot. "Yes."

He leaned down toward her. "You're half-naked!"

"Not hardly," she flashed back.

"The devil, you say —" The Evanses' butler opened the door. Grant's anger appeared to evaporate and was immediately replaced with what Phadra could only describe as a supercilious toadeating attitude. "Hello, Lady Evans, Sir Cecil. Thank you for hosting this affair tonight."

"You're late," Lady Evans snapped, the salt-and-pepper curls on top of her head seeming to bristle with indignation.

"My sincerest regrets, my lady," he said, giving Phadra a push forward through the doorway. "It's my fault. I was unavoidably detained at the bank."

"Sir Cecil has been with the bank for

thirty years and has never been detained when he had a social engagement." She snorted her disapproval before announcing, "Come, Sir Cecil, Miranda! We must form a receiving line now. There isn't a moment to waste. I can see guests starting to line up in the drive. Here, Phadra, hand Alexander your shawl."

"I thought I might like to keep it," Phadra started, and then felt the full force of Grant's stare upon her. His smile was pleasant, but his eyes burned bright with anger.

Well, he'd better learn now that he'd *married* her, not purchased her. Her head high, she slipped the sari down and unwrapped it from around her shoulders. Grant's eyes darkened, and his jaw tightened dangerously.

But the gasp of outrage didn't come from him but from Lady Evans. "Phadra! Why are you wearing that outrageous costume? And your hair's down. That is not the style. Not at all!"

"I set my own style, Lady Evans," she announced, her attention on her husband and the stern set of his face. If only her knees weren't shaking so!

"Obviously," her ladyship answered. She walked around Phadra as if viewing a

300

museum piece. "The material is pretty, but leaving this one shoulder bare is, ah . . . very daring."

"I took the design from a carving of a Phoenician girl I saw in the British Museum," Phadra said proudly.

"Yes, well . . ." Lady Evans made a face as if she'd just eaten something that didn't agree with her.

"Oh, Mama, let Phadra set her own style," Miranda said with sly insolence. "If she wants to dash around as if she has not even so much as stockings on underneath, what is it to us?"

Her words had the desired effect. Two hot spots burned on Phadra's cheeks, while her mother looked ready to swoon.

"It's going to be all right," Lady Evans managed to gasp out. She drew in a deep, steadying breath. "Besides, there isn't anything we can do about it now. Phadra, put on your gloves so that we can open our door to guests."

"I have no gloves, Lady Evans."

"You what?" the woman asked in a horrified tone.

"I don't like them," Phadra said. "The evening is hot, and I chose not to wear them."

Lady Evans looked to her husband anxiously. "She doesn't have any gloves? And she's wearing her hair down. What are we going to do?"

"Let her borrow a pair of Miranda's," her husband said.

"Yes, that's the very thing. Miranda, have a maid fetch a pair of your gloves."

"Oh, I'm sorry, Mama. I don't have another pair of gloves. There was an unfortunate accident and all of my gloves were —" She paused as if savoring the next word, "— ripped."

Phadra looked away. If she had any pride at all, she'd turn her back on these small-minded, selfish people and walk —

Grant's voice broke into her thoughts. "She doesn't need gloves."

"Doesn't need them?" Lady Evans asked as if he'd spoken a sacrilege. "They are a necessity!"

"My wife *chooses* not to wear them," Grant answered with the arrogance of a duke.

"But every lady —"

"My wife *is* a lady."

Phadra didn't know who was more surprised at his defense of her, Lady Evans or herself.

Sir Cecil decided the matter. "Beatrice, order the doors open and let's get this affair over with." The servants did as he commanded. Lady Evans had to scramble to her place beside Phadra in the receiving line.

Phadra leaned close to Grant, who was standing on her right, and whispered, "Thank you."

"Did you notice that Lady Evans listens to her husband when he speaks?" he asked in an undertone. He obviously didn't expect an answer, because he immediately went on, "What is going on between you and Lady Miranda?"

That was one of the questions she'd been dreading. "We don't admire each other."

"Don't admire?" He appeared to taste the words before concluding, "On Miranda's part, *hate* might be a better description." Phadra was thankful that at that moment the first guests entered the hallway and claimed his full attention.

Over the next half hour, as if by magic, the foyer filled with elegant guests. Grant treated her with the deference a man uses in introducing his wife to important people. Lady Evans made it her personal cause to draw attention to Phadra's dress. "Isn't it different? She's wearing little bells on her toes. Such an intriguing style, wouldn't you say?" the woman trilled, until Phadra struggled with the urge to throttle her.

Eventually Lady Miranda grew bored with the receiving line and wandered away, only to appear from time to time close to Phadra and talking loudly to the other guests. Words such as *misalliance* and *bluestocking* peppered her conversation. Phadra noted that she apparently was refraining from targeting Grant.

In fact, Grant was well received by all — especially by the women. Standing next to him, Phadra felt gauche and awkward. The sly side glances Miranda's gossip inspired started to feel like tiny darts. She didn't have to hear the words to know what they were thinking. They wondered what a man such as he, a man who could have had any woman he wanted, was doing with her. She didn't fit in. She wasn't one of *them*.

Holding her head high, her smile firmly fixed in place and so bright that her facial muscles hurt, Phadra desperately wished she could do it all over again. She wouldn't have done something so foolish as to tweak Miranda's nose and incur her wrath. She would have worn the most boring, staid outfit she could find, and good solid shoes.

"Phadra," Grant said, turning to her, "I'd like you to meet Lady Hollywise, Lady Sudbury, and Lady Fitzgerald. They are the wives of three of the bank's directors."

Phadra picked up on his cue and smiled graciously at the women. They returned her smile with doubtful ones of their own. Their gazes swept her person, starting with her wild curly hair and moving down to her belt made of braided gold cord and the skirt that flowed gracefully to her sandaled feet. Phadra caught her breath. If ever there was a trio that could give a "cut direct," it was this little band, who wore their husbands' status the way war heroes wore their medals. Phadra forced herself to say, "It is a pleasure to meet you."

They nodded in unison. Then, to Phadra's mortification, Lady Sudbury asked in an unusually robust voice, "Excuse me, Mrs. Morgan, but is it true you are wearing bells on your toes?"

"No, they're on her toe rings," Lady Fitzgerald corrected, smiling.

Lady Sudbury leaned closer and confided, "Lady Fitzgerald believes her feet are her best feature. She'd love to have a set."

Phadra felt her cheeks turn hot with embarrassment. To think that her feet were being discussed by the guests . . . She cast a glance to see if Grant had overheard the question, certain that he would appreciate the opportunity to gloat. However, his attention was being claimed by a lush and lovely brunette who pressed his hand warmly to her bosom.

The surge of jealousy startled her. She watched wide-eyed as Grant attempted to free his hand but the woman held on.

Her first impulse was to slap her husband's hand away from the woman's chest, but before she could act, Lady Evans pulled at her arm and said in a voice filled with genuine panic, "It's Dame Cunnington."

"Dame Cunnington?" Lady Sudbury squeaked even as everyone in the foyer stepped back to make way for two large footmen in plum and silver livery carrying a leather-and-silk-lined sedan chair through the front door and into the foyer. To Phadra's surprise, a very winded Alexei Popov, the poet, entered behind the chair and helped a tall, regal woman known as London's leading patroness of the arts out of the chair.

"She's one of your guests?" Phadra asked. If the Prince of Wales himself had joined their company, she could not have been more impressed.

"I had to invite her. She's my aunt," Lady Evans moaned unhappily. "I didn't expect her to show up. I haven't seen her for twenty years, ever since she told my mother I was too stupid to talk to." She stepped back a little farther behind Phadra as if to hide. "I wonder what she's doing here. She sent her regrets to our invitation, and, as I remember, the reply was very unpleasant."

Popov came toward Phadra, his arms outstretched. "Phadra, my wonderful darling, you look radiant," he declared in his accented English. Brushing a kiss on each of her cheeks, he pulled her over to Dame Cunnington. "Edith, this is Phadra Abbott —"

"Morgan," Phadra interjected.

"What?" Popov asked. "Ah, yes, your new name. Morgan." He frowned a moment, as if he didn't like the sound of it, before continuing, "Phadra, this is Edith, my new patron. She is wonderful, but she makes me run everywhere. I have told Edith about your salons, and she had already heard of you. Think, my darling Phadra — you were famous and then you, poof, disappear. Now you reappear married to a man who is supposed to marry another. You must tell us everything, darling, and did you ever find your father? Edith, you would be touched by this story —"

"Alexei, shut up," Dame Cunnington said. She looked down her hooked nose at Sir Cecil. "Hello, Cecil, are you still such a fool?"

In response Sir Cecil frowned and began to concentrate furiously on his thumbnail. Lady Evans stepped forward, her full mouth set in a grimace. "It's a pleasure to see you again, Aunt Edith."

"No, it ain't," the woman replied. "You don't like me any more than I like you."

"Aunt Edith," Lady Evans chastised, blinking as if hoping that if she blinked hard enough, the dowager would disappear, "we have many guests *listening*."

"I have eyes. I can see. This affair's a crush, Beatrice, just what you always dreamed of hosting. Too bad everyone is here to look at the man who jilted your daughter —"

"I was not jilted!" a voice screamed from the crowd. Miranda pushed her way to the front. She stared in open hostility at her great-aunt, her face turning a deeper shade of purple with each passing second. All conversation in the ballroom ceased, and the crowd pushed its way toward the foyer for a better view.

Miranda's going to throw a tantrum, Phadra thought only a second before Grant stepped between the two women. "You have the wrong of it, Dame Cunnington. Miranda and I had only an informal understanding, and she asked to be released from that because she found me —" He paused, searching for a word, and then finished softly, "— lacking."

Dame Cunnington flipped out a quizzing glass from her reticule and raised it to one eye. She gave Grant a slow perusal from his crisp dark curls to his polished shoes. "Lacking?" Her lips curled cynically.

In that moment of silence Phadra stepped to his side. If Grant could be generous and come to Miranda's defense, then so could she.

"I say, what is that noise?" Dame Cunnington raised her quizzing glass again. "That jingling sound."

Phadra wished the earth would open up and swallow her whole. She could feel the curious stares of dozens of pairs of eyes. "Those are my toe rings," she answered stiffly.

"Toe rings? You have *bells* on your toes?" Dame Cunnington demanded.

Phadra lifted her chin. "Yes."

For long seconds the two women studied each other. Finally Dame Cunnington smiled, a smile free of artifice. Motioning with her free hand at Phadra, she announced in her carrying voice, "I like your dress, dear, and the way you wear your hair down, without all of that fuss and nonsense.

Very fresh. Original. I will commend you to my friends." She turned back to Popov to reach for his arm. "Alexei, I desire a glass of champagne." They proceeded into the ballroom, the crowd parting to make a path for them.

"Did you hear that?" Lady Evans asked in awe. "She's never said that before. Ever." She looked up at her husband. "I've never heard her say anything nice to anyone."

"She didn't say anything nice to me," Miranda protested.

Her mother dismissed her with a wave of her hand. "We have to start the dancing. Now that Aunt Edith is here, we must start everything!" She flitted off into the ballroom.

Lady Sudbury leaned close to Phadra and whispered, "Dame Cunnington is very powerful, Mrs. Morgan. Almost as powerful as the Queen or one of the patronesses of Almack's."

"Very rich, too," Lady Hollywise added.

Phadra's lips formed a silent "Oh," aware that although many of the guests still watched her closely, here and there a smile was now directed her way. She turned to Grant. He stood alone and silent, his pensive features looking as if they could have been carved from granite. Excusing herself from the three bankers' wives, she went over to him.

He seemed to sense her approach and forced a smile that didn't quite reach his eyes. "The musicians have finished warming up. Lady Evans tells me that she wants us to start the dancing."

Phadra placed her hand on his offered arm and leaned close. "Grant, please, is there someplace we can go that is private? We need to talk."

He didn't look at her directly but instead casually studied the crowd before asking quietly, "About what?"

"About tonight. This dress. These silly toe bells. Our *marriage*." She tightened her hold on his arm. "What you did for Miranda was very gracious."

He reached out and with the tip of one finger pushed one of her curls away from her face. The gesture was so familiar that she caught her breath. "I did it for you, too," he answered softly. "Congratulations. You are launched in society."

"*We* are launched," she corrected.

The serious look on his face disappeared, and he seemed to relax. "There is no time to talk now." His other hand touched her bare arm, a reassurance. "We'll talk later. Right now, as the guests of honor, we are expected to lead the dancing."

"Lead the dancing? I'm a terrible dancer."

"What?" he said in mock surprise. "Something the esteemed Miss Agatha forgot to teach?" His teeth flashed in an easy smile, and Phadra discovered that she could stand rooted in that spot all evening and bask in the glory of his smile.

Lady Evans interrupted the moment. "Please, the maestro is waiting for you to take your places. Hurry, hurry!" She charged off in another direction.

Grant tugged at Phadra's hand. "Must we?" she asked with a smile, her feet already moving in that direction.

"We must," he said, and tucked her hand into the crook of his arm to lead her into the ballroom.

"But I'll make a fool of myself," she whispered, protesting one more time.

"Just do what the woman in front of you is doing and follow my lead. If it's a slow dance, you'll have time to copy her steps." He led her to their place on the dance floor. "After the first few steps, I'll guide us off the floor. But I warn you, I like to dance, Mrs. Morgan. I may have to give you instruction," he said, his voice so low, so silky, it gave his words an unspoken meaning — and a promise for the future. "Now put your hand on my arm."

"What?" she asked, as if he'd spoken in a foreign tongue.

"Put your hand on my arm, Phadra." He grinned at her, a pirate's smile that stole her heart. "Everyone is waiting for us in order to begin."

Aware now of the awkward silence from the crowd around them, Phadra quickly copied the lady to her right and placed her arm along his forearm. Grant adjusted her position so that he held her fingertips in his. Embarrassed, she looked up at him and lost herself in his silvery eyes, eyes that she had once thought were hard and uncompromising. Now she discovered warmth and laughter in their bright depths.

She couldn't wait for them to return home.

The maestro rapped upon his music stand, signaling for the attention of his musicians and the dancers. Grant gave her fingers a reassuring squeeze as, with a dramatic sweep, the maestro's arms came up, ready for the downbeat —

"Morgan!" a man's voice bellowed. "Grant Morgan, where are you?"

Phadra didn't recognize the voice. She looked around in confusion. The crowd buzzed with excitement. Grant obviously recognized the voice. He pulled Phadra to stand behind him while he turned toward the door.

Captain Duroy, dressed in his regiment's colors, his blond head bare and his hair disheveled, pushed his way through the crowd, flanked by two of his fellow officers. The men did not look prepared to enjoy a ball.

Grant stepped forward. "William, I'm pleased that you could join us." His voice sounded carefully controlled.

Swaggering onto the dance floor, the handsome young officer's face broke into an angry grimace. "This isn't a social call, Morgan." He advanced with several slow, unsteady steps and then stopped. "You knew I was going to offer for her. I *trusted* you."

The guests in the ballroom had fallen into complete silence. The man's words carried as if he'd shouted them. Grant reached his friend in three long strides and said something in a low voice. Every ear in the ballroom, including Phadra's, strained to hear what it was.

Suddenly Duroy shoved Grant in the chest, pushing him away. "No, damn you! I demand satisfaction!"

"William —"

"Name your seconds!"

"Listen to *reason* —"

"Name your seconds!"

"William —"

"Are you a coward, Morgan?"

Grant's back slowly straightened. In a voice so cold that Phadra barely recognized it as his, he answered, "Very well. But let us step outside to somewhere more appropriate — and we'll make the arrangements."

For one brief moment Captain Duroy's gaze moved to focus on Phadra. Then he turned his eyes back to Grant and agreed with a curt nod. He turned on his heel and left the room, the crowd backing away to create a path. Without so much as a word or backward glance to Phadra, Grant followed. The two other officers fell in behind him.

Phadra stood rooted to her place on the dance floor in stunned confusion. Slowly the reality of what she'd witnessed came home to her. With a cry of anger, she lifted her skirts and ran after the men, her merry little toe bells jingling with each step.

Miranda stepped in front of her. "Phadra, are you leaving so soon?"

"Get out of my way," Phadra demanded.

Miranda smiled, malevolence burning brightly in her eyes. "It's amazing. I didn't even have to say or do anything. You have a penchant for ruining things all on your own, don't you?"

Red rage engulfed Phadra. She doubled her fist, ready to swing at Miranda. Suddenly a hand slid under her arm. At the same time the smug expression on Miranda's face faded and she fell back. Dame Cunnington, her face schooled in careful nonchalance, pulled Phadra closer. "Don't make a scene."

"Don't make a scene?" Phadra practically choked on the words.

"Do you want to help him or hinder him?"

"Help him."

"Then stay and act as if nothing untoward has happened."

"I can't. It's impossible!"

"By all means, then, fly out the door and let everyone in this room assume the worst," the dowager answered tartly.

Phadra looked over her shoulder at all the faces watching her avidly. "And how will I help him if I stay?"

"You'll quell their tongues for the moment and, if your young man is as smart as he is handsome, he'll manage to talk his way out of this challenge. There will be those here tonight who will think nothing has happened — provided you don't make a scene."

"I don't know if I can!"

"Yes, you can." Dame Cunnington's words were slow and deliberate.

It went against all of her principles, but slowly Phadra straightened her shoulders and turned back toward the crowd in the ballroom.

"That's a good girl," the dowager whispered approvingly in her ear before raising her voice and saying, "Maestro, let the dancing begin!"

Chapter 14

Grant did not return to the ball.

After two of the longest hours Phadra had ever spent in her life, one of the Evanses' footmen approached her with a message on a silver salver. Immediately recognizing the black slashing handwriting as Grant's, she reached for it.

Dame Cunnington leaned close. "Don't open it here," she ordered out of the side of her mouth.

Phadra looked up and realized that she was the center of attention for all the guests standing close to them. She nodded and murmured, "If you'll excuse me . . ."

"Not without me!" Dame Cunnington declared, and followed Phadra from the ballroom and into Sir Cecil's study, haughtily staring down anyone who thought to follow them.

When she tried to break the seal, Phadra discovered her hands were shaking too badly. With a snort of impatience the dowager took it from her and broke the wax. She would have read it as well if Phadra hadn't quickly grabbed it back.

"So? What does he say?" Dame Cunnington demanded over Phadra's shoulder.

Phadra refolded the note, feeling no better now than before she'd received it. "He said that he will not be returning. He's sent the coach back to take me home when I'm ready."

"That's it?" Dame Cunnington frowned.

"That's it." Phadra closed her eyes and placed a hand to her forehead. Something was wrong. "Well, I'm ready to leave now. I'll have the coach ordered to the front door."

The dowager's hand on her arm stopped her. "You'll do no such thing. You'll stay here until midnight and not leave a moment before."

"I can't do that! Midnight's another hour away."

"You can and you will." She pulled Phadra closer and dropped her voice. "Obviously he couldn't talk that young hothead out of the challenge —"

"No!"

"Lower your voice and keep your wits about you," Dame Cunnington commanded. "Don't think for a second that any and all of those fine people out there are above putting an ear to the keyhole."

Phadra lowered her voice but protested, "This is all so ridiculous. I barely know Captain Duroy."

"There were no promises between you?"

"I can count on one hand the number of words either of us has ever said to the other. This is a complete surprise."

"Your husband didn't act surprised."

That acid observation forced Phadra to think, to remember. "Well, yes," she said slowly, "Grant did mention once that Captain Duroy wanted to offer for me, but I didn't give the matter a great deal of weight. I barely know him, and then Grant and I were forced into marriage —"

"Aha! The rumors are true. You were forced to tie the parson's knot," Dame Cunnington said triumphantly. "I knew that Evans wouldn't spring for an affair like this ball for someone else unless his arm was being twisted. What's the real reason Evans is involved? Knowing that coxcomb, there is something afoot!"

Alarmed, Phadra stepped back.

"Oh, don't go missish on me, dear. I can't stand Evans. He's little better than a crook, but I haven't ever been able to find out what his methods are, and then lo and behold, the man announces that he's marrying his daughter off to a man reputed to be the son of Satan —"

"Grant is nothing like his father!"

"He's not?" The dowager seemed disappointed with the revelation. She frowned. "Well, more's the pity for you. His father cut quite the figure in his day. I'm almost sorry there aren't more blackguards like Jason Morgan around. They liven things up." She narrowed her eyes thoughtfully. "I bet your Morgan knows Evans's secrets." She raised her eyebrows as another thought struck her. "I only hope he's around tomorrow after the duel to answer my questions."

"Tomorrow?"

"Certainly. Pistols at dawn. Matters of honor are always handled expediently. Men don't diddle around like women. Furthermore, that young cavalry officer appeared anxious to make you a widow."

Those words sent Phadra reeling toward the door.

"Now where are you running off to?" Dame Cunnington asked.

Phadra turned. "I'm going to find Grant. I'm going to do everything in my power to stop this!"

"You can't do that," the dowager said as if Phadra had just been spouting gibberish. "Only the participants can stop an affair of honor."

"Then I will convince one of the participants to back out of it."

Dame Cunnington gave Phadra a shrewd look. "You are a green one, aren't you?"

Phadra was in no mood for sarcasm. "Good evening to you, Dame Cunnington."

The dowager swiftly moved to the door and placed her palm against the wood to stop Phadra from opening it. "You can't leave yet."

"Whyever not?"

"Where have you been all of your life — rusticating in a convent? I told you, the ball's in your honor. You don't just walk out the door."

"Watch me." Phadra started to pull the door open again, but Dame Cunnington held it closed. Phadra turned to her with a defiant lift of her chin. "Dame Cunnington, I am not about to bow to silly social conventions when Grant's life is at stake. If that offends you, I beg your pardon, but get out of my way."

For a long moment the two women took each other's measure. Then the dowager's wide, generous mouth curved into a smile. "Damn me if I don't admire your style." She took her hand off the door. "You remind me of myself when I was younger. You can leave, but I'm going with you. This ball will turn into a dreadful bore without you!"

Popov was pleased to ride in the fancy hired coach instead of running beside Dame Cunnington's sedan chair. However, the dowager expected her footmen to run behind the coach carrying the sedan chair.

Popov and his patroness kept up a lively conversation on the way home, although Phadra didn't hear what they said. She was in her own world.

When the coach pulled up in front of her house, she opened the coach door and hopped out before Popov or the coachman could move. "Don't you want us to go with you?" Dame Cunnington asked.

"No."

"Killjoy," the older woman muttered.

Phadra reached up and gave the dowager's hand a grateful squeeze. "Thank you," she whispered.

"For what?" Dame Cunnington asked, sounding truly surprised. "Bringing you home? You did that yourself. If you'd listened to me, we'd all be back at the party at least until midnight to keep vicious tongues from wagging."

"If I have my way, they'll have nothing to wag about."

She started to pull her hand away, but Dame Cunnington held it tight. The gentle humor was gone from her eyes as she said soberly, "You can't stop a duel. You're a fool if you even try."

A coldness gripped Phadra's heart, and she shook her head. "Good night."

With a heavy sigh Dame Cunnington sat back in the luxurious coach. "Home, Alexei." The coach took off with a lurch.

Wallace stood waiting at the door in the lamplight. Racing up the steps, Phadra suddenly realized that she wasn't even sure if Grant was there or not.

Wallace evidently read her mind, because he said in a quiet voice, "He said he wanted to be alone."

"Where is he?"

"He went up to the attic."

"The attic? What would he be doing up there?"

"He goes up there sometimes to practice his fencing . . . and whenever he wants to be alone."

Phadra heard the gentle hint. She chose

to ignore it. "Where are the stairs to the attic?"

For a moment the servant's loyalties to his master and mistress seemed to war with each other.

Finally he said, "Up the back stairs and all the way up." As if he'd said too much, Wallace backed away.

The silk sari fell from her head down around her shoulders as she picked up the candle left on the hall table and walked toward the back stairs.

She hadn't had time yet to investigate and learn all the house's nooks and crannies, but she did know where the back stairs were located. Lifting her skirt with one hand and holding the candle in the other, she climbed the steep, dark stairs. The jingle of her toe bells sounded eerie in the blackness. As she started up the last flight, the sound of movement told her he was there. She blew out her own candle and set it down on the step.

Her footsteps slowed as she reached the top, and then she came to a complete stop. In the wash of golden candlelight from the attic, Grant appeared like a demon god living on top of the world.

He'd removed his jacket and neckcloth, leaving his shirt open at the throat. A faint breeze from the open attic windows played with the lace of his cuffs and ruffled his hair. His black breeches and stockings made his bottom half seem to disappear in the attic's darkness. For a moment he stood poised, one arm in the air for balance, another outstretched. In his hand he wielded a sharp, deadly rapier with a swordsman's grace.

When he moved, his actions were lighter, more elegant, than those of any dancer at the ballet. Candlelight caught and glinted off the rapier as the weapon silently slit the air, obeying its master's command in a well-practiced move. He lunged, and his shadow stretched across the wall and up the attic's low ceiling, dancing in ghoulish mimicry.

So complete was his concentration that she thought he wasn't aware of her presence . . . and for a moment she allowed herself to believe that everything was fine, that there had been no challenge.

A beat later he proved her wrong. His attention never wavering from his imaginary opponent, he said, "I've written out my last wishes. The document is on my desk. If I don't return tomorrow, then I expect you to deliver it to my solicitor." The rapier sliced the air and then flashed in salute. "His name is James McGovern. He's in Kensington, and he will ensure that your affairs are in order."

His calm acceptance shocked her. Her heart pounding in her throat, she asked, "So, is it going to be with swords, then?"

The touch of sarcasm in her voice was not lost on him. He smiled grimly. "No, pistols."

"Well, how convenient. The two of you won't even have to get close to each other to resolve this argument like rational men."

With a twist of his wrist he made the tip of the rapier whistle through the air. "Duroy won't accept my apology."

"Apology for what?"

"Our marriage."

Phadra raised a hand to her forehead, trying to understand. "This doesn't make sense."

"I knew he was going to make an offer for you." He picked up a rag and wiped off the gleaming blade.

"He doesn't know whether I would have accepted his offer. I'd laid eyes on the man twice in my life, and we'd shared only a handful of words. This is not grounds for a duel!"

"He demands satisfaction," Grant answered, as if those words explained everything. He tossed the rag aside and finally faced her. "Phadra, I'm going to delope."

The solemn tone of his voice caught her

attention. She took a step toward him. "I don't understand."

"I will not aim at Duroy. I'll fire my weapon in the air. It's a way of admitting that I wronged him."

"And what will he do?"

The corners of his mouth turned up in irony before he answered lightly, "I imagine he'll probably shoot me. William is known to be a crack shot."

Shocked, Phadra demanded, "You're joking, aren't you?"

"I'm deadly serious, Phadra," he said quietly. "That's why it is imperative for you to remember my instructions. Financially you should be fine. In the letter you will turn over to McGovern are my last requests. I've stated that you are to receive this house and the majority of my holdings except for a small bequest left to my sisters. Right now my holdings don't count for much because of the debt we paid off for the emeralds, but whatever you do, Phadra, do not sell off any of my investments. They will come back, and if my calculations are correct, within a year you'll find yourself well provided for —"

"No! I can't believe what I'm hearing!" she cried, interrupting the flow of calm, rational words. She leaned a hand against one of the painted brick columns that supported the roof. "This is madness. It makes no sense. A man has challenged you for no other reason than because he fancied me —"

"He planned to offer for you."

Phadra pushed away from the column. "But he didn't. Nor would I have accepted his suit if he had!"

Grant didn't answer, but she could tell by the set of his mouth and the resolve in his eyes that her argument bore no weight. She slapped her hand against the column, feeling a need to vent her anger . . . and her fear. "This is ridicul—"

"It's an affair of honor."

"It's outright stupidity," she snapped back. "And I'm going to tell Captain Duroy so! Now. This very minute!" She turned on her heel, prepared to charge down the stairs.

In a swift movement he blocked her way by pressing the tip of his sword against the column. The sharp blade stretched across her path.

"You'll do no such thing."

She heard the steel in his command and looked from the blade up to his face. "I can't let you do this," she whispered.

"And I can't let you disgrace me."

"What disgrace is there in making the man see reason?"

He stepped closer to her. "I didn't make

the rules of honor, Phadra. I don't determine whether they are right or wrong. I merely abide by them."

"Even if you die?" Her words hung in the air between them.

"Yes," he answered softly. He lowered the blade and leaned closer to her. "Phadra, if I don't meet my challenges, if I don't follow these rules that gentlemen of honor have set, then I don't have the right to consider myself one of them."

"This duel isn't about whether or not you are a gentleman!"

"Yes, it is." His voice was low and full of passion. "It's about wanting what my father didn't have. It's about honor and dreams. My dreams. I may have ruined my chances for a knighthood, but I will let *no one* say that I did not have honor."

That hurt. Phadra leaned her head back against the column. "It was honor that made you marry me," she whispered.

He'd heard the pain in her voice, and his expression softened. "Oh, Phadra . . ." He brushed her cheek with his fingertips.

She flinched, as if his touch hurt, and then to her horror realized that she was crying, silent tears that she couldn't stop. She attempted to twist away from him, but he wouldn't let her go. "I think what you need is a new dream," she finally said.

Grant leaned an arm against the column and rested his head against it, so that she was forced to stare up into his serious silver eyes and see as well as hear the truth in his words as he told her, "Some dreams you don't give up. You wouldn't give up your dream of finding your father, would you?"

"I already have," she started to answer, and then caught herself in surprise. In one clear, crystalline flash of realization, Phadra understood to her wonder and amazement that all of her dreams now centered on this one man. Somehow, at some time, in a way she didn't completely understand, he had become her dream, her reality, her destiny.

Almost as if bewitched by the revelation, Phadra raised her hand to place her palm against his lean cheek, reveling in the feel of his whiskers beneath her fingertips. He stood close enough to her that she could see the race of his pulse beneath the skin at his throat. She drew her fingers over his skin until she reached that warm pulse point. His heart was racing as fast as hers.

"Phadra?"

Phadra couldn't move. She couldn't even breathe.

He leaned close, his lips less than an inch from hers.

Her lips parted in surprise. She had to lean against the column for support.

Slowly he smiled, as if her reaction was everything he could desire and more, before he opened his lips and kissed her fully and completely on the mouth.

And Phadra kissed him back.

His sword clattered to the floor as he threw it aside. He buried his hands in her hair and pulled her closer to him. She didn't know if she wanted to laugh or cry as he kissed her shoulder, her throat, the pulse point beneath her ear . . . and when he took her in his arms and claimed her lips, she was lost.

Her body sang with its need for him.

His kiss deepened, growing more demanding. She hugged him closer, delighting in the feel of his chest against her breasts, the burn of his whiskers against her cheeks, his ability to turn her world inside out . . .

Her feet no longer touched the floor. Instead she clung to him for support, feeling the outline of his bandage and the hard, long lines of muscle beneath his shirt. She gave herself over to his guidance completely. He managed to loosen the clasp of the brooch that held her dress at the shoulder. The silk slipped to her waist held only by her golden belt. His finger unfastened the binding of her light linen bodice that served as her corset.

Surprised to find herself half-naked in the candlelight, Phadra pulled away.

"No," he commanded softly, then lowered his head and kissed one taut nipple. Phadra cried out at the sensation. As if with a will of their own, her arms wrapped themselves around his head, pulling him even closer.

Just when she thought she couldn't take any more he blazed a trail of kisses to her earlobe. "You're wonderful," he said. "I want you, Phadra. Now. Right here."

Deep inside her she heard his need, the sound of near desperation in his voice. Her body answered, begging to join with him, to become one. She slid one leg around his hips, needing to bring him closer, to fit him against her.

Bracing her weight against the column, Grant lowered a hand to cup her buttocks and pull her closer. His hand smoothed down the back of her haunch, over her knee, and up the inside of her thigh until his knowing fingers could slip through the slit of her undergarments and touch her intimately. She responded immediately with a start at first and then giving herself over completely to such exquisite pleasure.

"Give me this night, Phadra. I want this night," he said, his voice ragged. He kissed her again, deeply, fully, as if he could take the measure of her very soul with his kiss. His body pushed her back against the cool, painted brick of the support column. The hand that had pleasured her now began unbuttoning the buttons of his breeches.

Even lost in his embrace, Phadra was aware of these movements and so much more. In his kiss she could taste the desire that drove him — and, again, that fierce, almost overwhelming desperation. She ran her hands over his strong shoulders, the bandage, the muscles of his arm. A swordsman's arm.

And in just a few hours he would fight a duel over her.

As a drowning victim struggles to the surface for air, Phadra now warred with herself. She pressed herself closer to him, feeling the strong beat of his heart, the pressure of his chest against her breasts, the night's warm air, the sweat of their excitement. She wanted him inside her, making love to her. She wanted him to live. . . .

Almost as if from a distance, she heard herself say, "No." She made herself say it again, the sound stronger this time. "No." She slid her leg down and leaned back, taking his face in her hands. "Please, Grant. Listen to me. We can't do this. We can't."

His eyes were glazed with passion. After she spoke, he jerked his chin out of her hands. He leaned against her, letting her feel the tense readiness of his body, the strength of his arousal. "Yes, we can," he shot back in a harsh whisper.

Phadra pushed against his shoulders with the heels of her hands. "No! I can't do this if you are going to fight that duel tomorrow. I can't let you go off to die that way."

Grant stared at her as if he hadn't heard her correctly.

For one mad second Phadra wanted to call the words back. But she couldn't change her mind, not if there was a chance that she could get him to see reason.

To her dismay, he pulled back, gently setting her down on the floor. Embarrassed, she pulled her bodice up to cover her nakedness. He frowned in reaction and then turned his back to her. "Go away, Phadra." His voice was so low, she wasn't sure that he had said anything.

"You're upset with me," she said, fighting a rising sense of panic at the thought that she might have gone too far.

As he tucked his shirt back in and finished buttoning his breeches, the air was so quiet and still between them that she could hear the sounds of his fingers against the material.

"It's not right," she said.

"And you think that by refusing me, you will change my mind?"

She hated the question. She didn't know what she thought or felt. All she knew was the thrumming of unfulfilled desire. She stumbled over her words, trying to put her feelings in order. "I can't make love to you and then send you off to a fool's death. I can't do it."

"Go," he said again.

"Grant, please —"

He whirled on her, his handsome face contorted by anger. "Go, I said! You want me to give up my honor for you. I will *not* do that. Do you understand? You cannot have my honor!"

"Grant —"

"Go, damn you!" he yelled in a voice so ragged with emotion that Phadra took to her heels and ran down the stairs, her sweet little bells accentuating each step.

The sound of deep male voices by the front door woke Phadra at her post on the parlor floor, just inside the closed door. She could distinguish Grant's voice, but she couldn't hear what he was saying. The door shut.

Phadra scrambled to her feet. She hadn't meant to fall asleep. Her plan was to follow Grant to his assignation. In the wee hours of the morning, she'd decided that she had to talk to Captain Duroy. She had to make him understand that Grant hadn't stolen her from him. If it meant ruining her own reputation by revealing the story of how she had run away, then so be it. Cracking open the door, she saw that the hallway was empty.

She charged out of the parlor and ran to the front door, grateful to have the good, sturdy boots, from her days at Miss Agatha's, to wear. Not even Miranda's knife could cut through their leather.

Peeking out the front door, she saw Grant's tall figure and that of another man ride off on horses down the street. Phadra slipped out the door, saying a prayer that all had gone well and Wallace was ready to go. He was an unwilling accomplice, but — as she had pointed out to him the night before — his first loyalties were to her.

To her relief, Wallace led a rented team of horses out of a side alley. Phadra jumped when the door flew open behind her. Henny stood in the doorway, her hands on her hips.

"I can't believe you are going through

with this," she said.

"Henny! You scared me half to death."

"I'm hoping I'm going to scare some sense into you!"

"It's too late," Phadra called over her shoulder as she ran down the steps and climbed up into the open carriage beside Wallace.

With a snap of the reins, she and the butler took off after Grant. "Do you have any idea where they will be going?" Wallace asked.

Phadra looked up at him blankly before saying, "You mean there isn't one place where everyone goes to fight duels?"

Wallace groaned. "Not in a city the size of London."

Phadra chewed on that knowledge a moment before asking, "Where are most duels fought?"

"Well, I don't know that much about it myself, but I hear Hyde Park is a popular place."

"Are we going in that direction?"

"Aye."

"Then it must be Hyde Park," Phadra said with a confidence she was far from feeling.

"I hope we never find it. When the master finds out that I let you hoodwink me into

this, he'll turn me out without references."

"But at least he'll be alive to do so," she
replied with false sweetness. "Besides, I'll
give you references."

"Ha! Fat lot of good that will do me. References from a wife who doesn't know her
place."

"Wallace, I've already been over this
ground with Grant. We're all agreed. I don't
know my place. Now, can't you make these
animals go any faster?"

With another snap of the reins and a great
deal of grumbling under his breath, Wallace
did exactly that.

Phadra held on to the side of the carriage
with one hand and used the other to hold
her hat in place as they drove to Hyde Park.
It was going to be too pretty a morning for a
duel. Already the first rays of the sun were
turning the sky rosy and golden.

Pistols at dawn.

Grant and the other gentleman, who
Wallace assured her was his second, were
completely out of sight as they turned into
Hyde Park. And stopped.

At this hour the park appeared peaceful
and quiet. Too quiet.

"Where do you think they've gone?"
Phadra asked, straining to see through the

trees and wisps of early-morning fog for a sign of life.

"I'm not even certain we're in the right place," Wallace answered. He drew a deep breath. "Well, we've done everything we can. Better get you home."

Phadra put her hand down firmly on his, which was holding the reins. "Drive on."

Wallace raised his eyebrows but did as he was told, following the main path through the park. Phadra watched for any signs that riders might have recently turned off the path, but there were so many tracks that she had no success.

They rounded a turn and there, a quarter of a mile away from them was a small gathering of people beneath two huge, leafy oaks. Phadra pointed it out to Wallace. "Drive over there."

"I don't think this is wise."

"I don't care."

"It could be anyone. The young bucks fight duels here almost on a daily basis. It wouldn't look good if we stumbled into someone else's business, would it?"

"Drive."

Wallace turned the horses off the road and onto the grass. As they drew closer Phadra felt even more certain that this was the right place. In another second the wispy fog lifted enough for her to make out the bold red and blue of the officers' uniforms. She reached over and squeezed Wallace's arm, almost overcome with joy that they had found the right place.

They saw two men separate themselves from the group. Each took up a station away from the other, one man in uniform, the other in severe dark clothing. It could only be Grant!

Phadra's grip on Wallace's arm tightened. "Wallace, we must hurry. Can't these horses go any faster?"

They were still about four hundred yards away when Phadra heard one man shout an order. She couldn't hear what was being said over Wallace's telling her that the "damned cattle" were going as fast as they could without a road to travel.

Phadra couldn't wait. She climbed off the seat and, hanging her feet off the edge of the carriage, slid down to the ground, landing on her knees. She didn't worry about her bonnet, her dress, or Wallace's shouts for her to wait. Instead she struggled to her feet and ran with her heart pounding in her throat past the horses, heading for the clearing beneath the oak trees.

There was another shout. This time she heard what had been said: "Turn and fire!"

She ran faster, even as Grant raised his arm and fired into the air.

"No!" she cried. At that moment she stepped in a small hole, and her ankle twisted underneath her. She fell heavily to the dew-kissed earth.

A split second later another shot cracked the air.

Chapter 15

As he stood staring into the bore of William's pistol, a million thoughts invaded Grant's mind. . . . but the last thing he thought he would hear was Phadra's voice distinctly shouting, "No!" even as William raised his arm and fired into the air.

Phadra.

Phadra was *here!*

The shock of realization mingled with the sudden elated relief Grant felt that he was alive. Afraid that if he took a step in any direction, his knees would betray him by buckling, Grant stood very still. William lowered his arm. The acrid smell of gunpowder hung in the air as the duelists studied each other for a moment that stretched like eternity. Finally William said, "I couldn't do it."

"I'm glad."

His dry answer broke the restraint between them. William came forward with an outstretched hand. Grant met him halfway.

Their hands clasped as men of honor, and then they embraced as friends.

William raised his head. "I'm sorry, Grant. I shouldn't have challenged you. I let my hot temper rule my good sense. I beg you to forgive me."

"It's behind us, William."

William stepped back and answered softly, "Ah, but you have the girl."

Immediately Grant recalled the image of Phadra as she had been the night before: clinging to him and responding with wanton passion to his kisses, then demanding his honor, his pride. And he remembered her shout only moments earlier.

She was here. He could sense it. He looked over William's shoulder, past the men who served as their seconds, past the surgeon's dark carriage, his eyes searching for her. He immediately recognized Wallace sitting in the seat of a hired vehicle. As if sensing his master's scrutiny, the servant came to attention.

And there was Phadra — walking away from Wallace toward a grove of trees.

"Did you hear that shout?" Duroy was asking. "I realized then that I couldn't shoot you. We've been through so much together. Who shouted, anyway?"

"Phadra." Grant frowned. What the

deuce was she doing walking off that way? And she looked as though she was limping slightly.

"Phadra?" Duroy turned and stared in the direction in which Grant was looking.

"She's over there," Grant said. "The woman in the canary-yellow dress."

"I see her," Duroy said. "I say, that color makes her stand out, doesn't it? And the dress is rather different."

"It looks medieval."

"Medieval?"

"My wife sets her own fashion, William," Grant responded dryly. "I'm sure if you take a turn around the museum, you'll see a picture of a dress very much like it. And that silly hat, too." He started walking toward Phadra, who had disappeared behind a clump of shrubbery.

"Oh," William answered in a tone that said he understood nothing. He walked beside Grant. "What is she doing here?"

Grant handed his dueling pistol to Duroy. "She probably had it in mind to stop us."

"Stop a duel?" Duroy asked in an incredulous tone. "No one interferes with an affair of honor."

"When I catch her, I'll tell her you said so."

Duroy stopped abruptly, as if struck by a

345

sudden thought. "You know, Morgan, perhaps I should consider myself fortunate that I didn't marry the lady."

Grant stopped also and turned to the officer. "You don't even know the half of it, William," he said before turning on his heel and charging after his wife. Behind him, he could hear the men questioning Duroy and then bursting out into deep male laughter; Duroy must have told them that Phadra had planned on stopping the duel.

Wallace, his hat in his hand, intercepted him. "I told her not to do it, Mr. Morgan," he said, having to trot to keep up with his master's long strides. "I argued with her. But you know how she is. She doesn't always listen to reason. Even Mrs. Shaunessy told her it was a fool's errand —"

"Wallace, shut up."

The servant's mouth closed with a snap.

"Take that rig and bring it around to the other side of the park. My guess is that she is heading in that direction." He started to walk off. Over his shoulder he added, just so the servant would understand that he wasn't finished with him yet, "And I'll talk to *you* later."

Grant considered the subject closed and started off again. But Wallace's voice timidly called to him.

"What?" he practically roared as he turned on the servant.

Wallace jumped slightly but stood his ground. "Don't be too hard on her, Mr. Morgan. She only did what she thought was right."

Once again Grant was struck by the loyalty Phadra inspired in servants — servants whose wages *he* now paid! "I'll keep that in mind," he said curtly. "Now get that rig over to Knightsbridge." He walked toward the grove of trees where he'd spied Phadra last, his long legs eating up the distance between them.

Phadra knew he was following her . . . and she knew he was angry. At first she'd been relieved when Captain Duroy had fired into the air. Certainly her prayers had been answered. But then Grant had turned and recognized her. In that awful moment of recognition, she didn't have to read minds to know that she was in serious trouble.

Her ankle hurt, though not enough to prevent her from walking. Afraid that if she went back to Wallace, Grant would blame him for her actions, Phadra had decided the best course of action would be to run in the opposite direction. Maybe if Grant had time to reflect upon the duel and its possible consequences, he would understand that she only had his safety at heart.

She'd almost talked herself into turning around and facing him when she heard him call her name. His deep voice rang through the park, and in it Phadra heard his displeasure.

No. Now was not the time to turn and face him.

Her decision made, she came out of the park and quickly limped across Knightsbridge. The park might have been quiet and serene, but on Knightsbridge, London appeared wide awake and off to the business of the day. Dodging through the morning traffic coming into the city, she worked her way across the street. In her haste, the ribbons holding her bonnet, one that she had cleverly fashioned after a design in a Bellini painting, had come untied. As she avoided a farmer's cart the bonnet blew off her head.

"Phadra!" Grant's voice carried over the din of the traffic. She let the bonnet go.

Hobbling down the street, her mind worked frantically, formulating a plan. She'd hide from Grant, then walk home. It couldn't be that far. Later that night, when he was calmer, they'd talk. He'd see that she had his best interests at heart. He might even laugh about the whole unfortunate incident.

"Phadra!"

Phadra looked over her shoulder and then choked.

She could see Grant's tall figure on the other side of the road. He didn't look as though he was ready to laugh — or to abandon the chase.

And Phadra didn't feel ready to confront him. She ducked down the first side street she came to, pausing only long enough to see that he was weaving his way through the traffic. Her last glimpse was of him sidestepping a dogcart loaded with milk cans.

Phadra rounded a corner and took another street, brushing by fellow pedestrians on the narrow sidewalk in her haste. He wasn't far behind. She could sense his presence — and his determination — by the prickling sensation up the back of her neck.

He shouted her name, and she limped down an alley. Here the neighborhood appeared more shabby, the tall houses narrow and crowded. A heavyset man in a hurry almost knocked her over. To avoid him, she stepped out into the unpaved street and narrowly escaped having a chamber pot dumped on her head.

Catching a whiff of the contents, Phadra

covered her face with her hand and moved on. She couldn't keep running like this. Her ankle hurt, and she had a sharp stitch in her side.

Stopping at the threshold of another alley, this one smelling of rotting fish, she realized she had two options. One was to face Grant. The other was to hide and hope that he passed her by.

"Phadra!"

Hide.

Phadra dodged into the alley. A stack of rain barrels sat haphazardly against a building. Quickly she hid behind them and pulled her skirts in, angry that the first thing she'd pulled out of her wardrobe to wear was such a bright and frivolous color.

For long moments the only thing she could hear was the sound of her own breathing. She stared so hard at the entrance of the alley, waiting for him, that her eyes watered.

He called her name again. Someone yelled at him to stop bellowing. And then there he was, standing at the alley entrance.

The set of his face reminded her of the keen, hunting glance of a hawk. He carried his hat and her trampled bonnet in one hand. Phadra pulled back, held her breath, and prayed, *Not now, Lord. Please don't let him find me now, when he's so angry.*

As if in answer to her silent prayer, Grant moved on. She strained to listen for the sound of his booted footsteps until it disappeared in the distance.

She let out her breath with a sigh of relief. Safe. Of course, she still had to find her way home. That prospect seemed a great deal less daunting than facing Grant.

She had just emerged from her hiding spot when a noise startled her. Pulling back behind the barrels again, she watched as one of the alley doors opened and a greasy-looking man pushed an obviously pregnant woman out into the alley. She fell heavily to the ground.

" 'Ere, I told yer to get out and earn yer keep, and I meant it," he said.

"I'm so tired," the woman begged. Her face was swollen with bruises, and Phadra realized that she was little older than one of the girls at Miss Agatha's. "You told me that if I worked last night, you'd let me rest."

"We need the quid. Now, get on."

The woman was openly crying now, sobs of terror and exhaustion that tore at Phadra's heart. When she didn't move, the man kicked her. She cried out and scrambled to protect her swollen stomach.

The knave pulled back his foot again, and Phadra had had enough. She came out from behind her rain barrels and stood tall and proud. "You leave her alone," she commanded.

Her intervention stopped the man in mid action. He raised one eyebrow and peered through the greasy strings of his hair at her as if surprised by her presence. " 'Ere now, who do yer think yer are? This ain't none of yer business."

Phadra was too angry to be intimidated by a man only a few inches taller than herself. "You have no right to beat this woman."

"She's my woman. I can do wot I please."

Phadra quivered with anger. Her hands doubling up into fists, she took a step toward him. "You touch her again and I'll call the magistrate on you."

"Call the magistrate on me? For touching 'er?" he asked, as if that was the most wildly preposterous idea he'd ever heard of. "Wot do yer think they'll do? She's my woman. No one cares."

"I care," Phadra declared. "And I'll make them care."

"Please, miss," the girl at her feet whispered. "He's terrible mean. He'll hurt you."

"That's right," the man mimicked in a high falsetto. "I'll 'urt yer." He broke off into crude laughter that stopped abruptly, his eyes glittering dangerously. "So, the fancy miss'll turn me in to the magistrate if I touch 'er. Wot yer mean? If I touch 'er loike this?" He poked a grimy finger at the girl's neck. With a cry, the girl squirmed reflexively.

He looked up and grinned at Phadra, a soulless smile that warned her he would give no quarter.

He proved her right when he whispered harshly, "Or touch 'er loike this?" He dug those dirty fingers in the girl's hair and yanked it so hard that her head was lifted off the ground.

At the sound of the girl's cries, Phadra was overcome by a red haze of uncontrollable anger. Acting without thinking, Phadra jumped forward, clasped both hands together, and punched him in his soft belly for all she was worth. He let go of the girl, doubling over in pain and teetering backward. Phadra lost her balance and fell heavily to the dirty alley beside the girl.

Holding a hand against his stomach, the man whirled around, snatched up a good-sized piece of wood in his other meaty fist, and raised it into the air. "Bloody bitch! I'll beat yer to a pulp!"

He drew his hand back. Phadra covered

the girl's body protectively, closed her eyes, and braced herself for the blow — which never came. Instead she heard Grant's harsh, angry voice. "What in the bloody hell do you think you're doing?"

She opened her eyes to see Grant — tall, strong, and angry — holding the man up by his neck against the brick wall of the alley.

The man's feet danced in the air. His face was turning a purplish color.

Phadra rose up on one hand. "Grant! Grant, you're killing him."

"Scum like him doesn't deserve to live, especially when I'm having a bad day," her husband responded succinctly, but then he loosened his hold, and the man slid down the wall to collapse in the dirt.

Phadra scrambled to her feet and threw her arms around Grant's waist. "I'm so glad to see you!"

He pulled away slightly, his expression stern. "I can tell you are. You led me on a merry chase! It's a wonder you didn't get killed before I got here." The man started to crawl away. Grant scowled and barked, "I haven't given you permission to go anywhere."

The man cowered back against the wall. "Listen, guv, I didn't know she was yer woman," he wheezed out. "I wouldn't 'ave touched 'er if I knew she belonged to someone."

Phadra marched forward. "Belong? Is that what you think? That this girl belongs to you, and you can do whatever you like to her?" She almost picked up the discarded piece of wood and beat the man herself, but Grant's large hands came down on her shoulders as if he anticipated her thoughts.

"My wife isn't known for her sweet temper," Grant said calmly. "I'd advise you to crawl quickly back into whatever hole you came out of."

The man scurried his way toward the still-open door. He paused in the doorway. "Come on, Sarah. Get back in 'ere."

His order sent the poor girl into another fit of sobbing hysterics. Phadra shook loose of Grant's hold. "She's not going anywhere with you!"

Using the door for protection, the bastard shouted out, "Yer think yer so smart with that big 'ulking brute behind yer." When Grant took a step toward him, the man slammed the door shut, and they heard a bar come down on the other side. "Yer can keep 'er!" his muffled voice shouted. "She's no good to me breeding!"

His cruel words only made Sarah cry the harder, but that didn't bother Phadra, who fairly danced for joy. "Did you see that, Grant? Oh, I hope you didn't hurt your shoulder, but we showed him, didn't we? He'll think twice before he bullies another woman."

She stopped for a second and gifted him with her biggest smile, letting him see her undisguised admiration. Then she declared, "You were wonderful!"

To her delight, a dull red stain crept up his neck, as if he was completely unfamiliar with such open worship. He reached down and gently helped the girl up from the street.

And at that moment Phadra fell in love.

As she stood in a dirty alley on a bright summer's morn, with stains on her canary-yellow skirt and a sobbing pregnant girl at her feet, love took hold of her.

It swept through her like a great rushing wind and left a tingling sensation that told her she'd been changed forever. Love. Smaller than a hummingbird, brighter than a star, more mysterious than the folds of a rose. Poets sang its praises; souls died from the lack of it.

And she'd found it.

Grant reached down and picked up his hat and her discarded bonnet with a look of disgust. He clearly didn't feel what she felt.

Phadra could see it in his face, and the realization filled her with an inexplicable sadness. Why had she thought that a man such as Grant Morgan — a man who would run to the defense of strangers and attempt to rescue young women from their own follies, a man more handsome, worldly, and wise than she had ever dreamed possible — would fall in love with her?

"Miss." The girl's shaking voice interrupted her thoughts. "If I know Mad Bob, he's gone off to wake a few of his mates. He doesn't like being crossed."

"Then we'd best be going, shouldn't we?" Grant said easily, which was good for Phadra because she didn't think she could find her voice at that moment. He shot her a strange look, apparently concerned by her sudden quietness.

"Perhaps it'd be best if I stay here," Sarah offered timidly.

That snapped Phadra out of her contemplative mood. "So that brute can beat you again? Absolutely not." She took one of Sarah's arms, Grant took the other, and they walked out of the alley. "You can stay with us," she announced grandly, and then felt the jerk as Grant stopped short at her words. The look in his eyes clearly said that he thought she'd taken leave of her senses, but there wasn't any time to argue, because at that moment the alley door was thrown open and Mad Bob plus an assortment of disreputable characters stumbled out into the alley.

"Run!" Grant shouted.

They took to their heels, practically dragging the screaming girl between them. Phadra wanted to turn left, but Grant turned them right. Fortunately he was correct, and they found themselves headed for Knightsbridge, where Wallace waited docilely by the road with the hired carriage.

"Wallace!" Grant shouted. "Look lively, man."

Wallace turned round at the sound of Grant's voice, and then his eyes popped wide open at the sight of them being chased by several garbage-throwing arkmen. He climbed into the open carriage, ready to snap the reins.

Phadra threw open the door and scrambled in, tearing her hem in the process. Grant followed, pushing the hapless Sarah in before him. Wallace already had the carriage moving into traffic as Grant banged the carriage door shut. Daring to look over her shoulder, Phadra saw Mad Bob and his friends come to a halt at the street's edge. There were a few names called, fists raised, and fish heads thrown, but the riffraff didn't follow. She sank back into the cushions with a sigh.

"That was exciting," Grant said dryly, echoing her thoughts. He rubbed his wounded shoulder.

"Where are we going, sir?" Wallace asked.

Grant looked askance at Phadra. She put her arm around Sarah, who wiped her face with the dirty hem of her skirt.

With an impatient sigh, Grant reached inside his coat and pulled out a linen kerchief. He offered it to the girl, who burst into noisier tears. The drawing together of his eyebrows was a silent indication to Phadra that he would like to hear the watering pot between them silenced.

Imitating Henny's best comforting cooing, Phadra said, "There, now, it's not that bad. You're safe now."

"You don't understand, miss." Sarah sobbed harder.

Phadra shot a look at Grant to let him know she was doing her best. He rolled his eyes. "It *can't* be that bad," she murmured again.

"Yes, 'tis. I've done a terrible thing." And with that pronouncement Sarah threw herself into Grant's arms, crying and rubbing her face on his chest.

He looked so stunned by her actions that Phadra would have burst into laughter were it not for a cool male voice that interrupted them. "Well, Morgan, it's good to see you alive."

Grant and Phadra's eyes met, and then both of them turned their heads to the three distinguished gentlemen out for an early morning ride in the park. Grant forced a strained smile and answered dryly, "Thank you, Sir Robert, it's good to be alive." He made as if to tip his hat, but apparently remembered at the last minute that it had been thrown aside in their flight from the alley.

Phadra had never realized how naked one could feel without a proper covering for the head. She became conscious of the fact now — especially since the men sniffed the air as if smelling something unpleasant. Phadra's cheeks turned hot. She had no doubt the alley's fish smell lingered.

Grant spoke up, sounding for all the world as though they were taking a pleasant morning carriage ride. "Sir Robert, may I introduce you to my wife? Phadra, Sir Robert Dumbarton is the governor of the Court of Directors. The other gentlemen, Sir Henry Sudbury and Sir Victor Hollywise, are members of the Court." As he spoke he attempted to pry Sarah off him, but she only held on tighter.

Dumbarton flicked an interested eye over Sarah's hold on Grant and their stained clothing before he said, "It is my pleasure to meet you, Mrs. Morgan. I heard you made quite an impact on society last night. My wife promises you will become all the rage." Obviously he didn't expect any response from her, because he continued, "Morgan, I expect to see you later this morning at our meeting with Wakefield."

"Yes, Sir Robert," Grant answered immediately. He attempted one more time to pry the girl off. This time he was successful.

It was not a smart move.

The expression on the faces of the bank's leading members turned to shock as they glimpsed the size of the girl's pregnant stomach. They looked over at Phadra, then back at Sarah, and lastly at Grant with undisguised curiosity.

As if sensing their distress, Wallace discreetly urged the horses forward, and they pulled away from the bank's directors as Grant said, "I'll see you at ten, Sir Robert."

They drove off, but not before Sir Henry's gruff, carrying voice declared, "That girl's belly was as big as a tick!"

"That sort of thing is supposed to run in

Morgan's blood, isn't it?" Sir Victor questioned sagely.

That pronouncement would have sent Sarah into tears again, except that Grant had apparently had enough. He pulled her hands from his shirt, set them in her lap, and said, "Would you shut up?"

The stern command in his voice had the fortunate effect of bringing her to her senses. Her eyes opened wide in surprise, and her mouth shut.

"Now," Grant said, the voice of authority, "is there anyone you can go to, Sarah, who can help you? Relatives or friends, perhaps?"

Sarah's lower lip quivered dangerously. But when Grant raised a finger, a silent order for her not to break down, she took a second to compose herself and then answered, "My parents." She folded her arms protectively over her stomach. "I've done something very foolish, sir. I ran away. I thought things would be better in London instead of living on the farm and marrying Tom Hooper. I was wrong." She started to get teary again. Grant leaned back in the carriage with a sigh and handed her the kerchief that had fallen on the seat between them.

After a few moments he said, "Sarah,

we'll get you home to your parents. Where do they live?"

"Derbyshire, sir."

He patted her hand reassuringly. "Then we'll get you to Derbyshire." Almost as an afterthought, and with a quick glance at her stomach, he added, "And soon."

"Do you think that is wise?" Phadra asked. "I mean, letting her travel in her condition?" She cast a knowing look down at the woman's stomach. "Maybe she should stay with us."

"Phadra," he said through clenched teeth, his lips forced into a seemingly pleasant smile, "we need to practice economies. There is no *extra* for expenses such as a lady's maid."

"Lady's maid?" Phadra choked on the words. She supposed this was not the time to tell Grant about Jem's milliner's assistant.

"Oh, I can travel, miss," Sarah said eagerly. "Back home women milk cows and work the fields right up until their time. A stage ride will be nothing. Not if it means I'm going home."

"Will they want you?" Phadra asked gently. Her father didn't want her at all. She couldn't even imagine what he would say if she presented herself to him enceinte.

Sarah didn't mistake her meaning. "My

parents are kind people. I know I made a mistake, and I'll tell them so." She rubbed her palm across her stomach. "I would have gone home sooner if I'd had the money. I want this wee one to have something more than a life on a London street."

"There, it's settled," Grant said. He raised his voice. "Wallace, take us to the nearest post house."

Putting Sarah on the first stage out of London for Derbyshire was not as easy as it sounded. The stage was full. Grant paid a man double the fare to secure a seat for the girl inside the coach. He also slipped her a pound note to pay for food and expenses along the way. They stayed with Sarah until the stage left in case Mad Bob made an appearance.

Phadra watched all this while caught up with pride that this man, her husband, would go so far for a stranger. But she also had a feeling of alarm. Once again her actions were costing them money they could ill afford.

She had to tell Grant about the lady's maid. And forevermore, she vowed, she would be the most upstanding and frugal woman in society. Never again would his position at the bank be jeopardized by her. Never, ever, ever.

Grant leaned his head back against the carriage seat and gave a deep sigh of relief. "I'm glad that's over. This morning feels as though it has gone on for two days."

"It has been eventful, hasn't it?" she said noncommittally.

He opened one eye and peered at her as if to ask whether she was joking. Phadra forced a smile, feeling sick to her stomach. She had to tell him about the lady's maid. "Grant, we need to talk."

He'd closed his eyes as if trying to relax. "About what?"

"About . . . ," she started, and then stopped. He looked so tired. Certainly he didn't need to be upset — and she had a feeling that her hiring servants without consulting him might be something that would make him upset.

His hand came down on hers, which was resting on the seat. "About last night?" he prompted quietly. He turned his head toward her and opened his eyes.

What she saw in those bright, silvery eyes made her forget to breathe. He laced his fingers with hers. "In the attic?" He raised her hand to his lips. The touch of his lips brushing against the tips of her fingers seared a path straight to her soul and erased all thoughts of lady's maids and economies.

He smiled, and Phadra thought dizzily that no man should have the ability to smile at a woman and make her feel as if she'd been turned inside out.

Wallace pulled up to their house, breaking the spell.

Reluctantly Grant lowered her hand to the seat. "We'll talk tonight," he promised before he jumped down from the carriage and helped her down. He pulled out his pocket watch and then gave a start of alarm. "Good heavens, it's half past the hour. I have to change and get to the bank immediately for that meeting with Wakefield." He started to escort her to the door, but Phadra waved him on. Without a backward glance he took the steps two at a time and went in the house, calling for Jem to fetch water almost before he was through the door. She entered at a slower pace. Wallace followed after he found a boy to hold the horses.

An anxious Henny met her at the door. "Phadra darling, we have a terrible problem."

"A problem?"

Henny pulled back a moment and stared hard at her. "Mercy, what happened to you? You look as though you were in a fight with a ratcatcher." She covered her nose with her hand. "And you smell as though you lost."

"Ratcatcher. That's a very good description of the man . . . and *he* lost," Phadra said proudly with a touch of her husband's dry humor.

"And your bonnet. Where is it? Don't tell me you have been running around the streets of London without a headdress!"

"All right, then, I won't."

"Phadra Abbott, what is going on here?"

"It's Morgan," Phadra said proudly. "My name is Phadra Morgan." She drew out the sounds of her new last name as if they were music.

At that moment Grant ran down the stairs, still tying a clean neckcloth. Wallace appeared with another hat for him, not as fine as the destroyed one, but suitable.

Grant took it from him, placed his hand on the door handle, and then stopped. He turned to Phadra and ran his gaze up from her sturdy leather boots, past her stained and torn dress, to the top of her disheveled hair — and he smiled, a smile so full of promise that she thought she'd melt from the heat of it. "Tonight," he said. "We'll talk tonight." Then he was out the door.

Phadra didn't think she could move from the spot. She would stand rooted right there until he returned later in the day. Unfortunately, Henny had other plans.

She stepped in front of Phadra and gained her attention by waving her hand in front of the younger woman's face. "We have problems."

"Whatever is the matter?"

"Read this," Henny commanded, and handed her a letter addressed to Phadra. The seal was broken. When Phadra shot her a frown, Henny shrugged and said, "Who knew when or if you'd be back?" Before Phadra could read the note, Henny added, "It's from Dame Cunnington. She's holding a salon of her own, here, tonight."

"Here? Tonight?" Phadra repeated. Quickly she skimmed the note. Popov had always bragged about Phadra's suppers, and so the dowager was inviting herself and her guests for dinner. The postscript stated that she preferred her champagne iced.

She looked up at Henny, her eyes wide in alarm. "Dame Cunnington's salons attract the leading figures of the art and political worlds. Henny, what are we going to do?"

"Do about what?" came a clipped voice from behind her.

Phadra whirled around to see two young women standing on the steps. Their looks were identical to the miniatures Grant kept of his sisters — except in the miniatures they were smiling.

The one who appeared to be the elder stepped inside the door. She forced a smile, but her eyes remained suspicious. "I'm Anne Morgan Ballentine, Grant's elder sister. And this is our youngest sister, Jane Morgan Edwards." She appeared to catch a whiff of Phadra's alley perfume and backed away in sudden surprise. Then, in a voice cold enough to ice Dame Cunnington's champagne, she announced, "We've come to see what manner of woman our brother married in such haste."

Chapter 16

The meeting with Wakefield, the War Office's representative, went better than Grant had expected, although he doubted if Wakefield or even Sir Robert understood much of what was transpiring.

No, what gave him cause for optimism was Lord Phipps, who accompanied Wakefield. The portly little lord demonstrated a keen mind for finance and understood the intricacies of the government's financing of the war against Napoleon. He and Grant moved the meeting along to a satisfactory conclusion without their seniors being the wiser.

After the meeting, Grant made a point of paying his respects to Phipps. The man actually blushed. "Thank you, Morgan."

"Now, if you men in government would negotiate an end to Boney's embargo so British goods can start being traded again in foreign markets, I would bow down and kiss your feet."

"You mean that, don't you?"

"Of course I do. Good God, man, England is on the verge of bankruptcy, and that will destroy us faster than any fleet of warships."

Phipps's eyes narrowed thoughtfully. "One of the problems is that we don't have men in government who understand that fact. Parliament acts as if its members don't believe revolution can happen in Britain." He leaned closer to Grant. "We can't fight two battles, one against Bonaparte and the other against the weavers and tradesmen. What we need is more men like you, who understand how strained the financial markets are right now."

"Are you suggesting that I consider working in the government?" Grant asked in surprise.

"I'm suggesting the War Office, to be more specific."

"I'm flattered. However, my career lies with the bank."

"Are you so certain you couldn't find a similarly rewarding career elsewhere? I could say a word to Perceval."

The idea of being a topic of discussion between Phipps and the prime minister was a shock. "My lord, I deeply appreciate your offer, but unfortunately my circumstances are not such that I can entertain a move of that sort. At least, not right now."

Phipps looked pensive for a moment before rocking back on his heels and confessing, "I admit that I do begrudge you that change in circumstances. I'd looked in favor on Miss Abbott. You're a lucky man, Morgan. I wish she could have been mine, although I am not surprised you beat me out. How could a runt like me hope to compete with a gentleman such as yourself?"

"But you are a lord. You have a title."

"And I'm short and rather unhandsome," Phipps said morosely. "A title doesn't make a man."

"Nor do looks."

"Oh? It was a love match, then?" Phipps asked, his expression rather hopeful.

Grant almost answered bitterly, "No, a lust match," but wisely kept his own counsel. However, on the ride back to the bank, he realized that Phadra was rarely far from his thoughts. Nor were all the images that played through his mind erotic ones.

Instead he remembered clearly the sight of her standing up to Mad Bob in defense of that poor country girl. He was sure that his petite wife would be no less passionate in her defense of one of their own children. The idea of Phadra as a mother filled him with such a warm sense of pleasure and pride, Dumbarton asked him why he was smiling.

Nonplussed to be caught daydreaming, Grant mumbled something unintelligible, excused himself, and returned to his office, where his mind quickly drifted from the ledger sheets spread before him. Yes, Phadra would be a good mother — provided he could tame some of her more flamboyant ideas. The thought of taming Phadra brought him back to those hazy erotic images that had teased his mind ever since he had woken with his body intertwined with hers in the inn.

Those same images teased him now as the hours of the day dragged by until he thought he might go mad. He had no doubt that Phadra's appetites were as strong as his own — and he had very strong appetites, especially after having held them at bay for so many long years. At one point during the day, he actually entertained the notion of leaving work and going home then and there to bed his wife so he could think rationally again.

But he didn't.

His father, a man eager for immediate gratification, would have done it in a trice, but Grant was different from his father. He was a man, not a rutting stag. He was in control of his desires. He could wait until his responsibilities had been discharged before he rushed off in search of his own gratification.

And he would be gratified. He'd seen how quickly the flame of desire had been sparked in Phadra's large sapphire eyes when he kissed the tips of her delicate fingers in the carriage that morning. Just the thought of those fingers and what he'd like to teach them to do made him —

"Morgan!"

Sir Cecil's bellow brought him to his senses. He looked up from his desk to see the banker standing before him.

"I'm sorry, sir." Grant forced a smile. "Did you say something?"

"I've been trying to gain your attention for the past five minutes! Good God, where is your mind?"

That was a question Grant wasn't about to answer. Embarrassed, he pushed aside the papers that had been sitting untouched on his desk and tried to change the subject. "What may I do for you?"

Sir Cecil dropped a stack of papers at least six inches thick on the desk. "I need you to look over this for me," he said. "Draft a statement for me to deliver to the House of

Lords on the morrow."

Grant stood and placed his hands on his desk. "But it's already half past five." He riffled the top few pages. "And this concerns the effect of higher interest charges on the weaving industry! Sir Cecil, it'll take me hours to form some sort of opinion based on this report."

"Then you'd better get started."

Grant leaned across the desk. "I have a better idea. Why don't *you* get started and, for once, form your own opinions?"

For a long second Sir Cecil stared at Grant as if he could scarcely believe his ears. Then he shut the door quietly to ensure their privacy and said, "Perhaps you'd be wise, Morgan, to remember what exists between the two of us."

Grant straightened. "There is no longer anything between the two of us. I've paid Phadra's debt." He paused before adding, "And your debt also."

Sir Cecil grinned smugly. "That was good of you. I hope it didn't set you back too much. However, you still need my goodwill, Morgan. Oh, I know you believe we are quits, but you're wrong." He clasped his hands in front of him, evidently waiting for Grant to ask why.

Grant didn't want to ask the question, but

as the long moments stretched between them with his lordship grinning like a cat, he couldn't stop himself. "*Why* do I need you?"

Sir Cecil laughed triumphantly. When he had his title, Grant vowed, no one would force him into this nonsense again.

As if sensing his anger, Sir Cecil abruptly erased the smile from his face and said, "It's Dumbarton. He doesn't hold with dueling. I see nothing wrong with it myself. After all, gentlemen have to have a way to settle their differences, and —"

"Dumbarton doesn't approve of dueling?"

"The man's a bit of a Puritan, you know. He follows a rigid code of rules and expects his bank officers to do the same . . . but then I don't have to tell you that, do I? He's always admired you, truly he has. However, after hearing about the duel and the admittedly havey-cavey way in which you married Phadra . . . and then some nonsense going around about your cuddling a pregnant wench out in the middle of Piccadilly with your wife sitting on the other side of you — well, he finds it all quite confounding, and frankly, Morgan, so do I." Sir Cecil's expression turned to one of fatherly concern. "After all, I'd thought of you as a suitable husband for my Miranda. Of course, I'd always considered you more of a monk than a Bluebeard. This new pattern is somewhat a concern — especially since we'd considered you a valued member of the bank."

"*Had* considered me?"

Sir Cecil looked out at him from under bushy eyebrows drawn together in stern contemplation. "Nothing like that. Not yet, at least. I managed to assure Dumbarton that you are still the stalwart young man that we have always had so much confidence in. Of course, a banker's reputation is very important. It would be unfortunate for you and your ambitions if at some point I found myself unable to give you such a strong recommendation. Dumbarton and I were at Eton together, you know."

So. There it was.

Grant struggled with his pride, looking not at Sir Cecil but at the reports and their tightly written script. The words tasted bitter in his mouth when he finally said, "I'll draft the statement and have it sent to your house this evening."

Sir Cecil clapped his hands together in satisfaction. "I knew I could count on you, Morgan. If it is any help, I'll have my secretary stay and run it over to me when you're done."

Grant tightened his jaw muscles, biting

back the sharp retort.

His lordship appeared to take his silence as acquiescence. "Well," he said brightly, "I must be off. I dine with Sir Robert and some of the others at Fitzgerald's club." With that, he left Grant's office.

"Enjoy yourself," Grant muttered at the empty doorway.

He sat down at his desk and scanned the top sheets of the report. Actually, if he hadn't been so anxious to get home to his wife, he would have welcomed this opportunity to have his opinions presented in the House of Lords. Not that he thought Sir Cecil would add any eloquence to his words. If things had been different and money hadn't been so tight, he might have considered taking Phipps up on his offer of a position in government.

But then, if wishes were horses, beggars would ride, Grant thought wryly. With a sigh he began reading the report on the hosiery and lace industry around Nottingham, silently admitting to himself for the first time that he was secretly pleased he wasn't Sir Cecil's son-in-law. He tried not to think of his warm, willing wife waiting for him at home.

By the time Grant made his way home,

the lamplighter had preceded him on his rounds. He was surprised to see in the dim, foggy lamplight a line of vehicles up and down his normally quiet street.

Someone must be having a party.

It wasn't until he drew closer to his brick townhouse and noticed that every lamp and candle in the place was burning brightly that he realized *he* was the one hosting the party. What the deuce was Phadra up to?

The uncomfortable tightening in his loins that he'd suffered all day every time he thought of his wife was now forgotten, supplanted by a deeper and darker concern. He rushed up the front steps and was surprised when the front door was opened by Wallace in a dark green livery that could do a king proud.

Wallace took one look at Grant and acted as if he wanted to shut the door quickly — but then thought better of it.

"What is going on here?" Grant barked, even as he became aware of the loud hum of conversation and the clinking of glassware coming from his parlor . . . and his dining room . . . and the back of the house, where his personal domain, his study, was located.

Wallace, his face turning as pale as his lace ruffles, was saved from answering by the appearance of a young man in the fine trappings of a lord who stumbled out of the parlor and leaned against the door frame with a hiccup. He turned a bleary eye on Wallace, crossed his legs, and mumbled, "Water closet?"

Wallace pointed down the hall toward the back of the house, and the tipsy lord zigzagged his way down the hall.

Grant watched him go for a moment before he shoved his hat and walking stick into Wallace's arms and marched to the parlor door. The sight inside the parlor made him wonder if he'd wandered into the wrong house.

Dame Cunnington sat in her sedan chair in the middle of his parlor. The sides of the chair had been removed so that the conveyance served as a leather-and-satin throne while her liveried chair bearers stood behind her with more military bearing than most regimental officers. Her amorist poet Alexei Popov, sat at her feet, holding up a tray of sweetmeats and a glass of champagne for her enjoyment.

From this vantage point the dowager entertained a host of people who draped themselves nonchalantly on and across the backs of Grant's sofas or stood in small gatherings talking and laughing amongst themselves. To his astonishment, a group of young men, their hair overlong and their neckcloths tied in the manner of dandies, started throwing their glasses into his empty fireplace. Dame Cunnington cackled, and Popov tittered as if they'd done something clever.

Grant was on his way to stop this outrageous nonsense, picking a path through the ever-shifting crowd of unfamiliar faces, when he spied Mrs. Shaunessy. Or at least he thought it was Mrs. Shaunessy. Her red hair was bound up with an Indian cotton scarf, and her eyes looked as if they'd been outlined in kohl. She carried a tray full of crystal glasses filled to the brim with champagne.

Grant changed directions and was pushing his way through the crowd toward her when a woman grabbed his arm. He looked down and after a moment's astonishment recognized Lady Dumbarton, Sir Robert's wife, with a scarf of Indian cotton wrapped around her head, its ends hanging down her back in an outlandishly bohemian fashion. She looked a far cry from the staid and conservative lady to which he was accustomed.

"Mr. Morgan," she trilled. "We were wondering when you would make an appearance. Isn't this a marvelous crush?"

Pushed aside at that moment by an arrogant man wearing the single spur and well-cut coat of a Corinthian, Grant demanded, "Have you seen my wife?"

Lady Dumbarton squinted slightly, as if trying to think, and then offered an apologetic frown. "But here are Lady Fitzgerald, Lady Sudbury, and Lady Hollywise. They brought me here tonight, and I am deeply in their debt!"

Grant looked down at the quartet of ladies in outfits that resembled bedclothes. It took him a second to realize that they were attempting to copy the dress Phadra had worn to the Evanses' ball. Each had her hair styled with an Indian scarf, including the chubby Lady Hollywise, who didn't have much hair to speak of.

"This is a most successful soiree, Mr. Morgan," Lady Sudbury said.

"You won't believe who is here," Lady Fitzgerald chimed in, her normally somber expression alive with excitement. "Everybody who is *anybody!*"

Lady Hollywise tugged on his coat sleeve and whispered, "That was the Earl of Lofton who just shoved you aside. Twenty thousand a year, and holds Prinney's ear. The House of Lords doesn't move without Lofton's say-so. Brummell may even put in an appearance. And maybe Prinney himself!" The woman practically quivered at the thought.

And that was when Grant heard it — the faint jingling of bells. He looked around for his wife and then realized the sound was much closer. In fact, it was coming from Lady Sudbury.

As if reading his thoughts, she giggled and said, "Do you like them?" She held up her fingers so that he could see she had rings sporting tiny bells on every finger. "I have them on my toes, too." She lifted her skirts, and he realized that she was running around his parlor in her bare feet.

"We'll all have them by tomorrow," Lady Dumbarton announced. "We would have had them today, but Marian refused to divulge her source." She gave Lady Sudbury a glare for her perfidy.

"Oh, la," Lady Sudbury said. "I'll take you all on the morrow and we shall jingle merrily on our way! Well, Mr. Morgan, we must go mingle." She emphasized *mingle* to rhyme with *jingle,* then giggled at her own joke. "Don't you like our new hairstyles? Your wife did them. She is so clever —"

"Where *is* my wife?" Grant demanded.

"Oh, she's somewhere around here," Lady Dumbarton assured him. Leaning closer, she confided happily, "I don't remember ever having such a good time in my life. Such a stimulating group of people!" She drifted with the others into the crowd.

At that moment Dame Cunnington's loud cackle sounded over the crowd, and Grant turned in her direction. That was when he spotted another Indian-scarfed figure talking to a tall brunette beauty in the corner of the room. Certain that the shorter woman must be Phadra, Grant made his way toward her and, once he found himself close enough, grabbed her elbow somewhat forcibly.

The woman looked up in surprise, and he was completely stunned to find himself staring down into the sweet features of his youngest sister. "Jane?"

"Oh, Grant, it is so good to see you!" she cried, and kissed his cheek. "Rosalind is going to be so upset that she wasn't able to come."

"How is Rosalind?" Grant asked, his attention momentarily diverted by the thought of his middle sister.

"She hasn't had the baby yet, but the midwife assures her and David that it can happen at any moment. By the way, she sends her love and says that she deeply appreciates the money you sent, although it wasn't necessary."

"Not necessary? Has Oxford decided to pay its tutors more than it has in the past? Or has David chosen a different career?"

Jane blushed and smiled. "You know they need the money."

"So why are you here and not helping Rosalind? Is Timothy with you?"

"No, parish duties forbade him the opportunity, although he sends you his best. Actually, Anne and I came because we were concerned about you. Even Rosalind thought it best."

"You're here to check up on me?"

She placed both her hands on his arm, her face wreathed in smiles. "Oh, but we aren't concerned any longer. Phadra is wonderful, Grant! We're having so much fun getting to know her. She's perfect for you!"

"Perfect for me?" Grant repeated blankly. "Where is Anne?"

Jane frowned. "The last I saw of her, she was arguing with some poet, a De Quincey, in your study. Do you know him?"

"I haven't made his acquaintance," Grant observed dryly.

"He's fascinating, but when he started smoking this little pipe filled with cloves and then Anne asked if she could try it . . . well, I left." She looked doubtful about whether she should have shared this information with her brother.

"Anne is smoking?" he asked incredulously. He'd always considered her one of the most moderate of souls.

Jane nodded but protested, "Cloves. Nothing vile like tobacco."

"I'll go talk to her about this," Grant grumbled, and would have stormed off in the direction of his study, except that the woman Jane had been talking to pointedly cleared her throat, and Jane grabbed his arm.

With complete solicitousness she said, "Oh, I'm sorry, Countess, I should introduce you. Grant, this is the Countess Raisa von Driesen. Countess, this is my brother, Grant Morgan, whom you were asking about."

Grant immediately whirled at the mention of the woman's name. "*The* Countess von Driesen?"

The sloe-eyed beauty smiled knowingly and held out her hand. "It is a pleasure," she said in a seductive voice.

Grant was so stunned to discover that his youngest sister, the wife of a country vicar, had been talking to the most infamous courtesan in London that he left the countess's hand hanging in the air until Jane anxiously placed his hand against the countess's.

"My — ah, pleasure," Grant managed to choke out, completely nonplussed when the brazen woman pulled his hand to her lips and openly tongue-kissed the palm.

"I have heard so much about the father . . . and about the son," the countess whispered. She appeared ready to slobber over his hand again, and Grant jerked it away.

"Yes," Grant said with a frown. He looked down at his sister. "I've got to go find Anne. You're sure she was *smoking?*"

"Oh, I shouldn't have told you! Actually, I don't know. She may have changed her mind and only tried the snuff. She just wanted to try something different, Grant. She says she so rarely comes to the city anymore and occasionally longs to do something daring."

With a low growl, Grant turned and started to head to the study. Then he stopped, retraced his steps back to Jane, took her hand, and dragged her with him, ignoring her protests at leaving Countess von Driesen standing alone.

He pulled his sister out into the hall, where he saw a raspberry-colored Indian scarf on the head of a woman holding a tray of champagne glasses. Phadra. He reached for the other woman, but the face she turned up to him wasn't his wife's.

Frowning, he snapped, "Do I know you?"

The woman's eyes opened wide in alarm until Jane gently said, "It's all right, Meg. This is my brother, Mr. Morgan."

Instantly the girl smiled and bobbed a decent curtsey. "I'm pleased to meet you, Mr. Morgan. I'm your wife's new lady's maid, Megan Hartly."

Lady's maid! The blood coursing through his veins took on a dangerous sizzle. Phadra had hired a lady's maid after he had expressly told her there was no money for such things — or for champagne and wild parties at which his sisters took snuff and talked to courtesans, for that matter!

"Where's my wife?" he asked in a low, dangerous voice.

Jane pulled back. The young maid's eyes opened wide but she managed to whisper, "She's in the supper room, sir."

The supper room? "Do you mean the dining room?"

Meg nodded. "Mrs. Morgan instructed me to call it the supper room. She said that it sounds more elegant."

Grant turned to the dining room door and was surprised to discover it closed. He was certain that it had been open earlier. "Where's Wallace?"

Meg bobbed another curtsey and said,

"He's down in the kitchen helping Jem. It's a great deal of work to keep all of these glasses filled."

Grant only vaguely heard her complaint. Instead his complete attention was drawn to the closed dining room door. He crossed to it and tried the handle. The door was locked.

Locking the door to the dining room didn't make sense unless Phadra was planning some grand surprise. If she had something in mind for him bigger than his finding his house full of people, he didn't think he'd be able to recover.

He rattled the handle and ordered, "Phadra, open this door."

At the sound of his voice his wife made a muffled response. Then came a loud male grunt, and a second later Phadra cried out in a clearer voice, "Grant? Grant, help me!"

"What the devil —" He took a step back and rammed the door with his shoulder. The lock gave and the door flew open, banging against the wall. Quickly recovering his balance, he was shocked to see Phadra standing on one side of a food-laden table, her hand clutching a skewer as if to ward off Lord Lofton, who stood on the other side. Her chest heaved with exertion. Her eyes snapped with anger.

It didn't surprise Grant that she also had wrapped an Indian scarf shot through with gold around her unruly flaxen curls, but instead of looking silly, as most of the other women did, she looked regal and utterly individual. Even her dress, a classic design in layers of maize- and peacock-colored cloth as light as the sheerest linen, emphasized her uniqueness . . . until Grant realized that it hadn't been designed to hang off one shoulder, as it now did.

Lofton had been making love to his wife. Under his own roof. In his *supper* room!

He looked from the damning evidence to Lofton. The bastard had the courage to smile benignly and make a great pretense of removing an imaginary bit of lint from his sleeve. He looked up at Grant without any pretense of apology and said, "Your wife is quite delightful, Morgan. Such a challenge, but then we're both swordsmen and understand the chase, don't we?"

There was no mistaking the double entendre in Lofton's use of the word *swordsmen*.

Grant was pleased to discover that the control over which he prided himself was completely in place — even as he crossed to Lofton's side in two long strides, grabbed his high-and-mighty lordship by the seat of his breeches and the collar of his shirt, and, with almost superhuman strength, dragged the yelping bastard out of the room.

"Jane, open the front door," he ordered calmly. His sister, her eyes wide in astonishment, hurried to comply. Once the door was wide open, Grant tossed the yelling Lord Lofton out his front door and down his steps as if the worldly Corinthian was nothing more than a mangy, flea-ridden tomcat.

Grant brushed his hands together in satisfaction.

"What have you done?" Alexei Popov's accented voice screamed in horror.

The young poet charged through the crowd that had gathered to watch Lofton's humiliation. "Do you realize that you have just insulted one of the lions of society? That you've ruined this salon and disgraced my dear Edith?"

In answer, Grant grabbed Popov by his silver-trimmed lapels and sent him flying out the door after Lofton.

But his sense of satisfaction evaporated a moment later when he turned to confront the rest of the party. They stood as still as statues, expressions of shock frozen on their faces.

It was then that he realized that he might

have just sent his career sailing out the door with Lofton.

Phadra stood poised in the dining room doorway. She looked from him to her guests and then back to him. Two bright spots of color stained her cheeks. Her lower lip trembled dangerously.

"Phadra?" Grant said as he took a step toward her.

She shook her head, then gathered her skirt in her hands and ran through the crowd and up the stairs. Grant charged after her.

Chapter 17

Grant shoved several guests aside in his race to reach his wife. Dame Cunnington appeared to be the first to gather her wits and started haranguing him from her sedan chair about how she'd never been so insulted in her life and would see that his "betters" at the bank heard about his outrageous behavior. The other guests watched him pass in mute disbelief.

The door to his bedroom slammed shut when he was halfway up the stairs. The sound made him angry. What right did she have to slam *his* bedroom door? He had only come to her defense.

So why was it that when he reached the closed bedroom door, he felt as if he had to knock?

Conscious that everyone downstairs was probably straining to hear what was being said, he tapped softly.

No answer.

He rapped, the sound more forceful.

Still no answer.

Leaning close to the door, he said in a low voice, "Phadra, I am coming in. We have to talk."

"Go away."

"You can't tell me to go away from my own room," he shot back, not even bothering to keep his voice low. He turned the handle and entered. Phadra sat in the window seat, the dim candlelight reflecting off the gold threads in the scarf wrapped around her hair and making them glow. She turned away quickly and stared out the window when he entered, but not before he'd caught her wiping her eyes with the back of her hands.

Phadra crying? She never cried — or at least he'd never thought of her doing so. Lofton must have been more forceful than he'd imagined.

He shut the door. "Are you all right?" he demanded.

She seemed to be memorizing the lamp posts on the street below. The sound of their guests departing drifted up from the streets. Amid the good-byes and laughter, he thought he heard his name mentioned. This story would be all over London in an hour. The noise of coach wheels turning on the cobblestones grated on his nerves.

He was in no mood to hear his wife say,

"How could you have done that? How could you have thrown him out like that? He's a leading patron of the arts."

Grant frowned, irritated that only a few minutes before, he too had started to wonder if it had been such a wise idea. "Lofton attacks my wife under my own roof, and you're saying that I don't have the right to throw him out? What would you have had me do? Invite him to use the bedroom?"

A flush spread across her cheeks, but her eyes snapped with indignant anger. She stood, her hands clasped tightly in front of her. "Don't you think you may have overreacted?"

"Overreacted? I come home expecting a nice quiet evening, and instead I find my house full of radicals, drunks, and courtesans, all guzzling champagne and teaching my sisters how to smoke and take snuff. No, I don't think I'm overreacting," he said, aware that his voice was one note below a bellow. "What the blue blazes were they doing here, anyway?"

She squared her shoulders. "Dame Cunnington invited them."

"Really? So Dame Cunnington paid for all the champagne and the food?"

Phadra looked as if she'd rather cut off

her right hand than answer. She tilted her chin in that defiant way she had. "No."

Grant leaped upon that admission to justify all of his rash actions this night. "Certainly you can understand my anger, madam."

"No, I can't. Perhaps Dame Cunnington invited herself, but I was proud to host them. I welcomed the opportunity."

"You 'welcomed the opportunity,' " Grant repeated, his disbelief patent.

"Yes, I did. Dame Cunnington is a very powerful woman. Even the bank ladies agreed. I thought that by honoring her wishes tonight, I'd help you gain her favor. I thought you would want that after the disaster at the Evanses' ball. My only desire was to help you win favor with powerful, influential people so that they could see how wonderful you are and help you become knighted. I wanted to help you."

An uncomfortable feeling crept into Grant's mind that quite possibly Phadra could be telling the truth about her justification for hosting the soiree. He squelched the thought. "Even if you thought such a thing, what made you think I could afford it?"

"I paid for it."

Immediately his gaze flew to her ring finger. Phadra held her hand out for him to see the gold band and its fake emerald. "I still have it," she said proudly. "I used what was left of the five hundred pounds you gave me."

"I gave you five hundred pounds?"

"Yes, you did. At the inn after we were married. I offered to give back the money from the sale of the emeralds, and you told me to keep it."

"I did?" Grant searched his mind, trying to remember having said something so stupid.

"Yes, you did, and I have used the money as I think best — or at least I'd hoped things would go well tonight. I'd hoped that we would make a good impression. How was I to know that Lord Lofton was brazen enough to attack me in the supper room with a houseful of people outside the door?"

"You should have shouted the minute he turned the lock on the door."

"I was shocked at his effrontery, but I thought I could handle it. I thought I could reason with him."

"Not dressed like that, you couldn't."

Phadra stood still, as if suddenly turned to stone. She found her voice and said in slow, measured words, "What do you mean by that?"

Aware that he was treading on new and

possibly dangerous territory, Grant took the time to remove his jacket and throw it on the bed between them. He pulled at his shirt cuffs before deciding that he was completely justified in his feelings. He looked at her. "I'm saying that I don't necessarily blame Lofton for reaching a wrong conclusion."

"And what exactly is wrong with the way I'm dressed?"

"Proper young matrons don't walk around with their hair swirled up in scarves. Or in dresses that leave absolutely nothing to the imagination," he added, his eyes lingering on the way the soft material emphasized Phadra's lush curves, the high rise of her breasts, the length of her legs. Suddenly he didn't feel as anxious for a fight as he had only a second before.

She placed her hands on her hips, her brows coming together in anger. "I suppose you'd prefer me to wear those awful, stiff ruffled things Lady Evans chose for me."

Grant shifted uncomfortably. "Well, no . . . I mean, maybe. Certainly if you'd been wearing something like that, I wouldn't have had to defend your honor."

"You had to defend my honor because Lofton is vulgar and rude, not because of anything I was wearing. You can't convince me that anywhere in a book on manners there is an injunction that states that if you like the dress your hostess is wearing, you should try to take it off her over the roast veal!"

Anger surged inside him. "Is that what Lofton tried to do?"

"Grant, that's not the point! He shouldn't have behaved that way regardless of what I was wearing."

He shook his head. "You don't understand how the male mind works."

"Do you think the female mind works any differently?" With studied nonchalance, she added, "I saw that countess lick your hand as if you were a piece of marzipan."

Hot color flooded his face. "You saw that?"

"I did — and so did everyone else in the room. But notice that I'm not standing up here demanding that you wear gloves."

He frowned and took a step away from her. "That would be ridiculous. The woman is an infamous courtesan. Her lovers are legion and her reputation ruined."

Phadra tapped her foot impatiently before saying, "And what description would you give to Lofton? The man boasts of his conquests as being in the hundreds. Do you believe he is more circumspect in his encounters than the countess?"

Grant didn't like the way this conversation was going — especially since all he wanted to concentrate on was removing the rest of his wife's dress, laying her out on the bed, and making mad, mindless love to her. With that intent in mind, he edged his way around the bed toward her, saying, "Phadra, you are talking apples and oranges."

"I'm saying that you can't apply one standard to me and another to yourself," she retorted, moving several steps away from him. "Be honest. Between the two of us, you are the prettier one —"

"Men are not pretty," he interrupted, irritated that they were still talking and not doing something far more interesting.

"They are to women," she said, and held up a hand to ward him off while she made her point. Grant stopped and crossed his arms over his chest, impatient for their little argument to be done.

The look in her eyes told him that she didn't appreciate his attitude, but she continued, "Don't think that just because we are the softer sex, we are any less rapacious in our desires. When the two of us are together in a public place, no woman even notices me because they are so busy lusting after you."

"That's ridiculous."

"It's true. I've lost count of the number of gloves and kerchiefs dropped in your path while I've been standing right next to you, but I don't expect you to wear a mask over your head or do something to disguise the width of your shoulders or the strength in your thighs —"

"Phadra, this is nonsense!" he interrupted, embarrassed at her listing his physical attributes.

"Women are even bold enough to ogle a man's *equipment*." She let her eyes drift down to his nether region before saucily admitting, "And you, my dear sir, are very well equipped — but I don't demand that you wear looser breeches or longer waistcoats, do I?"

Grant blinked, surprised at her boldness. He backed up a step, fighting the urge to cover his groin, and stated flatly, "If you insist on emulating anyone, I'd prefer you follow Lady Dumbarton's lead and not the Countess von Driesen's."

"Why, certainly, Grant. I'll be more than happy to do so," she said with sweetness that immediately put him on guard. "After all, Lady Dumbarton is the one who compared you to her favorite stallion."

"The devil, you say!" Grant exclaimed,

and then felt himself turn a bright and burning shade of red. He hoped Phadra couldn't see how embarrassed he was. *Imagine, my wife and a group of ladies sitting around and talking about me as if they were —* his mind searched for an apt comparison — *as if they were a group of men sitting in a coffeehouse, leering at women.*

What was worse, Phadra stood there, hands on hips, eyes dancing with laughter, apparently feeling no remorse at embarrassing him this way.

The laughter died in her eyes and was replaced by sudden realization. She said with mild surprise, "You don't like the way you look, do you?"

He frowned. "I like the way I look."

"No, you don't," Phadra said with a shake of her head. "I've always known that you aren't particularly vain about your looks, but now . . ." Her brow crinkled as she puzzled over the problem. "It's not a lack of vanity, is it? You just don't like to look at yourself."

He took another step toward the door. "Phadra, this conversation has turned silly."

But Phadra wasn't listening. Instead she searched the room with her eyes before her clear, direct gaze met his. "There's no mirror in here. In fact, this afternoon we had to borrow a mirror from Wallace in order to do our hair. Your sisters mentioned that they took all the good mirrors with them when they married and that you'd never had the need for a mirror."

"So I don't have a mirror. What does it matter?" he asked in clipped tones. "I'm not a vain man."

Phadra walked thoughtfully over to his wardrobe and opened it.

"What are you doing?" he asked.

She ran her hands over the sleeves of the coats hanging there. "All your clothing is the same. The same colors, the same cut." She turned to him. "When we first met, my initial thought was that you wear your clothing the way most men wear a uniform. I thought it had something to do with your being a banker, but it's more than that, isn't it? You do it so that you can spend as little time as possible on your appearance."

"I have no idea what you are talking about —"

"This morning," she interrupted, "you were bathed, dressed, and out the door in less than ten minutes."

"So?"

"So you spent hardly any time at all on anything other than what was necessary.

You didn't primp. You didn't spend time on yourself."

"I was clean and shaved," he protested.

"But you didn't take any *extra* time."

"Oh, don't be ridicul—"

"I'm not being ridiculous," she said with a stamp of her foot. "I'm now realizing something important about you. You don't even talk about yourself."

"Yes, I do."

"No, you don't. You never talk about what you feel or think except to tell me what you want — such as to earn a knighthood and become a director at the bank. But you rarely talk about *why* those things are so important to you." She slid him a pensive glance. "Except for that night in the Evanses' garden when you told me about your father."

Grant shifted his weight. It was only when he bumped into the door handle that he realized he'd edged his way to the door.

Phadra leaned against the bedpost. "I remember thinking later that night that it was strange you hadn't already achieved those goals. I mean, with your extraordinary looks, you could have contracted a suitable alliance without having to resort to Miranda Evans. But you won't trade on your looks, will you? You told me that too, that day in the museum. 'I don't trade on my looks.' Those were the exact words." She paused and looked him in the eye. "Why not, Grant? Why don't you like the way you look? Is it because everyone says you look so much like your father?"

Grant placed his hand on the door handle and then removed it quickly, as if he'd touched a hot poker. Was he really so disturbed by her words that he'd let her chase him from the room? He stood his ground. "I didn't come up here to discuss this. I came up here to tell you that from now on I expect my orders to be obeyed."

"Obeyed?" she repeated as if she hadn't heard him correctly.

Grant took a step into the room, feeling a need to exert more control, to keep her sharp mind away from subjects too uncomfortable for him. "From now on, I expect you to consult me before you throw parties like this one tonight."

She didn't appear to take offense at his words, as he'd expected her to. Instead she asked, almost gently, "And I suppose you will expect to have a hand in choosing which fashions I wear?"

"I hadn't considered it, but yes, I do think that is a wise idea."

"And if I disagree?"

"I am your husband."

"And I'm your chattel?"

He frowned, not liking the word. "No, nothing quite as dramatic as that."

Phadra shook her head. "Then how else do you express it? I am to do *what* you order me to do, *when* you order me to do it, and *how* you order me to do it. Is that not correct?"

"Phadra —"

"I'm sorry, Grant, but I don't think I can live that way. I don't believe in it. The ladies and I were discussing this today, and we all agree that it's wrong for women to be treated as though we aren't partners in a marriage, just as it's wrong to treat us as if we aren't full and equal citizens of this country. The laws are wrong."

"British laws are designed to protect a woman and help a man cherish her."

"Is ordering me about to suit your mood considered 'cherishing'?"

"I don't order you about to suit my mood. I'm acting in our best interests."

"You don't know me well enough to know what my best interests are!"

"I know your best interests aren't chasing around after that vagrant father of yours," he snapped back, his voice rising. "I know that you would have been better off staying

406

at that girls' school rather than rolling your-self into debt in London. If you'd stayed where you were supposed to, none of this" — he waved his hand intending to encom-pass the house and their marriage — "would have happened!"

Phadra pulled back as if he'd struck her.

Grant wanted to call the words back, to deny them — but he stopped himself. He hadn't spoken anything other than the truth. She had to learn that he was in con-trol of his own house.

He just hated to see the hurt in her large blue eyes.

Phadra crossed her arms against her chest protectively and backed away even farther.

"Phadra, you know we aren't a love match." The second he said the words, he knew they were the wrong ones to say. She actually flinched when she heard them. He shut up and shoved his hands back into his pockets. This wasn't working. "Maybe we are too different," he muttered.

The silence stretched out painfully be-tween them. She was the first to break it. "All right," she said softly. She lowered her arms to her side and straightened her shoul-ders. When she lifted her chin, he knew he was going to be in trouble.

"Perhaps we *are* too different. Perhaps it

doesn't matter." She bunched her skirts up, giving him an excellent view of her shapely calves, and climbed up onto the bed. "It's obvious that you won't be happy until I understand my place." She slipped the sandals off her dainty feet.

He murmured something unintelligible, his mind suddenly reeling with the vivid memory of her legs wrapped around his hips up in the attic. He took a step toward the bed, his body moving of its own volition.

"Well," she said in an icy voice that demanded his attention, "henceforth I shall endeavor to stay in my place." Opening her arms, she fell back onto the feather mattress with a slight whooshing sound, spread open her legs, and stared up at the canopy.

After several long seconds he finally asked, "What are you doing?"

"I'm waiting for you," she said without looking at him. "Like a good and docile wife. Come and have your way with me."

Her words shocked him. "Have you gone mad?"

Phadra sat up, her scarfed hair bouncing with the movement. "I'm sorry. Do you not like this position? I can turn over onto my stomach if you'd prefer that position better." To his horror, she rolled over and spread her arms out to her sides like a martyr waiting to be tied to a cross.

He backed away . . . even as another part of his body cried *Yes!* at the sight of her delectable little bottom offered up to him. "Why are you doing this?" he ground out.

"Because I can't settle for a marriage that is nothing more than this, and I don't think you can, either."

Oh, yes, I could, he thought. And if she was paying any attention to his equipment, she'd see that fact. He moved back into the shadows and once again felt himself bump into the door handle. Did she realize how seductive she looked spread out on the bed?

She turned over and sat up, resting her palms on the mattress, the position emphasizing her cleavage. Dear God, he ached with the need to touch her, to take her. But he couldn't give in — not if he still wanted to be the one in control of this marriage. He placed his hand on the door handle and gripped it as if it were a lifeline.

When he still didn't speak, she shifted position again, sitting back on her heels in the position of a supplicant. "Grant, if you are going to insist that I live only to follow your command, to be little better than a servant, then I'd rather be locked up again in Miss Agatha's, where at least I was free to think my own mind."

"And is that the only way? On your terms?" His voice sounded harsh.

She blinked as if slightly hurt by his tone. Then she lifted her chin. "Yes." The expression in her eyes softened as she added, "I can't live my life as little more than a marionette."

The words hung in the air between them. Grant heard the almost desperate plea underlying them, but he couldn't shake the voice he heard in his mind, which was telling him that if he gave in now, he'd never be in control again. A man didn't let a woman run his life.

Only those weren't his words he was hearing; they were his father's words. He could hear his father saying them, emphasizing them, as they made the rounds of brothels and supper clubs, his arm around Grant's shoulders.

The sudden revelation shattered everything he'd ever believed about himself.

Grant turned the door handle and let himself out of the room. She called out to him. When he was halfway to the staircase, he heard her crying. He kept walking.

Downstairs, the guests were long gone, and most of the remnants of the party had been cleared away. A single candle burned in the hallway on a table. Picking up the candle, he walked purposefully into the dining room to the small liquor cabinet in the corner, set the candle on top of the cabinet, and took out a decanter of whiskey he kept for guests and one glass. Pulling the stopper out, he poured the whiskey into the glass. His hand shook as he poured, causing the mouth of the decanter to clink against the rim of the glass, and in a burst of violent rage he threw the decanter with all his strength at the far wall.

The crystal bottle smashed into thousands of pieces. "I am not my father," he said, enunciating each word clearly, distinctly.

The sound of footsteps made him turn with alarm to the door. A second later Anne appeared. A shawl was wrapped around her nightdress, and she was holding a candle. "Grant? Are you all right?"

He didn't want company. "I'm fine, Anne. Go back to bed."

She didn't move but stood in the doorway. He had no doubt that she'd heard the crash and could smell the peatlike scent of the whiskey in the air. She stepped into the dining room. "I thought you would be with Phadra."

He heard her unspoken question. "We're not a love match," he explained quietly.

Anne raised her eyebrows and sat down at the table, setting her candle in front of her.

Grant frowned. "I have no desire to discuss this."

Anne shrugged, as if his wishes were unimportant. "I like her."

"Why is it women are always so free with their advice?" he asked angrily. "Why can't you ever accept what a man says and leave it at that? Which reminds me, Anne, were you really smoking this evening?"

Anne waved a hand at him. "You aren't my husband, so don't adopt that tone with me. And please give me credit for some good sense. I didn't smoke. I was only teasing Jane." A slow smile spread across her face. "Of course, I seriously thought about doing it. Every once in a while it's fun to try the forbidden. Makes me feel like less of a matron."

"Matron? You're only thirty-one."

"And you are thirty and more than ripe for marriage. What I want to know is, why you are down here and not up sharing the marriage bed with your wife?"

He shoved his fists in his pockets and moved around the table away from her. "I didn't realize you were capable of being this direct, Anne," he said irritably.

"Bearing four children does that to a

woman, Grant. Now, what is the matter?"

He pulled a hand out of his pocket and combed his fingers through his hair before admitting, "We don't suit each other."

"I found myself thinking today that you two are very much alike."

"Have both you and Jane gone daft? She told me Phadra was perfect for me. I don't understand why two of the people closest to me can't see that we are complete opposites."

Anne leaned across the table. Her gray eyes, so much like his, caught the candlelight. "I find her much like you. She's good, kind, intelligent, generous —"

"Generous enough to waste hundreds of pounds entertaining!"

"She did it to help you," Jane's voice chimed in. She walked into the room, rubbing her back. "And you'd do the same if you thought it would help us. One of the reasons Anne and I are sleeping on the parlor sofas tonight is because you gave us the furniture from the bedrooms upstairs to help us set up our households, and would have given us the parlor furniture too if we'd let you. Believe me, Grant, not every brother is as generous as you."

She sat down in the chair next to her older sister. "Phadra thought that if she did a good job with the party, it would help your fortunes with the bank. She only wanted to please you, Grant."

He faced them across the table. "Well, it didn't help, did it?"

"Only because you decided to throw an earl out of your house by the seat of the pants," Anne observed dryly. "None of us expected the party to grow so big or so wild. And certainly no one thought that Lofton would attack Phadra."

Grant hated being reminded of his own part in the disaster. But when he'd entered this very room and seen Phadra holding off the bastard — "I don't want to argue about it, Anne. This is between myself and Phadra."

"Well, there is something I do want to talk about, brother of mine, and it is between us," Anne said.

"What is that?" he asked curtly.

"I heard what you said when I came into the room."

Grant went very still.

She pinned him with her gaze. "Father's dead, Grant. He's gone. You can't fight him. He's not here."

"I don't know what you are talking about."

"Yes, you do. Oh, I'll be the first to admit

414

that Papa left a reputation that may last forever, but when he was sober, he could also be a caring, loving man. We did have some good times. Not all the memories are bad, Grant."

"The ones I have are."

"But you've never told us about them," Jane said. "I mean, I know you and Papa used to go places together whenever you came home from school, and then it seemed that something terrible happened and Papa died in that duel, and now you rarely mention his name or let us say it." She paused. "I remember how scared I was, but you were there, Grant, and you kept telling me that everything would be all right." Her eyes filled with unshed tears. "And you were right. It did turn out fine, although I miss both Mama and Papa." She smiled up at him, her expression sad. "I love you, Grant, but I wish you had told us. Then maybe you wouldn't be so angry."

"I'm not angry," he denied, knowing even as he said the words that he lied.

"No, not now," Jane quickly agreed with him. "Because now you have Phadra."

Her answer surprised him. Jane went on, "This afternoon I was talking to Phadra about Papa and the picnics we used to have. Remember how much fun they were? And I gained the impression that she knew something about you and Papa. Something you haven't told us."

His sister's innocent observation made him suddenly feel naked.

Anne, who had been silently watching both of them, echoed Jane's question. "Does she know, Grant?"

At that moment someone pounded the brass knocker on the front door. Relieved to remove himself from his sisters' too-astute observations, he left the dining room and answered the door himself instead of waiting for Wallace.

On his doorstep stood a liveried servant. With a flourish he handed Grant a letter. "His lordship bids me to return with an answer."

Grant broke the seal on the letter and stepped toward the candle Anne held up for him. The letter was from Lofton. He demanded satisfaction and expected to meet Grant in the park at dawn. He gave Grant the choice of weapon.

Leaving the servant standing on his step, Grant went back to his study. In bold pen strokes, he wrote a reply agreeing to the meeting. His choice of weapon was swords. His expression grim, he also penned another quick note to Duroy asking him to serve as his second. He rang for Wallace.

"I don't understand dueling," Anne said.

Grant looked up to find her standing by the edge of his desk, her arm wrapped protectively around a white-faced Jane. "Most women don't," he answered, thinking of Phadra specifically.

"You're going to go through with it?" Anne asked.

"I have no choice."

Anne pressed her lips together and then spoke her thoughts out loud. "You're a fool, Grant."

"Go to bed, Anne." To his surprise, she did just that, taking an obviously upset Jane with her.

After Wallace and Lofton's servant left, Grant sat for a long time in his study alone. The ticking of a clock on the mantel measured the passage of time, but in his mind Grant lived in the past. For the first time he allowed himself to remember.

Scenes played in his mind, scenes of moments he'd thought he'd erased from his memory, never to be retrieved again. His father had taught him the finer points of swordplay and had encouraged his love for the sport.

And his father's laughter. Grant surprised himself that he could vividly recall the sound of that laughter. He fell asleep with the sound of it echoing in his mind.

The next morning Wallace woke him a half hour before dawn. Grant moved stiffly, his muscles, especially in his shoulder, sore from spending the night in a chair in his study instead of in his bed. That thought chased him as he silently climbed the stairs and entered his bedroom. No candle burned, but he could see in the moonlight that Phadra slept on the bed right where he'd left her. Still dressed in the yellow and blue dress from the night before, she hadn't even climbed under the covers but had snuggled under the jacket that he had so carelessly tossed upon the bed.

Grant moved quietly so that he wouldn't disturb her as he changed for his meeting with Lofton. When he was about to leave, he stopped and then walked over to the chest at the foot of the bed. Taking out a blanket, he tucked it around her. It was then he noticed that she held a book in her arms. Gently he pulled it away from her. Mary Wollstonecraft's *A Vindication of the Rights of Woman*. He should have known.

Setting the book aside on the bedside table, he noticed that the leather was damp. Pressing his fingers gently to the pillow under her cheek, he could feel the evidence of her tears.

A wave of regret washed over him. He'd botched everything he'd touched lately. If Phadra were wise, she'd put distance between them. They were both too headstrong, and judging by the way matters had been progressing, he couldn't ever imagine the two of them making a marriage work — no matter what Jane and Anne said. He ran the back of his fingers along the smooth line of her cheek, the skin warm and vibrant beneath his touch.

Then he quietly left the room.

Chapter 18

Under dark, threatening skies, Grant met Lofton in the park for the duel and dispatched him with a ruthlessness that was almost ungentlemanly. Those privileged to watch the duel were stunned by Grant's superior swordsmanship. He showed the earl no mercy. After he had unarmed Lofton for the third time, his sword point aimed at the man's heart, the earl finally, bitterly, admitted that his honor was satisfied.

Offering Grant his coat and hat, Duroy noted quietly, "You've made an enemy." But Grant's concern wasn't centered on Lofton. Instead he caught himself scanning the road for signs of his wayward wife.

She hadn't come to rescue him this time. He felt strangely disappointed.

Grant immediately left for his office at the bank, chased there by questions for which he had no answers. The day before, he had known what he wanted; he had known how to get it. Now, however, he didn't even understand himself, let alone know which direction to take. Unfortunately, throwing himself into his work didn't make the questions go away.

The summons from Sir Robert to meet him in the Court Room came late in the morning. When Grant arrived, he discovered the governor wasn't alone. All the members of the Court sat gathered around one side of a long table. With a sense of foreboding, Grant entered and stood at the opposite side of the table. He nodded his respects to Sir Robert and the others — except for Sir Cecil, who refused to look at him, staring at his thumbnail instead.

Sir Robert, sitting in the middle of the group, cleared his throat, gaining everyone's attention.

So, Grant thought, *I'm about to be sacked.* Lofton worked fast.

Clearing his throat again, Sir Robert placed both hands on the table, stood, and announced with great ceremony, "Morgan, you've got to control your wife."

"Control my wife?" Grant repeated. He looked around the table, surprised by the seriousness of their expressions and the intent way they appeared to be waiting for his answer. "Gentlemen, if I knew how to do that, I would have exercised the power days, weeks ago," he admitted candidly.

His response was evidently not the one Sir Robert sought. Dumbarton rapped the table with his knuckles, emphasizing each word as he said, "This morning my wife ordered the papers delivered to *her* before I'd had a chance to read them. When I informed her that I always received the papers first, she answered that I would have to wait my turn. She wanted to read about what Parliament was up to." He sat back in his chair and glared at Grant. "I never thought she knew what Parliament was other than that its opening signaled the beginning of the season."

"Excuse me, sir," Grant said, not certain that he understood the bank's governor correctly, "but you're saying that you are upset with me because you didn't get the papers first this morning?"

"I always get the papers first," Sir Robert answered. "It's my home. My papers. Or at least they were mine, until Lady Dumbarton met your wife. I ordered her to turn them over but she informed me, as cheeky as you please, that since she had brought most of the property into our marriage, I could deduct the price of the papers from that amount — and she went right on reading!"

"Well, at least she isn't jingling around!" shouted Sir Henry. "I know exactly where my wife is because she's wearing blasted bells, just like Mrs. Morgan. When I told her she sounded silly, she laughed at me. She said it was all good fun. I told her she was too old to be fun, and now she won't talk to me. Plus I have to put damned cotton in my ears to keep the jingling and ringing out. There's no peace in my house. No peace at all!"

"Your problems are only beginning, gentlemen," Sir James jumped in, the lines of his long face, so much like his wife's, set in a frown of displeasure. "When I left the house, my wife was dipping pen in ink to invite all of her acquaintances" — he looked around at the others sitting on his side of the table so that they knew their wives were included in that group — "to form a women's club."

"Certainly there is nothing wrong with that," Grant protested mildly.

"That's a matter of opinion, Morgan," Sir James shot back. "She's not planning a whist club or a music club or any of those other foolish things women do to keep themselves busy. Seems your wife told Emma some folderol about your saving a pregnant doxy from a beating by some jack named Mad Bob and sending her home to her parents. She put a queer notion in Emma's head that women of means should help their more unfortunate sisters living in the streets, and that's what Emma wants her club to do." He slapped his hand down on the table. "I informed Emma she already has a sister, who lives in Chelsea. She didn't need to go out looking for sisters."

"And was that the end of it?" Sir Victor asked.

"No!" Sir James practically barked at him. "We had a loud and angry argument, and then she said it didn't make any difference what I commanded her to do because she was going to do as she pleased. With that she walked out of the room as if she were the Queen herself, before I'd finished speaking!" He waved an accusing finger at Grant. "She's never gainsaid me, not once in twenty-two years of marriage, and then, within four and twenty hours of knowing your wife . . ." He clapped his hands together for effect, then sat back and grumbled, "A man doesn't want to argue with his wife. If I want to argue, I can go argue with my mistress. I need my wife to know her place." The others around the table nodded their agreement.

Sir Robert stood, commanding the attention of all in the room. "Morgan, Sir James makes an important point. You may have one of the finest financial minds in the bank, mayhap even this country, but frankly, I'm worried about your future here. A man's wife is either an asset or a liability. Yours is turning into a liability. Furthermore, there are those among us, Morgan, who have received particularly bitter complaints from the Earl of Lofton and Dame Edith Cunnington. I fear that if we were to take a vote now, you'd be summarily dismissed. However, Sir Cecil believes you should be given another chance and has argued eloquently on your behalf."

Grant shot a look at Sir Cecil. The man glanced up, turned red in the face, and then looked down at his thumbnail again, confirming Grant's worst suspicions. If Sir Cecil was championing his cause, he had to have another motive. The idea of a future spent at the man's beck and call didn't sit well with Grant.

Then Sir Robert grabbed his complete attention by announcing, "You have twenty-four hours, Morgan, to get your house in order. If you are unable to do so in that amount of time, we'll have no recourse other than to take action against you."

For several seconds Grant stared at him,

scarcely able to believe his ears. After all the time and service he'd given them, they'd sack him because of his wife?

He straightened his shoulders, made a perfunctory bow, and without another word turned on his heel and walked out the door. He left the bank.

The sky still threatened a storm by the time he reached his house. He stood on the walk outside and stared up at the black lacquered front door, still feeling confused by the sudden turn of events. Could anyone control Phadra? He hadn't even been able to make a wife of her yet! That knowledge surely would have set the directors' tongues wagging!

The bitter truth, he answered himself, was that perhaps they didn't suit each other. If that was the case, perhaps he should let her go. Annul the marriage.

He didn't like the solution.

The door of the servants' entrance opened, and Mrs. Shaunessy walked out and up the steps, her marketing basket over one arm. She stopped short at the sight of him. "Good day to you, Mr. Morgan."

Grant managed a smile. "Good day, Mrs. Shaunessy."

The woman walked past him, giving him a decidedly peculiar look, and went on her way. Grant watched her go, his mind still working over his problem . . . and then a thought struck him.

If he was entrusted with a matter for the bank, he would look for information and advice from someone who understood the situation better than he did. Why was his problem with Phadra any different? And whom did he know who understood her better than Henrietta Shaunessy?

Grant's long legs quickly closed the distance between them. He startled her when he slipped his arm through the handle of the basket. "May I help you?"

She slid him a suspicious look but let the basket go. They walked a few paces before she asked, "What do you want, Mr. Morgan?"

He gave her his most charming smile. "Why do you believe I want anything at all?"

At one time such a smile would have melted her resistance, but now she snorted in disbelief. "You give yourself away, sir. You never have time to waste." She took her basket from him. "What is it you want?"

They walked a considerable distance toward the small shopping district close to his home while he debated how much of the truth he should tell her. Mrs. Shaunessy stopped by a fruit vendor's stand before he'd reached a decision. She reached for the oranges and then pursed her lips in indecision. Finally she reached instead for a cluster of purple grapes. She looked up at him and smiled. "The oranges are Phadra's favorite but too expensive. Economies, you know."

He ignored her gentle jibe. "You've known Phadra for some time, haven't you, Mrs. Shaunessy?"

She snapped shut her purse after paying the fruit man and gave him a sweet smile. "Longer than you have, sir." Abruptly she turned on her heel and walked through the crowd toward the next stall.

Grant followed quickly, sidestepping the fruit man. "So how did you meet?"

She stopped suddenly and looked up at him. "Why do you want to know?"

Her effrontery caught him off guard. "Because she's my wife."

The redhead gave him a slow, hard look up and down before raising her eyebrows. "Is she, indeed?"

An uncomfortable heat stole up his neck. "She is."

Mrs. Shaunessy hummed her thoughts on that and casually walked over to an apothecary's shop where vinegars were set outside on display. She picked up a bottle, pulled out the stopper, and gave the contents a sniff. Her nose scrunched at the smell of it.

Grant stood waiting.

She set the vinegar down, pushed one of her outrageously red curls back under her bonnet, and said, "I met her the first day she arrived in London, green as fresh hay with that book of hers about women tucked under her arm. She needed someone to look after her."

"And you were where at the time?"

Mrs. Shaunessy's back stiffened. "I'd fallen on hard times, sir, and I'm not ashamed to admit it." She looked at him. "It isn't easy for a woman alone." There was a wealth of unspoken meaning in those words.

Grant took the basket from her. "Then she was lucky it was you who found her."

At his words some of her defensive starchiness seemed to relax. "Aye, there are those who would have taken her purse and *more* in no time," she confessed. "But something drew me to her. Maybe it was those big, shining eyes or the way she told everyone who passed that she'd come to London to start the search for her father. Said she wanted to make a home for him."

And there was something in the way

Henrietta Shaunessy said the word *home* that made Grant understand Phadra's appeal for the woman. Henrietta Shaunessy had been another of Phadra's strays — just like pregnant Sarah and Wallace and Jem and probably the little lady's maid.

Mrs. Shaunessy picked up another vinegar, sniffed it, and apparently found it to her liking. She held it out to the shopkeeper and then started to take out her purse.

"I'll get it." He started to reach for his coin purse.

"No. This is a gift for Phadra. I'll pay for it with my own."

While she handed her coins over to the shopkeeper, Grant watched the bustle and activity of the market even in spite of the approaching storm. Some vendors began moving their wares to shelter, but most tried for that last sale before the customers were driven back indoors. He began to enjoy the sight of commerce taking place and wondered why he hadn't ever made the trip down there before now. Someone bumped his arm.

Turning, he discovered a woman with a basket of flowers done up in nosegays. "Flowers, sir?" she asked, but the husky tone of her voice told him that she offered more than flowers.

430

"I'm done with my shopping, Mr. Morgan," Mrs. Shaunessy said, stepping smoothly between them and forcing the woman away with a hard stare. Mrs. Shaunessy looked up at him, her brown eyes sharp. "You know, don't you, that Phadra is one woman who won't hop in a man's lap just because he possesses a handsome face?" Without waiting for an answer, she started walking back in the direction of the house.

Grant followed. "What do you mean?"

The wind had picked up, and Mrs. Shaunessy placed a hand on the brim of her bonnet to hold it in place as she hurried along. "If you have to ask, Mr. Morgan, then you've just confirmed something I've long thought."

He reached out and pulled Mrs. Shaunessy up short under the branches of a good-sized oak. "And what is that?"

"That there are some men who are too handsome for their own good." She poked her finger at his chest impudently. "They are so used to having women throw themselves at them, they don't understand that occasionally they have to work for what they want."

"And you think I'm one of those?"

"I *know* you are one of those." She crossed her arms against her chest. "You should hear yourself, sir. You've ordered, berated, and growled. You've done everything but say what a woman wants to hear, and I think the only reason you haven't done that is because you don't know how."

"How to what?"

"Woo her. Win her."

Grant studied her a moment, as if she'd spoken in a foreign language. "Woo her?"

The plumes on Mrs. Shaunessy's bonnet bobbed and bounced in the wind. "Court her," she said with some exasperation, and then took the basket from his hands. "Mr. Morgan, I can't tell you how it's done. You have to think of that for yourself. But so far, in spite of being miserably clumsy about the business, you've been surprisingly successful."

"Successful?"

She rolled her eyes heavenward. "Can't you see? Are you that blind? The child is half in love with you already."

"She is?" This information astounded him, and then he discovered that he quite liked the thought of it.

"Yes," Mrs. Shaunessy said, then added darkly, "and I don't know how you did it. But love is a fragile thing, sir. It can be killed as quickly as it can be planted. If you take my advice, you'll treat her love as a very precious gift. Because it is."

Grant didn't answer. Already his analytical mind was weighing the possibilities. Phadra . . . in love with him. Could love make her bend to his will?

Mrs. Shaunessy shot him a suspicious look and, almost as if she could read his mind, frowned. "I'm beginning to regret I ever said anything. A woman could make better use of her time talking to a stone wall than trying to make her point with a man," she muttered. "Have it your way, then, but in the end, don't forget that Henrietta Shaunessy warned you!" She turned sharply on her heel and walked toward home.

Grant barely listened to her. Instead he stood under the oak, thinking. The more he thought, the more the challenge of winning Phadra intrigued him. After several minutes of concentrated mental activity, he smiled slowly and then walked down the street, back toward the market.

Outside the parlor windows, the rain began to fall, a dismal sprinkling at first, which grew steadily stronger as the minutes passed until it felt like the very heavens had opened up to rain down on London town.

Wearing her oldest dress, a serge uniform from her days at Miss Agatha's, Phadra sat on the floor of the parlor and watched the rain. Her hands absently twisted the bottle of scented vinegar that Henny had given her — "to improve your spirits," Henny had said. The cluster of grapes sat on a plate on a sofa table, untouched.

She'd already cleaned every square inch of the parlor, throwing herself into the household chore to escape the decision she felt she had to make, must make . . . and felt no closer to knowing her own mind than when she had woken late that morning with red-rimmed eyes and a dry throat.

She was a wife who wasn't a wife. A daughter without a father. A woman who'd lost her identity before she could gain it.

And in the middle of all the questions was Grant. Her chest tightened.

She'd come to London wanting something more from her life. Now she felt trapped. Trapped in a marriage to a man who didn't want her, just as her mother had been.

Squeezing her hands together around the cool bottle of vinegar, she wished Anne and Jane hadn't left that morning. Each had kissed her like a sister when they said their good-byes and had promised that everything would be all right. They'd even repeated the sentiment.

With sudden decision she came up on her knees and set the bottle of vinegar on the table, her fingers still loosely around it. *Enough!* She took a deep, slow breath and reached deep inside her, searching for strength. Tears welled up again, but she fought them back.

Yes, he was handsome, strong, noble, and a hundred other things that made him almost Sir Galahad reincarnated. He was also cold, dictatorial, stubborn, handsome — she decided his good looks weighed for *and* against him! — self-centered, arrogant . . .

A sound at the door interrupted her list of faults. "Henny, I asked you to leave me alone." She shot a look over her shoulder, bracing herself for another of Henny's well-meaning lectures, and froze.

Grant stood in the doorway, looking more devilishly handsome than she'd ever seen him. He'd removed his coat and neckcloth. His hair was wet; apparently he'd been caught in the storm. The thought struck her that he looked more casual than she'd ever seen him — except, of course, for that night in the inn.

Unbidden memories brought heat to her cheeks. She rose to her feet and made a pretense of centering the bottle of vinegar on the table. Had he noticed her blush? Could he see how just his presence seemed to throw all of her emotions in turmoil?

She drew another deep breath. "Grant, we have to talk —"

"I want to show you something —"

They both spoke at the same time, their words tumbling over one another, and then stopped.

For a second the only sound in the room was that of the falling rain outside. He broke the silence first, his silver-gray eyes solemn. "Come with me, and we can talk." He held his hand out to her.

Phadra didn't know if it would be such a wise idea right then to touch him. She pushed her hands into the folds of her skirt. "I've been doing a great deal of thinking about us."

"So have I."

"You have?"

He smiled, an easy, heart-stopping smile that set off strange fluttery yearnings inside her. "Why does that surprise you?" he asked, pushing away from the doorway. He crossed the room toward her, his steps slow and deliberate.

"Perhaps because I've never imagined you giving me a second's thought," she answered candidly, taking a shy, skittish step away from him before she forced herself to stand still.

Grant stopped, leaving the width of the sofa between them. "That's certainly not true."

"It's not?" she asked. Her throat tightened on the words, and she looked down at her hands, tightly clasped in front of her.

He came closer until he stood so near that his feet brushed the hem of her dress. That was when she realized that he was moving in his stockinged feet. The sight of the lines of his long toes through the thin stocking material seemed too intimate. It was the sort of thing that a wife, a true wife, one who shared her husband's bed, would accept as a matter of course. The lump started to form in her throat again. She looked away, staring hard at the colored bottle of vinegar instead.

"Phadra, look at me."

She didn't; she couldn't. Instead she squeezed her hands together and said, "I've been doing a great deal of thinking." The words came out rehearsed, but at least her voice didn't shake, even with the rest of her body literally humming at the nearness of him. She forced herself to get the words out in a rush before her resolve wavered. "I don't think you will ever be the kind of husband I need or —" She paused slightly, knowing she was about to lie. "— desire." *Why did he have to stand so close?* she thought. She could feel the heat of his body right through her serge uniform. Drawing in a slow, deep breath, she finished in a voice so low that she was almost whispering, "And I don't think I can be the wife you want."

Again, the only sound in the room was that of the falling rain — and her own hammering heart.

And then he touched her. One long finger traced the line of her chin, tilting her head up. He studied her features intently, and she was certain he read the truth as plainly as if she'd written it on paper for him. His hand came down on her shoulder and followed the curve of her arm until his hand covered hers.

"Come," was all he said, and she released the tight hold of her hands and let him curl his fingers around hers. Their fingers laced together — and he smiled. "Come."

Phadra didn't want to follow him. She knew she shouldn't. But when he turned and walked to the door, she followed.

He led her down the hallway toward the back stairs, moving silently on his stockinged feet. She caught herself tiptoeing, as if they didn't want Wallace or

Henny to know what they were up to. At the stairs he pulled her arm through his and shot her a glance that was so boyish in its appeal, she almost missed the step.

On the second floor he drew her down the carpeted hallway toward the bedroom, the one they had yet to share.

Phadra slowed her steps to a stop and dug her heels into the carpet. "I'm not so sure this is a good idea," she said stiffly.

Grant didn't say anything but opened the door and stepped aside, waiting patiently for her to enter.

Phadra frowned at him. "No." If she entered that bedroom, she'd be like a Christian entering the lions' den, and could get gobbled up just as quickly, too. But then, through the open door, she caught a flash of color that had not been there before and the fresh, full scent of . . . flowers.

She took a step to the door and peered in. Her breath caught in her throat in wonder. He'd transformed the bedroom into a flower garden. Marigolds, asters, roses, bluebells, gladioli, and daisies created a riot of color. The rain fell gently now, and its light breeze made the curtains billow and teased the flower heads.

Phadra walked in, her mouth open in surprise — and delight. The flowers had been arranged around a blanket laid out at the foot of the bed. On the blanket sat an orange. "What is this?" she asked, turning back to Grant.

He'd closed the door and was leaning against it, watching her. To her amazement, he looked slightly embarrassed. "A picnic. It's a pretty poor one, but after I purchased the flowers . . ." His voice trailed off.

"A picnic?" She mouthed the words.

"I thought it would please you. Mrs. Shaunessy said oranges are your favorite." He took a step to stand beside her before saying, "It does look rather silly."

"No," Phadra said immediately. "It doesn't look silly."

His eyes met hers. "It doesn't?"

"No." She looked away first, all too aware of his presence, of his nearness. Even over the heady scent of flowers, she could make out the clean, strong scent of his shaving soap and realized that he'd shaved. For this? For her?

Phadra shifted nervously and stepped away from him, around to the other side of the blanket. She faced him. "Grant, why are you doing this?"

He frowned slightly. "It's only a picnic, Phadra."

She looked around at the flowers, the

blanket . . . the bed. She shot him a skeptical look.

Grant ignored it. Instead he stepped into the makeshift bower and sat down on the blanket, stretching his long legs out. He looked up at her standing straight-backed and proud. "Join me."

Her eyes flashed down at him and then looked away, but in that blink of a moment he'd seen what she wouldn't have wanted him to see: the vulnerability, the hurt. At that moment he realized what Mrs. Shaunessy had been trying to tell him. His brave, proud Phadra. Didn't she understand? He'd honor his wedding vows. He'd never abandon her as her father had done. He always honored his word.

Grant sat up. "When I was a child, we used to have picnics every time Father came home. And if the weather was bad, Father used to order the servants to set it up in the sitting room, and we'd play and tumble over the furniture as if we were outside." He raised his knee and leaned forward to balance his arm on it, watching her intently as he confided, "Those were my favorites, the indoor picnics on rainy days."

"I don't remember ever being on a picnic," she said, her voice almost wistful. How fortunate he was to have come from a family with siblings and a father, however errant, making an appearance in his life. "Mama and I may have had them. I don't remember."

"Then join me." He held his hand up to her.

Phadra wanted to take his hand. She wanted to with every beat of her heart — but she couldn't.

"Phadra?"

Dear sweet Lord, how she loved the sound of her name on his lips. She struggled with indecision.

"Phadra, it's only a picnic."

No, Grant! she wanted to shout. *It's so much more. Because if I give in to you, I'll never have that part of myself back. I'll never be whole. Not ever.*

Closing her eyes, she drew in a deep breath. "Grant, I don't think either of us knows how to be a good husband or wife to the other." There. She'd said it.

Phadra's direct honesty caught him off guard — and it stung. Once he'd decided to marry, it had never occurred to him that any woman would find him lacking. He rose up on his knees. "I don't think either of us knows the other well enough to make that judgment."

She looked at the blanket spread out on

the floor, the flowers — and the man. "And how will we get to know each other? By tumbling around on the furniture?" Immediately her cheeks grew warm at the double entendre of her words.

His eyes danced, and a slow, easy grin spread across his face. "We might."

Her whole being responded to those words. Traitorously, her whole body suddenly felt warm. Her breathing stopped. And there, at the very core of her, she felt the very distinct singing of desire.

Outside, the rain started coming down harder, the sound mingling with the rapid beating of her heart. No other sound disturbed them. It was as if they were alone, isolated from the rest of the world.

And it would be so easy to set their differences aside.

Grant reached up to her again. Almost against her will, she placed her hand in his and felt the warm reassurance of his fingers closing over hers. He didn't have to pull very hard to bring her down to the floor closer to him. His eyes had turned darker, smokier, and Phadra could swear she could feel his heart beating as rapidly as her own was beating at that moment. "Phadra?" He didn't just say her name; he tasted it, savored it.

She couldn't answer. What little of her sanity she had left warned her that this wasn't what she wanted. That if she gave in now, she'd regret it later.

But another part of her, almost all the rest of her, wanted to whisper, "Oh, yes . . ." Perhaps she really had said those words aloud, because slowly, almost reverently, Grant leaned closer until his lips touched hers.

And that was all it took. In the next second she rose up to meet him. His arms wrapped around her, pulling her closer to him, and in that moment Phadra knew that the spark she'd tried so hard to deny had a life of its own.

Chapter 19

For one brief second Grant sensed her resistance — and then felt her capitulation as she practically melted into his arms. Fierce pride surged through him, mingling with the heady, sweet need of desire. He didn't kiss but devoured — and Phadra met him all the way.

In a sudden decision, he rose to his feet in one fluid motion, lifting her up in his arms. Her lips broke from his. "What are you doing? What about your shoulder?" Her arms tightened around his neck as he stepped over the flowers.

"My shoulder's fine, and for this first time I want us on this bed. Our bed." The bed ropes creaked slightly as he laid her on the lavender-scented sheets and stretched out beside her.

When her hands came up to his shoulders to hold him off, he saw the slight hesitancy, the apprehension in her eyes.

"Phadra, don't be afraid. I won't hurt

you. I won't . . ." He let his soft promise drift off as he lowered his head and kissed the soft skin under her chin. So sweet. What did she have to fear? He was her husband. . . . He wanted this, and if she didn't realize how much he wanted, needed, their joining, she was about to find out.

But then, she was Phadra. Unique, unpredictable Phadra.

And she was his. Even without the marriage ceremony, some elemental part of him knew that she was his, had always been his — maybe even from the moment when he'd first seen her standing in proud defiance in Sir Cecil's office. Suddenly he didn't want to wait or linger. He wanted to be inside her, claiming her, possessing her.

Again her fingers pressed into his shoulders, refusing to let him come closer. "Grant, are we doing the right thing?"

He wanted to groan his frustration, to push aside her resistance. But he didn't. Instead he held himself back, his lips poised six inches over hers. Looking into her bright, clear eyes, he whispered, "Oh, Phadra, for once let's set reason and arguments aside and just kiss."

The resistance in her fingers relaxed; her lips parted slightly. Never had he received a sweeter invitation. He leaned closer, burying his fingers in the wild mass of her glorious hair, and kissed her — joyously, fully, wantonly — and, dear sweet God, she met him with a passion to rival his own. Her arms slipped around his head and pulled him closer to her. Why had he been such a fool and wasted time fighting with her when kissing her was so much more pleasurable, so much more fulfilling?

Slipping his fingers down into the folds of her dress, he started searching for the hooks and buttons. Releasing them would let him come so much closer. He lowered his mouth to nuzzle the underside of her chin, the curve of her jawline, the hollow behind her ear. A sound escaped from low in her throat, a feminine sound of need and the pleasure of discovery. It set off an answering response thrumming through his veins. And her hair . . . it smelled of sunlight and wild grass. Her skin tasted warm and rich, like honey. He wanted more, so much more — and so he practically roared with frustration when he'd undone a line of hooks and still found his way barred by heavy material.

He broke the kiss and leaned back. "This damn dress has more trappings and hidden folds than an officer's uniform."

Her lips, ruby red from kissing, curved into an innocently teasing smile. "And have you tried to undo many officers' uniforms?"

He arched an eyebrow in mock challenge. "What do you think?"

"Well . . . ," she hedged before he wrapped his hands around her waist, pulled her up to him, and kissed her as if he could drink her soul. It felt so right. Dear God, it felt so right.

When he finished kissing her, he didn't know who was more befuddled, Phadra or himself. Drawing in a deep breath, her wide eyes glazed with passion, Phadra reached up and under the front collar of the dress. Her fingers twisted and released the hidden button from its buttonhole, letting the neckline fall open to reveal the curves and valleys of her breasts.

"Beautiful," he murmured, bending his head toward them. Then her hands stopped him.

"Now it's your turn," she said.

Startled, Grant stared at her for a moment until he saw the gleam of challenge, and hunger, in her eyes. He tipped back his head and laughed. "Are we to be equal in this also?"

She came up on her elbows to look him straight in the eye. "Can we?"

"Oh, yes," he promised, and pulled his shirt over his head and tossed it aside.

Phadra's reaction was everything he wanted and more, for when she reached up to run her hands over the hard lines of his chest, her fingers lightly touching the bandage, he stopped them. "Now it's your turn." Her eyes opened wide, blinking in surprise. "Everything equal," he reminded her, finding this love play intriguing. He rolled over on his back and, with a pretense of casualness he was far from feeling, placed his hands behind his head as if he had all day.

Phadra looked at him, and then a slow, sure smile spread across her face as she accepted his challenge. Kicking off her shoes, she stood up on the bed, her feet shifting to help her keep her balance. She reached down and gathered her dress up around her waist, then slipped it over her head. Her hair caught in her skirts before tumbling down wildly around her face and shoulders, several long curls brushing over the high curves of her breast.

She looked beautiful, wanton, desirable. For a blessed moment he forgot to breathe. "Willful wife," he whispered, and then rose up on his knees to meet her. "Wonderful wife." His hands pushed up the cotton of her petticoat, his palm running up the back of her leg. "Willing wife," he finished as almost reverently he bent down and placed his lips against the tender white skin of her inner thigh.

She gasped, as if the sound had been surprised out of her, and then seemed to hold her breath as he tasted her, his lips touching first the inside of one thigh and then the other, working his way slowly upward.

She tasted as cool and smooth as buttermilk. He didn't want to frighten her, but how he wanted to taste her, to touch her! Gently he urged her to open to him, and she obeyed, her weight relaxing in his arms, the very essence of her dewy and soft. For a second her hands fluttered as if she didn't know what to do with them . . . and then she laid them against his head, her fingers curling in his hair. Her breath escaped in a low, sweet moan, and he smiled.

Suddenly Grant was done playing games. He lowered her to the bed in his arms, his skillful fingers unlacing her corset, loosening the tapes holding her petticoat.

"Grant?"

"Don't, Phadra. Don't let it frighten you."

She looked at him then, her eyes clear and sparkling. "I'm not afraid. I want this."

"Oh, Phadra, when you look at me like that . . ." His voice trailed off as he lowered his head and closed his mouth over her breast, drawing the sensitive nipple in with his tongue as if sipping nectar.

She cried out his name, the sound lost in the rhythm of the rain. Her hands smoothed the muscles of his back before pressing him against her, a silent plea for more. He obliged while pushing and pulling the last of her cotton and linen undergarments down around her knees, at which point she helped him by kicking them off her feet until she lay naked, open and panting for him.

Grant rolled off the bed and onto his feet. Unbuttoning his breeches, he hooked his hands in the waist and pushed them down over his hips. He lay back on the bed and, cradling her in his arms, kissed her, running his hand down the smooth, soft skin of her arm, over her back, and along the curve of her buttocks. "You're beautiful," he whispered as he slipped his hand between their bodies to the very sensitive center of her femininity. She was ready for him. More than ready. At the first brush of his fingers against her, her flesh quivered as if aching for his touch.

He was barely able to control his own body as she arched and moved naturally to his touch. He didn't want to scare her. He didn't want to hurt her. But he wanted her.

Nothing he'd known before this moment

compared to this primal desire racing through his body. Grant lifted himself up and on top of her, letting her feel the strength of his heat between her thighs. She moaned slightly, the sound captured in his mouth, and moved against him.

She pressed her breasts, the nipples hard and firm, against his chest, her arms hugging him closer, and Grant accepted that as her consent. Ever so steadily, he pressed himself into her.

Nothing could feel sweeter, or tighter, than Phadra. The feeling of her adjusting to fit his size was almost his undoing, and yet the desire to please, to make her first time wonderful, overrode his own needs. His mind half mad with lust, he pushed through the barrier of her maidenhead and claimed her as his wife, burying himself deep inside her.

His penetration into the deepest recesses of her body shocked her. He held himself still, letting her accustom herself to the feel of him.

"Are you all right?" He raised himself, favoring his good arm, and looked down at her, his gray eyes smoky.

"I don't know," she confessed. "Are we still taking turns?"

His eyes turned light with surprise and

then laughter, a laughter she could feel to the very core of her being. It felt good.

"No," he admitted gently. "In this we're as one." Then he kissed her so deeply, so tenderly, all fears were erased from her mind.

When he moved, she discovered she moved with him. He began whispering her name with each stroke, the sound hypnotizing her and encouraging her to meet him and find pleasure.

She didn't know what she was searching for; she didn't know what he wanted. But it seemed right to have his body cover hers, and as she relaxed he became her guide, taking her to places she had never known existed.

He kissed her now, his tongue entering her until she felt herself full of him — and still she wanted more. When she wrapped her arm around the still-sensitive area near his wound, he pushed away from her, telling her to lower her hand until it rested on the hard curve of his buttocks so that she could better communicate what she wanted.

This felt natural, felt *right*. She let him know that she wanted more. More, more, more . . . her movements came faster, and he kept pace with her, kissing and stroking her until . . . until . . . with a startled cry, she found it.

Hearing her gasp of wonder, Grant pushed deeper inside her, surprised by the strength of her release. Her eyes opened wide with knowledge and deepened with sudden understanding as contraction after contraction flowed through her and to him. Then, and only then, did he seek his release, letting his seed spill into her in the most satisfying, most soul-fulfilling act of sex he'd ever experienced.

For one long moment he held her to him as if he'd never let her go, and then, rolling to his side and gathering her close to him, he fell asleep, his senses filled with the touch and taste of Phadra and the steady rhythm of the rain.

Cradled in the haven of his body, the heady scent of their lovemaking mingling with the fragrance of flowers, she listened to the rain and relived over and over what had passed between them.

It was better than fairy tales, magic, and Chinese fireworks rolled up into one.

For the first time since her mother's death, she felt close to another human being.

For the first time in her life, she felt complete.

Phadra didn't remember falling asleep

but when she woke it was to find herself held in his arms, her back hugged against his chest, her buttocks curved to fit his hips, and the heat of him moving inside her body. He wouldn't let her stir but held her body in place with those wickedly knowledgeable fingers while he took her to heights she hadn't thought possible. It was possessive. It was hard. It was wonderful.

Afterward they sat on the bed while he peeled the orange with his long, tapered swordsman's fingers and talked — about nothing, about everything. Even when they sucked the juice from the orange and no words were exchanged, she felt the two of them to be in perfect harmony.

"It's just as you said," she whispered, half to herself.

"What is?" He looked over at her, offering her another slice of the orange.

She took it, her fingers brushing lightly against his, and even that slight contact excited a response from her body. "I feel as though a part of me has joined with you and become one."

Grant leaned toward her, his long legs stretching out intimately against hers, and pulled her closer. "That's the way it is supposed to be between a man and a woman."

"Like this?" she asked, her eyes looking

up into his light gray ones.

He brushed the back of his fingers against her breast. The nipple tightened, and deep inside her she felt again that heady rush of desire. "Yes," he said solemnly.

Suddenly he sat up. "Come. I'm hungry for something more than a piece of fruit." He went over to his wardrobe and threw it open. He chose a red silk dressing gown and offered it to her.

"What are we going to eat?" she asked. She felt almost decadent as she slipped her arms into the hugely oversized garment that smelled like him and let the fluid silk cascade over her body.

He pulled on his breeches. "There'll be something down in the kitchen."

"We can't go down to the kitchen like this. What will Wallace or Henny say?"

"Nothing, I imagine," he answered, opening the door for her. "I gave them all the day off and asked them to let us have the house."

"You didn't!" she gasped.

He leaned against the door, his eyes alive with amusement. "Phadra, Henny and Wallace are probably thinking it's high time the two of us got together."

His words sounded so close to the truth that Phadra didn't argue but followed him through the hallway, feeling like a naughty child as she trailed him down the back stairs to the kitchen dressed in nothing but the silk dressing gown. While she sat on a high stool, he sliced some cold capon from the night before and offered it to her with a loaf of crusty bread and a glass of champagne.

Again she found him to be a good companion. Never had the conversation between them been so easy — but then she realized that she'd always felt free to speak her mind to him. As it grew dark, he lit some candles and then insisted on heating water to make a bath for her. As he rolled out the large copper tub and placed it in the middle of the kitchen, he talked about raising his sisters in this house after their mother had died.

"Anne and I did it all, taking care of the little ones and everything." He poured the heated water into the tub.

"What do you mean, 'and everything'?"

Grant shrugged. "Father left debts. Matters that had to be settled." He smiled at her. "My lady's bath awaits."

"Grant . . . ," she started uncertainly.

Before she could utter another protest, he slipped the robe off her, lifted her up, and lowered her into the warm tub. "You need this."

And she discovered she did. The warm water soothed the tenderness between her thighs. She sighed at the luxury. "I've never had anyone prepare my bath for me before."

He dropped to his knees beside the tub. "We've done several things you haven't experienced before," he said, grinning. He picked up the bar of soap that he had fetched a moment earlier and dipped his hands into the water.

"What are you doing?" she asked, edging away as far as she could in the tub.

"I'm giving you a bath," he responded evenly, and brought his hand out to show her the bar of soap. He then lathered his hands and began rubbing the soap across her neck and shoulders, his hands slipping underneath her hair.

It felt heavenly. Her tense muscles relaxed. The soap had the clean, masculine fragrance he used every day. Finally he removed his hands; thinking him done, she closed her eyes, sinking deeper into the water.

His hands dipped lower and then brushed the crests of her breasts. Phadra came up with a start. Unrepentant, he flashed her a smile that deepened his dimples and stole her heart — and warned her that he had something other than a simple bath in mind.

She tilted her head in his direction, arching one eyebrow suspiciously. "Did you plan this?"

"All of it, or just the bath?" he asked, his knowing fingers lingering a moment between her legs before sweeping up the inside of her thigh. He lifted her leg and made a show of lathering it, his strong hands kneading, caressing the muscles.

Phadra was finding it hard to breathe, let alone think coherently. "Any of it," she managed to say before breaking off in a sigh as he kissed and nibbled a sensitive spot on the inside of her knee.

He looked up, his quicksilver eyes warm and admiring. "Perhaps it would be better to say that I thought it would be fun."

Phadra pulled her leg from him and sat up in the tub. She covered her breasts with her arm. "Fun? Grant Morgan is actually unbending enough to have *fun?*"

Grant sat back on his heels. Gently he reached out and twisted one of her wet, unruly curls around his finger. "Actually, Grant Morgan isn't unbent at all." She didn't even begin to understand his meaning until he leaned over, kissed her, and then rose to his feet and began unbuttoning his breeches.

The modest part of Phadra wanted to

hide, but another part of her surged with pride. There was no doubt as his breeches fell to the floor that this man wanted her. And she wanted him. Already her need thrummed through her body — but still she was slightly shocked when her staid, conservative banker stepped into the tub.

"It's not big enough for both of us," she protested.

"Yes, it is," he said. "Trust me." Lifting her up as easily as if she were a doll, he sat down in the tub and brought her down on top of him.

"Grant, this is —" She struggled for a word as he shifted himself to cradle intimately against her. His hands wrapped themselves around her breasts. "Ecstasy," Phadra finished, leaning forward until her breasts flattened against the soft, wet mat of hair on his chest.

Phadra sighed with the contentment of a well-fed cat, her head beneath his chin as he stroked and lathered her. "Phadra?" his low, deep voice asked.

She looked up, her nose so close to his lips. "Can you do it again?" he asked.

"Oh, yes," she answered, the slow glow of desire starting in her belly. She started to stand up, but his broad hand held her in place. "Here?" she asked, shocked.

He smiled, a wicked smile. "Phadra," he chastised with mock seriousness, "you dare to question the Lord of Love?"

Her eyes met his. She was surprised by his lazy teasing. Then his strong hands molded and shaped her buttocks, lifting her and then setting her down so he could fill her. Phadra sat up straight, her eyes wide with surprise at the sensation of warm bath water and hot, hard man.

He laughed quietly a moment before gently instructing her to move. Phadra still wasn't sure what he meant until he lifted his mouth up to hers and began stroking a gentle rhythm with his tongue. Almost without conscious thought, Phadra slowly began to copy that rhythm. Her movements became more sure, less hesitant, as his eyes closed and his body arched to meet hers, giving her a sense of her power.

He let her set the pace. His breathing became harsher, more labored. His hands stroked her arms, and he whispered words to her, love words that made her feel strong and wonderful. And then her need took over, driving her to a pace that sloshed the water back and forth in the tub and onto the brick floor. This was what it was about, her heart sang. This give-and-take between a man and a woman. This was marriage. This was love.

He came, his body thrusting up into hers and holding her while he shouted her name to the world around them. Throwing her arms around his neck, Phadra gave in to her own wild release, collapsing on top of him.

Long, wondrous minutes passed before either of them moved. He moved first, his hand relaxing and then tiredly caressing the small of her back. She felt his face curve into a smile, and he released a sigh of pure satisfaction. Lifting her a moment, he settled the two of them more comfortably in the tub.

"I hope Henny and Wallace don't ever come back," she said, rubbing her cheek against his shoulder.

He chuckled, the sound low and warmly masculine. "If they did come back right now, I don't think I could move even if my soul depended on it."

"Me neither," she agreed, tracing a swirling line in the damp hair on his chest. The emerald on her ring winked at her.

"Grant?" she asked, raising her head until she could look him squarely in the face. "We're going to be all right, aren't we? I haven't ruined you completely, have I?"

For a second she thought she saw a hesitation beneath the lids of his half-closed eyes, but then just as quickly it wasn't there and she could believe she'd imagined it. "We'll be fine," his deep voice reassured her. Then he hugged her so tightly, she chose to believe him.

Later, after they'd managed to find their way back to their bedroom, she wrapped a dry bandage around his chest and shoulder. He folded her up in his arms and they made slow, lazy love one last time. He warned her she would be sore in the morning, but she didn't care. She didn't care about anything but having him hold her close and listening to the steady, strong beat of his heart.

Dear Lord, she loved him. The truth of it went straight to the very core of her being. She loved Grant Morgan. And then she said those words aloud, softly, against the silky hair of his chest, as her eyes closed and she drifted off with a sigh into the deepest sleep she'd had since the moment they'd met.

Grant didn't know if she'd meant for him to hear that quiet declaration. For a brutal moment, he wished that he hadn't heard it.

But he had . . . and then bit by bit, measure by measure, a miracle began to happen. Those words, simply said and honestly given, began to work magic upon him. A magic he'd never known he needed.

It was as if he'd lived his life in a shell as rigid and hard as stone and then, in the next minute, that shell began to break away piece by piece, freeing the man inside. Freeing *him*.

The rain had stopped and the brilliance of a full moon beamed through the window down on him, gilding the bed and everything on it with a sheen of silver. There, bathed in silvery light, Grant Morgan, the man who knew what he wanted and how to get it, realized that the course of his life had been unalterably changed.

The realization was humbling . . . and the woman next to him was a treasure more precious than gold.

Grant wasn't there when she woke the next morning. Phadra sat up on the bed, disappointed to find herself alone in a room filled with flowers and the earthy scent of their lovemaking. A note lay on the pillow next to her.

He'd written that he'd gone to the bank, would return before noon, and wished her a good morning.

The note seemed sparse after what they had shared the night before. But then, that was the type of man he was . . . always economical, with both words and money. Wincing slightly as she moved and discovered that she was indeed sore in places she hadn't dreamed existed until the previous day, she amended her verdict. Economical, yes, but not when it came to making love.

The thought filled her with happiness. Outside the bedroom window, the sun shone in the kind of clear sky that followed a day of rain, and birds sang — or was that her heart? Suddenly Phadra realized that she felt better than she ever had in her life. She bounced out of bed and started dressing. Her body's stiffness all but disappeared, and she found herself humming. The dress she chose was one of her favorites, a yellow and rose design copied after a painting of Helen of Troy. She felt as though she could launch a thousand ships that morning!

A timid knock sounded on the door. In answer to her call, Meg, the lady's maid, entered. "Oh, Mrs. Morgan, you're already dressed," she said. Meg started to bob a curtsey and then stopped, knowing Phadra didn't like the formality. "Mr. Morgan told me not to disturb you. Oh, look at the flowers!"

Phadra grinned, absurdly pleased at Meg's reaction. "Come help me carry them downstairs. I'm sure they need fresh water, and I want to make sure there's a bouquet in every room of the house." As Meg helped to gather the flowers, Phadra fastened her bronze bracelets around her wrist and then picked up the gladioli. "When did he leave?"

"Mr. Morgan left over an hour ago. Said he had to get to the bank and finish some business."

That sounded so much like Grant that Phadra smiled to herself.

They took some of the flowers downstairs to the dining room, and Phadra ordered Meg to bring down the rest while she searched for vases. Meg hadn't been gone for more than a few seconds when a voice in the doorway caught Phadra's attention. "I suppose you're pleased with yourself," Henny said sagely. She walked into the room. "Someone made a terrible mess in the kitchen last night."

Phadra threw her arms around the older woman's neck. "Henny, isn't this day wonderful? Isn't the world wonderful?"

Henny made a pretense of feeling Phadra's forehead. "She's not running a fever," she said to the world in general. She cocked her head and studied Phadra's face. "But she looks flushed, and there is a slight giddiness."

Phadra laughed, kissed her on her cheek, and practically danced away. "Yes! You're right," she admitted. "I'm in love. Wonderful, wonderful love. And he loves me."

"Ah, child," Henny said expansively. "I'm so happy for you."

"Not as happy as I am for myself," Phadra blurted out. "Henny, he is the most honest, caring . . . *handsome* man I've ever known. And he loves me, Henny. He loves *me* —"

Someone rapped on the front door. Since Wallace wasn't readily available, Phadra thumbed her nose at propriety and crossed into the hall to open the door herself. Immediately she wished she hadn't done it. Miranda Evans stood on the front step.

"Ah, Mrs. Morgan," she said with false sweetness. "Is your husband here? Or has he already left for that important meeting at the bank?"

Phadra didn't like the emphasis she'd placed on "that important meeting," as if she knew something Phadra did not. "He's not here," she replied, and pointedly refused to invite the woman in.

At that moment Meg came down the stairs, her arms full of flowers. "This is the last of them, Mrs. Morgan."

Phadra had turned at the sound of the maid's voice. "Yes, thank you, Meg. Please put them in the dining room."

"Oh, flowers," Miranda said with obvious interest. "From your husband?"

"Yes," Phadra replied with a proud lift of her chin.

"Well, how nice," Miranda said benignly, but Phadra caught the hint of a secret smile. And Phadra's instinct was confirmed as Miranda continued smoothly, "Then I guess Grant will be able to report to the directors this morning that he has managed to bring his wife in *line*." She shook her head with a commiserating "tsk" before adding, "This morning I overheard Father telling Mother about Sir Robert's ultimatum. It must be so embarrassing for you to know that Grant will lose his position, his livelihood, if he can't control you. Makes a person wonder what you've done, hmm? But then it seems Grant has brought you in line nicely for the price of a few posies —"

Phadra slammed the door in her face.

"Phadra?" Henny's worried voice said from behind her. "You can't believe everything that she-devil has to say."

Phadra didn't answer. She couldn't. What Miranda had said was true. The evidence was in the way he'd planned her seduction, the way he'd manipulated her. She leaned her forehead against the cool wood of the door and let wave after wave of pain at his betrayal wash over her.

He didn't love her. She was merely a

468

means to an end. How could she have been so stupid, so naive?

And then suddenly it was almost more than she could bear. *Fool, fool, fool,* she told herself over and over, not even feeling the hot tears that rolled down her cheeks.

Henny gathered her in her arms. "Phadra, what is it?"

It almost hurt to talk, to repeat Miranda's words, but Phadra made herself say them, hoping Henny would deny them for her. That Henny would say it was all malicious spite on Miranda's part.

But Henny didn't. Instead she stared at Phadra. A terrible sense of foreboding tied Phadra's insides into a knot. "Henny, why do you look that way? Tell me, Henny."

Henny cupped Phadra's face in her hands. "It's nothing."

Phadra pushed her away. "Tell me."

Henny looked toward Wallace, who had quietly joined them in the hall. "Tell me, Henny," Phadra commanded again.

The lines on the older woman's face drooped sadly. "He asked me questions about you. I told him I thought he should pay some attention to you. . . ." Her voice trailed off guiltily.

Phadra turned on her heel and walked into the dining room. He'd been asking

Henny questions about her. So he could learn how to bend her to his will; how to make her *obedient* and *acceptable*.

And it had worked, hadn't it? That morning when she'd woken, she would have followed him into the fires of hell if he'd asked her to.

For the price of a few posies.

She'd been such a fool.

"Meg, throw out all of these flowers. Every single one of them." Phadra turned to the doorway, where Henny and Wallace hovered anxiously. They looked so worried, as if they thought she was going to break down into tears.

No, she was done with that. She was her own woman now, completely and unalterably.

"Henny, I want all my belongings packed and ready for me to leave this afternoon. Wallace, summon a hack. We leave for the Bank of England. Now."

Chapter 20

Phadra wanted, needed, to deal with Grant herself, so she ordered Wallace to stay with the hack. He agreed reluctantly. "If you need me, miss, just shout. I'll be right to your side," he promised, opening and closing one meaty fist.

Hoping that matters wouldn't come to that, Phadra stepped out of the hack and paused, momentarily overwhelmed by the Bank of England's elaborate facade of ornate columns, stone banisters, and carved statues. The heavy doors had been propped open to allow the summer air to circulate inside.

Saying a quick prayer for courage, Phadra stepped across the threshold into enemy territory. Huge windows allowed the room to be filled with bright sunshine, and there was a crowd of people doing their business in the Pay Hall this fine morning. To her right stood an officious young man, who appeared to be charged with the responsibility of making sure that all went well there in the bank's great hall. She walked over to him. "Excuse me, but I wish to speak to Mr. Morgan. Can you direct me to his offices?"

The officious young man lifted an eyebrow, taking in her bold bronze bracelets, unique style of dress, and sandaled feet. "May I ask your business, madam?"

Phadra forced a tight smile. "I'm his wife."

"Mrs. Morgan?" His watery gaze swept her dress again, making her conscious that all the other women in the Pay Hall wore gloves and bonnets. "Of course," he whispered. He then snapped his fingers to gain the attention of another young man standing by a set of doors leading out of the room. He signaled the other man to join them.

"Wilcomb, this is Mrs. Morgan." At the mention of her name, Wilcomb's mouth practically dropped open, and again Phadra found herself being studied rudely. "She wishes to speak to Mr. Morgan. Will you escort her to his offices?"

Wilcomb frowned. "That's not possible right now. He's in a meeting with the Court," he said, nodding at the double doors.

The meeting.

She lifted her chin, her voice businesslike and brisk. "I wish to see him. Now."

"I'm sorry, but that's not possible, Mrs. Morgan. They've been in there this past hour and more. I'm under orders not to allow any interruptions."

Phadra looked in the direction of the doors. No interruptions? "Well," she said pleasantly, "I'll just have to wait, won't I?"

"Yes, Mrs. Morgan. I'm very sorry," Wilcomb said, as if he truly regretted not being able to honor her request. "Although I'm sure they will be done shortly. Perhaps you would like to wait in Mr. Morgan's offices for him?"

"Oh, no," Phadra said smoothly while taking a sidestep or two toward the double doors that led to the Court of Directors' meeting room. "I'll wait for him over there. Would it be possible for you to get me a chair to sit in while I wait?"

"Why, certainly," Wilcomb responded, and, turning to the other man, started to tell him to fetch the chair when Phadra made her move.

She broke into a mad dash for the set of doors and slipped through them before the startled young men could gather their wits and give pursuit. She heard a shout behind her and the objections of bank patrons who were jostled aside in the men's hurry to stop her.

Behind the doors was a small anteroom that led to another set of doors. In front of them, at a small desk, sat another officious young man. He rose. "May I help you?"

"I'll only be a moment," Phadra replied, moving swiftly for the doors.

"Wait, I don't —" But she'd already entered, slamming the door behind her.

Phadra came to an abrupt halt as she realized that she'd done it. She'd gained entrance into the palatial splendor of the hallowed Court Room of the Bank of England.

She didn't know what she'd expected. Looking up and around the room, she took in the cream-and-gold columns, the ornate ceiling and wall medallions, the thick carpet apparently woven specially for the room — and the long mahogany table in the center of the room at which were seated the twenty-five directors of the bank.

At her entrance, every man at the table had turned in her direction except for the one standing at the end of the table closest to the door — her husband. No, she hurriedly amended. She would not call him husband.

The three junior bank officers tumbled through the door behind her. Phadra quickly sidestepped them and went to stand beside Grant, holding herself proudly apart from him.

"What nonsense is going on here?" Sir Robert demanded, slamming his palm against the table.

Phadra defiantly held her head high and remained silent. She didn't answer, and she wasn't about to leave the room until she'd said her piece. Wilcomb immediately started making an excuse: "She wanted to see her husband, sir. We told her she couldn't. That we were under orders, but then she just rushed in here —"

"We tried to stop her," the first young man interjected.

Sir Robert held up his hand for silence, and the three young men came to attention. He sat back in his chair. "Good morning, Mrs. Morgan. As usual, your behavior is irregular."

At the mention of her name a low buzz of recognition started among the directors sitting around the table, and several craned their necks to get a good look at her. Sir Cecil did little but stare at his thumbnail. She refused to look at Grant. Every fiber of her being was aware that he stood only a hand's width away from her. She could smell the spiciness of his shaving soap, sense his slightest movement beside her, even swear that she could feel the heat from his body — the textures of which she now knew almost as well as her own, after what they had shared the night before. But she couldn't look at him. If she looked at him, her hard-won resolve would crumble.

She took a step forward, placing the tips of her fingers on the table's dark, glossy surface. "If it please you gentlemen," she said in a clear, ringing voice, "I have something to say."

Sir Robert's eyes narrowed with speculation. He looked from her to Grant and back before lifting his fingers, signaling for her to speak.

She could feel Grant's eyes on her, and her heart raced. Her voice shook slightly when she started speaking. "I understand that this group of men has informed Grant Morgan that if he values his position at the bank, then he must exert more control over his wife. I've come today to solve your problem."

"And what are you suggesting, Mrs. Morgan?" Sir Robert asked.

Phadra looked around the table, meeting the eyes of each and every one of them before announcing, "I'm suing Grant Morgan for divorce."

The word *divorce* set off an astonished,

almost angry, murmur from the directors as they sat up in their chairs and turned to their companions. Phadra refused to turn and look at Grant, struggling instead to control her own reaction at saying the word out loud. Only that morning she'd met the day full of hopes and dreams for the future. Now she felt that the very life had been drained out of her.

"That's it," she said, the words becoming harder to speak over the lump in her throat. "That's all I have to say."

One director snapped angrily, "We've never had a divorced member of the bank. It's not to be sanctioned."

"But we need Morgan," another argued. "Whitehall wants to deal with him and him alone."

"I will not countenance divorce," the other shot back.

"Think of the scandal," another man added, and looked down his hooked nose at Phadra as if she were some new species of beetle climbing across his table.

Sir Robert spoke, commanding the attention of everyone in the room. "And what do you say, Morgan? Does your wife's announcement change your decision?"

All heads turned to the man standing behind her. Phadra straightened her back and clasped her hands together to keep them from trembling. This confrontation, carried out in public, was harder than she could ever have imagined.

Grant answered, his voice low and firm. "No, sir, it doesn't change my decision. I am determined to resign my position with the bank."

Resign?

Phadra whirled around in surprise.

"And you were about to tell us why, weren't you?" Sir Robert said. "That is, before we were so rudely interrupted."

Looking directly into her eyes, Grant said, "Because I love my wife."

If the carpeted floor had opened up beneath her feet, Phadra could not have been more surprised. "Do you mean that?" she whispered, oblivious to the others in the room.

"With all my heart." And there in the silvery-gray depths of his eyes, Phadra saw the truth. The magic of it stole her breath away.

"Then I guess our business is done," Sir Robert announced. He rose from the table.

"Wait a moment," Sir Henry said. "What about Morgan? Are we just going to let him resign without another word? Don't we need him?"

Sir Robert started walking around the table. "You have your choice, Henry. The peace and harmony of your home or Morgan and his independent wife."

For a moment Sir Henry appeared to weigh the choices. He shook his head and, rising from the table, said, "I have to say, Morgan, I'm sorry that we will not have the benefit of your intelligence and widely acknowledged financial acumen . . . but if this is the price I must pay to get my wife out of those toe bells, so be it."

"As you wish, Sir Henry," Grant answered, and then he did an amazing thing. He threw his arm around Phadra's shoulder and hugged her close as if they were any young couple wandering around a country fair instead of a banker and his wife standing in the columned glory of the Court Room in the most powerful bank in England.

Sir Robert paused a moment before them, his keen eyes resting briefly on Grant before he offered his hand. "Good luck to you, Morgan," he said. He gave a nod and a smile to Phadra. "I have a feeling you may need it."

In the face of Sir Robert's good humor, the other directors filed out without further objection. Three or four of them stopped to shake Grant's hand and offer to help him in any way possible in his new career, whatever that might be. Phadra watched them go without regret. Sir Cecil was the last one to approach them. "If I ever need any help on anything, Morgan, can I bring it by for you to look at?"

Grant shook his head. "Do your own work, sir."

Phadra could have sworn that the man looked close to tears, but he didn't say another word and scurried out of the room behind the others. Slowly Phadra looked up at Grant. "Are you sure you'll have no regrets?"

"Are you still planning to sue me for divorce?"

No! she wanted to shout, but instead appeared to consider the matter until his lips curved into a wide, easy grin. "You're incorrigible! I guess I shall have to remind you," he said, and then he kissed her, right there in the Bank of England, until she couldn't remember what day it was or her reason for being there.

When at last he broke for air, he slid her a speculative glance. "I think I may have found the way to control my wife."

Phadra raised her eyebrows and tilted her head. "Through kisses? I pray that you try."

He laughed, the sound full and rich.

Taking her hand, he led her out of the bank into the light of a glorious summer day. They stood on the steps for a moment as if seeing the world through new eyes.

"Wallace is waiting for us in the hack." She nodded to the hired coach waiting down the street.

"We'll have to get him out of there and ask him to join us for the walk home," Grant noted soberly.

Phadra turned to him. "How badly off are we?"

"It'll be tight, but if we watch ourselves —"

"And practice economies," she interjected.

He smiled. "I've taken some tremendous risks with investments, Phadra — the ones I was telling you about the other night. If they pay off, then we never need worry again. If they don't, well, there will be something else. Phipps has talked to me about a place in government. What would you think about that?"

"You don't think they'd find me a bad influence on their wives and not let you work for them?" she asked, for the first time admitting obliquely how much the opinions of the directors had stung.

Grant squeezed her hand. "Some men aren't intimidated by a woman with strong

481

opinions and honest emotions. Phadra, I don't want you to change."

She bowed her head. "Well, there are a few things I wouldn't mind changing, Grant. I do have a tendency to be impulsive, and sometimes matters do get out of hand."

He tilted her head up so that she was forced to meet his piercing gaze. "And sometimes I am dictatorial and —" He paused for strong effect. "And occasionally I do lose control."

She flashed him a smile. "No," she said in mock denial.

He hooked her arm in his, and they started down the steps. "The point is, Phadra; we each have faults, but I realized last night that I don't want a wife who is nothing more than an ornament or a slave to my wishes. I want an intelligent wife. A woman who can think for herself, who can teach our children and help them to grow strong and healthy. I realized I want a woman who will be a partner to me in every way." He stopped and turned to her. "I want you, Phadra. I love you."

And right there, in the middle of Threadneedle Street, Phadra reached up and threw her arms around her husband and held him as if she'd never let him go. Not now. Not ever.

Epilogue

1815

"Someone told me, Sir Cecil, that you knew Morgan well when he worked for the Bank of England."

Sir Cecil looked up from the contemplation of his thumbnail and frowned at the member of the Royal Geographic Society, Mr. Marpledon, sitting in the coach seat opposite him. He didn't like being reminded of those days. No man wanted to be reminded of how opportunity had slipped through his fingers.

"He did some work for me," he muttered noncommittally, and then for some perverse reason added, "My daughter was engaged to him for a time." What he wouldn't give to go back to that moment in time! He'd finally been able to buy a husband for Miranda, but the bastard had, after only four months of marriage, sent her home to her parents, threatening to horsewhip her if she ever darkened his door again.

Between Miranda and his wife, his life was a living hell. Even his mistress was starting to sound like a shrew.

"Was he as wealthy then as he is now?" the second gentleman, Sir Lloyd, asked with undisguised curiosity.

Sir Cecil frowned. "I certainly don't know."

The men's speculation was undeterred. Sir Lloyd turned to his companion. "I overheard in my club last week that the prime minister offered Morgan a title and the man refused it."

"Refused a knighthood?" Marpledon repeated incredulously.

"No," Sir Lloyd said. "He offered Morgan a peerage for his service to the government. Morgan said that he deeply appreciated the honor but did not want or expect anything for his service to his country."

"Amazing," Marpledon said. "Can you imagine any man in England not willing to sell his soul for a peerage?"

"I suppose it depends on the man and what he values most," Sir Lloyd answered.

"Amazing," Marpledon said again, and Sir Cecil echoed the same sentiment in his thoughts.

Suddenly their conversation stopped as

each man looked at their companion, Sir Julius Abbott, sitting next to Sir Cecil. Sir Cecil shifted uncomfortably. "Doesn't he ever say anything?"

Sir Lloyd shook his head. "Not that anyone's heard, not since we met him at the pier in Portsmouth. The lads who found Sir Julius in that Berber village said the same. All he does is stare off into space. Fever can do that to a man. The lads didn't even realize he was a white man until they'd been in the village several weeks."

Sir Cecil frowned. He'd been hoping that by worming his way into this midmorning expedition to deliver Sir Julius Abbott to his son-in-law, Grant Morgan could be convinced to help him handle some present difficulties he was suffering. Looking at Sir Julius sitting next to him staring off into space, he doubted Morgan would be pleased at all. First, Sir Julius didn't look anything like his former robust self, and second, there was no treasure. Mayhap there never had been a treasure. The thought made Sir Cecil sad.

At that moment the coach turned off the road, its wheels rumbling along the fine cobblestones of the drive. Sir Lloyd sat up. "We must be here." He rolled up the coach's window flap and craned his neck.

"I'm anxious to see Morgan's estate, Bell Haven. They say the design is very original."

"So I've heard," Mr. Marpledon agreed. "I also heard it was designed by his wife. Can you imagine letting your wife design a house, let alone an estate of this magnitude?"

"I've met Mrs. Morgan," Sir Lloyd said. "She's a very unconventional woman but completely charming. I admire her work on behalf of several social causes. She and a cousin of mine are very actively working to improve the conditions at several London hospitals, and when you hear them talk about it, they make sense, too."

Sir Cecil found himself searching the woods for his first glimpse of Bell Haven. All this could have been his if only he hadn't listened to his wife and acted so hastily in marrying Phadra Abbott off to Morgan that day in the inn. Even Beatrice agreed now, especially when Miranda was having an unusually bad day. Morgan wouldn't have sent her packing. He was a man who understood his responsibilities. Sir Cecil's thoughts turned to what he had just heard from Sir Lloyd. Imagine not accepting a peerage.

Through the autumn foliage they caught their first look at the estate. It was unusual, completely done in white marble and looking as lovely as a fairy castle. Two huge, graceful fountains with sparkling waters greeted the visitors as the coachman maneuvered the coach along the circular driveway in front of the house. Liveried servants snapped smartly to attention and rushed down the steps to greet them.

A servant opened the door, and Sir Cecil started to climb out. Then he saw Morgan's butler waiting at the top of the steps. Wallace, his name was. The two of them had tangled once when Sir Cecil had tried to push his way into Morgan's London house.

He sat back down on the upholstered seat and turned to the two men from the Geographic Society. "Maybe you should go in without me."

They looked surprised, especially in light of all the favors he'd had to call in for permission to accompany them, but honored his request. Gingerly they helped Sir Julius out of the coach, talking to him as if he were a three-year-old instead of a man.

Sir Cecil sat back in the coach. Yes, he'd made the right decision. Morgan wasn't going to be happy with anyone who brought such an unwelcome burden as an addle pated father-in-law into his life. Perhaps later, in town, he would be able to speak to

Morgan and beg his assistance before Sir Robert insisted that he resign his position on the Court.

Inside the grand foyer of the house, Phadra shifted restlessly beside Grant. He reached down and took her hand. "Are you all right?"

She drew in a deep breath and released it. "I don't know. See, my hand is shaking."

"You don't have to see him."

She gave his hand a reassuring squeeze. "I must. I've waited too long."

At that moment Wallace opened both sides of the double door. He shot his employer a speaking look. With a sense of foreboding, Grant pulled Phadra closer to him, wrapping his arm protectively around her back and resting his hand along the side of her body, which was heavy with child. This would be their second child, and it was due in two months' time.

With each day of their marriage, she became more precious and important to him. He prayed that this moment would not hurt her.

As the visitors came up the steps, Grant tightened his hold on her. He immediately recognized the men from the Royal Geographic Society, and there was no mistaking which man was Sir Julius. His haggard, almost skeletal appearance was a complete shock. He looked so fragile, as if a good breeze could blow him away.

Phadra leaned away from her husband's embrace and then started to move forward. Grant's first instinct was to pull her back, to protect her — but he let her go, his body tense and ready for whatever happened.

Slowly Phadra approached the man. "Papa?" The soft yearning he heard in her voice wrenched Grant's heart. He shouldn't have done this. He should never have conducted this search for Sir Julius.

In response to her call, Sir Julius turned his head, the action stiff and mechanical. He narrowed his eyes as if trying to see who spoke to him.

Phadra stopped. She stood no more than a foot from him, waiting for him to make the first move.

Sir Julius frowned, as if perplexed by something, and then he whispered hoarsely, "My baby."

"Oh, Papa," she said, her eyes filling with tears, and then she reached out to him and cradled him protectively in her arms.

Grant met with the gentlemen from the Geographic Society and took full responsibility for Sir Julius, signing over a tidy donation to their organization at the same time. Henny reported that she, Wallace, and Jem had managed to see Sir Julius safely to his room after he had been thoroughly checked out by a doctor Grant had sent for from London. The man had lain down on his bed, fully clothed, and fallen asleep.

"He gives me the shivers," Henny confessed with a shudder, "seeing him this way. Who would have thought that Phadra would be right all these years and that the man had been held in slavery by heathens, waiting for someone to rescue him?" She shook her head. "What does the doctor say?"

Accustomed by now to Henny's motherly bossiness, Grant dutifully answered, "He believes that the man will recover with good food and a good home." *And love,* he added silently. If anyone could bring her father back to life, it was Phadra.

He went to search for his wife. He found her where he thought she would be, in the music room. She sat at the pianoforte, staring out through the floor-to-ceiling windows into the garden beyond. Still never one to bow to convention, she'd tied her wonderfully curling hair at the nape of her neck, the way he liked it.

He came up behind her and placed his hand on her shoulder. "Are you all right?"

Phadra gave a little start. "Oh, Grant." She reached a hand up and pulled him down to sit next to her on the music bench. "I was so deep in thought, I didn't realize you were there."

She looked out the window again. With unconscious grace her hand rested on her belly. Grant placed his hand next to hers and suddenly felt the baby move. "This will be a strong one," he said with a smile.

"Yes," she agreed readily. "We do make beautiful babies."

His eyes met hers. "We do."

Smiling absently, she lightly touched an ivory piano key. Grant reached out and took her hand in his. "We don't have to have him live with us. There are places for people when they become like him. I don't want this to distress you."

He didn't have to say who "him" was.

She turned her head to him in surprise. "Oh, no, Grant. Is that what you think? That I'm upset we found him? I'm not, truly. In fact, I wish we could have found him sooner . . . before he became like this, though the doctor says he can fully recover." She laced her fingers through his. "It's just that I keep thinking about how he's lost so much and about how I came so close to being just like him."

"Phadra, you could never —"

"Yes, I could have. I mean, if you hadn't chased after me that night I ran away from Evans House, none of this" — she looked around the room and then at him, her love for him brimming in her eyes — "would have happened. I probably never would have found Papa, and then who knows what might have become of me. But there never would have been *us*. Papa spent his life searching for treasure when everything that is valuable and important was right here, within his grasp."

On her other hand the fake emerald caught the late-afternoon sunshine in its dark depths. Over the years he'd offered to replace it with a real one, but Phadra wouldn't let him. She always said that it reminded her of what was important, of what was real.

He pulled her hand up to his lips and gave her fingertips a light kiss. "And I would have been hollow, too, Phadra. If we hadn't met, I wouldn't be complete."

She smiled then, her eyes full of promise. "Yes, that's what it is. Together we're complete, like the circle of this ring." She held up the emerald. "Remember what you said when we married, that it was good and solid? It has been, hasn't it?"

"Yes. And it will be. We're still beginning."

At that moment they were interrupted. "Hug," shouted a small, demanding voice. "Me want hug."

Three-year-old Lizbeth Morgan, her wild, curly hair flowing down her back, hurled herself between her parents and scrambled up onto her father's lap laughing. Grant settled her in place and wrapped his arms around daughter and wife.

Lizbeth snuggled in happily.

Over her head, her parents looked into each other's eyes and smiled. Phadra whispered, "Yes, together we're a circle. A bright and shining circle."

And as the sun shone down on them through the paned windows, they silently vowed that what God had joined together would remain so for eternity.

A man of sense
can only love such a woman. . . .
A Vindication of the Rights of Woman
Mary Wollstonecraft

About the Author

Cathy Maxwell spends hours in front of her computer pondering the question "Why do people fall in love?" The question remains for her the great mystery of life and the secret to happiness.

She lives in beautiful Virginia with children, horses, dogs, and cats.

Fans can contact Cathy at
www.cathymaxwell.com
or P.O. Box 1532, Midlothian, VA 23113

The employees of Thorndike Press hope you have enjoyed this Large Print book. All our Thorndike and Wheeler Large Print titles are designed for easy reading, and all our books are made to last. Other Thorndike Press Large Print books are available at your library, through selected bookstores, or directly from us.

For information about titles, please call:

(800) 223-1244

or visit our Web site at:

www.gale.com/thorndike
www.gale.com/wheeler

To share your comments, please write:

Publisher
Thorndike Press
295 Kennedy Memorial Drive
Waterville, ME 04901